MISSING

ALSO BY J. T. GODDARD

Traces
Tracks
Piracy

Missing

A Gavin Rashford Novel

J. T. Goddard

Prologue

The rain came suddenly, icy slivers blown on the prairie wind, and the young man turned up his collar. The weather had been warmer earlier and so he hadn't worn a hat, a decision he now regretted. He moved as close to the garden walls and fences as the path would allow, trying in vain for some shelter. The early leaves on the trees were just starting to unfurl and did little to shield him from the deluge.

The road was empty at this time of the evening, the only other movement a few fast-food wrappers skittering across the asphalt. A dozen or so cars were parked along the street, wheels tight to the curb. Some distantly spaced streetlights provided a sickly yellow illumination, enough for him to navigate the small piles of dog faeces and the regurgitated remains of what appeared to be a Chinese meal.

It was nearly midnight and he smiled to himself as he remembered his evening. There had been a fancy dinner, where he had chatted with the other guests and told self-deprecating stories about himself. He had avoided alcohol, even though there was plenty on offer, and restricted himself to a single glass of wine. Throughout he had realized that he was on display, and at the end of the meal he was pleased that the woman he had chosen had accepted his request to walk her home. That had been at eight thirty, the sun just setting on a balmy spring day, and the sky had been darkening dramatically.

At her house she had invited him in for a nightcap, and then one thing led to another, and now here he was, heading back to his dorm cold and wet on the outside but warm and happy on the inside. His thoughts were interrupted as he heard a vehicle approaching, his shadow suddenly clear in front of him as the headlights shone on his back.

This was a small town and normally quite safe, but nonetheless a frisson of fear ran through him as a pick-up drew up alongside. It slowed, matching his pace, and the window wound down with an electronic hiss.

"Cold wet night for a walk," said an almost familiar voice. "Can I give you a lift?"

He kept walking even as he looked across, but then he recognized the university decal on the side door, and relaxed.

"Thank you," he said, and dashed across to the curb. He paused and spoke through the open window.

"Are you sure it's no trouble?"

"None at all. I'm going your way."

The door opened and he climbed into the cab, reaching over to shake hands.

"Cheers," he said.

The driver nodded, then accelerated away, sheets of rain dancing through the headlights as the windshield wipers beat out the metronome of the night.

CHAPTER 1

Pfft.

With every tap on the keyboard, Rashford imagined he could hear another puff of air leave the room.

Pfft.

The speaker read out the text written on the slide. His voice was a monotone, bereft of passion or variation.

Pfft.

Rashford looked around the room. It was a university classroom, the seats arranged in fixed rows. Each chair was formed from a single piece of molded laminate and had a retractable writing pad that folded flat against the side. There were perhaps forty seats, most of them empty.

Pfft.

Three people sat in the front row. They appeared to be paying rapt attention to every word, leaning forward and focusing on each slide.

Pfft.

Rashford counted twelve additional people. There were three pairs, two singles, and a group of four young women who huddled together. The audience were mainly seated towards the middle of the room. Rashford sat in the back row.

Pfft.

The four women were whispering to each other. They seemed to be paying attention to a computer held by the one who was second from the left in the group. One of the others pointed at the screen, and they all laughed, softly.

Pfft.

The lecturer droned on.

Pfft.

Rashford looked out of the window. The late spring sunshine gleamed on the wet pavement. Drops of moisture glistened on the grass, recently mown with the first cut of the year.

Pfft.

There was a splash of yellow from a forsythia bush, and some emerging leaves on the trees. A robin sat on a branch. Rashford hoped it was singing.

Pfft.

Seven members of the audience were looking at their phones, pale blue light emanating from their laps like so many alien babies.

Pfft.

Rashford estimated that most of the people in the room were in their early to mid thirties. The three in the front row were a bit older, perhaps mid-forties. He estimated that the four women were in their late twenties. The speaker was in his sixties.

Pfft.

The lady sitting across the aisle from Rashford looked to be older than the others, but younger than the speaker. Late forties, perhaps, thought Rashford, so about his age. She had short, cropped hair, jet black with a grey streak over the temple, and wore a light apricot-coloured jacket offset by a vibrant purple scarf. She had flipped the laminated writing pad over across her lap and rested a notebook on the surface. She held what looked like an expensive fountain pen, and every so often she wrote a note.

Pfft.

The man at the front of the room stopped talking and looked around. There was a moment of silence, and then the three people in the front row started to clap. One, a slim blond-haired man in leather jacket and shiny black trousers like an aging rock star, jumped to his feet.

"Bravo!" he said.

The rest of the audience engaged in some desultory applause.

The young woman folded away the computer.

The leather jacketed man walked up to the podium and shook the speaker's hand, enthusiastically, then turned to the room. He picked up the microphone in one hand and brushed a long lock of hair away from his face with a practised gesture. Rashford stifled a laugh as he realized that the other half of the man's hair was green, the seam running straight back across his scalp. From behind it had looked like a shadow.

The woman across the aisle looked towards him, then made another note on her pad.

"Would anyone have any questions for our speaker?" said Leather Jacket.

It appeared that nobody would.

"Well then," he said, brightly. "Obviously we have so much to process, it will take a while for our lesser minds to comprehend. Please join me, once again, in thanking Professor MacDowell, our distinguished speaker today."

The applause was more animated this time.

'People must know this is over,' thought Rashford, then chided himself for being uncharitable. The leather jacketed speaker continued.

"We will now have a twenty-minute health and nutrition break," he said. "Please reconvene at ten promptly and Dr. Hazleton here will facilitate our discussion session."

One of the two women in the front-of-room group got to her feet. She lifted her glasses from her chest to her face, the lanyard sparkling as she nodded at the audience.

"May I request no electronic devices at our next session," she said. "That way we can concentrate on the conversation."

One or two people nodded; the remainder kept looking at their phones. The four young women picked up their bags from the floor.

Rashford got to his feet and turned left on the aisle, heading out of the door at the back of the classroom. The lady in the apricot jacket followed him.

Out in the corridor, Rashford looked around, confused as to where he was standing. The bright fluorescent tubes threw shadows from the conference delegates who were milling around. The walls were painted bright yellow and were festooned with posters, display cases, and notice boards. There were no signposts. The lady in the apricot jacket stopped beside him.

"You look lost," she said.

Rashford nodded.

"I am," he said. "I came in though a different door. How do you get outside?"

"Outside?"

She looked at him shrewdly, then nodded, as though she had made a decision.

"The quickest way is through here," she said.

He followed her through an unmarked door which led into a narrow corridor. The walls were painted a dull grey, bare of ornament, and illuminated by some low-energy light bulbs.

"The bowels of the academy," she said, over her shoulder. "This way."

It was only a short corridor, terminating in a fire door covered with warning signs to indicate that it had to be kept closed at all times, that it was not an exit door, and that an alarm would sound if it was opened without authorization. The woman pressed the metal bar and the door swung outwards. She stepped through into the sunshine. Rashford hesitated.

"It's okay," she said. "Maintenance uses this as their smoking area. They disengaged the alarm so they can shelter in the corridor if the weather is bad."

Rashford laughed and followed her outside.

He found himself in a grassed area, completely square, and surrounded by the brick walls of buildings. None of the walls had windows, and each contained a door, the one by which he had entered and others on the walls opposite. There were no trees or flower beds, nothing except for a substantial wooden structure against the blank wall to his left. In front of the door through which they had arrived, a wooden picnic table and two white plastic chairs were arranged around a large, galvanized metal bucket.

Rashford walked over and saw that the bucket was filled with sand, the surface of which was dotted with stubbed out cigarette butts. He turned back to the woman.

"I guess it's okay to smoke," he said.

"Absolutely," she said. "This is the only haven on campus. We're proud to be completely smoke-free, you know. But central administration figured it wasn't worth a strike, and as long as people only break the rule here, things are fine."

"Out of sight, out of mind?"

"Exactly."

Rashford looked around a second time.

"What is this place?" he said.

"A mistake," she said, laughing. "Apparently someone misread the blueprints. This was supposed to be a big glassed-in atrium, a central space to link the four buildings together, but they forgot to put the weight bearing struts for the glass roof into the walls of two of the buildings. It was a question of taking the whole thing down and starting over or having this little secret quadrangle. Central administration went with option B."

Rashford took out his cigarettes and lighter and offered the pack to the woman, but she shook her head and reached into her purse. She withdrew a small silver case that she opened to reveal a number of dark brown cheroots, one of which she removed. Rashford leaned forward with his lighter, observing with delight that her nail polish matched her scarf, and that every finger sported a sizeable ring. She noticed his glance.

"It keeps the students on their toes," she said, inhaling deeply. "It makes them wonder what I'll do next."

Rashford rested his back against the picnic table, taking deep drags on his cigarette, and then leaned back. He tilted his face to the sky as he exhaled.

"God, I needed that," he said.

The woman laughed, a pleasant sound.

"Yes, well, I'm not surprised. Ninety-three power point slides in a seventy-minute lecture is a bit excessive, even for old MacDowell."

"You counted?"

"Hash checks," she said, showing him the open page of her notebook. A series of four short vertical lines with a fifth crossed through were sketched messily over the page.

"It looks like the wall of a prison cell," laughed Rashford.

She looked at him.

"Indeed," she said.

Rashford looked around the smoking area, noting again that no windows faced out onto the space. More than ever, it reminded him of exercise yards at the different prisons he had needed to visit at various times in his career. Here there were no watchtowers, though, no razor wire, no searchlights, no armed guards. He turned to face his guide, who had a quizzical look on her face.

"What do you do?" he said. "Here, I mean."

He waved his arm around, vaguely encompassing the space.

"Here? Here, I smoke," she said, laughing, then laughing again at the confusion on his face. She waved her own arm, indicating the wider area beyond the grass and the walls.

"But there," she said, "out there in the real world, I'm a professor. Linda Benoît, professor of linguistics."

She held out her hand. Rashford shook it, noticing again the bright purple nail polish and trying not to catch his fingers on her rings.

"Pleased to meet you," he said. "I am ..."

"Oh, excuse me," she interrupted, dropping the handshake and turning away. Rashford saw her lift her phone to her ear, listen a moment, and then assume the hunched over position ubiquitous to people sending texts.

As her thumbs flew across the keyboard, Rashford turned away and lit another cigarette. He walked around the picnic table and then sat down again, relaxing in the sun. He wondered what it would be like, to be allowed out into such a space for only an hour a day, to mill around with others or, if in isolation, to prowl the perimeter of the grassy cage.

He snapped out of his reverie as Professor Benoît approached him, her phone in her hand.

"Sorry about that," she said. "Where were we?"

"You had just told me you were a professor of linguistics," said Rashford, "and I ..."

"And you were going to introduce yourself," she said, annoying Rashford with her second interruption in as many minutes. He nodded, sourly.

"Just tell me your name," she said.

He looked at her for a moment. She met his gaze, her eyes steady.

"My name is Gavin Rashford," she said.

She nodded, then looked thoughtfully at him as she began to speak.

"You're originally from central Saskatchewan, the Saskatoon area, but you've lived a long time in the south, Regina or Swift Current. You're not Aboriginal but you speak at least one Indigenous language. You're not married, and you're not an academic. You were something in law enforcement, but you recently retired."

She paused.

"How am I doing?"

Rashford stared at her. He realized that his mouth was open, so he closed it. She held up another cheroot, and he automatically leaned forward with his lighter.

"How ..." he said, but she interrupted him a third time.

"I told you that I'm a professor of linguistics. I know everyone at this university, and you're not employed here. I know nearly everyone who might be remotely interested in Professor MacDowell's talk and you're not on the list. Only someone who has been there would make the link between calendar ticks and a prison cell, and you don't look like a criminal. You're not wearing a wedding ring."

"Fair enough," said Rashford. "All good clues. But what are the indicators for language and place?"

"Here I rely on your phonology," she said, "the process of specific sounds you use to pronounce words, and your morphology. You used 'I guess' as an introductory syntax and your reference to the prison cell was a semantic strategy to establish context. I think you would change your tone and your vocabulary if you were talking to someone else, a colleague or a suspect perhaps, but that is because I prefer Bloomfield over Sapir, and have an anti-mentalistic bias to support my belief that clear insight is more useful than methodological orthodoxy."

Rashford realized two things. First, that his mouth was open again. And second, that he had no idea what she had just said.

He stared.

She laughed.

"You'll catch flies," she said.

He closed his mouth.

"Sorry," she said, laughing again. "I'm just teasing. It's all about your name tag."

She pointed to his chest, where his name tag was pinned to his jacket pocket.

"It's green," she said, "which means you're a speaker, not a regular delegate. So, I googled the program and looked up your name and biography on the speakers list."

She waved her phone at him.

"I was kidding about a call," she said, laughing again, her eyes crinkling with amusement.

Rashford shook his head, bemused.

"Gotcha," she said.

Rashford looked around, hoping to change the subject.

"What's that?" he said, pointing to the wooden structure on the other side of the grass.

"It's a planter box," said Benoît. "One of the maintenance guys plants geraniums and such in there, to give this space a bit of colour. Come and have a look."

They walked across the lawn. As they got nearer, Rashford realized that the structure was about eight feet long, four feet across and four feet high, made of planks nailed to a strong two-by-four frame. The container was full, the top of the soil newly turned. Two thirty-litre bags of sheep manure were leaned against the side wall.

"Bruce will dig the manure in when it's planting time," she said. "It makes for a lovely burst of colour, especially in the afternoon. This is the east wall, so the sun shines from over there, where we were. You can sit at the table and have a quiet smoke, and the sun on the green grass and red flowers make this a very special place."

Rashford nodded, looking around admiringly.

"Isn't it a bit early to be planting geraniums?" he said. "Winter's not over yet!"

"We have a lovely microclimate here," said Benoît. "There's lots of sun, shelter from the wind, and we have this cover if it suddenly turns cold."

She pointed at a folded sheet which was hanging from the back side of the planter. It was tacked onto the lip of the wood, and had weights sewn into the lower edge.

"We just flip that over and it protects the plants," she said.

"Good idea," said Rashford, then checked his watch. "Well, I'd better get going, I have a meeting I'm supposed to attend, in the Robert Stamp Building. Do you know where that is?"

"Yes," she said. "You need to go out of the other door, not the one we came through. When you're in that building, just leave by the main door. Stamp is just across the pathway; you won't miss it."

"Thank you."

"You're going to the Speakers' Reception, I assume?"

"Yes. Will you be there?"

"No, I think I'll give it a miss. I've got some marking to finish."

Rashford stubbed out his cigarette in the bucket ashtray, nodded at the professor, and started to walk across the lawn.

"Wait," Benoît said, and he paused, looking back at her.

"If you fancy another smoke break, find one of the janitorial or maintenance staff. Tell them you're looking for the SQ."

"The SQ?"

"It's like a code, it means 'secret quadrangle'. You're a stranger, so they will probably ask you who told you about it. Tell them it was LBC. That's the code for me, Linda Benoît Cheroots. Then someone will show you the nearest corridor."

"Got it. SQ. LBC. Thank you."

"You're welcome. Enjoy the conference. I'm sure we'll meet again."

Rashford nodded and walked away across the grass. The second door opened onto another short grey passage, then another door led him back into the lights and bustle of the university.

<h1 style="text-align:center">CHAPTER 2</h1>

The Robert Stamp Building was surprisingly easy to find. A low three storey structure built from grey concrete, the three broad steps leading up to the front door were flanked by mock columns in the Corinthian style. Above the door, a large round window filled the space between lintel and roofline. Three bands of smaller windows extended the length of the building.

It looked so much like a school that the plaque by the door was almost superfluous. The plaque informed all who entered that this was the original Normal School for the area between Regina and Saskatoon. When the university was established in Wheatville, the building had been relocated to the centre of the new campus, then completely gutted and modernized. The outer façade, however, remained true to history, the spiritual home of teacher education in the region.

Rashford entered into a large atrium, the light pouring in from the rondel window supplemented by the diffused illumination provided by wall-mounted sconces. A series of informational messages, including one informing anyone who cared that the Speakers' Reception was in board room 310 on level three, scrolled through on wall-mounted screens. For the technologically challenged, a makeshift notice board which had been structured from an A-frame sandwich board stood in the middle of the atrium, conveying the same information.

The modern interior would have perplexed most educators who had entered the Normal School in its earlier iterations. Rashford followed the signs, stepping with amazement on the escalator to the second floor, then turned abruptly and took a second escalator. He was decanted at the third floor, where an arrow on a second notice board directed him to the meeting. He walked down the corridor until he reached the LaGrange Board Room.

The door was open, so he entered, finding himself in a large space with a small, raised dais at one end. On the dais was a podium lectern, together with a microphone on a stand. Strategically placed around the room were a dozen or so tall round tables, each covered with a white linen drop cloth.

Rashford looked around. A few clusters of people stood next to some of the tables, chatting to each other. Some individuals stood off to the side of the room or placed their drink on one of the tables and waited, forlornly, for others to join them. Most people, however, were lining up next to a table at the end of the room opposite to the dais, a table which he now realized was a makeshift bar.

As he started towards the bar, his way was suddenly blocked by a young woman in a light summery dress. She was about five and a half feet tall, perhaps thirty centimetres shorter than Rashford, with long blonde hair tied in a high ponytail that had obviously taken her some time to perfect. It blossomed out from a tight stem and was then tied off again in three sections. These were separated by tight elastic bands, the hair between pouffed out to give a bubble effect. She thrust her hand out towards him and, looking down, he was distracted by the swell of her large breasts, which seemed all the more noticeable on her slim frame.

"I'm up here," she said, sternly.

Reddening, he raised his eyes to hers, and was relieved to see she was smiling.

"Drinks tickets," she said, still holding out her hand.

"Oh, right," said Rashford. He reached into his pocket for his wallet. "How much are they?"

She laughed.

"No, silly, they're free," she said. "We're not allowed to sell the drinks, but we have to track them. Then the university pays us later, based on the tickets."

"Who's 'us'?" said Rashford.

"We're the Social Committee for the Student Union," she said. "We're catering the event this evening. All speakers get five tickets, which they can exchange at the bar for a drink."

He realized she was holding a roll of paper tickets, from which she tore off a strip of five. Handing them to him, she looked around, and then whispered in a conspiratorial way.

"My name's Mandy. If you need any extras, just let me know and I'll see you right."

"Thank you," said Rashford, laughing as she winked at him. As she moved away, he turned, and then headed for the bar. He exchanged one of his tickets for a bottle of beer, then looked around to survey the room.

The people present were of all ages, most dressed casually like himself but a few in suits or formal business skirts. The majority had the same green name tag as himself, although a few wore tags that were royal blue in colour. Rashford wandered around the edge of the room until he saw someone who was standing, alone, at one of the tables. Rashford walked over.

"May I?" he said, raising his beer and nodding towards the table.

"Of course," said the man, looking pleased that someone had joined him. A thin man of medium height and inky-black hair, he looked to be in his early thirties and was wearing a grey suit with a white shirt and a red tie.

"Marc Claydon," he said, extending his hand.

Rashford placed his beer bottle on the table and then shook the man's hand.

"Gavin Rashford," he said.

The two stood silently for a few minutes, surveying the crowd.

"What's your talk about?" said Rashford.

"It's about the use of plant dyes in clothing made for Hudson Bay Company employees in the sixteenth century," said Claydon, his eyes shining. "It's my PhD thesis. The traders and voyageurs of the time had very brightly coloured clothes. How did they get that material?"

"I thought they just bought it," said Rashford.

"Everyone thinks that!" exclaimed Claydon. "But what if they're wrong? I've found references in old journals to 'boiling leaves for colour,' and I think they did it themselves. In fact, I think it's an early example of gendered expressionism, no doubt influenced by the interaction of the masculine heterogeneity found among European trappers of the time with the collective communalism of the First Nations people with whom they traded."

Rashford nodded.

"Early Eurocentric colonialism practised by the dominant patriarchal hierarchy," he said.

Claydon nodded enthusiastically.

"Exactly, Well said, indeed. I might borrow that line, if I may?"

Rashford nodded, once again thanking Bettina Blackeagle for the words he had just used. He still had no idea what they meant, but he had obviously put them in the correct order for a change.

"What's your field?" said Claydon.

"A bit more on the applied side," said Rashford. "Nowhere near as erudite or scholarly as your work, I'm sure."

Claydon preened visibly, then tried to be magnanimous.

"Oh, I'm sure it's just as important," he said, managing through his tone to imply that he rather doubted this fact.

Rashford laughed.

"Perhaps," he said. "Actually, I'm giving a talk on the value of FILTER in helping to overcome racist attitudes on both sides of the First Nations and Settler Community divide."

Rashford took a swallow of his beer and waited for Claydon to ask a question, but the other man just nodded, distractedly.

"They're going to introduce the speakers," he said, looking across the room at the podium. "Please excuse me."

He took his beer and left Rashford standing at the table.

The first speaker was the President and Vice Chancellor of the university. She gave the customary land acknowledgement, although Rashford noted that she didn't offer to give any back, and then welcomed all present and thanked them for their contributions to the conference. Contributions not yet made, thought Rashford, wondering why no similar closing event was planned.

The President concluded her remarks by referencing another important event she had to attend and left the room in a flurry of handshakes. Rashford noticed Claydon hovering on the edge of the cluster, trying unsuccessfully to break through to the inner circle.

A second speaker approached the lectern and introduced herself as the academic coordinator for the conference. She welcomed all those who were going to be speaking and thanked the seventeen colleagues who had served on the planning committee. As she then referenced each individual by name, department, and type of contribution to the work of the committee, Rashford quietly went back to the bar and exchanged another token.

"It's only just started," said a soft voice beside him. "Do you need more tickets yet?"

Rashford turned and saw Mandy smiling up at him.

"No, I'm good, thanks," he said, keeping his voice low. "What do I do with the left-over tickets?"

Mandy shrugged.

"Just give them to someone who looks like they need more," she said. "Or keep them as souvenirs. They only become valuable when they're used. Before that, it's all just potential and possibility."

"Just like life," said Rashford.

"Yes," said Mandy. "All potential and possibility."

She winked at him, again, and then walked away. He was not certain, but it seemed to Rashford that she put a bit more wiggle into her hips than was strictly necessary for a conference room. He shook his head and returned to the table, imagining how his friend and former colleague Gayle Morgan would respond to that interaction, had she been present.

"Eh up, she's putting her'sen on a plate for yer," she might have said, adopting the broad northern English accent of her youth. "Is tha' gunna go all Gary Puckett on me?"

Smiling at the thought, and humming the tune to 'Young girl' in his head, Rashford drank his beer and refocused on the room, where someone was being thanked for selecting 'the absolutely delightful' shade of green used on the name tags. The academic coordinator then gave way to the program chair, a large black man with a shaved head. He did not thank anybody but placed a thin silver computer on the lectern, then got straight to the point.

"Some of you have made lots of presentations," he said, "and some of you haven't. It doesn't matter. My advice is the same."

He flicked a switch and the screen behind him lit up with a projected image of the word 'ADVICE'. As he spoke, he tapped the keyboard of his computer; the word faded away, to be replaced by a line of text.

"As program chair, my first piece of advice is, keep to your allotted time. If you've got a forty-minute slot, which is the norm, then only speak for twenty minutes. You need to allow five minutes for introductions and late comers, ten minutes for questions, and the last five minutes for thank-you's and goodbyes. Don't drone on."

He tapped the keyboard again.

"Second, keep it simple. If you're showing slides, just show them. Don't use all the transitions and sounds and fancy fonts and all the other blather that gets in the way of your message. You want people to remember what you're saying, not how technically clever you are. Use a big clear font so that people at the back can read it as well."

Another tap on the keyboard.

"Finally, keep it focused. No more than three bullet points on a slide. Talk to the bullet points, don't read them."

The man turned and looked at the screen. In black print on a light grey background, the three bullet points were clearly legible to Rashford.

- Keep to your time
- Keep it simple
- Keep it focused

The program chair turned back and faced the room.

"That's my advice," he said. "If you all do that, it will be a great conference. Any questions?"

Rashford thought for a moment, then put up his hand. The man noticed and pointed at him.

"Yes, your question please."

"What if you don't have a PowerPoint?"

Rashford was sure that he heard a collective intake of breath, and that people edged away from him. The program chair just smiled.

"No PowerPoint?" he said. "Goodness me. What on earth are you planning to do?"

"I was just going to talk for a bit," said Rashford, feeling a bit flustered. "Then ask for questions and try to get a bit of discussion going."

The program chair clapped his hands together and laughed delightedly. His carefully cultivated cadences seemed to shimmer into more of a Jamaican accent.

"I'm guessing you're not an academic, good sir," he said.

Rashford confirmed this was true.

"Well," said the program chair. "Welcome. Most people here are academics and would rather bask in the brilliance of their own rhetoric than engage in conversation. Colleagues, don't look at me like that!"

He raised his voice and wagged his finger at the crowd.

"You know it's true, and I'm as guilty as all of you as well. The gentleman has raised an important point, a mirror if you will, and we would do well to reflect on that image."

He grinned at his own pun and a few people groaned appreciatively. He turned his gaze back to Rashford and his accent slipped even further.

"In the absence of PowerPoint, mon, your plan is perfect. I might come to that session myself. For the rest of you, remember my advice."

He pointed back at the screen, then left the podium to a scattering of applause. Rashford was surprised to see Mandy replace him at the microphone.

"On behalf of the Student Union," she said, "thank you for coming to this reception. Please drink as much as you like because we only get paid for the tickets you redeem."

She continued for another two or three minutes, describing the various projects to which the money raised would contribute, but very few people were listening. Rashford noticed how the academics had clustered together and were talking, a low hum of voices that overcame even the microphone. As Mandy finished and looked around, Rashford caught her eye by raising his arms above his head and clapping. She smiled, but everyone else ignored him as much as they had ignored her. Rashford finished his beer and started to leave the room.

As he moved away from the table, a hand touched his shoulder. He turned around and found himself face-to-face with the program chair, who had two beer bottles hanging by their necks between the fingers of his right hand.

"D'you have time to stop awhile and chat," said the program chair, peering at Rashford's name tag. "Mister Rashford?"

Rashford leaned forward and peered at the other man's navy-blue name tag.

"Certainly, Doctor York," he said.

"Patrick," said the program chair, doing a complicated shuffle that ended up with them each holding a beer and shaking hands.

"Gavin," said Rashford, standing straight again.

"That's called the conference dip," said Patrick York, laughing. "You lean forward slightly when you shake hands so that you can read the name tag and then say hello by name. Experienced attendees do it so smoothly that you'd never notice unless you were looking directly at them. You're just pleased they know your name!"

Rashford laughed, then raised his beer bottle so that it clicked against the other.

"Cheers," he said.

"Cheers," said Patrick. "I meant what I said, you know. About tomorrow. When are you speaking?"

"Zero eight thirty," said Rashford.

"Oh dear, the hangover shift! Well, nobody will be able to nod off to your slides, will they? Your session sounds like it will keep them on their toes!"

"Hangover shift?"

"Yes, there are two bad, or at least, less optimal, times to be scheduled at a conference. The first is the first session on the second morning, because everyone spent the night before drinking and catching up with people whom they haven't seen all year. Hooking up as well, sometimes, with 'conference husbands', as the sisters say."

York shook his head, smiling.

"The second time is the last session on the last day, because a lot of people check out of their rooms early and then either go for a last lunch or make a dash for an early flight. So, at both those sessions, engagement can be low, and attendance can be … well, let's just say, attendance can be a bit sporadic."

Rashford shook his head.

"I had no idea," he said.

"No," said Patrick, casting a glance at his companion. "You said that you weren't an academic, so what is it that you do?"

"Actually, you said I wasn't an academic," said Rashford. "I just agreed. I'm a police officer, well, to be accurate, a recently retired police officer."

"Touché," said Patrick. "And a good one, to notice that small slip by my good self. What are you doing here? Investigating something, or someone?"

He dropped his voice and looked furtively around the room. Rashford laughed.

"No, nothing like that," he said.

"What, then?"

"Well, last year I did this exam, they call it FILTER. That stands for Focused Indigenous Language Training for Emergency Responders. It's a big thing in Alsama, and I did well on my exam. My boss asked me if I'd come here and talk about it, explain how it works, answer questions, that sort of thing. I said yes, but then we wrapped up a big case I'd been working on for a few years.

"That was towards the end of the year. In January I got promoted, and got a new assignment, but it wasn't very exciting. I decided to retire, I'd got my twenty years in and had a decent pension. To be honest, I'd forgotten about this. A month ago, the Chief Superintendent called and asked me if I could still give the talk. They were going to cover all my expenses, and I had nothing else planned, so I said 'yes Ma'am' and here I am."

"Cool," said Patrick. "Well, I for one am looking forward to your talk. I'll pace myself tonight, so I can get up early in the morning."

"Pacing is always good," said Rashford, finishing his beer and putting the empty bottle on the table. "And that's enough for me. See you in the morning, I hope."

They shook hands again, then Rashford left the room.

CHAPTER 3

It was still early evening, just after seven, Rashford walked around the campus for nearly half an hour, trying to get his bearings. He was about to declare himself officially lost when he saw a member of the maintenance staff driving past in a marked pickup truck. He waved his arm and the driver slowed down, then stopped. The window whirred down.

"Yes, sir, can I help you?" said the driver, a young Cree guy in his mid-twenties.

"Tansi," said Rashford.

The young man looked at him in surprise.

"Mânan'tow," he said. "Umm ... ki'ya maka?"

He blushed.

"Sorry, I don't speak Cree."

"Ekosisi!" said Rashford, then, switching back to English. "Never mind. I wonder if you can help me?"

"I'm not sure. What do you need?"

"I'm looking for the SQ," said Rashford.

The man looked at him.

"Really? How do you know about that?"

"LBC told me. She took me there earlier."

The man nodded.

"Okay, jump in," he said, reaching across and unlocking the passenger door.

Rashford pulled on the handle to open the door and then climbed into the truck. The driver moved into gear and drove slowly off. Rashford had only just figured out how to lock his seatbelt when they stopped in front of a door clearly marked 'No Entry'.

"She's not as crazy as they say, you know," said the young man, as Rashford unclicked his seatbelt.

Rashford paused, his hand on the door handle.

"What do you mean?"

"Well, all that jewelry and stuff, and the weird colour combos. And the way she likes young black guys. That's just her trying to be cool and trendy."

Rashford nodded.

"How do you know her?" he asked.

The man hesitated.

"I took a class from her," he said, finally. "She was the best instructor I had."

"What do you study?" said Rashford.

"Did," he said. "Not do. Past tense. I used to be a student here, but I got to party too much, you know. So, I got academic probation, and then got advised to take a break. Now I'm driving truck, mowing lawns, that sort of thing. But I'll reapply one day."

Rashford nodded.

"Well, good luck with that," he said, climbing down out of the truck. He opened the door in the wall, revealing another grey corridor lit by low-wattage bulbs. He waved at the driver, who slowly started to leave, then entered the corridor.

***

The door closed behind him, and he followed the passage, turning at two sharp bends before the passage ended at another door. He pushed this open and found himself in a short cross corridor. The door behind him closed and, to his surprise, seemed to simply disappear.

There was no handle and no evident door frame. It was only when he looked carefully that he saw the thin crack marking the outline of the door.

He considered the options to his left and right and thought that the warning signs on the door to his left looked familiar. Walking down to it he pushed open the metal handle and found himself emerging by the picnic table. A man was sitting at the table, smoking a cigarette. He turned as Rashford entered, looking up and breaking into a huge smile as the two recognized each other.

"Gavin, mon, what'cha doing here?" said Patrick, jumping to his feet. "This is a secret place, mon!"

"Just came for a quick smoke, Patrick," said Rashford, taking out his cigarettes and lighting one. "I didn't think anyone would be here, this time of night."

"Just me, relaxin'," said Patrick, laughing. "Then off to my last meeting of the day. Then the party. You know about the party, huh?"

Rashford shook his head as he walked around and sat opposite Patrick.

"No. What party?"

"There should be a notice in your package," said Patrick. "The Student Union throws a first night party at all the conferences we host here. It's invitation-only, for all the key people. You know, organizers, speakers. People like us!"

He looked at his watch.

"It's nearly seven thirty," he said. "Sorry but I'm going to have to go. The party starts at nine, over in the Three-Legged Rabbit. That's the student pub on campus. Come to the downstairs room, the main floor is a regular bar."

He stood, waiting, as Rashford finished his smoke and stubbed it out in the metal bucket.

"I'll see if I'm still awake."

Patrick laughed.

"Just come by and show your face. I'll see you then, just after nine."

He led Rashford to the exit door and opened it.

"I've just got to tidy up," he said. "See you in a couple of hours."

Rashford left through the corridor, wondering why he felt rushed, and not sure what Patrick York needed to tidy up. He crossed the wide corridor, still brightly lit and busy with students, and went outside.

He walked along the broad pathway and turned right to head to his room. Like all delegates, he had been given a room in one of the student residences, which were mainly empty during the semester break. His was one of the spacious suites on the seventh floor, normally reserved for visiting professors and other special guests of the university. It had been booked and paid for by the North-West Mounted Police, and he was pleasantly surprised find a large queen-sized bed and windows that looked out over a small park and flower garden.

The room had a tiny kitchenette attached, with a stove and fridge as well as the ubiquitous microwave and kettle, so he stopped at a convenience store and bought some orange juice, bagels, and cream cheese for breakfast. Coming out of the shop, he realized that he was opposite the 'No Entry' door where the young maintenance guy had dropped him. The door was just closing on a dark clothed figure whom he might not have noticed if not for the flash of a purple scarf.

Rashford stood for a moment, thinking, then shook his head and walked to the residence. He dropped his purchases off in his room, took out a heavier jacket, and then went to find a place to eat.

In the end he decided to eat on campus at the Three-Legged Rabbit. The other options were a 'choose your own fillings' sandwich shop and an all-night coffee place offering a variety of microwaved meals. At the pub he found basic comfort food. He settled for a steak and mushroom pie with French fries, washed down with a cranberry soda, and followed that with a coffee and a slice of homemade almond cake with a honey glaze. 'Allegedly homemade', he thought to himself, not sure who in the back room of a student pub would have access to a licensed kitchen in their home. Wherever it was made, though, it tasted pretty good.

As he ate, he quietly observed the students who were milling around, together with a smattering of older adults he assumed were staff or faculty. Some were playing darts, others a game of pool, but most just ebbed and flowed in different groups as people came and went from the bar. Nobody came to disturb him, and he read over his notes for the morning.

He knew what he was going to say and, as he had told Patrick York, it was going to be short and focused. He hoped, though, to be able to speak without notes, and so he worked on memorizing the main points. He finished a second cup of coffee and glanced at his watch, noting with some surprise that it was almost nine o'clock. He folded his notes neatly and put them in his pocket, then went outside.

The pub was located on the edge of campus, so as attract trade from both the student and local communities. This also meant that the car park was exempt from the campus smoking ban, and a small corner had been designated as the smoking area. A covered shed similar to a bus shelter provided some protection from inclement weather, and three metal posts contained receptacles that served as ash trays.

Rashford walked over, nodded to the half dozen other individuals who were standing around, and lit a cigarette. Nobody spoke to anyone else, each aware that they were the new social pariahs. Yellow light from the pub windows spilled into the street, exacerbating the darkness of their corner and the illicit isolation of their enjoyment.

Finishing his cigarette, Rashford stubbed it out in one of the ashtrays, and nodded again to his fellow smokers. He was about to leave and walk back to his apartment when he recognized the tall figure of Patrick York walking up to the pub. The man seemed to pause, straightening his shoulders as if bracing himself for a potential challenge, then pushed open the door and stepped across the threshold. Rashford thought for a moment, then walked back across the parking lot and followed York into the pub.

This time, instead of going through into the bar, Rashford turned to his right and went through the side door located under a green emergency exit sign. The door was marked with a stapled sheet of handprinted paper as being 'Reserved for Private Event'. He went down a flight of stairs and found himself in a large room. Obviously, this was the original basement, which extended the whole length and width of the building.

The walls had been left, or repurposed, as exposed brick, and the ceiling was low enough that he had to resist the urge to duck his head. The lighting was a soft mauve, created by low wattage red and blue bulbs interspersed with regular white ones. A mixed track of music played softly in the background; the lyrics audible but not overpowering.

There were perhaps fifty people in the room, some standing to chat but most sitting on one of the many upholstered armchairs and couches which dotted the area. A table to his left contained ice buckets with a selection of beers and ciders, and an array of opened bottles of red and white wine. Rashford picked up a bottle of red wine and read the label. When he saw that it was a blend of national and imported wines, he put it back and selected a beer instead.

"Wise choice," said a voice at his elbow. He turned to see Marc Claydon standing next to him, a glass of red wine in his hand.

"This is rubbish," said the doctoral student. "The label says it's Canadian wine, but if you read the label, that's only three per cent. The rest is a tanker load of swill from Chile or somewhere, a place where they've used the good wine for their own bottles, and this is the stuff left over."

"Well, I wouldn't go quite that far," said Rashford. "They still have quality control rules, I'm sure."

"Right," said Claydon. "And every global company works terribly hard to ensure it meets all local, national, and international laws and regulations, irrespective of the impact on its bottom line."

He emphasized the word 'terribly' in a fake English accent, making Rashford laugh, then placed his glass back on the table.

"Well, it can be someone else's problem, I'm having a beer."

He reached past Rashford and took a bottle, then turned and faced the crowd.

"Anyone you know?" said Rashford.

"A few. Mainly profs. You?"

"Nope. See you later."

Claydon looked at him, open-mouthed. Perhaps he was not used to being summarily dismissed, thought Rashford, feeling ridiculously pleased that he had got his own back.

Still enjoying the frisson of petty revenge, he moved away from the bar towards an empty armchair he had seen. It looked quite comfortable and was in a corner next to the emergency exit. With his back to the wall, and a secondary escape route close at hand, he was able to relax and observe the crowd.

He amused himself by focusing on one individual at a time, then watching that person as she or he or they manoeuvred through the party. One bearded man, whom Rashford estimated to be in his late fifties, stood out because of his brightly hued tartan waistcoat. He wandered from group to group, chatting for a few moments and shaking hands, but all the time circling in towards a group of young women. One person in that group was a brunette with shoulder length hair, who kept looking up from her conversation and scanning the room until she saw the waistcoat, fixing it with a frank stare.

Rashford smiled to himself as the coloured waistcoat joined a group next to that with the dark-haired woman. He chatted to the group, focusing on one man in particular, who then took him by the arm and walked him across to the group of women. He was obviously making introductions, and everyone shook hands and smiled.

The brunette contrived to be the last person to be introduced, and Rashford noted the longer handshake and the meeting of eyes. He knew, without a doubt and contrary to appearances, that the two were previously and intimately acquainted. He was not at all surprised that after her friends moved away, the two engaged in a short but intense conversation, before splitting up.

Rashford watched the brunette as she moved through the crowd, pausing briefly to chat with a few apparent friends and acquaintances before leaving the room. Three minutes later the coloured waistcoat reached the door and followed her out. 'A conference husband,' thought Rashford to himself, 'off for an early night'.

He started to watch another person, a tall Black fellow with a shaved head and piercing eyes who was wearing a soft grey linen suit. Somali or Masai, thought Rashford, watching the man as he seemed to glide through the crowd. Some people gave him a high five as he went by, or a complex series of handshakes and fist bumps ending in a clasped fist, but to most he seemed invisible, a ghost drifting by, one to whom they paid no attention at all.

Rashford idly noted that most of the people in the crowd were white, but some twenty per cent he would consider Black, of either African or Caribbean descent. Another half dozen appeared to be of Asiatic appearance, and a couple were possibly of Indigenous background.

The majority of the men were in casual jackets and jeans, a few were in dark blue or charcoal grey suits. The women, who made up over half of those present, were more diversely dressed and shone brightly in the dim light. Rashford noticed that it was the white women who tried to engage with the Somali-Masai as he glided past; they were graciously acknowledged, but he seldom stopped for more than a second or two.

The women of African background, however, appeared to ignore him, and it was at those groups he stopped to chat. At the third group a woman stood at his approach, her shawl a sparkling cascade of reds and golds interspersed with silver thread. She was nearly as tall as him, with a close shaven head and huge copper rings hanging from her ears.

She said something sharp, her body language echoing the staccato thrumming of her words, then slapped him hard across the cheek. The other women in the group laughed, and as she sat down, she joined in, banishing him to the outlands of past memory. The Somali-Masai rubbed his cheek, shook his head, and walked to the next group.

Rashford was trying to decipher what he had just witnessed, drink his beer, keep his eye on the progression of the ghost, and scan the room, all at the same time, when someone in a sundress plumped onto the arm of his chair. It was only as she reached one arm behind his back, pulled him towards her so that his face was nestled in her bosom, and kissed his forehead, that he realized it was Mandy. He struggled to sit up straight, reaching to put his beer on the small side table, and she relaxed him from her grip. As soon as he was upright, she slid off the arm of the chair and onto his lap. He automatically put his arms around her waist.

"Hello," she said. "How are you?"

She reached across him and placed a large, and largely empty, wine glass on the table next to his beer, then settled back.

He was uncomfortably aware that he was in a public place with a girl almost half his age sitting on his lap. He was also aware of her perfume, and the shine in her eyes, and the proximity of her breasts. He was also aware that she was probably aware, or soon would be, of the effect this combination of factors was having on him.

She pulled his head down and whispered in his ear.

"This is a nice dark corner. Nobody can see."

As if to illustrate, she lifted his left hand from her waist and placed it on her breast.

"You were admiring them earlier."

"Yes ... But ..."

"It's okay," she said, softly. "I like it. Don't you?"

Rashford tried to move his hand, but she pushed his wrist more firmly. Through her dress, he could feel the nub of her nipple on his palm.

"We can't, you're too young, I'm too old," said Rashford, gabbling, trying to release his hand.

"It's not like we're going to get married," she said, pouting a little. "Anyway, I'm twenty-nine."

"Twenty-nine? Are you a graduate student?"

"I wish," she laughed. "No, I'm what they call a 'mature' student. This is my second go-round at university."

"You're still too young."

"How old are you?"

"I'm forty-eight, for heaven's sake!"

"Forty-eight?"

She looked at him, her face scrunched up to indicate she was thinking hard. Then she smiled, leaned back again, and nibbled at his ear.

"Don't you see, that's just perfect," she said.

"What is?"

Rashford tried to move his head away from her lips and at the same time lift his hand from her breast.

"The half your age plus five rule. Half of forty-eight is twenty-four, plus five is twenty-nine. That's me. So, we're good."

She snuggled in close against him again, but he pushed her away.

"Mandy, stop it, please," he said. "That rule is for kids and, anyway, isn't it plus seven?"

She pouted.

"Whatever. It's just a bit of conference fun. I thought you liked me?"

"I do, I do," said Rashford. "But I can't do this, not here, not now."

She gave a great sigh, then got off his lap and stood up. Facing him, she leaned forward, resting her right hand on his chair back as she put her head next to his ear.

"This is what you're missing," she whispered, using her left hand to pull down the neck of her sundress. Rashford could not help but look down and see her smooth tops of her breasts.

"I like fit, older, men," she said.

"So do I," said Rashford, his voice squeaking as he reached out and pushed her away, again.

She laughed; he thought far too merrily given the circumstances.

"Later," she said, picking up her wine glass, blowing him a kiss, then turning and disappearing into the crowd. Rashford fell back into his chair, breathing heavily, and reached to the side table to pick up his beer.

"Looks like you'll be needing that, mon," said a voice.

Rashford started, then looked around to see Patrick York standing at his shoulder, a beer bottle in his hand.

"How did ..." he started, then saw the Emergency Door behind them and understood.

"Another secret passage?" he said.

"Place is full of them if you know where to look," said Patrick. "And of course, it helps to have a master key."

"Right," said Rashford.

They were both silent for a few moments, each sipping their beer.

"So, Randy Mandy has you in her sights, does she?" said Patrick. "Good luck with that, mon."

"No, no," said Rashford, "she was just, umm, saying hello."

Even to his own ears that sounded lame. Patrick just shook his head.

"Of course, you were. She was. Whatever. Just be careful. She's a popular girl, but she can be a real bitch if she doesn't get her way."

Rashford was surprised by the vehemence in Patrick's tone but decided to ignore it.

"What have you been up to?" he said.

Patrick shrugged.

"Oh, you know, had my meeting. Just finished, actually. Then came here. Oh, there's Lin-Lin."

He waved, enthusiastically, and Rashford saw an answering wave from the crowd. It came from near the Somali-Masai ghost, who then moved towards them, and it was only as they got near that Rashford saw the purple scarf and realized that his waving partner was Linda Benoît.

The four met and shook hands, Linda asking him if he was enjoying himself.

"Just fine, thanks," he said, but York spoke over him.

"He's met Randy Mandy," he said.

Linda Benoît raised an eyebrow.

"Has he, now. Well, good luck with that."

They chatted for a few more minutes and then Linda, together with the ghost, who Rashford had discovered was indeed Masai and was named Issack, eased back into the crowd. Patrick watched them go with a sour look on his face.

"Everything alright?" said Rashford.

York looked at him, seemingly about to say something, then just nodded his head.

"Just fine, thanks."

"Well," said Rashford. "I think I'm off to bed. I've got an early start in the morning."

"Yes," said Patrick, nodding. "Eight thirty. I'll be there, unless some emergency comes up. I'm program chair, so I have to fix every problem, but I hope to be there. I want to hear what you have to say. Good night."

They shook hands, and then Rashford made his way to the door. As he crossed the room he saw Issack, seemingly floating in space, his arms around Linda Benoît as they swayed to the music. He held her tight to his chest, the grey of his suit enveloping the black of hers, and her purple scarf ran down between them like an illuminated landing strip on a cold foggy night.

Back in his room, Rashford made himself a cup of mint tea. While it steeped, he took a quick shower, revelling in the hot water. Wrapped in a towel, he took his tea to the window and looked out. The park was full of people, mainly couples, walking along next to each other and chatting. Sometimes they would shake hands, then go their separate ways; sometimes they would hold hands, then leave the park together. Rashford stood there, sipping his tea, musing on the mating rituals of humans. He started thinking about Mandy, and the glimpse she had given him of her breasts. He felt himself stirring and was grateful for the interruption of a knock at his door, although he did wonder who it might be at that hour.

He walked over and opened the door a little, peering out through the crack.

"Yes?" he said.

Mandy pushed her way in and closed the door behind her. She was wearing a long blue raincoat over her summer dress. 'It must be getting cold out', thought Rashford. She reached up and put a finger on his lips, the age-old signal for him to be quiet, to not say anything. Then she turned and opened the door, reaching out to hang the Do Not Disturb sign on the outside handle.

Turning back, she unbuttoned her coat, and it was only as she took it off and threw it over a nearby chair that he realized she was no longer wearing her dress. She was naked apart from her sensible slip-on shoes and her black panties, which were decorated with bright yellow butterflies. He stared at her.

Mandy reached out and took his hand, then lifted it to the tightly plaited base of her ponytail, wrapping his fingers around the upright column.

"I left my hair up," she said, "so you can be in control."

Then she sank to her knees, taking his towel down with her.

Chapter 4

Later, as they lay in bed, Rashford raised himself on one elbow and looked down at her.

"Like a sleepy golden dawn," he said, softly, gently stroking her hair. At some point she had undone the ponytail and her blonde hair was splayed out across the pillow.

"Oh, good," she said, giggling and clapping her hands at the same time. "Does that mean I get to stay the night, so you can love me in the morning?"

"Umm," said Rashford. "I was just .... Umm. You know your Leonard Cohen?"

She huffed.

"I'm an English major," she said. "He was most of our first semester, third year. In my contemporary poetry class I wrote a three-thousand-word paper analyzing the comparative mythologies between his poem 'For Anne' and Shakespeare's 'Sonnet 18'."

Rashford just looked at her.

"That sounds like something Professor Benoît would say," he said.

"You guessed! Yes, she was the prof for that class. I liked her. Before."

"Before what?"

Mandy pulled him down and kissed him.

"Never mind. Let's not talk about her. I'm having such a good time and I don't want to spoil it."

Rashford kissed her back.

"Okay," he said. "But no, I don't think you should stay until morning. I have to get up really early, to prepare for my talk, and I need to focus."

She pouted at him, then smiled.

"It's okay, this has been wonderful. I've waited a long time for an evening like this. Thank you for making my first time so special."

Rashford sat bolt upright and stared at her, then dropped his head back on the pillow and exhaled loudly. He closed his eyes, then spoke in a strangled voice.

"Your first time?"

She laughed out loud.

"Oh, the look on your face," she said.

Rashford opened his eyes. She was sitting up, her arms wrapped around her knees, her head tilted to one side and looking directly at him. Her hair hung down like a veil. She reached down and stroked her fingers across his chest.

"I meant the first time I've made love," she said, softly. "I've had sex before, loads of times actually, but that was different."

Rashford figured that this was a good time not to say anything, so he didn't. He just lay there as she continued talking, her fingers pulling gently at his chest hair, her nails scratching softly across his nipples.

"When I came to university," she said, "I was eighteen. I had no idea what to do, how to behave. On that first day we were all lining up to join different clubs. This boy next to me in the queue asked me if I'd like to take a break and go to his room for a cup of tea. I said sure. So, we walked over to the dorm.

"When he went out to fill the kettle, I got undressed and climbed into his bed. I figured that's what we were really there for, and I wanted to get back to make sure I could sign up for the Poetry Society.

"Well, long story short, he came back, looked surprised, said 'oh', plugged in the kettle, got undressed, got into bed, and we did it. Then the kettle boiled so he got up and made tea, then we did it again, drank our tea, and went back to the lines. That was my first time."

Rashford reached out and held her hand. She gripped his tightly.

"I'd fooled around with boys at home," she said, "but I'd never gone all the way before. The next day, after one of our classes, I met him in the hall. He asked me if I'd like another cup of tea. This time he didn't even bother with the kettle. Come to think of it, we didn't even get into bed, he just lifted my skirt."

Her voice started to tremble a little, and he grasped her hand more tightly.

"That was my second time. I didn't even know his name."

Rashford spoke softly.

"It's okay," he said. "You don't have to tell me this."

"I want to," she said.

Rashford watched a single tear roll down her cheek.

"I don't think I ever saw him again," she said. "Later, someone told me that he'd gone home, he didn't like being away from his friends. A couple of days later, another boy asked me if I'd like to have tea with him. When we got to his room, he said he wanted doggy. I had no idea what he meant. He laughed at me and told me to strip, then kneel on the bed. Then he slapped my breasts as he did it. It hurt, but he used really crude language and made me tell him how much I liked it."

She was crying more freely now.

"There were more guys that first few weeks. Once two of them came, and they each took it in turns while the other watched and took pictures on his phone. I just couldn't stop it. I didn't know how to say no.

"Then one day I was in one of the washrooms. Between classes, you know. A couple of girls came in and were chatting. They obviously didn't know I was in the stall.

"They were talking about this girl who would spread her legs for a cup of tea. 'Jeff says he wonders what she'd do if he offered her a cookie as well,' one of them laughed. The other said, 'yeah, she's a right slut, they call her Randy Mandy.'"

Rashford put his arm around her and pulled her to his chest as she sobbed.

"I couldn't believe it was me they were talking about. It was horrible. I went home that weekend and told my mom I was quitting university."

She sniffled.

"Do you have any tissues?"

Rashford extricated his arm and found the box on the bedside table. He passed it to her. She took one and blew her nose noisily.

"My mom asked me what was wrong, and when it all came pouring out, she told me not to be so stupid. 'You got yourself in this mess,' she said, 'so get yourself out. You're smart enough to do that.' But I couldn't go back."

She sniffed, then blew her nose again.

"I got myself a job in a retail store, selling clothes, and just kept away from people. I hung out with my cousins and that was all. Seven years later, one of them told me he was going to go back to university. He was like me, he'd dropped out once, but then he'd got into trouble and spent time in jail. Now he was out and trying again. He asked me if I'd go back with him.

"So, we both reapplied and got accepted. When I came back to school for the second time, everyone had forgotten about my awful nickname. So, I was free to study."

'No, they hadn't,' thought Rashford, but he didn't say anything.

"I went back to campus and just got on with my studies. I didn't go to anyone's dorm for tea, or anything else. I found I liked my classes, and I did pretty well at them. My cousin made it through his first year and then quit again!"

She laughed.

"After Christmas I had an introductory science class, and my assigned lab partner was this guy called Emmanuel. He asked me to call him Manny. Manny and Mandy, we laughed about that. He was really smart, an Afro-Canadian from somewhere in Nova Scotia. He said his people had come up as Black Loyalists, back in the 1780s, and settled outside Halifax.

"We got on really well and after a late lab would go for a coffee or a drink. Except Fridays. On Fridays he always said he had to rush off, for an appointment.

"One Sunday afternoon towards the end of the semester we bumped into each other near the pub. We decided to have a drink, then something to eat, then the next thing that happened was we were back at my place and in bed. We missed all our classes on Tuesday and Wednesday."

Mandy stopped speaking and looked at him.

"It was good with Manny," she said, after a moment. "Not as good as this, but better than what I'd had before."

Rashford nodded, smoothing her hair with his hand. She dropped her head back onto his chest.

"Anyway, on Thursday at our lab, he asked me out to the movies on Saturday. He said he thought the next day would be his last Friday commitment anyway, but even if it wasn't then he was going to cancel his regular appointment as he didn't want to do that anymore. 'Do what?' I asked, and he said, 'do LBC'."

Rashford started upright, bumping her head with his chest.

"What?" he said.

She thought he just hadn't heard her and spoke more clearly.

"He said, 'I don't need a guaranteed A and I don't need to do LBC anymore'. And I said, 'what's LBC?' and he said it was a nickname for one of the profs, who apparently 'Liked Black Company'. He said she took a different guy to her house each semester, they didn't have to do any assignments, just turn up there on a Friday night and have dinner with her and some friends, and they were guaranteed an A. He was going to tell her he wanted out, and then I never saw him again."

She sat up and reached across to the nightstand and pulled out another couple of tissues. Rashford tried not to be distracted when her breasts brushed his stomach. She wiped her eyes and blew her nose again, then settled back at his side.

"What, he just left?"

"He just disappeared. I waited outside the theatre, and he never showed up. I texted him, I called, but there was no answer. He just ghosted me. After that, it was like he had never existed. He wasn't around campus; he never came to class. Nobody knew where he'd gone, or why."

"Did you talk to his prof, the one he was seeing?"

"Not then, no. How would I know who she was? There are a lot of women profs here. I could hardly go round asking them if they liked to have sex with young black students, could I?"

"No, I suppose not," said Rashford. "If that's what they were doing."

"What else could it be?"

"I don't know, but let's not jump to conclusions without some evidence."

"Oh, right, you're a policeman, I forgot."

"That's not the point. Anyway, what did you mean, 'not then'? Did you talk to someone later?"

"Yes, but much later, and way too late. I finished the semester, and my exams, and that was it. I asked around when I came back, for second year, but my cousin was having issues then and that took up my time. I just forgot about Manny."

Mandy sniffled again. Rashford reached across and pulled her to him, kissing her eyes, nose and mouth before moving down to her throat, and then her breasts. She pushed his head down so he was kissing her stomach. He paused, looking up.

"We can pretend it's the morning," he said, "but then you'll really have to go."

"I know," she said, pushing his head down again.

The next morning Rashford found himself smiling as he showered and dressed. He made himself a toasted bagel with cream cheese and ate it while the coffee brewed. Then he reread his notes as he drank his coffee, trying to focus on his talk instead of his recurring visions of Mandy in the throes of passion. Shaking his head didn't help, so he took a second coffee in his takeaway mug and went to find the secret quadrangle.

This he did without any difficulty, arriving just after seven thirty to find that two maintenance men had had the same idea. They looked at him, quizzically.

"LBC sent me," said Rashford, raising his coffee mug in salute. They raised theirs in return and he joined them at the picnic table. There was silence as he lit his cigarette, the communal hush that surrounds such sacred acts as the first smoke of the morning. It was only after he had stubbed out the butt in the ash tray bucket that they engaged in some desultory talk about the weather, and the chances of the Toronto Blue Jays for the coming season. Rashford passed his packet around and they each took one, and the proffered light, before he lit his own second cigarette.

"Do either of you work in that garden bed?" said Rashford, pointing at the wooden structure on the other side of the lawn.

"God, no!" said the younger of the two workers.

"She'd kill us," said the other.

"Who would?" said Rashford.

"LBC", the two exclaimed, simultaneously.

"That's her baby", said the first worker. "She built it, she brings in the soil and compost, she plants it. None of us are allowed to touch it."

"Except Bruce, of course," said the second. The first nodded.

"Bruce?" said Rashford.

"Yeah. He's probably the longest serving gardener here, isn't he, Fred?"

The older worker nodded.

"I reckon. He was here before me, any road, and I've got my ten-year pin. I dunno, he might have been here when it was still a college. It only became a university twelve years ago. That's when she came, I think, when they started recruiting proper profs instead of just teachers. Anyways, he's the only one I've ever seen digging in there, helping her get the soil ready for planting, I guess. He can climb up the step ladder to dig a bit easier than she can."

"You'd think she had a sack of gold buried in there," said the younger man. "My mum's a gardener and she taught me a lot. One day I noticed that the geraniums had started to die back, so I began dead-heading them. LBC caught me and she went ballistic."

"Got a right temper, that one," said Fred. "Glad I'm not her fella."

"Or her girl," said the other gardener. "Word is, she goes both ways."

"Nah," spat Fred. "That's just the haircut. Right, c'mon young Jeff. Time we were moving, it's nearly eight."

They both got up from the table, nodded at Rashford, stubbed out their cigarettes, then walked across the grass and out through the far door. Rashford lit a third cigarette and studied his notes, but his mind was full of disparate pieces of information, and he found it hard to focus. Eventually he gave up, stubbed out his cigarette, and went to find his room.

***

The talk had gone well, he thought. There were twenty-three people in the room, plus himself and the young student who introduced him. Rashford had been required to provide the conference organizers with a short biography, a copy of which had been printed in the program, and the student proceeded to read it out to the group. The voice of the student trembled and stumbled with nerves.

Some in the audience followed along, reading from their own programs, presumably checking to make sure the student did not make any mistakes. Others simply gazed out of the window, no doubt wondering, like Rashford, why the fellow had not simply said 'read the blurb'. Only three people were actually looking at the young man as he ploughed on to the end.

In the far back corner of the room, to the left, sat Marc Claydon. He was wearing a jacket and tie and held a large notebook in his lap. He nodded briefly at Rashford, but otherwise did not move. Also seated at the back of the room, but on the right as he looked out, Rashford saw Patrick York sitting on the chair nearest to the door. With his shaved head, black turtleneck, and black leather jacket, he looked more like a gangster than an academic. He too held a notebook, albeit a smaller one, and nodded in greeting. Rashford nodded back.

In the centre of the room, by herself, sat Mandy. She was wearing a blue high-necked shirt under a cream blouse, and a pair of stone-washed jeans with artfully placed rips at the knees. She did not nod at him, simply smiled when they made eye contact. Rashford felt himself blushing and hurriedly looked down at his notes. He remembered the words of wisdom Gayle Morgan had given him.

'Don't be scared,' she had said. 'They're just people. Imagine them all sitting there without their clothes on'.

'That's not helping right now', he thought, trying to scan the crowd without seeing a naked Mandy sitting in the middle row.

The introduction finally over, Rashford stood as the young man led the applause, then moved to his reserved place in the front row. Rashford waited until he was seated before speaking.

"Thank you for those kind words," he said. "I couldn't have written them better myself."

A few people chuckled, Patrick York barked out a sharp laugh, and the young man turned crimson. Rashford hurried on.

"As many of you know, when the western provinces left Canada and declared the independent state of Alsama, a lot of people wondered why the First Nations and the Métis had not become involved. After all, their treaty relationships and other legal understandings were with the Crown, in Canada, not with the provinces.

"It was only later, when the dust had settled, that it became known that secret negotiations had taken place. Before inviting the Americans to help them establish their independence, the western provinces held high-level talks with the various Treaty Council chiefs. They agreed that, in order to keep their jobs, all public servants in Alsama would have to learn an Indigenous language.

"They also agreed to a two-year grace period, after which all public sector jobs would be designated bilingual, English plus an Aboriginal language. The provincial premiers hoped that this would minimize any resistance to their plans. The Treaty Chiefs hoped that it would serve as a conduit to promote Indigenous engagement in the public service, as more Aboriginal people know English and a first language than the other way around. They had seen what had happened after Canada was declared bilingual, when many of the top government and private sector jobs went to Francophones, who all spoke English.

"Once this agreement was in place, the Treaty Chiefs made sure that it would be adhered to. The first item on the legislative agenda for the new state of Alsama was the creation of the FILTER program. FILTER, as you perhaps know, stands for Focused Indigenous Language Training for Emergency Responders. The Treaty Chiefs wanted to make sure that police officers, paramedics, firefighters, and so on, were all able to communicate with the Indigenous population.

"As you know, there have been too many cases where a lack of communication and compassion, exacerbated by a healthy dose of racism, has led to bad outcomes. The hope was, and is, that by learning an Aboriginal language, the first responders would develop a better understanding of, and greater empathy for, the people they served.

"I took the FILTER program; I decided to learn Cree. I did quite well. I am now able to speak to the people in their own language, and to listen to what they have to say."

Rashford stopped talking, and slowly looked around the room. He was pleased to see that everyone was looking at him, and that Mandy had gotten dressed.

"I actually think it's the listening that's most important," he said, "and I'd like to do that now. Please, let's have a conversation. Would anyone like to start, with a question or a comment?"

There was silence. Some people shuffled uncomfortably in their chairs, others looked down at their feet, or out of the window.

Rashford had been in this situation before, sitting in an interrogation room, waiting for a suspect to break. He had learned that most people cannot stand silence, and rush to fill the void with words. He stood patiently, watching, and saw a young woman hesitantly raise her hand.

"Yes, miss?" he said, immediately and cheerfully. "What is your question? Or comment?"

"Megwetch," she said, softly. "Why did you choose Cree?"

"Great question," said Rashford. "Tânehki? Because it's one of the strongest Indigenous languages left in use north of the Medicine Line, and because it's the language spoken by most of the First People in the areas where I live and work."

Another person raised a hand.

"Is it the easiest to learn as well?" he said.

"I've no idea," said Rashford. "That was not a criterion for me."

"What's the Medicine Line?" someone said, and Rashford explained that it was an old name for the border with the United States.

Now that the silence was broken, the questions came thick and fast. Rashford was able to answer most of them, and in those cases where he could not then he posed the question to the larger group. If there was still no satisfactory answer, he wrote the question down on the back of his notes and promised to try and find an explanation. As he came to the end of the allotted time for his presentation, he moved to the back of the room and left a pen and piece of paper on an empty chair.

"If you would like an email with the answers to those outstanding questions," he said, raising his voice and his arm at the same time in order to get everyone's attention. "Just leave your address on the list here. I'll send out a mass response and bcc anybody who wants to know."

He wrapped up his talk by thanking the organizers for their work, the student for his introduction, and the audience for their participation. He was gratified by the enthusiastic response he received and took a mock bow. This prompted laughter and more applause.

As the attendees left the room, a number paused to write their email addresses. Others came to the front, continuing to ask questions as they crowded around. Rashford saw Marc Claydon on the outside of the group and nodded to him. Claydon, delighted to be publicly recognized, straightened his posture and beamed.

"Great talk, Gavin," he said loudly, letting everyone know that he was on first name terms with the man at the centre of attention.

"Thank you," said Rashford. "Good luck with yours."

Claydon preened.

"Yes. Session seven point three. Hope to see you there."

Without waiting for a response, negative or otherwise, he left the room. The clamour of questions surrounding Rashford continued until a deep voice cut through the hubbub.

"My apologies, Mister Rashford," said Patrick York. "I am afraid you will have to continue these conversations outside. The next presenter would like to come in and set up for their session."

Rashford nodded and turned back to the seven or eight people still clustered around.

"Look," he said, "I'd love to keep chatting but I'm afraid that I have another session to go to, as I'm sure you do as well. This is my e-mail address. Please send me your questions and I shall try to answer them."

He wrote his email on another piece of paper and this was passed around, people entering it into the contact lists of their phones. York accompanied him as he walked to the door.

"It was a good talk," he said. "Well done. Which session are you going to next?"

"I thought a coffee and SQ," said Rashford. "Want to join me?"

"Sounds like a plan, mom," said York, slipping back into his Caribbean accent.

Rashford picked up the sheet of paper from the chair at the back of the room and glanced at it as he followed York out of the door. There were eleven e-mail addresses listed, but what made Rashford smile was a cryptic note at the bottom of the list, which looked a bit like an email address but was something else entirely.

Even though it was not a very elegant code, he got the message as 'later2030@m.icu' he read. He folded the sheet of paper and put it in his pocket.

"Where's the best place for a latte with an extra shot?" he said.

"Follow me, mon," said York.

Chapter 5

There was nobody else in the secret quadrangle, so the two men took their coffee and sat at the bench. They chatted about Rashford's talk, and some of the questions that had been raised.

"You really got them engaged," said York. "You should have been a teacher!"

Rashford laughed.

"No thanks. Those folks all wanted to be there; they were already interested. Teachers have to work with whomever turns up. I don't know if I could do that, talk to people who aren't paying attention, who just don't seem to care."

"It's a challenge for the profession, that's for sure," said York. "Even at university level. Some students seem to think that because they've paid for the program, they are entitled to the degree. They don't seem to understand that you actually have to earn the credits, and that not everyone will pass. And their parents are worse!"

"Parents?" said Rashford. "Of university students? You're joking."

"Sadly not, mon. I had one who phoned me to tell me that her daughter couldn't focus because the room was too hot, and we didn't have air conditioning. She thought the girl should get an A but not have to turn up. I looked it up. The girl was twenty-eight."

"Hardly a girl," said Rashford. "What are they called, 'helicopter parents'?"

"Used to be. Drone parents, we call them now. They don't just hover, they follow you around, on social media and real life, trying to wear you down."

Rashford shook his head, then sipped his coffee.

"What about you," he said. "What do you teach?"

"Oh, this and that," said York, vaguely. "I'm more of an administrator."

Rashford looked at him.

"'This and that'?" he said.

York looked at the ground, quietly smoking his cigarette.

"You're a cop, right?" he said.

"Used to be, yes" said Rashford. "Now I'm retired."

"Maybe you can help me, then."

"Help you with what? How?"

There was a pause as York took another drink of coffee.

"My PhD is in Island Studies," he said. "Specifically, pre-colonial social customs and mores in the Caribbean. I study the cultures and communities that existed before and during the sixteen hundreds, up to the time of the pirates and buccaneers."

"What on earth are you doing here, then?" said Rashford.

"I'm on sabbatical. I normally teach at UWI, the University of the West Indies, at the Cave Hill campus. That's in Barbados. But I came here to look for someone."

Rashford sat forward and took another cigarette.

"Oh, yes? Who?"

"My half-nephew, I guess. My wife's younger sister's adopted son, anyway. They live in Kingston, Jamaica. He came here to study, and then just disappeared."

"Disappeared?"

"Yes. Last year. I had no real plan to go anywhere for my sabbatical, I was just going to hunker down and write a book. We have a little house on the east side of the island, the Atlantic side, so I can sit and watch the waves as I write. No sandy beaches and half-naked tourists to distract me!

"Anyway, my wife's sister was going frantic, so I said I would try to help. I called up here and got a sabbatical visitor thing organized. I was supposed to give them two lectures, one in each semester, and they gave me an office. My sabbatical stipend from home is enough to cover rent and the meal plan at one of the guest dorms, so it's all good."

"Why do you say, 'supposed'?" said Rashford.

"Oh, the guy who was organizing this conference got sick and they needed someone to step in at short notice. I wasn't doing much anyway, so I volunteered to do that instead of one of the lectures."

"What happened to your half-nephew?"

"Chad. That's his name. I don't know, I'm trying to find out. He got a place here, to study General Arts, and came up last fall, a year ago. He flew home for Christmas, and all was good. He was really enjoying himself, and he told the family he liked the people. His grades weren't brilliant, just C's, but he said that would improve in second semester, as he had a sure-fire straight A lined up in one class. Then he flew back, and nobody saw him again."

"No contact at all?"

"There was for a bit, emails every couple of weeks, a Zoom call on his stepbrother's birthday, that sort of thing. He posted pictures of the snow, said it was cold, but he was able to get warm once a week, his studies were going okay, that sort of thing. Then, in late March, early April, it all stopped. There was nothing."

"Was there any warning?"

"No. My sister-in-law said it was like he just dropped off the planet."

"And this was last year?"

"Yeah."

"Have you spoken to any of his profs?"

"Of course. They don't know anything. They all say he was an average student, laughed a lot, popular with his classmates, yada yada. Only one said he was a troubled soul, but I think she's just crazy."

Rashford laughed.

"Really? Why?"

"Well, it's a bit embarrassing. I'd been here about a month and was working my way through meetings with Chad's teachers. This one prof said she was busy, but I could go to her place for dinner, and we could chat. So, I went there, and she's made meat patties, rice, and beans. It was like being in a tourist place at home."

"Maybe she was trying to make you feel comfortable?"

"Ya mon, I don't think so. She served me Red Stripe beer, for heaven's sake. And what she was wearing! I've got handkerchiefs bigger than that skirt. I'm a married man, you know. But she didn't care about that."

He shook his head at the memory.

"You see it at home, you know. White girls on holiday throwing themselves at black guys. I've been there myself, when I was young. But up here? And she's no girl, she has to be fifty at least. I swear, every time she passed me a plate her cleavage got bigger."

Rashford laughed, but in a rather forced way, as an image of Mandy came into his head.

"Sounds like she was being invitational," he said.

"You think? Man, she was dressed for access, that's for sure."

Rashford laughed out loud this time.

"So, what happened?"

"Nothing. I tell you, I'm a married man. She eventually gave up and told me that Chad had tried hard but hadn't really lived up to his potential. Then she more or less threw me out."

"Who was she, this prof?" said Rashford.

"Her name is Benoît," said York. "Professor Linda Benoît."

Rashford looked sideways, raising his eyebrows. York nodded, then gave a big sigh.

"Yes. Lin-Lin."

"You know," said Rashford, "I thought you were looking a bit discombobulated when we met her at the Student Union party."

York bit back a laugh.

"When she was with Issack? Yes, poor guy doesn't know what he's in for."

"What do you mean?"

"It's all in the chase for Lin-Lin," said York. "And anyways, she prefers them younger. Much younger."

After finishing their coffee, the two men walked across the grass to the door on the far side of the secret quadrangle.

"Someone's been busy," said York, pointing at the wooden structure. The bags of compost were gone, and the surface looked as if it had recently been dug over.

"Apparently it's your friend," said Rashford. "She won't let anyone else plant anything."

"My friend? You mean, Professor Benoît? Really? She's a gardener?"

"So it would seem."

"How could she get up there and dig it over? Does she bring a stool or something?"

Rashford laughed.

"Perhaps," he said. "I think she permits one fellow to help her, someone called Bruce. He's one of the maintenance staff here."

They left the secret quadrangle and went through the passage back into the noise and bustle of the conference. York left to go and observe another session, while Rashford wandered around and looked for somewhere he could get an early lunch. He needed to think.

Rashford left the campus and walked along the wide avenue that led into town. On one side of the road were a series of large houses with compact front gardens. The houses had been subdivided into student apartments, and the gardens covered in gravel or asphalt, filled now with cars and bicycles instead of roses and birdsong.

On the other side of the avenue, to his right, the ground sloped down to the river. The banks were manicured, with spring flowering trees and shrubs strategically placed amid the freshly mown grass. He saw a couple walking, and a young woman on a bicycle, and realized that there must be a path alongside the river. As he approached a traffic light, he saw that the cross-street terminated, with a row of stone bollards between the sidewalk and the road. The cross-street continued for a short distance after the bollards and stopped with a view of the river. He turned right and descended a series of wide steps to the path below, and then turned left onto the path.

He walked along the riverside path for about ten minutes, passing an occasional wooden bench. He saw only a few ducks and a solitary magpie, then came up to a floating dock tied tightly to the bank with thick yellow mooring cables. On the dock were some chairs and tables, each with a bright beach umbrella rising from the central hole.

On the edge of the path was a food truck, a converted motor home carefully balanced on large metal jacks. A large sign indicated that it was called 'Dances with Gravy'. The menu, written in multicoloured chalks on a board, promised a variety of 'authentic Indigenous food'. He considered the options, then made and paid for his order.

A few minutes later, with a large bowl of buffalo chili and three pieces of fried bannock, he went out onto the dock and claimed one of the outer tables. One of the servers followed him out, carrying his large glass of soda water with cranberry juice. Rashford thanked her and ate his lunch, carefully eyeing the two large Canada geese which swam up and down a few feet away, obviously hoping for some pieces of thrown bannock.

The waitress came out to clear his plate and to ask him if her had enjoyed his meal.

"Very much, thank you," he said. "Am I allowed to smoke here?"

"Yes," she said. "I'll bring you an ashtray. But, not over the dock, remember."

Rashford looked around.

"What, up on the hill?"

"No, here's okay. You just have to hold your hand out over the water and lean your head out when you take a drag on your cigarette."

Rashford looked at her.

"You're joking, right?"

"No, it's some bylaw they passed last year, about smoking in open air eating areas. They were thinking of patios, not docks, but it applies here. Apparently, the Council is going to review it later this summer, but until then it's the rules."

Rashford shook his head, then pulled out his cigarettes and engaged in a complicated ritual to light and smoke his cigarette. Every time he took a drag he leaned out over the edge of the wooded dock, blowing the smoke at the Canada geese. He tapped the ash into the river and the geese swam over to investigate, glaring at him with pure malice when they realized it was not a piece of bannock.

The server had placed the ashtray on his table and as he finished his smoke, he looked from his hand to the metal saucer. He decided that as he was extinguishing his cigarette, not smoking it, it was okay to bring it over the dock and stub it out. He managed to complete this task without a bylaw officer jumping out of the bushes.

Rashford sat back in his chair and took a drink of his soda, then looked up as a young woman on a bicycle stopped and dismounted. As she walked towards the food truck she stopped and looked at him.

"You gave the talk this morning," she said.

Rashford realized that it was the girl who had asked the first question, wondering why he had chosen Cree.

"Yes, I did. Tân'si. Ki'ya maka?"

She blushed.

"Mânan'tow, but I'm sorry, that's all I know. Tân'si. Ki'ya maka? Mânan'tow. I don't speak any other of my language."

"You are Cree, yourself?" said Rashford.

"Yes, from Grandmother's Bay. It's in the north but I was brought up in the city. My folks wouldn't speak Cree at home, only English. Except when they were fighting, then I learned some good words!"

"I bet you did," said Rashford, laughing. "Are you eating here?"

"No, I work here. I'm just coming for my shift."

"I see. Well, please could you ask my waitress if I could get another cranberry and soda? Thank you."

"Sure, I'll do that."

The girl went to the food truck, opened the back door, then disappeared inside. A few minutes later she came out again, this time carrying his drink. Rashford lit another cigarette and was leaning out over the river as she appeared. She put his soda on the table and picked up his empty glass, then laughed.

"Josee got you as well, did she?" she said.

Rashford looked at her. She simply shook her head.

"There's no bylaw, she just doesn't like the smell of tobacco smoke. So, she tries to make it difficult for people. Sorry about that."

Rashford brought his arm in and relaxed in his chair, giving a sigh of relief. She laughed again.

"Are you a student at the university?" he said.

"Yes. Third year General Arts. It's pretty cool but I don't think it will get me a real job!"

Rashford thought for a moment, then made his decision.

"I'd like to ask you a question," he said. "It might sound a bit weird, but I'd appreciate an honest answer."

"Okaaay," she said, looking at him carefully and moving back a step.

"No, no," said Rashford, hurriedly, feeling the blush of his embarrassment. "Nothing personal, I promise, just weird."

The woman relaxed a little.

"What I was wondering," said Rashford, then paused for a moment to collect his thoughts, and to determine the best way to ask the question.

The woman waited.

"What I was wondering," he repeated, "was do you remember any strange things, from your first year?"

"What kind of strange things?"

"Someone disappearing, for example. Towards the end of the year."

"Well, there were a couple, you know. Girls who got pregnant and had to leave to have their babies."

"No, I'm thinking of guys, now."

"A few, I guess. People who had partied too much and who decided they were never going to pass their exams, so what was the point? They would leave early, so they could get the best pick of the summer jobs while everyone else still had classes."

"But you kind of expected them to leave early, right?"

"I guess. You could usually predict who would be an Easter graduate."

"Was there anyone else, though? Someone who seemed to be doing okay, and then just wasn't there anymore?"

She thought for a few moments, then nodded.

"There were rumours, yes," she said. "But I don't remember

anything specific. There was just something about an international student who left suddenly."

Rashford looked at her.

"An international student?"

"Yes, I think so. But I can't really remember. I'm sorry."

"That's okay. Thank you anyway."

The woman nodded, then left him with his drink and another cigarette. As she entered the food truck the other waitress, Josee, came out. She glared at Rashford, ostentatiously waving her hand in front of her face, then set off jogging down the riverbank pathway.

Rashford smiled to himself, stubbed out his cigarette, and finished his drink. As he got up to leave, he tucked a ten-dollar tip under his glass. The young Cree woman came out and told him the tip was too big, but he waved her concern away.

"Thank you," she said. "Can I have your phone number?"

Rashford stopped. He turned back to face her.

"At the risk of being really stupid," he said, "why?"

It was her turn to be flustered and embarrassed.

"I mean, I'll talk to my brother," she said. "He might remember something. There weren't many First Nations guys on campus, so they hung out with the international students more than I did."

Rashford nodded in appreciation.

"Thank you," he said, "that would be great."

She took out her own phone and entered his number as he recited it to her. Then she sent him a quick confirmatory text. His phone beeped and he looked at it.

"Test received, Shyanne," he said. "I hope to hear from your brother."

"No promises," she said, "but I hope so too."

She shook his hand softly.

"Tênikeh," he said, and walked back along the riverbank to the campus.

Rashford checked the conference program and selected two sessions to attend that afternoon. At two o'clock, he joined three other people to hear Marc Claydon talk about the different ways sixteenth-century voyageurs may have individualized their garments by colouring them with plant-based dyes.

To his surprise, the session was informative and interesting. Claydon was brief and witty as he introduced each of his slides and contextualized his topic within the wider social and cultural events of the day.

At the end of the talk, it turned out that Rashford was the only person to whom the topic was new. The other three asked a series of astute and penetrating questions, which Claydon carefully contrived to have one of his audience members answer with a clear and relevant response. They all appreciated the opportunity to display their knowledge, and Rashford thought it was an excellent teaching strategy. As he left the room after thanking Marc for the talk, Rashford felt that he had learned more than he had realized was possible about the clothing habits of fur traders. Quite what he was going to do with that knowledge, he wasn't sure.

The second session he attended was quite different. The room was packed, and Rashford was fortunate to find an empty chair at the back. A number of younger people, whom he assumed to be graduate students, sat on the floor along the sides of the room. Two sat in the central aisle itself, right underneath the podium. There was a general hubbub of noise, which quietened down as someone moved to the podium and turned on the microphone.

"Hello, hello. Testing, testing. One, two, three. Can you hear me at the back? Charles, can you hear me?"

A man sitting three chairs along from Rashford lazily raised his arm in the air and called back.

"Yes, I can hear you," he said.

"Thank you," said Linda Benoît.

The room quietened even further. Benoît stepped back from the podium, coughed lightly, then returned to the microphone. She was wearing a dark red dress, saw Rashford, one that came down to just above her knees. Her legs were clad in light purple tights which matched her scarf. A pair of shiny black patent leather boots completed the ensemble. She raised her hands above her head like a boxing champion after a particularly hard bout.

"My Lords, Ladies, and Gentlemen," she declaimed into the silence. There was a pause, broken only by a sudden guffaw. Benoît fixed the perpetrator with a glare as someone shushed him.

"Sorry," he said, in a way that did not really support the claim.

"My Lords, Ladies, and Gentlemen," Benoît said again, more softly this time. "Thank you all so much for coming out this afternoon. We know there is a full program, and we appreciate your spending your time with us."

'She sounds like a flight attendant,' thought Rashford to himself, thanking passengers for choosing their airline. He didn't think he had made that thought audible, but one of his neighbours turned and looked crossly at him. Rashford kept his gaze forward.

"I know you didn't come to hear me," said Benoît, laughing in a self-depreciating manner, "but before I introduce our speaker, a few house-keeping comments."

She stopped and peered around the room, seeming to catch everyone with her eye. Rashford certainly felt skewered, even at the back of the room, and was convinced she had recognized and remembered him.

"We have a full house here today," said Benoît, "so please try to keep disturbances to a minimum. No 'alleluias' or speaking in tongues, okay?"

A few people laughed and she smiled with them.

"I know, I know it's not a revivalist meeting and he's not the new messiah, but he's pretty special in our field."

At this a young Black man in the middle of the crowd and seated across the room from Rashford jumped to his feet, waved his arms around frantically, and shouted 'Alleluia!' in a loud voice. The crowd roared in appreciation.

"Thank you, Jeremy, now please sit down," said Benoît, laughing. "That, ladies and gentlemen, is my teaching assistant, Jeremy Beals. After the talk he will be walking around the room with a hand-held microphone. If you would like to ask our speaker a question, please get Jeremy's attention."

Jeremy turned a full circle, waving to the crowd, and then sat down. Benoît quietened the audience again.

"Finally, our guest has asked that his talk not be recorded or videographed. Photographs are fine, as long as no flash is used. He will also be willing to pose for photographs after the talk."

There was a murmur from the front row, which Rashford could not hear. Benoît nodded, then leaned back into the microphone.

"Yes, and he will also sign copies of his latest book."

There was another murmur, and some giggles from people in the front few rows.

"Actually, he will sign any book. Or article. Or body part," said Benoît, smiling.

Now the whole audience laughed, some shaking their heads. Rashford felt that he was at the taping of a popular television comedy show, with a frontman warming up the audience before the star appeared. Front-person, he corrected himself. Benoît held out her right hand and metaphorically calmed the waters with an extended patting motion. When there was silence, she spoke again.

"I know that many of you will have read one of his seven books. Some of you will have read all of them. Or his thirty-nine refereed articles, especially those that won the Richmond Award, the Jamieson Medal, or the Aurelias Prize."

There was a smattering of applause.

"I had the great honor and pleasure of having our guest as a student in the first graduate class I ever taught," she continued. "To say that he made a challenging event even more difficult than I had anticipated is an understatement."

She laughed, spreading her arms wide.

"I was a new PhD, I was smart, I was nervous ... and here was someone who was still a student, who was smarter, and who was not nervous at all. To say we clashed would be another understatement.

"But we got through it, and by the time I was seeking tenure, he had his own doctorate and was teaching his own classes. He was kind enough to write me a letter of support, from an ex-student, which helped my file no end. He taught with us for only a year before being lured away to a rather famous university near Boston, I forget its name."

She laughed again, and a number of the older audience members sniggered.

'That must be an inside joke', thought Rashford, perplexed.

"We collaborated on a book together," said Benoît, "and then I came west to my professorship here, and he went south and west to his."

She paused, then took a deep breath, and raised her voice a fraction.

"So, without further ado, please help me welcome to the podium my ex-student, an award-winning scholar in his own right, all the way from Palo Alto, California, Professor Benjamin McHale."

There was a rockstar-like burst of applause from the audience, some of whom came to their feet in a show of welcome. Rashford could not hear the drum roll as the guest bounded up from the front row, but he was certain there had to be one somewhere. As the man came onto the stage, Rashford recognized the bi-coloured hair.

The leather jacket had been exchanged for a maroon smoking jacket with white piping at the seams. A striped Paul Smith shirt with a paisley collar hung loose over a pair of skinny black jeans, which in turn were hemmed to hang above his blue Blundstone boots. He swept on stage and embraced Linda Benoît enthusiastically, planting a loud kiss on each of her cheeks.

Laughing, she kept clapping as she extricated herself from the clinch and backed away from the dais. Turning to the room, he put his hands on his hips and nodded appreciatively. Then he stepped to the podium and slowly, deliberately, flipped the loose bang of hair back over his ear. Only then did he lean into the microphone.

"A thousand thank you's, Professor Benoît," he said. "They say you never forget your first time, and I confess that I remember with great fondness losing my academic virginity while under your ..."

He paused, looking around the room, raising his eyebrows in a dramatic way.

"... tutelage," he finished. The audience roared, Linda Benoît turned bright red before hurrying to her seat, and even Rashford smiled.

"Gotcha," he thought.

Benjamin McHale was an excellent teacher, thought Rashford. Part flamboyant showman, part erudite academic, he roamed the dais like a polar bear in a zoo.

The first thing he had said was 'I refuse to be tethered to the expectations of the stage managers.' He had then clicked off the microphone and carried both it and the stand to the far corner of the front space of the room. Returning to the centre, he had paused, hands in his pockets. He then held out his arms, palms upwards, like a magician trying to convince the audience he had no tricks up his sleeves.

McHale began to speak, and Rashford realized he could clearly hear every word. Looking more closely, he noticed the small microphone pinned to the burgundy jacket, and the looped wire extending into the side pocket. Freed from the podium, McHale walked up and down, focusing on different parts of the room, making eye contact with as many people as possible, sometimes nodding and smiling to recognize someone he knew.

Twice he stepped carefully over the graduate students crouched at the front and walked up the centre aisle itself. The audience turned in their chairs as he passed, like gazelle monitoring the passage of a lion, wondering if he would bite. At one point he was within five feet of Rashford and paused, as if sensing a threat, an outsider to his domain. He scanned the back row, slowly, acknowledging 'Charles', his gaze passing over Rashford with only a subtle flicker to indicate that he saw someone out of place. Turning, he walked back down the aisle, stepped over the students again, and returned to the dais.

Rashford was impressed at the performance. McHale spoke of his early days as a teacher in the inner-city, observing that in those times the children were called underprivileged or ghettoized. Later, he observed, the language changed, and they were referred to as urban, as marginalized, as 'Black or Afro-Canadian'. The currently preferred designation, he said, was BIPOC – Black, Indigenous, People Of Colour.

Whatever you called them, said McHale, they were people, with hopes and dreams, excluded from the dominant society by structured and institutionalised racism. He spoke of prejudice and persistence, of resilience and resistance, and in measured tones laid out a dozen issues that needed to be addressed if the education system was going to serve all segments of society.

His talk concluded with a flourish and a joke, and the audience rose to its feet as one, Rashford included. McHale pretended not to hear the adulation, cupping his ear with one hand while encouraging more noise with the other, but Rashford could see from his smile that he was satisfied with a job well done.

After a full minute of applause, McHale indicated that people should sit down, and they did, still chattering. He spoke again, softly, reminding his audience that he was willing to answer questions and inviting Jeremy to walk around with the microphone. The young student stood, then made his away along the row to the first raised hand. The man took the microphone and stood up.

"Introduce yourself, please," said McHale, "and then ask your question."

"Certainly," said the man, clearing his throat. Rashford saw that he was a white man, mid-to-late thirties, wearing a brown corduroy jacket with patches on the elbow, and had thick framed glasses. The man cleared his throat again.

"Umm, my name is John Nicholson, and I am a grade nine social studies teacher at an urban high school with a large BIPOC population. I am here at the university to study for my masters' degree, as I hope to be a principal one day. Professor McHale, you spoke about issues that need to be addressed by the school system and I agree with you."

McHale nodded in appreciation, stroking his chin with his left hand while keeping his eyes directly focused on the speaker. Nicholson continued.

"In fact, my colleagues and I face at least ten of those issues every day. My question is, what do we do about it? How can we address those issues with workable strategies that have meaningful results? How do we move from the theoretical to the empirical, from the philosophical to the practical?"

He passed the microphone back to Jeremy but did not sit down. The eyes of the audience swivelled back to McHale, who now used his right hand to brush the blond part of his hair back over his ear. He looked slowly around the room, then up to the ceiling, then back down at Nicholson. There was silence, albeit one tinged with expectancy. Then McHale spoke.

"How the heck would I know? I'm an academic!"

The room erupted, Rashford included, and Nicholson simply shook his head and sat down, laughing along with everyone else.

As Jeremy wandered the room, passing the microphone from hand to hand, the questions flew quick and easily to McHale. There were no more difficult moments, each response requiring only a generic answer or a simple affirmative. Rashford sat quietly, attuned more to the people around him, and looked up sharply when he heard a murmur from Charles.

"Ego over evidence, I'm afraid," Charles said to the woman in the chair next but one from Rashford. "He puts on a good show, though. Fine grasp of the language."

The woman nodded, and Rashford sat back in his chair, glad he wasn't the only one who felt that way. The questions continued for another five minutes, then McHale brought the session to an end. Linda Benoît returned to the dais and thanked McHale for his captivating and inspirational words, then Jeremy brought forward a large bunch of flowers and an envelope of appreciation. McHale accepted the gifts modestly, slid the envelope into the inside pocket of his jacket, and then posed for photographs with most of the graduate students, and many of the older academics.

Some people stood around in small groups, chatting, but others started to leave. Rashford followed them, leaving the room and walking out into the cool afternoon sunshine. As he descended the steps, he became aware of a person coming up behind his shoulder. Turning, he saw it was York. The man spoke softly.

"Did you enjoy the performance?"

"Very much," said Rashford. "Were you inside? I didn't see you."

"Oh, I was down the front. We BIPOC folks have to be visible these days, you know. We can't hide at the back like you honkies."

Rashford laughed out loud, and was pleased that York joined in.

"Fancy a smoke?" he said.

"Yes please. I need to get some of that hot air out of my system."

York led them to another door, one Rashford had not previously noticed. 'Garden tools for repair: Maintenance Personnel only' said the sign, but the door opened to York's touch. Inside they found a collection of tools hanging from hooks on the wall, mainly garden forks, rakes, and spades but with a selection of hoes and mattocks as well. A wheelbarrow with a flat tire stood in one corner, a folded green tarpaulin in its barrow.

They traversed the usual grey passage and emerged across the quadrangle from the picnic bench. As they walked over the grass, Rashford noticed that a spade now stood against the wooden planter, together with a large 60L bag of garden soil and a small stepladder.

York sat on one side of the bench with a heavy sigh, bringing out his cigarettes. Rashford sat across from him, taking the offered smoke and clicking his lighter. The two men sat quietly for a few moments, studying each other. York broke the silence.

"It's so easy to be a fucking armchair expert," he said, bitterly. "Pardon my French."

Rashford nodded. York continued.

"That was a perfectly reasonable question from the teacher, and McHale just clipped it away over square leg."

Rashford looked at him.

"Excuse me?" he said.

"I said, he just clipped ... oh, right. You probably don't understand cricket, do you?"

Rashford shook his head.

"Not a clue," he said. "I know you're in until you're out and that the other team is out until it's their turn to be in. I saw that on a t-shirt once."

York laughed.

"Right," he said. "Alright, let's try a hockey analogy. The teacher made a perfectly fair play and McHale took him into the boards with a high stick and a hip check from behind that the refs ignored. How's that?"

"Brutal," said Rashford.

"Indeed," said York. "So many words, so little meaning."

He shook his head and took a long drag of his cigarette, then lit a second from the first before flicking the butt into the gravel bucket.

"These guys are part of the problem, you know. All their journal articles and books, using us as their subject so they can build their careers by looking smart to other white people. Especially women. Did you see those girls, those super-smart graduate students pawing all over him and trying to be the one he takes back to his room tonight?"

Rashford had an uncomfortable image of Mandy riding him, hair flying as she shook her head, calling his name as he caressed her breasts. That was different, he thought, shaking his head to clear his thoughts. York looked at him, at first strangely, then with comprehension. A large grin appeared on his face.

"Oh, mon, you scored, didn't you? Who was it? Let me think."

Rashford reddened and lit another cigarette. York snapped his fingers.

"That blonde, the one who was all over you at the opening reception."

Rashford reddened even more, and York laughed.

"That's it," he said. "You scored Randy Mandy! Oh, mon, how was that?"

Rashford inhaled deeply.

"Why do you call her that?" he said.

York shrugged.

"I dunno, exactly. I think that's what Linda Benoît called her. Something to do with her, umm, enthusiasms, in first year."

"Do you think it's fair, though," said Rashford. "Ten or eleven years later, carrying around that same moniker with her? What were you like when you first went to university?"

"That was different, mon."

"Different? How?"

"Well, first I'm a guy, so it was expected, you know, to sow your wild oats. And second, there was no internet. She's on there, mon. Taking two guys at once."

"And they were just 'sowing their wild oats', right? And what was she? Just a convenient furrow? Are people going around saying, 'oh, there go the blokes who got her drunk and took advantage of her'? Is it Bobby Bastard and Pete the Prick, is that what they're called?"

"Hey, calm down, mon."

"I am calm. And I've got friends in IT who owe me favours. They're going to take down that film, and trace it to the appropriate phones, and to the people who owned those phones eleven years ago, and I am going to track them down and beat them into the little shitty molecules of nothing they deserve to be."

York just looked at him.

"And that will make it right?" he said, eventually.

Rashford laughed.

"I'm not a knight," he said. "I'm an ex-cop. I don't care about right. What I do to them won't make it right, no. And it won't remove the shame and hurt of the last ten years. In fact, Mandy won't even know it's been done. But it will make things even, and that's about as good as I can promise right now."

York nodded, slowly. He passed Rashford a cigarette.

"You like her, huh?"

It was Rashford's turn to nod.

"Yes, I do. She's bubbly and fun to be with, and she's resilient, and persistent. All the things that McHale said were the positives in the world. That's Mandy. This is just a fling, I know that. For both of us. She's going to go on to a good life, husband, family, everything. I'll not be part of that, except maybe as a memory, one of the good things that happened in her university years."

The two men sat and looked at each other. It was a few minutes before York spoke.

"Ex-cop, eh?"

"Yes."

"But still with contacts in the force?"

"A few."

"Hmm."

There was silence again.

"Why?" said Rashford.

"Just thinking," said York. "Remember I told you about Chad? My half-nephew?"

"Yes. Well, a bit. We kind of ended up talking about Professor Benoît."

"Indeed, we did, mon. But really, I'd like your help in finding Chad. Or in finding out what happened to him. I'm getting nowhere. I'll pay you."

"I'm not a private eye."

"I know, and this isn't official like that. But you've got skills, and your time is valuable."

It was Rashford's turn to sit in silence.

York looked at him in a hopeful but questioning way.

"Just thinking," said Rashford.

He reached for another cigarette. York waited, patiently. At last, Rashford spoke.

"I'll do you a deal," he said. "I need an introduction to Professor McHale. Can you get me one?"

York scoffed.

"I'm the Program Chair," he said, his tone of voice capitalizing the title. "I can do anything ... as long as it's conference related."

"If you set me up a meeting with him, I'll help you with your problem. Okay?"

York nodded.

"Okay," he said. "Thanks."

"Today's Saturday," Rashford said. "The conference runs until tomorrow afternoon, and I'm booked in my room until Monday. Get me a chat with McHale as soon as possible, and I'll help you over the next two days, alright?"

"Oh, thank you, mon, that's great," said York, extending his hand in a high five.

"No promises, mind," said Rashford, "but I don't really have any real schedule here, not now that my talk is finished. So, I can wander around and ask questions, see what I can find out."

"Thank you, thank you, thank you," said York.

"What's his full name?" said Rashford, taking out his notebook.

"Sobers, Chad Sobers, no relation to Gary," said York.

Rashford looked at him. York laughed.

"Oh, right, you don't do cricket, do you? Gary Sobers, one of the finest players the game has ever seen, and originally from my home patch of Bridgetown, Barbados."

Rashford shook his head and got the conversation back on topic.

"I know you're busy with conference stuff, but can you spare me an hour tomorrow morning? Bring all your notes and papers, anything related to Chad, and talk me through what you've got."

"Sure," said York, taking out his phone and scrolling through it. "I've got an early meeting with the program committee, then I need to check everything is up and running. I should be free about nine-thirty, I can block an hour then."

"Great," said Rashford. "Nine-thirty it is. Where do you want to meet?"

"How about the student pub? They're doing breakfast throughout the conference, and I bet we'll be able to find a quiet corner."

"See you there," said Rashford. He checked his watch.

"It's nearly six," he said. "I'd better get going. I need to grab a bite to eat and a shower, it's been a long day."

York raised an eyebrow.

"A shower?" he said. "Sounds like your day might not yet be over, mon."

Rashford felt his face reddening and left the table quickly. As he entered the passage, he continued to hear York's laughter.

CHAPTER 6

Rashford and York met in the Three-Legged Rabbit at nine thirty the next morning. Rashford was glad of the late start. The previous evening, he had just finished his shower when his phone rang. He did not recognize the number, so answered cautiously.

"Yo, this is Pia," said a male voice.

"Sorry, who?" said Rashford.

"Pia. Piapot Starblanket. You spoke to my sister, Shyanne. You gave her this number."

Rashford remembered his conversation with the young woman at the café.

"Oh, yes. Sorry, my mind was miles away. How can I help you?"

There was a moment of silence.

"Well," said Piapot, "you asked me to call you, so that question is the wrong way round."

Rashford laughed.

"You're right. Sorry. Listen, can I call you back? I just got out of the shower."

"Sure. I'll be here."

"Thank you. Sorry about this."

Rashford clicked off his phone and hurriedly got dressed. He got his notebook and pen, then sat down at the small table in his room. He looked at his phone again, then hit recent calls and redial.

"Piapot Starblanket, tân'si," said the voice.

"Mânan'tow, ki'ya maka?" replied Rashford, automatically.

"You speak Cree?" said Piapot, incredulously.

"Ekosi. Kinisinitohten?"

"Not really," said Piapot, self-consciously. "Let's do this in English, oaky?"

"Sure," said Rashford. "Sorry for the confusion earlier."

"You white guys sure say 'sorry' a lot, don't you?" said Piapot. "Shame you don't back it up with some action."

"Sorry," said Rashford, then laughed.

Piapot laughed as well.

"So, how can I help you?" he said.

"Your sister said you might be able to answer a couple of questions for me, about your university days."

"Are you a cop?"

"I used to be, but this isn't official. I'm checking into something for a friend."

Rashford crossed his fingers as he said this, hoping that Patrick York wouldn't find that too presumptuous a statement.

"Go ahead," said Piapot.

"He's looking for his half-nephew, a fellow called Chad. From the Caribbean, possibly Barbados or Jamaica. He started at the university here last year."

"Last year? That's after me, then. I left a couple of years ago."

"Yes, I know. But I'm trying to see if there's a pattern. When you were here, did you ever hear any rumours, stories about international students just disappearing?"

Piapot was silent for a while.

"I left in my second year, Christmas time, but there was something from the year before," he said. "A guy who everyone thought was going to do well but then quit early. Like me, except I wasn't doing so well in my classes. Too many parties, too much fun, not enough studying."

He laughed.

"That was the year before?"

"Yes, maybe three years ago? I can't remember the guy's name. Something biblical. Eli or Abraham or something."

"Emmanuel?"

"Maybe. I can't remember. Sorry."

"But nothing from your year?"

"Not that I heard. You could ask Lenny, he might know."

"Who's Lenny?"

"He's an international student, from Nigeria. We hung out together, played basketball, you know? Anyway, he was a couple of years ahead, in school. He's graduated now."

"How do I get in touch with Lenny?"

"Well, the thing is, he don't like cops much. He's gay, and where he's from, the LGBT plus folk get hassled pretty good. Plus, he deals a bit on the side, you know, for people who can't make it to the government store. It might be best if I called him and explained the situation. Introduced you, as it were."

Rashford's phone beeped that he had another call but he ignored it, focusing on what Piapot was saying.

"That would be great, thanks."

There was a moment of silence before Piapot spoke next.

"Is there, like, a finder's fee?" he said.

Rashford laughed.

"I really hadn't thought," he said. "What do you think would be reasonable?"

"Fifty bucks," said Piapot.

Rashford considered this for a moment.

"How about twenty for making the call, another twenty if he actually calls me back, and ten more if he tells me anything useful."

It was Piapot's turn to consider.

"Sure," he said at last. "That'll work."

"Shall I give the money to Shyanne? How do you want to do this?"

"Yeah, give it to Shyanne. I'll tell her it's coming. And remember, môniyâw, if you cheat on me, I'm a Cree warrior, named after a great chief. I'll track you down and get my payment."

Rashford tried to keep the smile out of his voice.

"I'm sure you would," he said, "but don't worry. I'll leave an envelope with Shyanne at the food truck."

They spoke for another minute and then Rashford ended the call. He checked his voice mail and listened to York telling him that McHale had agreed to a meeting. He left McHale's cell phone number and wished Rashford luck.

Rashford was sitting quietly, thinking about what he had learned so far, when there was a knock on the door. He checked his watch, but it was only seven o'clock, so he opened the door cautiously. He was surprised to see Marc Claydon standing in the hall.

"Good evening," he said. "Can I help you?"

"I saw you come in earlier," said Claydon. "I was going to go and have a beer. Would you like to join me?"

Rashford heard the underlying plea in the voice and realized that Claydon had one of two motives. Either he was lonely but too shy to go and drink alone, or he wanted to be seen in the company of a better-known speaker. Or perhaps some combination of the two, thought Rashford, looking quickly around the room. Everything looked neat and tidy, so he grabbed his jacket.

"Sure," he said, "but just a quick one. I'm meeting someone at eight thirty."

"Great," said Claydon, his evident relief confirming Rashford's earlier thoughts. "To the pub, then?"

"Yes," said Rashford. "But would you mind waiting in the lobby? I just have to make one more call."

"No problem," said Claydon, and walked off down the hall with a spring in his step. Rashford closed the door and then called the number he had been given.

"McHale," said a surprisingly soft and diffident voice.

Rashford explained who he was, and that he had a few questions.

"I'm busy today and tomorrow," said McHale. "My plane is an afternoon flight on Monday."

"Perhaps Monday morning, then? Would ten o'clock work for you?"

"Sure. I don't really know this campus, so why don't we meet outside the student pub, the main entrance. They might serve coffee there, or we can find a place somewhere else."

"Thank you," said Rashford. "See you tomorrow."

It was still quite early so the bar at the Three-Legged Rabbit was quiet. Claydon bought them each a beer, which they took to a corner table. They looked at each other.

"Cheers," said Rashford, raising his glass. "Are you having a good conference?"

"Cheers," said Claydon, bumping his glass against Rashford's. He took a sip before responding. "It's okay, you know. You saw how many people came to my session. I'm not quite the McHale of plant dyes, I'm afraid."

"Not yet, perhaps," said Rashford, earning a grateful smile. "But you know what, I learned a heck of a lot more from your presentation than I did from McHale."

"Really?"

"Yes. Not just the talk, but the questions as well. It was a really interesting session."

"What was?" said a voice behind him. Rashford turned and saw Shyanne standing there.

"Hello," he said. "What are you doing here?"

"We've just finished our shift," she said, as Josee emerged from behind her. "We just dropped in for a quick drink."

"Would you like to join us?" said Rashford, indicating the two empty chairs at their table.

"Does he smoke?" said Josee, pointing her lips towards Claydon and making a clicking sound with her tongue.

"I don't know," said Rashford, but Claydon interrupted.

"No, I don't," he said.

"I'll sit there, then," said Josee, moving to the chair opposite Rashford but next to Claydon. Shyanne laughed and sat down in the fourth chair. They all looked at each other.

"Would you like a drink?" said Rashford, then realized that everyone had spoken at once.

"My name is Marc."

"Did you talk to Pia?"

"My name's Josee."

There was a self-conscious pause. Rashford leaned forward and waved his hand.

"Me first," he said. "Would anyone like a drink?"

"Vodka tonic, please," said Josee.

"Screwdriver, please," said Shyanne.

"Sure," said Marc.

Rashford went to the bar and bought the drinks, then carried them back to the table. The three were chatting amiably to each other. He put the drinks on the table.

"You're not having another?" said Claydon.

"No, I'll finish this, then I have to go."

"Oh," said Shyanne. "That's a shame."

He looked at her, noticing the not so innocent smile that played around her eyes.

"Sorry," he said, "I have a prior engagement. But I have to come and see you tomorrow, at the food truck. When is a good time?"

"Tomorrow? I start at eleven," she said, "finish at seven. Why don't you come then, and we can have the drink you're missing today?"

She was speaking softly. Rashford looked around and saw that Marc and Josee had their own conversation going and were paying no attention.

"Sure," he said. "See you then."

He nodded at the drink in front of her.

"Don't drink too many of those," he said. "They'll creep up on you."

"These? Oh, you can't get drunk on these. The orange juice is an acid, and the alcohol is a base, so they cancel each other out. Basic high school chemistry."

Rashford looked at her and shook his head.

"Maybe where you went to school," he said.

Shyanne laughed.

"I'll show you tomorrow," she said, then leaned the other way and said something to Josee.

Rashford nodded, finished his beer, then stood up. "Right, you three," he said. "Have fun."

They all ignored him, so he turned and walked away. He left the pub and crossed the street back to the residence. He hung up his jacket and used the washroom. He was just drying his hands when there was a knock at the door.

He opened it to find Mandy standing there, her long hair hanging loose. She was carrying her purse and holding up a brown paper bag and a bottle of wine.

"Let's get French," she said. "Pastries and a Bordeaux."

"Mais oui," said Rashford, standing aside to let her enter. As she passed him, she turned her head and spoke over her shoulder.

"I brought a frilly maid's uniform as well," she said.

Chapter 7

Now, sitting at a table in the corner bar of the Three-Legged Rabbit, Rashford smiled at the memory of Mandy serving what she called a 'replenishment snack'. She had come back into the bedroom wearing only a frilly pink apron, white rabbits leaping across her bosom, holding a glass of red wine in one hand and a *pain au chocolat* in the other.

"No crumbs or spills," she said, "or I'll have to lick them off."

His memory of how easily French pastry could crumble was interrupted by the return of Patrick York, bearing refilled cups of coffee. Rashford took both their plates and put them on an adjacent, empty, table.

"That was good," he said. "I needed that."

"Uh-uh," said York. "All that post-shower excitement, I guess."

Rashford didn't say anything, hoping the steam from the coffee would obscure his blush.

"I know, gentlemen don't tell," said York. "Your secret is safe with me, mon."

Rashford hurried to change the subject.

"So, what do we know?" he said.

"You're the cop, you tell me," said York.

"Ex-cop," said Rashford, automatically, "but okay, I'll go first."

He paused to marshal his thoughts.

"We know that last year, about this time, your half-nephew, Chad, disappeared. He was an average student, male, from the Caribbean."

"Jamaica," said York. "He was born in Jamaica."

"Right. So, he was a first year General Arts student, doing okay but not brilliant, and he just disappeared, no word to anyone. Is that correct?"

"Yes."

"Okay. We also know that three years ago, a similar thing happened. A first-year General Arts student, one who was actually quite bright, disappeared about this time. He was a domestic student, but not from here. He came from an Afro-Canadian community in Nova Scotia."

"Afro-Canadian? So, he was Black?"

"Yes, I think so."

"So, they have three things in common. First year, General Arts, Black."

"Correct," said Rashford. "And male. Now, I don't know if anything similar happened two years ago, but I'm waiting to hear from someone who might know."

Rashford paused, considering his next words carefully.

"I heard a whisper," he said, "about Emmanuel, or Manny, the guy from three years ago. Apparently, he had some sort of arrangement with a professor here."

"An arrangement? What kind of an arrangement?"

"As far as I can figure, something that involved sex for marks. He was guaranteed an A, apparently. But he never collected, obviously."

"So, what, you think Chad might have had a similar arrangement?"

"Well, you said that he had a sure-fire A lined up, and that he got warm once a week."

York looked at him.

"That's true," he said, "and yes, I guess you could interpret that in that way."

He paused, moving his coffee cup slowly around the table.

"So, if we assume that is correct, young Black guys who are given good marks in exchange for sex with their teacher, just disappear. How does that add up?"

Rashford took his time with an answer. This was a difficult moment.

"I'm not exactly sure," he said. "But this whisper I heard. It also said that the prof concerned 'liked Black company', so her nickname was LBC."

York rocked back in his chair, his coffee spilling.

"Whoa! What?"

"Keep your voice down," hissed Rashford, looking quickly around the room. There were a few other delegates getting their early-morning breakfast, but nobody appeared to be paying them any attention.

"That's insane, mon, what you are saying?"

"Why?"

"Well, she's ... she's a prof ... and she's old!"

"Yes, and right now she has a bright young thing, a bright young Black young thing, as her teaching assistant. Is that a coincidence?"

"Is he in General Arts?"

"I don't know," said Rashford. "I've still got to check that."

York drummed his fingers on the table.

"I can check with my sister-in-law," he said. "She has all Chad's things, the university sent them back in a box. I'll ask her whether he kept an agenda or diary, something like that. I'll call her later today."

"Good idea," said Rashford. "Maybe we can find out what classes he was taking. You do that and I will see if I can learn anything about whether someone disappeared two years ago. I might also dig into our good professor a bit, as well."

"Can we meet again, perhaps later this evening?"

"I have a meeting at seven," said Rashford. "Can we meet before then? Say five?"

"What, the marvellous Mandy again? You got stamina, mon."

"No, not her, someone else," said Rashford.

York just stared at him and shook his head.

"Which reminds me, though," said Rashford, finishing his coffee. "You said that Mandy could be a real bitch if she didn't get her way. Why did you say that?"

York shrugged.

"Just gossip, I guess. Actually, I think it was Lin-Lin who told me that, in passing."

"Lin-Lin?"

"Linda Benoît."

"Just a bit of drive-by character assassination, then?" said Rashford.

York looked at him.

"You might be right," he said. "See you at five, back here."

———

Rashford left the pub and returned to his room. It was empty, although he could still smell Mandy's perfume. There was a folded piece of paper on the small table. He picked it up and saw that it was a note, which he took over to the window to read.

'Dear Gavin,' he read. 'I'm sorry I missed you, but I guess it's better this way. I have a gig this evening, so I won't be able to see you tonight, and I suppose you'll be leaving tomorrow. Thank you for making this a better-than-great conference! I had a lot of fun and hope you did as well! Enjoy the rest of your weekend and good luck in your future! xxx Mandy xxx'

Rashford was surprised at how upset he felt. He had been looking forward to coming back and waking her up from her morning slumber, although even in his own mind he realized this was a selfish notion. Mandy had made it clear from the beginning that theirs was a quick fling, nothing serious, and he had to accept that.

At the same time, he felt that he had been played again. He remembered the weekend fling he had enjoyed with Sarah, the administrative assistant to Chief Superintendent Pollard. He had thought he was the pursuer then, only to discover that she was the raptor, and he was the prey.

He had returned to Pollard's office on the Monday after the weekend in the Stone Hall Castle. He had been delighted that Sarah had stayed for both nights, calling her mother to cancel their perogy dinner. As he talked with the Chief Superintendent about his next assignment, he had heard Sarah come into the outer office. Then he had heard the tell-tale sound of wood being filed.

Pollard had laughed.

"Sounds like Sarah got lucky again this weekend," she said, gleefully. "I wonder who the lucky guy was this time?"

Rashford did not remember much of the rest of their conversation. As he left, he paused by Sarah's desk. She looked up at him with a sparkle in her eyes, but his voice oozed displeasure. He nodded at the ledge which ran around the top of her desk, a series of notches cut into the wood.

"You told me that was all a joke," he said, "a bit of fun to liven up your day."

She had the grace to blush.

"Well, yes, that seemed the right thing to say. I'm not the office bike, you know, available to anyone who wants a ride. I'm pretty picky."

"And the young farmer?"

She laughed.

"Yeah, he was an ox, that one. Amazing how much muscle you need to grow canola."

She sat back in her chair, tapping a pen against her teeth, looking up at him with a smirk.

"Really, Gavin. Do you really think I'd spend my Saturday nights eating perogies with my mom? After a week sitting here, I need a proper romp."

Rashford felt himself reddening again, although whether with anger or embarrassment he didn't know. Sarah chose to pile on the agony.

"Anyway, I figured you weren't interested in Slutty Sarah. When I showed you my tits up in Fort Qu'Appelle, all you did was throw me out. So, I thought I'd try Saintly Sarah instead, and that worked."

She looked up at him, meeting his gaze frankly.

"Not that you weren't pretty good yourself. I was only expecting a six or a seven, that's what the rumour mill had said, but you were pretty close to an eight. And look, you got two notches."

She gestured to the ledge at the edge of her desk, which had two new and deeply carved vees cut into its surface.

"I don't normally stay a second night, but you had gone to so much trouble to make it romantic, I figured you deserved more than a quickie. And you liked me being all subservient and amenable to your wants, didn't you? You liked it when you found my boobs all by yourself."

Rashford took a deep breath. He remembered the way she had carefully put down her wine glass and kissed him. How she had pulled back, tilting her head to one side and looking at him with questioning eyes. He remembered sliding her blouse off her shoulders, and his delight at discovering that her bra had a clasp in the front.

"Goodbye, Sarah," he had said, and left the office. He took the stairs down, not the elevator, and pushed outside past the startled young constable on the front desk. Two days later, he had called Chief Superintendent Pollard and thanked her for the new assignment. Then he had advised her that he had decided to take an early retirement. She had tried to persuade him otherwise, but he couldn't bear the thought of going back to her office and seeing the ever-expanding trophy board of her administrative assistant.

Three weeks later he had received his initial clearance papers from the Force and started to move into his new life. Gayle Morgan had come over to console him and they had split a bottle of single malt, but all he got from the evening was a headache. He had told her he was going to take some time and figure out what to do next, but he hadn't mentioned his liaison with Sarah, not even when Gayle gleefully informed him that there were now eight notches on the famous desk.

And now here he was, a few months later, still getting paid but recognizing that his paycheques would finish soon, once HR got their act together. And wondering if he was just a number on whatever scorecard was kept by Mandy.

'Ah, well,' he thought, 'I suppose this is the new world now. Equality in all aspects, including choosing bed partners.'

He folded the note and put it in his pocket, then made some coffee and took it to the window. He was looking out across the small garden when he stopped, staring at one of the early lilac bushes.

"What kind of gig, I wonder?" he said, but the bush did not answer.

At five o'clock Rashford was back at the corner table in the Three-Legged Rabbit. He had two beers in front of him and was waiting for Patrick York to arrive. The man appeared at ten past the hour.

"Sorry, mon, but the last session went long."

"No worries. Hope you don't mind but I started."

Rashford held up his beer glass, which was almost a quarter empty.

"I'll catch up," said York, pouring his bottle until the amount of beer in each glass was the same. He then raised the bottle and drank directly from the neck. He put the empty bottle down on the table, burped, then sat down.

"Right, where were we?" he said.

Rashford grinned.

"Your turn to go first," he said, sitting back and crossing his arms.

York nodded. "Okay, then, you were right. I talked to my sister-in-law, and she checked Chad's diary, his day timer. Every Friday evening, Chad had blocked off , for 'LBC'. And in one email he talked about being made a teaching assistant. He was pretty pumped about that."

"Good to have that idea confirmed," said Rashford. "Anything else?"

"Not really, no. What about you?"

"Well," said Rashford, leaning forward and putting his hands on the table. "A few things."

In turn, he raised his forefinger, middle finger, and ring finger, enumerating each point.

"One, I had lunch with a gay Nigerian. Two, there was another missing student. Three, I tracked the backstory of Professor Benoît, back to when she was plain old Lionel Bishop."

York stared at him with an open mouth.

"You'll catch flies," said Rashford.

York just stared. Rashford took a drink from his own glass, then pushed the other one across the table.

"Drink. It'll get flat."

York picked up his beer and took a sip. Only then did he close his mouth.

"I'll start at the beginning, shall I?"

York nodded, still looking stunned. Rashford brought out his notebook and flipped through a few pages. He glanced at the book, but otherwise spoke without reading his notes.

"So, Lenny Afololo is, or rather was, an international student from Nigeria. He identifies as gay and was persecuted for that back home, so he came to Canada as a student refugee. He graduated last year but still lives in town and hangs around campus. He says it's his safe place."

York nodded again.

Rashford did not mention Lenny's point that it was also where most of his customers were.

"There aren't too many international students here, and even fewer Indigenous ones. I got Lenny's name from the brother of a Cree girl I met in a café."

"Of course, you did," said York.

"They used to hang out together," said Rashford, ignoring the comment. "They called themselves the IDIOTS, which stands for ... just a moment." Rashford picked up his notebook and read out the acronym again. "IDIOTS. Indigenous, Decolonized, International, and Other Types Society."

York laughed out loud. Rashford continued.

"Anyway, they elected a president, secretary, everything, just like the other student clubs and societies, but they were basically secret. Lenny Afololo was the founding president and he's stayed in touch. He's sort of the President Emeritus now."

"And Chad. Was he in this society?"

"He was. In fact, they gave him a special title. They called him LBC, or 'Lonely By Choice'."

"What does that mean?"

"It means that, because he accepted the position of teaching assistant to Linda Benoît, he couldn't join their regular Friday night meeting. The IDIOTS got together at a bar downtown every Friday, then danced the night away at various clubs. But if you worked for Professor Benoît, you had to go to her place for dinner every Friday and be prepared to stay the night."

"Really? Why? No, wait, I know. That old white woman was perving on Black students!"

York had started to raise his voice, so Rashford urged him to calm down.

"No. No, you've got it wrong."

York paused and looked at him.

"I have? How?"

"It seems this was all made clear in the contract."

"Contract? She made Chad sign a contract?"

"She didn't make him sign, Patrick," said Rashford. "Lenny said it was always offered, no strings attached, and lots of people didn't want to sign one. Himself included. But Chad did."

"What did it say, this contract?"

"It said that you agreed to be her teaching assistant for the semester. I think she sort of scouted people in the first semester, then invited four or five likely candidates to a party at Christmas. She explained it all there, so they could think about it over the holidays and let her know in January. If more than one said 'yes', then she made a decision."

"That's it?"

Rashford paused.

"Umm, no. Not really." He hesitated again. "No, there was more."

"What sort of more?" said York.

"Well," said Rashford. "These Friday dinners. You had to wear coconut oil all over your torso, and the only clothing was a laplap."

"Laplap? What's that?"

"It's from Melanesia or somewhere, in the Pacific. It's a sort of sarong. A piece of coloured cloth you wrapped around your waist. That was it."

"Just like a towel?"

"Yes. And then you had to serve the food and drinks, like you were some sort of servant at a colonial dinner. The guests all called you the 'special waiter'."

York sipped his beer, looking pensive. Then he cleared his throat.

"Well, that's sort of weird, I grant you, but it's not exactly dangerous, is it? And I don't suppose it's even illegal. Stupid and childish and not what you'd expect in this day and age, but not illegal. And especially not if he agreed to it."

"Well, if it was a quid pro quo for marks then it might be illegal," said Rashford. "It would certainly be against a whole bunch of university policies. But the thing is, that's only part of it."

When Rashford had finished explaining what he had discovered, York sat back in stunned silence. Eventually he found his voice.

"Holy shit," he said. "Can you prove that?"

"Not yet," said Rashford, "but I'm working on it."

York went to the bar and came back with two more beers.

"I know you're going out," he said, "but this news needs lubrication. And you learned all this at lunch?"

Rashford nodded.

"Okay, then, what about points two and three?"

"Yes. I was going to get to that. But first, the last bit of point one. I've asked Lenny to do a discreet check and find out if Jeremy is a member of the IDIOTS, and also to check whether or not he is General Arts. He's going to send me a text with the information."

York nodded that he understood, and that Rashford should continue. He did.

"Point two, the other missing student. Lenny told me that two years ago, the year before Chad and a year after Emmanuel, who I told you about, another fellow disappeared. His name was Simon Lepani, and he was from Papua New Guinea."

"Papua New Guinea? Where's that?"

"It's an island north of Australia."

"How the heck did he get here?"

"I'm not sure. It seems that one of the teachers at his school was an international volunteer placement with a mission agency and took quite a shine to him. The missionary got called back to Canada because her parents passed away unexpectedly. It might have been something to do with COVID, Lenny wasn't sure. Anyway, they left her some money, quite a lot as it happened, and she used some of it to sponsor Simon to come and do a Canadian degree. She gave up being a missionary and was going to have him live in her house, but then she was killed in a car crash. His fees had been paid so he stayed at the university, although he had to move into a dorm room."

"And he became a teaching assistant?"

"It seems so, yes. Lenny says he was quite excited about it, because it meant he had one less class to worry about and could increase his working hours. He did something in retail, computers apparently."

"And then he disappeared?"

"Yes, around the end of the year. He never showed up for any of his final exams, anyway. The rumour was that he had gotten homesick and without his sponsor, he had no real reason to stay in Canada. It was too cold for him, said Lenny. So, everyone just figured he had gone home."

"Are people from Papua New Guinea black?"

"I asked Lenny that, and he said he thought they were all sorts of colours, from light brown to black. I checked and it seems that's right. Simon himself was more on the lighter side of the spectrum, apparently. He would certainly fit in the BIPOC category, that's for sure."

"So, another young male Black student?"

"That's what it would seem like, yes."

"Was he in General Arts?"

"Apparently."

York looked at him, nodding slowly.

"Okay, then," he said. "So, there is definitely a pattern. Now, your point number three?"

"Here's where it gets even more interesting. It seems that about a dozen years ago, a young graduate student named Lionel Bishop decided that they were really a woman, rather than a man. After their masters' degree they took a year out from their studies and started the transition, the social side of it anyway. Changed all their ID and what they call 'public facing' documents, driver's licence and health card and stuff. Then they enrolled in a different university, as Linda Benoît, and studied for their doctorate."

"As a woman?"

"I'm not sure what they call themselves, actually. I've not talked to them yet. But yes, presenting as a woman, at least in public."

"You said 'the social side of transition'. What does that mean?"

"I had to talk to one of my colleagues about this stuff. They're trans and were happy to chat about it. There's a social transitioning process, of changing your gender marker and name, the way you dress and groom yourself, that kind of thing. Then there's a medical transition as well, when you physically change yourself, by surgery, to the new identity."

"And she hasn't done that? He?"

"Use 'they', it's easy and is the preferred term unless they tell you something different."

"Okay. So, they haven't done that?"

"I don't think so. It's possible they have started hormone therapy, so that they could develop that cleavage you noticed. And it explains the scarves they always wear. Even if they had a tracheal shave, to reduce the size of their Adam's apple, it would still be visible, and they might be a bit self-conscious about that. My colleague said that it all gets complicated, because your medical records and your social documents might be different, and even the professionals can get confused.

"But I've not found anything out either way, yet. The other stuff is all public record. It happened in Ontario, and remember this was before the separation of Alsama, but back then all name changes had to be published in the Ontario Gazette. You could ask for a non-publication order, but it seems they didn't request one, because the change was published."

York sat there silently, shaking his head. He took another drink of his beer.

"How does this affect what we know?"

"I'm not sure yet," said Rashford. "It sure complicates things, though."

"What do we do now?"

"Now?"

Rashford looked at his phone.

"We're running out of time right now," he said.

"Yes," said York. "I've got to go to a bunch of meetings."

"And I have to go and meet my seven o'clock. Tell you what, let's think about this overnight. No sense in rushing into things."

He stood up, finishing his beer as he did so. He looked down at the other man.

"Can you meet tomorrow?"

"Yeah, as long as we're not too late. The conference wraps at two but then I'll have close-out meetings."

"How about a quick chat at noon?"

York thought for a moment.

"Well, I still gotta eat, so sure. Noon here, at the pub?"

"See you then," said Rashford. "And I probably don't have to say this, but not a word of this to anyone. Not until we figure out what's going on."

"My lips are sealed, mon," said York, drawing his finger across his mouth.

CHAPTER 8

Rashford wandered along the street and down the steps to the riverbank. As he walked along the path he turned things over in his mind, trying to sort out fact from supposition, truth from fiction. He had not progressed very far in his mental gymnastics when he came up to the food truck. It was not quite seven, so he leaned against a tree and had a smoke. The two Canada geese swam over and peered at him with cocked heads, then huffed and swam away when they realized he didn't have any food. 'Or perhaps they recognize me,' he thought.

The back door of the food truck opened, and Shyanne came down the steps, calling back to someone inside that she would see them on Monday. She saw Rashford and waved, disappearing behind the food truck for a moment and then emerging pushing her bicycle. She walked over to him.

"Hi you," she said. "Are you ready for that drink?"

"Sure," said Rashford, pulling the envelope out of his pocket. "But first I need to give you this."

She took the envelope and opened it, looking up when she saw what was inside. She grinned what Rashford could only describe as a lasciv-ious grin.

"Fifty bucks? And I haven't done anything yet!"

Rashford shook his head.

"It's not for you," he said. "It's for your brother, Pia. He said I should get it to him through you."

"Oh," she said, moving her face into a mock pout. "I see. Typical misogynistic behaviour, treating the woman as a conduit for your own nefarious goings on, assuming that I'll be patient and accommodating to your every whim."

"Nefarious?" said Rashford.

She grinned at him again.

"It seemed to fit with the cadence and the context, and my Gender and Women's Studies prof says that really important."

"I bet she does."

Shyanne laughed. "Come on, then," she said, wheeling the bicycle down the path. Rashford followed along beside her, smiling and nodding as she chattered on about her day, her classes, and the behaviour of some of the guests at the food truck that afternoon.

"Josee got one group good," she said, giggling. "There were four of them, visitors, Asian I think, and she had them all standing up to smoke over the edge of the dock. I guess one had had a bit too much to drink at lunchtime. That big Canada goose came over and squawked at him, and he fell in the river!"

She was still chattering on as they left the river path, crossed a busy road at the traffic light, and then made their way up a suburban side street to a small two-storey duplex. She took the bicycle around to the side of the building and chained it to a metal grill, then came back and climbed the front steps. Opening the door, she beckoned him in.

"We're drinking here?" said Rashford, bemused.

"No, silly," she said. "But I have to get changed. I'm not going out in my work clothes."

Rashford nodded, then followed her into the small front room of the house. In the middle of the floor was a black bear skin, its head raised and staring at the door. Rashford stopped in his tracks.

"Wow," he said. "You don't see many of those."

"My grandad killed it," she said, proudly, "and my kôhkum dressed the hide the old way, with a scraper knife and some lye soap. It was a gift when I came back to school the third time, for my perseverance."

"Is your grandad a hunter?" said Rashford.

"Not really," she said. "He will bring a moose and perhaps some deer every fall, for the family, but he does not think of himself as a hunter. He is a trapper, still practises the old ways."

"Why did he shoot the bear, then?"

"He didn't. Shoot it, I mean. He was in camp one night, on his trapline north of the Churchill River. It's just upriver from these beautiful rapids, and there is a deep pool where you can catch suckers."

"Suckers?"

"Yeah, whitefish. They're a type of catfish, I guess. Not as good as walleye, but less bony than jackfish. Anyway, he was in camp, and this bear started sniffing around, looking for food. My grandad said he thought it must have been hurt or something, because it didn't seem scared. It didn't run away when he shouted at it. In fact, it came closer."

She subconsciously lowered her voice, almost to a whisper, and Rashford could imagine her grandfather telling her the story.

"First it knocked the frying pan off the fire, and then it ate the suckers. Granddad said he didn't mind that, he had enough to share. Then it came and started digging into his pack, ripping up his clothes. Grandad said he didn't even mind that, they were old clothes anyway. But then it got hold of his small medicine bag, where he kept his snuff, and started shaking the bag around, holding it in his teeth like a dog with a toy.

"Grandad told him to put the snuff down, he only had the three tins, and he was supposed to be on the trapline for five weeks, but the bear didn't listen. The bear stood up on his hind legs, still shaking his head, the snuff tins rattling and banging. So, grandad took his knife and went over to the bear and asked nicely for it to give him the tins back. He shook the knife to show he meant business.

"The bear looked at him and raised his paws, showing off his claws, as though he was saying, 'you've only got one claw, but I've got ten.' All the time he kept shaking his head, like he was saying 'no no no'.

"Grandad said a third time, 'give me back my snuff boxes.' This time the bear dropped the small medicine bag, and jumped at my grandad, teeth bared, claws flashing. My grandad jumped right back towards him, inside the reach of its paws, and stabbed with his knife while trying to avoid its teeth and claws. They fought for what seemed ages but was probably only a few minutes. Grandad got cut up pretty bad, and the clothes he was wearing were ruined, but he killed the bear."

"With his knife?"

"Yes."

Rashford looked at the rug, which was probably five feet from nose to tail. He thought that standing on its hind legs, it would have been much bigger, and he couldn't imagine jumping into its embrace, knife or no knife. He shook his head.

"So, you got the trophy," he said.

"Yes. My grandad made me a necklace of the claws from one paw. And he gave me the pelt."

"The claws? I thought that was something only the hunter could receive?"

"Yes."

She looked at him, then came to a decision. Taking a deep breath, she spoke.

"Well, there was something else. You see, I was out on the trapline with grandad that trip. Me and my kôhkum would go for berries when he was out checking his snares. We had both gotten very tired, so we were having a nap in the tent. I woke up when I heard my grandad talking about his snuff boxes. I came out and was just in time to see the bear wrap his paws around my grandad, so I ran to the fire and picked up the big cast iron frying pan and banged the bear on the back of the head. He turned his head to look at me, and that's when grandad killed him. So, he said I should take the claws."

Rashford stared at her. She shrugged.

"When I got back to school, we had to write a 'what I did this summer' sort of essay. My teacher wouldn't give me a mark, he said I was supposed to write a truthful story, not fiction."

Rashford smiled at that.

"Stupid môniyâw," she said, laughing.

He laughed with her.

"What about Pia? Does he go trapping?"

"No, he's a city Indian," she said. "He likes his comforts, Pia. He's not comfortable about sleeping in a tent, or cooking food on a fire."

"You said that he dropped out of university? What does he do?"

"I'm not really sure. He runs a business with a friend of his, from high school, and they seem to make enough money to get by. Why?"

"Oh, I was just wondering. He wanted a finder's fee for connecting me with someone, that's the envelope I gave you. I just wondered what he did for a living."

"Like I said, I'm not really sure," she said. "Okay, I have to get changed. You sit there, I'll just be a minute."

She left him sitting on a large, overstuffed armchair and ran lightly up the stairs.

It was over forty-five minutes before she reappeared. She had kept shouting updates from what was apparently her bedroom, so he knew she had had a shower, washed and dried her hair, and agonized long and hard over what top to pick. Rashford had spent the time checking his phone for non-existent messages or emails and looking casually around the room.

It was a typical room in a student house, he supposed. In addition to the chair on which he sat, there was a second armchair and a well-worn three-person couch, upholstered in what had originally been a bright striped pattern but was now muted by usage and, perhaps, multiple laundries. In the centre of the room stood a large flat screen television, mounted on some sort of wooden cabinet. To one side was a battered-looking table, surrounded by six mismatched dining room chairs. On the cross walls flanking the stairs there was the ubiquitous Matisse print of a blue nude silhouetted on a white background, and the almost equally ubiquitous black and white on red portrait of Che Guevara, the red star on his beret gleaming.

There were anomalies, though. On the opposite wall, next to the door through which they had entered, in a similar style to the revolutionary poster but restricted to black on red, was the image of Louis Riel. Hanging above the television was a photograph of a First Nations woman, wearing a deerskin jacket and her hair in braids, standing behind a large grizzly bear. She had her hand on the shoulder of the great beast but did not look in the least afraid. Smoke or fog billowed around the pair. Rashford went over and peered more closely, and decided this was no photoshopped image, but perhaps one taken in a museum or a wildlife interpretive centre, using a taxidermy model. He had to admit that it was a very striking photograph.

Standing against the wall was a replica Secretary's Desk, with four narrow drawers and a flap that would pivot down to provide a working surface. The desk was situated so that anyone sitting at it would be able to look up and see the photograph.

At one point Shyanne had appeared at the top of the stairs and called down to him.

"What do you think? Is this too risqué for a first date?"

Rashford just stared. She was wearing a bright red dress that hugged her body like a second skin. It had a deep-cut vee-neck and fell to her ankles, but there was a hip-high slit in one side and as she posed, she pushed her leg out. He saw she was not wearing stockings, or anything else as far as he knew.

He thought she looked fabulous, and totally inappropriate to be accompanying him for a drink.

"Maybe save that for when you go to pick up your Oscar," he said.

She giggled, then gave a large theatrical sigh.

"Okaaay, I'll go and change," she said, disappearing back into her bedroom.

"And it's not a date!" shouted Rashford, but there was no response.

Rashford continued to poke around. He found a small kitchen, and a fridge full of Tupperware boxes with 'don't eat me, I'm Shyanne's' written on them. A large box of chocolate covered peanuts had a similar admonishment, this time signed by someone called Derek, and the almond milk apparently belonged to Frieda.

The third door off the living room led into what was presumably Derek's bedroom, as here the posters were of NHL players and Playboy models. A game consul stood on a side desk, with the joy sticks thrown loosely onto the floor. The bed was untidy, and a variety of different coloured socks were scattered across the carpet. Rashford smiled to himself, remembering his early years at university. He closed the door gently and went back to sit in the chair and wait for Shyanne.

When she eventually reappeared, Rashford was only slightly mollified by her choice of clothing. She was wearing high-waisted leggings which were a shiny metallic blue in colour, topped by a tight white tee-shirt. The leggings were cropped, and she showed an expanse of ankle above red low-top canvas shoes that had thick white shoelaces and were dotted with white glitter. As she came down the stairs, she shrugged herself into a tan leather jacket that had fringes running from shoulder to chest, under her arms, and from the hem.

"Did your dad kill the jacket as well?" said Rashford.

"No, silly, this is suede," she said.

She took something from her pocket and handed it to him. He looked down at the thin metal chain, to which were attached five highly polished bear claws. Each was just under two inches long, dark grey and mottled with black streaks, curved to a stiletto point. He held the necklace gently, then handed it back to her.

"It's beautiful," he said. "You must be very proud to have earned that trophy."

She nodded, then pirouetted in front of him.

"What do you think?"

Rashford tried to phrase things carefully.

"Well, umm, people will certainly notice if you get cold," he said, at last.

She looked down at her herself.

"You can see my boobs?"

"Very much so, yes."

She sighed, then turned and went back upstairs.

"I'll leave the necklace here," she called back over her shoulder.

When she came back down, he saw that she had changed. The tee-shirt was just as tight but was now black.

"Well?" she said, in a challenging tone.

"Much better," he said, "you look great. Where are we going?"

"Just to a bar," she said. "There's a good band there, and one of my cousins is playing tonight."

She grabbed his arm and pulled him to the door.

"Come on," she said. "Hustle hustle, or we'll miss the bus."

"Bus?" said Rashford.

They walked quickly down the street and turned the corner towards the university. Rashford tried to ask where they were going, and why they were taking a bus to get there, but Shyanne just hurried him along. Rashford saw the glass-sided shelter ahead of them, illuminated by the lights of the adjacent convenience store, and was relieved to see three people already waiting. Shyanne noticed the queue as well and slowed her pace.

As they approached, a man came out of the small shop, unwrapping a tube of candy. Rashford saw that he was wearing a dark khaki blazer over a blue button-down Oxford shirt, with a pale green plaid Madras necktie. He had on skinny black dress jeans and brown lace-up shoes.

"Marc?" said Rashford.

The man stopped, then came forward and offered the candy to them both.

"Would you like a mint?" he said.

"No, thank you," said Rashford. Shyanne just shook her head.

"Where are you going, all dressed up?" said Rashford, looking at Claydon.

"Nowhere special," said Claydon. "I was at the Three-Legged Rabbit but there was nobody there I knew, so I thought if I'm going to be on my own, I might as well be somewhere new. I was just going to wander until I found somewhere, I don't know this town."

"Come with us," said Shyanne, brightly. "We're going dancing."

Rashford looked at her.

"We are?"

"Yes. Come on, Marc. It'll be fun."

"I don't really dance," said Claydon.

"Neither do I," muttered Rashford.

Somehow Shyanne shimmied around so that she was in the middle, her arms linked through theirs. She pulled them towards the bus stop.

"C'mon," she said, a teasing note in her voice. "Josee will probably be there."

Just then the bus arrived, the doors opening with a pneumatic hiss. Shyanne released their arms and followed the other people in the queue up the steps, tapping her card on the square metal reader as she passed the driver. Rashford and Claydon stood awkwardly in the door area.

"Umm, we don't have tickets," said Rashford, looking at the driver. The man looked back.

"Three fifty each, exact change only, no change given," he said, nodding at the small sign that displayed the same information. Claydon looked at Rashford.

"Do you have cash?" he said. "I don't, only cards."

Rashford sighed and pulled out his wallet. He found a ten-dollar bill.

"No change, eh?"

"Nope," said the driver, a large man with a prominent paunch. "Make your minds up, I've got a schedule to keep."

Rashford pushed the bill through the slot next to the pass reader. The driver pushed a small button on his side of the glass partition, and a ticket whirred out from a black box on Rashford's side. The driver repeated the process and a second ticket appeared. He nodded at Rashford and put the bus into gear. The door hissed shut behind them and they walked down the aisle to where Shyanne had claimed the entire back seat. They sat next to her, one on each side.

"Why are we on a bus?" said Rashford.

Shyanne giggled.

"Sorry, I wasn't thinking. It's free with my student card."

Rashford just looked at her. She grabbed his arm and pulled him to her, smiling.

"Don't be grumpy. We can get a taxi back, or an Uber."

Claydon looked around, then turned to them.

"I've never been on a bus before," he said. "It's remarkably comfortable."

Shyanne stared at him.

"What, never-ever?"

"Never-ever," he said. "I'm from downtown Toronto, we either walk or get an Uber. Sometimes the train. But never a bus."

For the next twenty minutes, Claydon and Shyanne chattered about the benefits and pitfalls of public transit, while Rashford stared out of the window and watched the terraced row houses of the town centre transition to more suburban semi-detached homes with small gardens, and then to an almost rural landscape of new-built homes on what appeared to be large acreage lots. The bus stopped and started, people getting on and off, and the traffic became lighter.

A light rain began to fall. The acreages gave way to a more industrial looking landscape, with large warehouses and a paved parking area full of yellow school buses. Their bus drove through a pool of light emanating from a gas station and pulled up beside the small convenience shop.

"Here we are," shouted the driver, "end of the line."

"Thank you," said Shyanne, getting up and walking back down the aisle. As she passed the glass partition she paused and thanked the driver again.

"Great ride, Steve," she said.

"You're welcome," he said, then closed the door behind them as they exited down the steps.

"You know this route?" said Rashford.

"Yes," said Shyanne. "And like I said, it's a free ride, nice and comfortable, and then I get an Uber back later. The buses stop running out here at eleven. Come on."

She led the way along the side of the convenience store and towards the back of the gas station. To their left there was a brushless car wash, the red and blue neon lights shining though the pebbled glass walls, and a small stand which contained two vacuum cleaners. They walked alongside the gas station, past the row of black, green and blue bins that held garbage, compostable food debris, and recyclables, and came out into a large car park. Opposite them was a long, low wooden building with planked sides.

Shyanne led the way through the rows of parked cars and pick-up trucks. Rashford and Claydon exchanged glances, then followed. As they approached the building, Rashford saw that there was one entrance, a porch with steps leading up to the door. A large Miller Lite roundel hung on the door itself, the neon light blazing, and three large spotlights illuminated the entrance area.

Moving closer, he noticed the line of nine large Harley Davidson motorbikes, the chrome gleaming in the light spilling out from the doorway of the bar. They were parked parallel to the building, which had long overhanging eaves. Rashford stepped towards the bikes and a dark figure emerged from the shadows, moving into the light.

Rashford stopped and looked at the man, who was about his height but much thinner. He wore his hair long, tied back in a ponytail, and had on a black leather vest over a taut tee-shirt. His muscular arms were covered in full-sleeve tattoos.

"Stay away," he said.

Rashford held his arms out to the side, palms open.

"Just looking," he said.

The man nodded.

"Eyes only, no hands," he said.

Shyanne had stopped at the foot of the three steps which led up to the door.

"It's okay, Brian," she said. "He's with me."

"Still can't touch, Shy," said the biker, not moving his eyes from Rashford.

Rashford nodded and stepped back a pace.

"They're nice bikes," he said, then walked along the line to join Shyanne and Claydon at the steps. Brian stepped back into the shadows under the eaves. They walked up the steps and Shyanne pushed open the door.

CHAPTER 9

Once they were inside the door, Shyanne stopped. Rashford and Claydon stepped up beside her. Shyanne spoke quietly to Rashford.

"Brian must have really upset someone," she said. "He loves this band. He'll be pissed that he's on guard duty for the bikes."

Rashford nodded, then looked around. He saw that they had entered into a large rectangular room. To his immediate right, the bar was parallel to the long edge of the room. The wall behind was covered in mirrors, shelves full of glasses, rows of liquor dispensers topped with a variety of bottles, and for some reason a plethora of cuckoo clocks. There was a narrow shelf underneath the dispensers, with wicker baskets full of small packets of peanuts, pork rind scratchings, and potato chips.

The bar itself was covered in some sort of vinyl material, with long faded bar mats interspersing the rafts of draught beer pumps. A young woman stood behind the closest set of pumps; a dishtowel was flung haphazardly over her shoulder. Beyond her, chatting to a group of tattooed and leather vested men whom Rashford assumed belonged to the Harleys, a large barman was laughing at someone's joke.

The bar stopped at the wall which formed the far edge of the rectangle. The wall was bare, with the central area cut out and a stage placed in the recess. Some microphones stood on stands, amps and play-back monitors lined the edge of the stage, and large speakers mounted on heavy metal scaffolds stood off to each side.

As his gaze shifted to the long wall opposite the bar, Rashford noticed that the general hum of conversation was faltering. A dozen or so tables were placed along the wall and as he scanned them, he realized that most were filled. The top wall, extending in front of him on his left, was also lined with tables. They were also busy with customers, unlike the general tables scattered around the middle of the room. These formed a horseshoe design on three sides of a small dance floor, which had been roped off with thick yellow cord attached to pylons placed at each corner. There were two entrances to the dancing area, one on each side, and the tables were placed at least a metre away from the ropes.

"Where do we sit?" he said, quietly, as Shyanne looked around and then waved at someone on the far side.

"Over with Pia," she said, and Rashford believed he heard some relief in her voice, that her brother was already in the bar. Shyanne called hello to the young woman behind the bar, who nodded and then used her dishcloth to flick an imaginary speck of dirt off the bar counter. Shyanne led them through the central tables and down the far side of the room, to a table about one third of the way along the wall up from the stage.

As they crossed the open area, Rashford realized that most of the people to his left, along the top wall of the bar, were white. They had round, red faces, and short cut tousled hair, and most wore checked shirts and clean blue jeans. Some wore baseball caps, some sported black Stetson hats. The women were generally slim, wearing denim jackets over white blouses and tight blue jeans capped with finely tooled leather boots. A few wore white straw Stetsons, or a brightly coloured kerchief around their hair. Men and women alike watched silently as the three newcomers crossed the floor.

Pia was a large man with dark black hair tied in a braid. He had some tattoo lines across his cheeks, and more around his neck. He was wearing a buckskin jacket similar in design to that worn by Shyanne, but his was dark and stained, some of the fringes torn away, a small round lapel button with yellow, red, white and black quadrants the only decoration.

He was sitting at a table with four other men, all of whom stood when Shyanne arrived. They each gave her a fist bump, then drifted away and found seats at other tables. Rashford reached in and shook Pia's hand.

"Mister Piapot Starblanket, I presume?" he said.

"That's me," said Pia, nodding. "You must be Rashford. Who's the Indian Agent?"

Rashford choked back a laugh as Shyanne slapped her brother on the shoulder.

"Be nice!" she said. "This is Marc. He's Josee's friend."

Pia nodded.

"She's in the washroom," he said, pointing with his chin at the large sequin-covered purse that hung on the back of the seat to his left. A small glass of clear liquid, with ice, stood on the table in front of the chair. Rashford noted that Pia's own glass was empty.

"Can I get you something?" he said.

"Sure. I'll have a soda water with blueberry," he said. Then he looked at Claydon with a glare.

"What's your problem?"

Claydon shut his mouth and stood back half a step.

"N, n, nothing," he said, stammering slightly.

"Breaking another of your fucking stereotypes, am I? I'm a male Indian so I must be an alcoholic drunkard? Sorry to disappoint."

"No, it's not that."

Claydon looked to Rashford for support, but Rashford had no idea what the problem was either. Claydon cleared his throat, then reddened slightly.

"It's just that most people I know," he said, "have cranberry with their soda."

Piapot looked at him, incredulous. Shyanne stifled a giggle. Claydon was still standing, not sure what to do or say, when Josee came bouncing across from the washrooms and called out his name. He turned to her with great relief, and they sat down, Josee looking at Rashford and waving her hand in front of her face.

Shyanne laughed.

"No," she said, "he's been with me for the last two hours and he has not had a cigarette!"

"Two hours?" said Josee, widening her eyes.

Still laughing, Shyanne shook her head and sat down in the empty seat on Pia's right. Rashford took the drink orders and went to the bar.

As he approached, the bikers moved apart and left him with a clear four feet in which to stand. He did so, and the large male barkeeper walked over to him. He raised an eyebrow, the unspoken question.

"Two draught beers," said Rashford, "anything local is fine. One screwdriver, and one soda with blueberry."

The man nodded and turned away to make the drinks. One of the bikers walked up to the gap behind Rashford and stood in it. Rashford turned and nodded at him. The biker looked him up and down.

"Don't see many cops in here," he said.

Rashford nodded.

"I can believe it."

The biker said nothing, just stared. Rashford stared back. The biker looked up to the ceiling, as if to collect his thoughts, then returned his gaze to Rashford.

"So, why are you here, then?" he said.

"The thing is," Rashford said, "I'm not a cop. I'm retired. I'm just here for a drink with my friends."

The biker shook his head.

"You're a friend of Pia? I don't think so."

"No, not Pia, Shyanne. I'm speaking at a conference, up at the university, and she invited me here to listen to the band. Apparently, they're pretty good."

The biker nodded.

"And, after the set?"

"Up to Shyanne, really. She brought me here, and she said she'd make sure I got back okay."

The biker laughed.

"Did she now? Well, we'll see about that."

He nodded over Rashford's shoulder.

"Your drinks are ready," he said, and walked away.

Rashford turned and saw that the four drinks were neatly arranged on a small tray. A slip of paper indicated how much he owed, and he tapped his card on the offered device, adding a twenty per cent tip. The barman nodded in appreciation, then turned away to serve another customer. Rashford picked up the tray and walked back to the table.

"Any hassle?" said Pia, glancing back towards the bar.

"Nah," said Rashford, "he was checking out who I am and where I'm from."

"That's Malcom," said Pia, "the number two of that motley crew."

"Number two?"

"Yeah. Do you see the fat guy he's talking to now? That's Edward. Not Ed or Eddy, Ted or Teddy. Edward. Edward the Executioner. He's the number one."

Rashford took a sideways look and saw Malcom standing with his back to the dance floor, leaning over the shoulder of a large, bearded man who was sitting on a bar stool. The man looked up and turned around, scanning the tables. He caught Rashford looking at him. Rashford was reminded of a hawk, the perfect stillness of the gaze holding him fast. He broke away with difficulty, took his beer, and seated himself next to Shyanne. As he sat down, he glanced across again, and saw the big man laughing, his jowls wobbling, as he raised a glass in a mock toast. Rashford ignored him and turned to Shyanne.

"What kind of place have you brought us to?" he said.

"It's a roadhouse, a country bar. You've met the bikers, that's their side. You've got all the farmers along that side, and all us Indians along this side. Any strangers who come in have to sit in the middle."

"Do you get many of them? Strangers?"

"Some. But for whatever reason, they don't tend to come back."

Rashford nodded.

"Yeah, I can see that."

"It's perfectly safe," Shyanne laughed.

"No fighting inside?" he said.

"Nope," said Pia, interrupting. "And none outside unless it's been pre-arranged. No ad hoccery allowed. Save that for your own time, your own place. This is a shared space."

"Like an African watering hole," said Claydon, nodding. "I saw that on television once. All the animals need water, so when they go to the watering hole, nobody eats anyone else. The lions and zebras stand next to each other and drink."

Pia shook his head.

"I guess," he said. "I'm not sure who are the zebras, though. Here it's pretty much all lions."

<hr>

Marc Claydon revelled in the attention of the table as he spoke about his research. Josee kept asking questions about the plants people picked to use as dyes, and both Shyanne and Pia contributed comments from time to time. Rashford, with his back to the wall and a clear view of the room, let his gaze wander, only half listening. Suddenly, his attention was drawn back by a sharp intake of breath from Josee.

"No," she said, "you can't say that."

"What? Half-breed? But that's what Adams called himself."

"He can call himself what he wants. But you call him Métis."

Piapot nodded, then spoke quietly.

"There was always some stigma, back in the day," he said. "The people whose parents were French voyageurs, they called themselves Métis. The ones with Scottish heritage, they would often call themselves half-breeds. And Howard Adams was a great scholar so, like Josee said, he could call himself what he wanted. But you, and anyone else, you use the word Métis. Okay?"

Claydon nodded.

"I'm sorry," he said, contritely. "I didn't mean to offend. I've never actually met one, you see."

"Met one what?" said Shyanne.

"Met a Métis person," said Claydon. "I do all this research on voyageurs, and their families, and everything, but it's all from books, you know. Maybe you know someone?"

This last appeal was put to Shyanne, who blushed and dropped her eyes.

"I'll, umm, I'll see what I can do," she said, quietly.

Piapot cleared his throat.

"My turn to buy a round," he said. "Come on, môniyâw. You can help me carry the drinks."

He stood up from the table and Claydon followed him across the room. The two women exchanged glances, giggling softly.

"Are you going to tell him?" said Rashford, looking at Josee.

"Maybe later," she said, then looked at him frankly. "How did you know?"

"Your earrings," said Rashford. "They are blue with the white infinity symbol, that's the Métis flag."

Josee touched them with one hand and smiled at him.

"Correct," she said. "Don't tell him, will you?"

"Not my story to tell," said Rashford, laughing, then looking up as sounds of an argument came from the bar. He made to stand but Shyanne caught his arm.

"It's okay," she said, "Pia will handle it."

Rashford noticed the rustles around him as men straightened in their chairs, ready to rise if called. He settled back down in his own seat. After a few minutes, Claydon walked back over, carrying a tray. Piapot walked behind him and then sat down at the table with a laugh.

"What was all that about?" said Rashford.

"Nothing," said Pia.

"He tried to con me!" said Claydon, his face going red. "I was ordering the drinks and this biker fellow next to me, he just picked up his glass and poured his drink on the bar. Then he said, to me, 'oi, you knocked my arm and I've spilled my drink. You owe me a new one.' The cheek of the man!"

Rashford laughed.

"You're lucky that in his shock, he didn't knock the next arm, and so on. You might have owed the whole bar a drink."

"That's not right," said Claydon. "I wouldn't give the man satisfaction. I didn't buy him a drink. Honestly!"

"I did," said Pia, in answer to the unasked question. "Keep it light, you know."

Rashford nodded.

"And, anyway, what kind of person calls their child Slider?" said Claydon, huffing. "Ridiculous name."

"It was Slider?" said Josee, starting to get out of her chair. "I'll go and have a word ..."

Pia pulled her back down.

"It's sorted," he said. "Just a joke. Okay?"

Josee folded her arms and shrugged.

"If you say so," she said.

Claydon was still muttering about the appropriateness of Slider as a name. Piapot interrupted him, speaking softly so that Claydon had to lean forward in order to hear.

"Some people say it's because he's long and thin and can slide in easily through almost any open window, no matter how small. A good man to have along if you're doing any B and E."

"Break and enter," whispered Rashford, noticing Claydon's incomprehension.

Piapot continued.

"Other people say it's because he keeps a long thin stiletto knife in his boot, like the Italians or the Corsicans, and you never know you've been stabbed until he's sliding it out of your gut."

Claydon sat back with a jerk, looking across to the bar.

"Really," he said, his voice squeaking.

"But me," said Piapot, "I went to school with him. And I happen to know that he fancied himself as a great pitcher, but he could only throw one type of pitch. And everybody knew, so they saw it coming, and let it go, then hit every other pitch out of the park."

"What sort of pitch did he throw, a knuckleball?" said Claydon.

Piapot just sat back in his chair, taking a great swallow of his soda and blueberry as he shook his head.

"No, Marc," said Rashford. "He used to throw a slider."

"Oh," said Claydon, nodding thoughtfully. Then he looked up and smiled.

"Oh, now I get it. His name is Slider because that was his pitch. Ah, very funny."

Everyone at the table laughed and reached for their drinks. Shyanne turned to her brother.

"Before I forget, this is for you," she said, handing him the envelope. "It's from Gavin."

"Ekosi," said Piapot, nodding at Rashford, who dipped his head in acknowledgement. Piapot put the envelope in his inside pocket. Just then the outside door opened, and a man stepped inside. All conversation across the bar stopped immediately. From his seat Rashford could see the tall man stop and survey the room, much like he had. When their eyes met, they nodded to each other. Rashford stood and waved.

"Over here, Patrick," he called.

Chapter 10

Patrick York picked his way through the tables and made it to their group safely, ignoring the scandalized looks from the farmers and the inquisitive ones from the bikers. He stood at the table and waited to be introduced. Rashford did the honours, then asked if York would like a drink. He did, so Rashford went over to the bar and bought him a beer. When he got back York was sitting next to Shyanne, with his back to the wall, so Rashford sat in the empty chair next to him. There was a small zone behind his right shoulder that he couldn't cover but he thought that Piapot's men would assist there.

Patrick thanked him for the beer, then kept talking to Shyanne and Piapot. Rashford coughed, loudly, and York turned back to him.

"Yes, mon?"

"Yes, mon, indeed," said Rashford. "What the hell are you doing here?"

York laughed.

"Following you, I guess," he said.

Rashford looked at him.

"Really?"

"No, of course not. I heard this was a really good place for music, so

I got an Uber to bring me out here. There was nothing happening on campus, and it is Saturday night, mon."

He looked around.

"Nobody told me it was only for white folks, though."

Rashford laughed.

"Well, this is the multicultural table," he said. "We've got First Nations and settlers and everything in-between."

"And we're in-between rednecks and bikers, I see."

"Yeah. But it's okay, according to Marc this is a waterhole where we're all safe. There's lions and zebras but nobody eats anyone else here."

"Uh-uh."

Suddenly there was a cacophony of noise, as seventeen different cuckoo clocks all chimed at once in a discordant clamour. As the sound faded away, Rashford realized that the band had just emerged onto the stage.

York took a swig of his beer, then turned back to speak with Shyanne and Piapot. Josee and Claydon were still chatting away, so Rashford focused on the four-person group. A woman with bright red hair appeared to be the vocalist, although she carried a tambourine as well. There was a lead guitar player with a yellow amplified acoustic guitar, a bass player with a long-necked base that had a black body and a white pickguard, and a drummer. They started playing some covers of country classics, with '*Ring of Fire*' followed by '*The Gambler*' and then '*Friends in low places.*' Rashford tapped his feet to '*Walking after midnight*' and hummed along to the ironic Willie Nelson classic '*I don't go to funerals.*' As the final chorus came to an end, he realized that half the crowd were singing along, and joined in with "and I sure won't be at mine."

The band paused to a smattering of applause and the lead singer introduced herself, then the rest of the people on stage with her. She wiped the sweat from her forehead with a red checkered kerchief, then spoke out clearly over the crowd.

"I know y'all have been waiting for this, what do you say to a bit of two-step?"

There were whistles and hollers from the farmers along the back wall, and from some of the tables down the side. Josee shushed whatever Marc was saying and clapped her hands. Shyanne reached across to Rashford, her eyes shining.

"This is my cousin coming on," she said, excitedly.

"Our cousin," said Josee, pointedly, and Piapot nodded.

A long, drawn-out note wailed from off stage. As it died away, the drummer started a slow beat on his large drum, skittering the cymbals at the same time. The lead singer spoke over the beat.

"We are delighted to have a special friend back with us today," she said.

The bass guitar joined in, increasing the speed of the beat a fraction. Another, sharper, wailed note came from off-stage. The acoustic guitar player started picking, speeding up the tempo even further. The crowd started to clap in time to the beat.

"Please welcome," said the singer, her voice rising even further. "Please welcome, one of the best fiddle players in this part of the world, and one of the best Métis fiddle players in any part of the world."

The crowd roared and the beat got faster, now joined by the mournful sound of a train horn echoing through the night, the slow slide of the bow a counterpoint to blurring fingers across the frets of the guitar and the staccato beat of drum and tambourine.

The voice of the singer could hardly be heard, even as she screamed into the microphone.

"Ladies and gentlemen, please give a great big western welcome to … Amanda Robicheau!"

The crowd roared and the fiddle picked up the pace as well, the notes sharper and somehow cleaner, cutting through the bar and sending shivers down every spine. The crowd were on their feet, Rashford included, and clapping madly as the beat somehow got faster. Then, suddenly, there she was.

The fiddle player emerged from behind the drums, walking slowly, her fiddle held horizontally to her chin. Although her fingers flashed over the neck and finger board, the bow was moving slowly, almost hypnotically. Her long blonde hair was pulled behind her in a braid, and she wore a Métis sash over her right shoulder and down, tied in a knot at her left hip. Her top was a loose shift that hung over her blue jeans and white cowboy boots. She increased the speed of the bow and her fingers danced over the strings with every chord.

Rashford stood with his mouth open.

Shyanne grabbed his arm.

"That's our cousin," she said. "Isn't she great?"

"Mandy?" he said.

Once the set was finished, Mandy came over to their table, eyes shining, and flopped into the empty chair. Shyanne had been to the bar and had a glass of white wine waiting, together with a glass of iced water. Mandy drank half the water down first, then took a sip of her wine.

"Thanks, cuz," she said. "Who else is ..."

She had started to look around the table and appeared to suddenly realize who she was sitting next to.

"Gavin!" she squealed, slamming down the glass onto the table and reaching around to hug him tightly. "You're here!"

She kissed him hard on the lips, and he could not help but reciprocate. Eventually he felt a tap on his shoulder from Patrick. He broke off the clinch and looked around. Everybody at the table was staring at them. Piapot broke the silence first.

"Umm, I guess you two know each other?"

"I sure hope so," said Josee, softly. She giggled but stopped when Shyanne gave her a dagger look.

"This is my friend," said Mandy, looking across the Shyanne. "The one I was telling you about!"

"Oh," said Shyanne. She glared at Rashford.

"Why didn't you tell me?"

"Tell you what?"

"That you had a girlfriend. Instead of coming on a date with me?"

"Date? What date?" said Mandy.

"It's not a date," Rashford protested, realizing that he was starting to blush. He turned to Shyanne. "I told you it wasn't a date."

She harrumphed and crossed her arms, turning away so that her back was to him. Only Josee could see the small smile that played around her lips.

Mandy continued the cross-examination.

"Why are you here, then?" she said. "If not on a date with Shyanne, who did you come with? This Black guy?"

"Whoa, keep me out of this," said Patrick York, holding his hands up in mock surrender. "I just wandered in here for some music."

Mandy nodded, then glared at Josee.

"Is he with you?"

Josee sat straight in her chair and glared back.

"I hunt my own," she said. "Don't need your sloppy seconds."

Mandy shook her head in disgust, her hair flying.

"I know you," she said, looking at Marc Claydon. "Did you bring him?"

"No, not me," said Marc, only just stopping himself from saying that he had never seen Rashford before in his life. "I came to see Josee. And to hear you, of course," he added, rapidly.

"What about you, cuz?" Mandy said to Piapot. "Is this môniyâw one of yours?"

Piapot held his hands up as well.

"I never met him before," he said, truthfully, omitting the details of their earlier conversations.

Mandy squirmed around in Rashford's lap, her arms still around his neck. Her voice dropped ominously low as she spoke to the back of Shyanne's head.

"That leaves just you, cuz," she snarled.

Shyanne turned slowly round in her chair; her face was downcast. She lifted her eyes slowly to meet Mandy's. Behind her, Josee raised her hand to her mouth. The three men all stared at Rashford, whose mouth dropped open.

"Help!" he mouthed.

Suddenly Mandy raised her arms, then slapped them down on the sides of her thighs, and the three women dissolved into great gulps of laughter and guffaws. She turned back to Rashford and gave him another kiss.

"Oh, the look on your face," she laughed.

Over the next ten minutes, Rashford discovered that Shyanne and Mandy chatted together a few times every day on social media. They had quickly realized that they had both met Rashford, albeit in different contexts, and when Shyanne found out Mandy's concern that she might not see him again, they had decided to cook up some fun by arranging the 'accidental' meeting.

Mandy drained the last of her wine and kissed Rashford on the cheek, then stood up.

"Gotta run," she said. "Time to get ready for the second set. Josee, teach them how to do the *Red River Jig*!"

With that she left and walked back to the small door in the wall next to the stage. Josee got to her feet.

"C'mon then," she said, gesturing to the three men. "On your feet,"

Rashford, York, and Claydon looked at each other, and then to Piapot for assistance. He just shook his head and held out his hands.

"You heard the lady," he said, making himself comfortable and picking up his drink. Shyanne picked up her drink as well, then leaned her shoulder in against her brother.

"This should be fun," she said.

"C'mon," said Josee, "or else we'll do this out on the dance floor, not here where it's dark."

The three men scrambled to their feet and stood in a ragged line in front of the table. People at the other tables nearby rearranged themselves so they could watch.

"Okay," said Josee. "This is pretty easy. First, stand with your feet apart, about in line with your shoulders. Stay on the balls of your feet and keep a bit of a bend in your knee. Good."

She walked around them, checking their stance.

"Okay, so this is basically a heel toe tap step, which goes back to front and then side to side. And you have a little hop in there."

Her feet moved rapidly across the floor. York nodded, Rashford thought he could see a pattern, and Claydon looked stricken.

"Now you try," she said. "Right foot first. Hop, heel, toe, tap, kick. Now the left foot."

Shyanne giggled.

"The other left, Marc," she called, and there was some appreciative chuckling from the others at the surrounding tables.

"Okay, stop," said Josee. "Now switch and try to go side to side. Right foot first. Step, heel, toe, tap, kick. Now the left foot. Good."

They tried a few times, York dancing on one leg after being kicked by Rashford, Claydon off the beat by half a second compared to the others.

"Stop, stop, please," said Josee, trying to keep a straight face. Shyanne was biting the knuckles of her hand, trying not to shake, and Piapot Starblanket simply sat there, serene, tears of laughter running down his cheeks.

"Now let's put this together," said Josee. "Ten of each. And remember, keep your backs and arms straight. All the movement is below the waist and the elbows. Back in line, please."

They shuffled into an approximation of a line. Josee turned to the other tables.

"Randy, Johnboy, come up here and assist, will ya."

It wasn't a question, and the two men got up from their tables and took their places at each end of the line. Josee nodded.

"Remember, we'll start with the right foot first, so just balance on it a bit, so you remember."

They all raised their right heels and stood poised, like long distance runners waiting for the starting pistol.

"We'll start slowly. All together, now, hop, heel, toe, tap, kick. And the left foot, hop, heel, toe, tap, kick. Excellent. And the right foot."

She clapped her hands to beat the time, starting out really slowly for the first set of ten steps. Then she started clapping a bit more quickly.

"And now the side to side," she said. "Step, heel, toe, tap, kick. And the left foot. Step, heel, toe, tap, kick. Well done! Keep it going."

The clapping got louder as some of the other drinkers joined in, but Josee kept the overall beat quite slow. Then suddenly she speeded up, and both Johnboy and Randy backstepped, stomping their toes twice and then kicking out one foot across the other before returning to the hop-step kicks. Rashford and York both stumbled, crashing into each other as they tried to stay upright. Claydon almost made it to the end of the sequence before banging into a chair and falling into the seat.

Josee applauded, and Johnboy shook Claydon's hand before he went to sit down. Shyanne and Piapot wiped the tears from their eyes and choked back gulps of laughter.

"It's easier to music," said Josee.

As they settled themselves in to watch the second half of the performance, York said it was his turn to buy a round of drinks.

"You can pay," said Rashford, "but maybe I should go."

York scoffed.

"I think I can handle some honky bikers," he said.

"It's the rednecks I worry about," said Rashford.

Piapot spoke out. "He's right," he said, then turned and looked over his shoulder. "Leon, go help carry the beer, eh?"

A tall man about the same size and shape as both York and Rashford, but with much thicker arms and the shoulders of a weightlifter who bulked up on steroids, stood up from one of the back tables. He walked a pace behind York, who made his way through the tables to the bar.

Four young men stepped away from the back wall and walked across to the bar, using a route which would intercept York. Rashford saw the sinewy muscle of their arms and necks and wondered if any of them were canola farmers.

The two groups arrived at the bar at more or less the same time, the farmers perhaps a fraction behind. York made his order, and the largest of the farmers spoke loudly to the barman.

"Make sure you disinfect those glasses pretty good, Jake," he said.

His three friends all laughed.

"Can you smell banana?" continued the large farmer.

York tensed, and Leon stepped up next to him and placed a hand on his shoulder.

"I think it's lovely when people are comfortable with their sexuality," sneered the farmer, and York started to turn. The farmer stepped back half a pace and raised his right arm back to his shoulder, making a fist. A man suddenly stepped between them.

"Edward says, not here, not now," said Malcom. He stood easily, facing the farmer. "We're all here for a good time, let's not spoil it."

The farmer froze in place, then slowly dropped his fist and turned away. The other three followed him, and Malcom turned to York.

"Just drink your drink, dance your dance, and go home after the last set, okay?" he said.

He did not wait for a response, simply nodded at Leon and then turned back to the other bikers standing around the bar. York picked up the tray, then went back to the table, Leon following a step behind. As he sat down, York released a big sigh.

"I guess we're the zebras," he said.

Just then the cuckoo clocks chimed again, and the band reappeared on the stage.

CHAPTER 11

The band started the second set with a series of three old cowboy songs, played in a slow tempo. '*The Cowboy's Lament*' was followed by '*The Dying Cowboy*', with '*When the work is done this fall*' finishing the medley. Some of the farmers along the back wall sang along, and a few older couples went to the dance floor and glided gracefully around, receiving applause as they left.

They were replaced by slightly younger couples as the band moved to an assortment of Ian Tyson ballads, played to a faster time signature and provoking more energy among the crowd. The dance floor was full, and the room reverberated as people sang along to '*Springtime in Alberta*', '*Rockies turn to rose*', and '*Barrel racing angel*'. Then the tempo increased again as the band moved into '*Navajo rug*', and the slow mournful cry of Mandy's violin from off stage sent shivers down Rashford's spine.

When she emerged, she was still wearing her white cowboy boots but had swapped the jeans and tunic for a checked pinafore-style dress that flared at her waist and hung down to her knees. Her hair was now loose, brushed out in waves, and the Métis sash was still tied from shoulder to hip.

Finishing the tale of Katie pulling the Navajo rug from the fire, the lead singer paused. As the band kept playing a steady monotone beat, she stood at the microphone and caught her breath, smiling at the audience and nodding in appreciation at their applause.

"Ladies and gentlemen," said the singer, "are you ready to dance?"

There was a loud roar from the crowd, and some sustained clapping. Rashford noticed that a number of the people from his side of the room had started to get to their feet and were slowly making their way down towards the dance floor. Some of the couples already there looked at them and returned to their seats, others simply moved across to one side and left an area clear.

"We're going to play a bit more Métis fiddle," continued the singer, "but I see we have some visitors here tonight, so let me tell you what to expect. We're starting with the '*Louis Riel Reel*', then the '*Wigwam Polka*', and then '*Cut Knife Hill*'. Is that right, Amanda?"

She looked across the stage at Mandy, who stood holding her fiddle in a relaxed position, her toe tapping to the beat and her bow tapping lightly on her thigh. Mandy nodded.

"And then," said the singer, lowering her voice to a breathy whisper. The crowd fell silent, or at least to a sustained murmur.

"And then," she said, "if you've been really good, we'll finish with '*Oayache Mannin*', which for those of you don't speak Michif is also known as the '*Red River Jig*.' But you're gonna have to earn that one!"

There was a loud burst of laughter and applause. Still holding onto the microphone stand, the singer leaned back and made eye contact with her band members. The tempo of the beat began to increase, as did the volume. Some people in the crowd began to stamp their feet to the rhythm, others to clap their hands. The singer looked across at Mandy, who raised her bow and straightened her arm.

"Please welcome back, the incredible Amanda Robicheau!"

Mandy drew out a long slow note and then clipped the bow against the strings, echoing the drummer. The group moved smoothly into the first notes of the reel, the fiddle rising above the backbeat of the guitars and drums. The lead singer slapped the tambourine on her thigh, and Mandy moved to the centre of the stage, her fingers flying.

Rashford just stared in awe as she moved from one tune into the next, the intricate finger movements flawless, dancing over the strings with each chord. The bow knifed up and down, pulling some notes on the upward stroke and others on the down, then whipping flatly across the frets. Her eyes were closed, and Mandy played with a passion he had seldom seen in a musician.

From one corner of his eye, he saw that most of the couples had left the dance floor, which was now populated with small clusters of men and women who faced each other as they danced. Their feet moved quickly across the dance floor, and Rashford could not discern any coherent pattern. Then he heard the music change again, the fiddle stopping as the drum maintained a staccato beat.

"Watch this," said Shyanne, waving towards the group on the dance floor. Rashford saw a group of four men move out from the rest of the dancers and edge towards the stage. The bass guitarist joined the drummer in keeping the beat, and Mandy drew a long soulful note from the bow. The four men nodded, then vaulted onto the stage.

As they turned to face the crowd, Rashford recognized Johnboy and Randy together with two other men he did not know. They stood, frozen in place with one knee slightly bent. Then Mandy brought her bow across the fiddle in a banshee wail, and as the music became a recognizable tune so the dancers started to perform the '*Red River Jig*'.

The crowd started to cheer, and the band played louder and faster. Suddenly Mandy started to tap her foot, then seemed to take a deep breath before breaking into the jig herself. Her feet were blurs as she danced in a tight circle on the stage, stepping out the hop-heel-toe steps and stomps, her hair flying but her back straight and the fiddle rock steady in her hand. Two on each side of her, the dancers maintained their furious pace. On the dance floor, people stood and stared, and at the tables the audience rose to its feet as one and roared its approval.

The ovation continued long after the music had come to a crescendo and the band had left the stage. They reappeared, Mandy included, and took a bow, then played a slow set of classic tunes like '*Loch Lomond*' and '*The Leaving of Liverpool*'. The jiggers returned to their seats, and the couples returned to the dance floor to waltz the encore away.

Once the band had finished their set, the jukebox started playing and people got up and danced as the fancy took them. Rashford went to the bar and got another round of drinks for their table, including a glass of wine for Mandy. He was waiting for Jake to serve him when he sensed a presence at his shoulder.

"Make this the last round, eh?" said Malcom, quietly. "Then take your friends and go home. The rednecks are looking for a rumble."

"We're just waiting for the band to come out," said Rashford. "We're not here to cause trouble."

"I know," said Malcom. "But thing is, just by being here you cause trouble. Do you know how many people here have lusted after Amanda Robicheau, and got absolutely nowhere? Then you turn up and she's all over you. And Josee with the civilian. And Shyanne with the Black dude? What's all that about?"

Rashford turned and saw Shyanne, smiling broadly and leaning in closely to whatever York was saying. She was patting him on the forearm with one hand and twirling a lock of hair around the fingers of her other hand.

Rashford turned back to the biker.

"Like I said, we were all at the conference, up at the university. We came here to listen to the band. That's it. End of."

Malcom looked at him, nodding slowly.

"Last round, okay," he said, and it wasn't a question. He turned and faded away into the crowd. In his place Rashford saw Piapot emerge.

"Need a hand?" said Piapot.

"Thanks," said Rashford. "I was just getting a warning."

"What, 'drink up and leave', I guess," said Piapot.

"Got it in one," said Rashford.

The two headed back to their table and distributed the drinks. As Claydon reached for his, Piapot stopped him.

"Just a moment," he said.

He looked around the table at the group, then nodded, slowly.

"We have had a good evening," he said. "Soon our cousin will be back with us, after she has changed. Please do not waste your drinks. We will celebrate this night with her, and then we will leave."

"But why are we leaving?" said Claydon, peevishly. "We're all having a great time, why can't we have another round?"

"Or two?" said York.

Piapot shrugged.

"You can do as you wish," he said, "but I will be leaving after this drink."

He gestured at the blue concoction in front of him, condensation bubbling on the glass.

"And," he said, gesturing towards Shyanne and Josee, "I shall be taking my cousins with me."

There was a finality to his tone of voice that even Claydon could hear.

Rashford looked across the table.

"Can we discuss this?" he said.

Piapot nodded.

"Sure," he said. "But not here. Later."

Just then Mandy appeared from the door next to the stage. She walked through the crowd towards them, stopping to chat and shaking hands with audience members at their tables. It took nearly ten minutes before she reached them, during which time Claydon reached for his glass several times only to be dissuaded by a glance from Piapot.

As Mandy approached the table, Rashford realized that she was carrying the Métis sash that she had worn over her shoulder. As she reached them, she carefully handed the bundle across to Josee, who placed it in her large sequin-covered shoulder bag and zipped the top closed.

"Can I see it?" said Claydon. "I've read all about them, but I've never seen or touched one."

"Perhaps later," said Josee. "You heard Piapot. We're leaving after this drink."

Mandy looked across with a quizzical look on her face.

"We are?" she said.

"I'll tell you later," said Shyanne in a loud whisper, winking at her cousin.

Mandy nodded, then sat down beside Rashford and gave him a quick kiss on the cheek. He raised his glass and called for attention.

They toasted Mandy for her brilliant musicianship and chatted happily about their evening. Rashford noticed that Piapot did not look at the group when he spoke, his eyes constantly ranging around the room as he sipped his drink. Finishing, he placed his glass emphatically on the table.

"Now, we leave," he said, getting to his feet. "Drink up or leave your glass, but it's time to go."

Claydon complained that he was not finished, but York pulled his arm.

"Come on," he said, "listen to the wind."

Half out of his chair, one hand still on the table and the other with elbow raised, Claydon stared at him.

"What the heck does that mean?" he said.

"Old sailors' saying," said York, smiling. "I bet even your voyageurs knew that one."

"They weren't sailors," muttered Claydon, but he allowed himself to be brought to his feet. Josee took his arm.

"Come on," she said, and they joined the group as they followed Piapot Starblanket across the room. Checking back over his shoulder, Rashford was not surprised to see Leon, Johnboy, Randy, and five other men get up from their tables and walk close behind.

***

Once they were outside, Rashford called out to Piapot.

"Now what?" he said.

Piapot checked his phone.

"I called an Uber for you," he said. "It's a people carrier so there will be room for the six of you. I've booked it to go to Shyanne's place, after that you're on your own."

The group stood at the bottom of the steps and Claydon walked over towards the line of motorbikes.

"Look at these, they're really cool," he said, then stepped back with an 'eek' as Brian materialized in front of him.

"Back off, suit," he said, standing up from his kneeling position behind the bike and towering over Claydon. He had been tightening something and held a large adjustable wrench in his hand. Claydon stepped back hurriedly.

"It's okay, Brian," said Piapot. "He's with me."

"Still can't touch, bro," said the biker, not moving his eyes from Claydon, who was starting to shiver. When Rashford stepped forward and took his arm, pulling him back to the group, Claydon nervously smiled in acknowledgement and then stood between Josie and Shyanne. Brian stood quietly, watching.

"If we're still at that waterhole, I hope the magic is holding," said York. "I'm starting to feel more and more like a zebra."

A vehicle approached and turned into the parking lot, its headlights illuminating the tableau. The minivan pulled up alongside them and the driver wound down his window.

"I can only take six," he said, looking at the large group.

"Yes, that's us," said Rashford, pulling open the sliding door. He stood back and indicated the three rows of seats.

"Patrick," he said, "why don't you and Shyanne go in first. Then Marc, you and Josee. Mandy, you go next, and I'll sit next to you."

As they all clambered inside Rashford turned to Piapot.

"Thank you," he said. "It's been a great night. Will you be okay?"

Piapot scoffed.

"Me?" he said. "No problem, man. We're the biggest lions here."

Rashford laughed and they shook hands, then Rashford got into the van, pulling the door closed behind him. The driver waited until he was settled, then put the car in gear and drove out to the road. As he did so, his vehicle was illuminated by several headlights. York leaned across Josee and tapped Rashford on the shoulder.

"We got trouble?" he said.

"No, we're good," said Shyanne. "That's just Edward making sure the rednecks stay and have another drink."

Rashford looked out of the rear window and saw the motorcycles come to a halt in the gateway of the car park, filling the space. Even from inside the minivan, he could hear the rumble of the engines. As they turned and drove along the road parallel to the building, the door to the bar opened and he saw a group of farmers spill out, only to stop when confronted by Piapot and his friends. Someone shouted, and he saw arms outstretched towards their van, pointing. Then they were out of visual contact, and he settled back in his seat.

"Let me know if anyone follows us," he said to the driver, a young man with a turban who nodded enthusiastically.

"Certainly, I will do that, sir," he said, and continued down the road.

Chapter 12

They arrived at Shyanne's without incident. As they wandered into the small living room, a young Black couple who were sitting on the couch and watching television looked up, smiling. As they realized that Shyanne was accompanied by others they jumped to their feet, rapidly fanning the air with their hands. The sweet smell of marijuana lingered.

Patrick York laughed.

"It's okay, bro," he said, "don't mind us."

The young man looked at him, then across at Shyanne.

"Wah gwaan?" he said.

"Mi deh yah, yuh know," said York, laughing, then walking over and bumping fists with the other man, who just looked even more confused.

"Cheugy," said the young woman who had stood up next to him, her tone dismissive. "Don't pay him no mind."

She flashed a glance at York.

"Bro," she said.

Shyanne laughed.

"Calm down everyone, this not a bait up," she said.

She turned to the group who had clustered around her.

"Okay, this is Derek, he lives here. And that's his friend, Alvita. She doesn't but she might as well. Guys, you've met my cousins, right, Josee and Mandy."

The two women nodded at the couple, who nodded back.

"Then these are Gavin, who's Mandy's friend, and at the back there, that's Marc, who's with Josee."

Marc waved his arm, causing Alvita to raise her eyebrows. She looked back at Shyanne.

"And Cheugy here?"

Shyanne laughed again.

"This is my friend, Patrick, who as you can see is from your part of the world."

"Right," said Alvita, her tone still dismissive. She nodded towards Marc, her voice rising.

"Where are you from?"

"Um, me? Toronto," he stammered.

"Thought so," said Alvita. "And you?"

This comment was directed to Rashford.

"Regina, Ma'am," he said, smiling.

She didn't smile back.

"So, you're from the same part of the world?" she said.

Marc Claydon looked at her.

"No, I just said, I'm from Toronto. He's from here. Well, Regina. That's near here."

"Yes, well the distance between Regina and Toronto is about two thousand kilometers, and that's the same distance as between Kingston and Bridgetown. Just because we're all black doesn't mean we come from the same place."

Shyanne looked at her.

"What's your problem?" she said, her tone icy.

Alvita glared back.

"I'm fed up with you giving me a hard time for hanging out with Derek. He pays rent, he can have friends over whenever. You're not our mummy."

"Whoa, chill out. Who said what?"

Rashford stepped forward, his arms outstretched.

"Okay, okay," he said, soothingly. "Let's try again, shall we."

He turned to Alvita and Derek.

"Hello," he said. "Sorry, we didn't mean to disturb you. We've just been to a pub, to listen to some music, and stopped off here after the show. We didn't expect you to be back, Derek, or to have company. Where's Frieda?"

Shyanne turned and looked at him, her eyes narrowed.

Derek spoke.

"She went out earlier, I don't know where she is," he said.

"What are you, a cop?" said Alvita.

"Retired," said Rashford, then saw Shyanne's expression.

"I saw her name on the almond milk," he said. "I was looking around while you were getting ready."

"Me gaan," said Alvita, heading for the door. Derek looked around, then followed her.

"Sorry," he said, quietly, as he sidestepped Shyanne. "I'd better go with her."

"We'll talk tomorrow," she said.

He nodded, then left without looking directly at anybody else.

Once Derek had left, Shyanne turned to the group and held out her arms.

"Welcome to my house," she said, emphasizing the 'my'. "I rent out a couple of the rooms, to Derek and Freida, but it's my house. They just stay here; it helps me with the mortgage payments."

Marc Claydon whistled softly as he looked around.

"Nice place," he said.

"Thank you," said Shyanne. "I try to keep it clean."

She picked up the ashtray from the small coffee table and took it into the kitchen, where she dumped the roach into the green plastic tub on the counter. She rinsed out the ashtray under the tap as she spoke.

"Who would like a drink?" she said. "I only have beer and wine, I'm afraid. No spirits."

She came back into the main room. Everyone looked at each other. Patrick York broke the silence.

"I'll have a glass of red wine, if you have one," he said. "Please."

Mandy looked at Rashford.

"A white wine, please," she said. "Just a small one. I'm tired."

"Same for me," said Josee.

"Um, could I have a beer, please?" said Claydon.

Shyanne nodded.

"One red, two white, one beer," she said, then spoke to Rashford. "You?"

"Sure, I'll have a beer, thanks," he said.

As she turned away, she spoke over her shoulder.

"Make yourselves comfortable," she said. "Gavin, please can you push the television to the side? And if anyone needs the washroom, it's upstairs."

She went through the door into the kitchen.

"I'll give you a hand," said Josee, placing her shoulder bag on the floor behind the couch and following Shyanne.

Rashford pushed the cabinet across to the wall, York helping to balance the television. Once it was in place, the four stood awkwardly, then Mandy took Rashford by the hand and pulled him over to the same overstuffed armchair in which he had sat earlier. He sat in the chair, and she perched on the arm, leaning into his shoulder. York and Claydon looked at each other, then both went to the couch, sitting at either end. They all looked at each other.

"That was, um, interesting," said Claydon, clearing his throat. "Why did she call you 'cheugy'? What does that mean?"

York laughed, self-consciously.

"Oh, that's street talk," he said. "It wasn't very complimentary; I can tell you that!"

Rashford raised an eyebrow.

"I guess my patois is a bit out of date," said York. "She was basically saying that I'm an old guy trying to be cool, mainstream now but hanging onto things that were hip years ago."

Claydon nodded, sagely.

"She thought you were a bit of boomer, did she? I see."

Mandy giggled.

York hurried to change the subject.

"So, Mandy," he said, "where did you learn to play like that?"

Mandy smiled.

"From one of my uncles," she said. "He had studied under John Arcand, and then he taught me."

Just then, Shyanne and Josee came in, holding a variety of cans and glasses. Josee held out two large glasses to Claydon and Rashford, who each took one, and then she offered them two cans from her other hand.

"One's an IPA," she said, "it's the last one. The other is a brown ale."

Rashford nodded to Claydon.

"You choose," he said, then accepted the brown ale after Marc took the other can.

Shyanne was holding four glasses, two in each hand, the stems held between her fingers. She reached out to Mandy, who took one of the white wines, and then passed the glass of red wine to Patrick. Josee leaned over and took another of the white wines, leaving Shyanne with the final glass, which she then raised in a toast.

"Welcome to my house," she said. "Hey hey!"

"Hi hi," said Marc Claydon, phonetically.

They all raised their glasses and then took a sip, before stopping and looking at each other.

"Well, that was, um, interesting?" said Marc Claydon, repeating himself.

Shyanne walked over to the second armchair and flounced herself into it, emitting a loud sigh. Josee went and sat on the couch between Claydon and York. Shyanne took a large gulp of her wine.

"Well, that was a Pinot Grigio moment," she said, laughing. "I'm sorry about all the drama. Alvita can get a bit like that, sometimes. She's a bit brittle, she grew up in a rough part of Kingston."

There were murmurs of sympathy and agreement from around the room. York looked around.

"Who's that?" he said, pointing to the black and red portrait of a bearded man.

"That's Louis Riel," said Shyanne, Josee, and Mandy, in unison. They all laughed.

"Yes, Louis Riel," said Shyanne, softly. "He was the leader of the Resistance. He is our hero."

York looked at Rashford, the obvious question in his eyes. Rashford nodded.

"It's a long story," he said. "Maybe another day?"

There was another silence as people sipped their drinks.

Marc Claydon looked around and cleared his throat. He looked across at Mandy.

"Umm, I was wondering, can I see your sash? Please?"

Mandy shrugged.

"Sure," she said. "It's not a secret or anything. Josee, where did you put it?"

"Here," said the younger woman. "In my purse."

She stood up and went behind the couch, reaching down and picking up her bag. The beads and glass sequins glittered in the lamplight as she passed the bag across to Mandy. Mandy carefully unzipped the top and withdrew the folded sash. She gave it to Josee, who turned and held it out to Marc. He carefully placed his drink on the floor by his feet, then reached out with two hands and took the sash.

Holding it on his lap as though it was an icon or a religious relic, Claydon stroked his hand softly over the material, smoothing it down.

"It's beautiful," he said, quietly, staring at the sash as though committing each strand to memory. "This is a Celebration Sash, you know."

"There are different kinds?" said Rashford.

Claydon looked at him, then around the room.

"Yes," he said. "In the old days, each family made their own. It took time, maybe three hundred hours, but it was easier and cheaper to buy wool and weave your own than to buy one from the big fur trading companies."

"Three hundred hours?" said York, incredulous. "That's, like two months, even if you can find five hours a day!"

"Well, they didn't have looms, of course," said Claydon. "They used a technique called finger weaving, and they had all winter to make one."

"Is this one of the things they used your dyes for?" said Rashford.

"Yes!" said Claydon, nodding vigorously. "As I said, every family had their own design, so they used different colours."

"That helped at dances," said Josee, laughing.

Claydon stared at her.

"What do you mean?" he said.

"Well, if a guy saw a pretty girl, he could tell straight away whether or not she was a cousin!"

Shyanne and Mandy laughed, Claydon shook his head.

"I didn't think of that," he said, murmuring to himself. "I'll have to add that to my dissertation."

He looked up, raising his voice.

"Anyway, after the 1885 Resistance and the hanging of Riel, people were scared to wear the sashes. A lot of family patterns were lost. In the late twentieth century there was a bit of a revival of Métis culture, and the Celebration Sash was created. It's also called the 'ceinture fléchée' or arrowed sash, because of the design."

He held it out in front of him.

"Here, you see, there are seven rows of herringbone stitching, they look like the fletches on an arrow."

York leaned forward and peered at the design.

"That's like the feather bit, on the back?" he said.

"Yes, it stabilizes the arrow after you fire it. It's called a fletch."

"Why did they pick those colours?" said Rashford.

"Good question," said Claydon, leaning back against the couch. "Each one has a meaning. Let me see if I can remember."

He closed his eyes, then started to speak.

"Blue is for the earth," he said. "Green is for fertility, yellow is for prosperity. White is for our connection to the creator. Black is for the period of suppression and dispossession, and red is for the blood that was shed."

He opened his eyes.

"And blue and white together, of course, is the colour of the Métis flag."

"Like these," said Josee, softly, raising her hand to her earring.

Claydon stared at her in astonishment. Shyanne reached across and patted his arm.

"You see, Marc, you have met a Métis person," she said.

———

There was a moment of stunned silence, then Claydon started to speak rapidly, hardly taking a breath, his questions tumbling over each other. Josee reached over and held his arm just above the wrist, laughing.

"Whoa," she said, "one thing at a time!"

He stopped, turning red with embarrassment, then took a deep breath.

"Okay," he said. "Sorry. I just feel like such a fool. Why didn't you tell me earlier? How does it work, if you're all three cousins, but you and Mandy are Métis, and Shyanne isn't? What ..."

"Let's start with those," said Josee, firmly. "First, don't feel like a fool, we were just having fun. We wondered how long it would take you to figure it out. I mean, it's not a secret, we're proud to be Métis, but that doesn't mean we go around telling everyone. We're not evangelical about our identity."

Claydon nodded, his blushes subsiding.

"I understand," he said. "It's your own business."

"Exactly," said Shyanne. "And you have to remember; western concepts and ideologies look at Indigenous relationships through the patriarchal cultural lens of the colonizer."

Rashford laughed.

"That sounds like your Gender and Women's Studies prof," he said.

"Well, she is right," said Shyanne, huffing.

"Being an uncle doesn't just mean that you're the brother of a parent," said Josee, nodding. "For our people, for the Métis and the Cree and for other Indigenous peoples, being an uncle is a nurturing role, not a biological relationship. It's a term of respect for someone who is there to help you as you grow into an adult person."

"We call them nohcâwîs, which means 'my little father'," said Shyanne.

She turned to Rashford.

"I think I told you; I grew up in Grandmother's Bay, in the north?"

Rashford nodded.

"My dad got a job in the city and so we moved south, my brother and me. But all our relatives are still up there."

Mandy smiled. "Josee and me, we're from Stanley Mission, on the Churchill River," she said. "It's about thirty kilometers from where Shyanne's family lives."

"Thirty by river," said Josee. "It's about an hour and a half by road."

"Stanley was our local 'big city'," laughed Shyanne. "It used to take about three and a half hours to get there by canoe, because that's the way the current goes. It could take all day to get home. My grandparents would go down every month to go shopping at the store, and to visit people."

Josee smiled.

"You have to remember," she said, "that there are less that four hundred people at Shyanne's place. There are sixteen hundred at Stanley."

Mandy nodded.

"We're from the Métis side, but there's a Cree side as well. And we're all related, including to people in namīpithsīpihk. That's what we call Grandmother's Bay."

"My dad is brother to Mandy's mom," said Josee, "and one of his brothers was nohcâwîs to Piapot."

"Shyanne's brother?" said Rashford.

"Exactly," said Josee.

There was a moment of silence.

"My head hurts," said Patrick York. "How do you guys keep track of all this?"

Josee laughed.

"Usually, it's one of the old kôhkums who remembers everything. It's their job. They used to sit around at dances and feasts to make sure we didn't speak to the wrong boys!"

"Things sure got harder for them when social media came along!" said Shyanne, laughing. "Now people can hook up without the old people knowing, and sometimes that can cause some stress."

"Maybe you need to bring back the family sash idea," said Claydon.

Mandy yawned, then stepped off the arm of the chair.

"I'm sorry, people, but it's after midnight. I'm going to have to go," she said. "I'm wiped."

She walked over to Josee and picked up her sash.

Rashford put down his beer and stood up.

"I'll walk you home," he said. "Sorry guys, stay and enjoy yourselves."

"No worries, mon," said York. "I'll make sure Marc gets back to the residence safely. See you tomorrow?"

"Noon at the Rabbit?"

"Sounds good."

Rashford nodded his head in acknowledgement, waved his hand at the others in the group, and followed Mandy to the door.

Chapter 13

R ashford called Chief Superintendent Pollard just before eight o'clock on Monday morning. As he had hoped, she was in the office early and answered her phone herself. He still could not face the idea of chatting to Sarah and being reminded of how he had been manipulated. Pollard asked him how his talk had gone and seemed pleased by his report. There was a pause.

"You could have waited to tell me this when you got back," she said. "What else has happened?"

Rashford cleared his throat, then recounted the story of the three missing students. He explained his conversations with Patrick York, and the ongoing situation with Jeremy. When he had finished, Pollard let out a great sigh.

"You never learn, do you?" she said. "I asked you to go and give a talk, not to get embroiled in a mystery. I know you're not officially retired yet but that's because of HR being slack, nothing else. I mean, you don't even have your Force identification card anymore."

There was a pause.

"Do you?"

"No, Ma'am," said Rashford.

Pollard sighed again.

"What do you want from me?" she said.

"I'd like your permission to stay here until the weekend," said Rashford. "I'll get a hotel room, but I'd like to follow this through. Also, I'd like permission to contact Senior Constable Morgan, if it becomes necessary."

"Morgan? She's got her own job to do, you know. She's not here just to be on call as your personal lackey."

"No Ma'am."

"Why Morgan?"

"We've worked closely together before, Ma'am. We get on well, and she is located not far from here."

Pollard was silent. Rashford could here a clicking sound, and thought she was probably tapping a pen or pencil against her teeth. At last, she spoke.

"Okay," she said. "On one condition. If Senior Constable Morgan is busy when you call, she will not just drop everything to assist. You'll have to wait until she's free. And secondly, do not under any circumstances pass yourself off as a serving police officer."

'That's two conditions', thought Rashford, but he didn't say anything.

"Understood?"

"Yes, Ma'am. I've been telling everyone here that I'm retired."

"Good."

"On that note, though, I wonder if I could trouble you for an introduction?"

"An introduction? To whom?"

"My understanding is that the university hasn't linked the three students," said Rashford. "I'm going to go over to the administrative offices this afternoon and ask to meet with the Registrar. They might ask me for identification and, as you pointed out, I don't have any."

Pollard made a short shark barking sound which he assumed was a laugh. He could visualize her teeth appearing in her barracuda smile, her lips not moving.

"Have them call me," she said. "I'll be here all afternoon. I'll tell Sarah to put them through."

"Thank you, Ma'am."

"Talking of Sarah, she was asking about you on Friday. She is of the opinion that putting you on a campus full of nubile young undergraduates was not necessarily the best move on my part. Should I have any concerns in that regard?"

Rashford gulped, thinking of Mandy, then decided that as she was a 'mature student', and had nearly graduated, she didn't count as the type of naïve eighteen-year-old student Sarah was probably implying.

"No, Ma'am," he said.

"Good. Right, find a cheap hotel, keep your receipts, and I expect you here with a full report next Monday. You have a week, Staff Sergeant."

"Yes. Ma'am. Thank you, Ma'am."

She grunted, and just before the phone clicked off, he heard her voice rise.

"Sarah, coffee please," she said.

***

Rashford checked his phone and saw that it was almost ten. He left his room and walked over to the Three-Legged Rabbit, joining a shivering couple in the smoking area. He smoked two cigarettes, then saw McHale walk up to the pub and stand outside, looking around. This time he wore his black leather jacket over a white tee-shirt and blue jeans with ripped knees. Rashford strolled over and said hello, introducing himself. They shook hands and McHale looked at him.

"You were at my talk," he said. "Back row. You didn't look comfortable."

"I don't go to many conferences," said Rashford, shrugging.

McHale raised his eyebrows but said nothing. He led the way into the pub and was surprised when the bartender said hello to Rashford.

"Come here a lot, do you?" said McHale, once they were settled with coffee in front of them.

Rashford shrugged again.

"It's cheap, the food's good, and it's a convenient place to meet people."

"I suppose," said McHale, looking around. "It's all a bit ... dark and dingy, though, isn't it?"

Rashford laughed.

"Pubs are never at their best in the daylight," he said.

"True," said McHale. He sipped some coffee then returned his cup to the table and looked at Rashford.

"What do you want to talk about?"

Rashford nodded, then put down his cup.

"Tell me about your time as a graduate student," he said.

"My time ... why on earth is that relevant to anything? I thought you said you were working on a case."

Rashford nodded.

"I am."

McHale peered at him intently. Rashford suddenly realized how stressful that look must be to an unprepared graduate student. He held the gaze. McHale nodded.

"Very well. I went to the University of Toronto, of course. I was doing my master's degree, but my advisor suggested I move straight into the doctoral program."

He swept back his hair with a practised sweep, moving the blond lock away from his face. Rashford thought it a somewhat precious habit but did not refer to it.

"I'm sure he realized your potential," he said, instead.

McHale beamed.

"Indeed, he did," he stated.

"And Professor Benoît? Where and when did she come into the picture?"

McHale stiffened in his chair. He picked up his coffee cup and took a long, slow sip. Then he nodded to himself and returned the cup to the table.

"They. Not she. The preferred pronoun is they."

Rashford smiled.

"Yes. Actually, I knew that, but I didn't know if you did. Thank you for confirming that, Professor. So please continue. Where and when did *they* come into the picture?"

McHale took a deep breath.

"Are they in trouble?"

"Possibly. We are still trying to determine facts, not make accusations."

"Yet."

Rashford was silent. McHale nodded.

"Very well. Yes, I knew Linda when they were still figuring out who they really were. We became close."

He noticed the look on Rashford's face.

"Not in that way! Pah. We were just friends."

Rashford apologised and McHale continued.

"We were almost the same age. They had finished their PhD and I had just started mine. I had left what we called the 'real world' of teaching and joined the academy and wasn't sure how it was going to work out. They were trying to figure out who they were and weren't sure how that would all work out either."

"Kindred spirits?"

McHale nodded.

"If you like. I helped them when they started the transition. The clinic was near my place, so they stayed in my spare room for a while."

"Who else knew?"

McHale shrugged.

"No idea. I didn't tell anyone. And it was only for a short while. They had already started the social transitioning process, you know."

Rashford nodded.

"Yes, changing themselves from Lionel Bishop to Linda Benoît. Getting all their identification sorted out. That was all done before they started their doctorate."

McHale smiled.

"You are well informed," he said. "Yes, all that was in place. Then they started thinking about medically transitioning as well. That's why they were at the clinic."

"And staying with you?"

"Exactly. They underwent an operation, to reduce the size of their Adam's apple, and started hormone therapy. It helped a little bit, they started to grow breasts. But they also had some reactions to the medication, so they stopped taking it."

"Without finishing the treatment?"

McHale nodded.

"Correct. They thought it best to leave it for a while, and then restart everything. But I don't think that was the only reason."

Rashford sat back in his chair.

"Really?"

McHale lowered his voice.

"It was a financial thing as well, I think," he said. "They realized how expensive it was going to be. This isn't something you can do on your provincial health plan, you know!"

"I imagine not," said Rashford.

"Anyway, that's all I know," said McHale, putting down his coffee cup and starting to stand.

Rashford looked up at him.

"One more thing," he said. "Your letter of reference, the one you wrote when they were applying for a job here. Why did you do that?"

McHale stared back.

"It was what they wanted. And I felt that they would benefit from a new start, in a fresh place. Some people were starting to put two and two together. So, it seemed like a friendly thing to do."

He stood and extended his hand.

"They're a good person," he said. "Whatever you think they've done, I don't think they did."

Rashford nodded.

"I'd appreciate your not mentioning this to Professor Benoît just yet," he said.

McHale looked at him.

"I thought you might want that. Well, 'I'm leaving, on a jet plane', as they say," he said, smiling. "I've no reason to talk to them over the next few days."

"Until the beginning of next week would be helpful," said Rashford.

McHale raised his eyebrows.

"Indeed? It's obviously a complicated investigation. Very well, no contact until next week."

"Thank you," said Rashford.

McHale nodded, then turned and walked away.

Rashford finished his coffee, mulling on what he had just learned. He still had ninety minutes before his meeting with Patrick York, so he decided to go for a walk. He went down to the river and walked along the bank, past the 'Dances with Gravy' food truck and continuing along the path for another two kilometres before turning around. He arrived back at the Three-Legged Rabbit just before noon, York was already sitting at the corner table. They nodded at each other.

"I took the liberty of ordering you a sandwich and a coffee," said York. "My treat. It will be here in a minute."

Thank you," said Rashford, dropping into the opposite seat with a sigh.

"Long night?" said York, sympathetically.

Rashford shook his head.

"No. Mandy really was tired, so I dropped her off at her place and then went back to my room. But I couldn't sleep. I've been up since five, checking online, making phone calls to places down east where they are already awake, trying to pull some bits and pieces together. What about you?"

York scratched his head.

"Umm, well, Josee said she'd look after Marc," he said, grinning and blushing at the same time. "And then after they'd left, well, umm, let's just say, Shyanne wasn't too tired."

Rashford was saved from a response by the arrival of their waiter, carrying a tray which held two large cups of coffee and two plates, each with a club sandwich and fries. Once they had everything organized, and some extra ketchup had been delivered, York moved the conversation into a different area.

"So, what have you found out, since five o'clock this morning?"

Rashford took a long drink of his coffee.

"Well, a few things," he said. "First, I heard back from Lenny."

"The head honcho of the IDIOTS?"

"Exactly. He told me that yes, Jeremy is a member, but he is like Chad, he is the LBC member this year."

"This year?"

"Yes. It turns out that there is one every year. Apparently being 'Lonely By Choice' is an annual thing."

"Anything else?"

"Yes. Three things, actually. First, Jeremy is in General Arts. So that's another check mark. And second, Lenny told me that he had never put two and two together before, but now that he thinks about it, all the LBC guys have failed to finish their year. They all just disappeared."

York finished his sandwich before speaking.

"That is certainly strange. And nobody at the university has picked up on this?"

"It doesn't seem that they have, no. I can't double-check that until later, the offices were closed on the weekend and I've been busy this morning."

York nodded, then reached over and took one of Rashford's fries.

"I thought you were leaving this afternoon," he said.

"I was," said Rashford, nodding. "Now I'm not too sure. Something is going on here and I want to figure it out."

York laughed.

"Cop instincts, eh? They never go away, do they?"

Rashford smiled, pushing his plate over towards the other man.

"Help yourself," he said.

"Thanks," said York, squeezing open another sachet of ketchup. "I'm not sure why I'm so hungry this morning."

Rashford said nothing, just shook his head, then took their cups to the bar and had them refilled. Coming back, he put the fresh coffee in front of York. The man nodded in appreciation.

"Thanks," he said. "Now, you said that Lenny told you three things. What was the third?"

"Right," said Rashford. "The third thing is that the final obligatory dinner is going to take place this week, on Friday. Jeremy is going to miss another IDIOTS night out. Apparently, it was supposed to be last week but got postponed because of the conference. I think I'll stick around for it."

"Until Friday?" said York. "What are you going to do for the rest of the week?"

"Oh, I'll think of something. There are a lot of things going on that I need to get straight in my head."

"As I said before, cop instincts!" said York, laughing. "Well, I hope you can manage without me. I'm going to go to Calgary for a couple of days, to see my auntie. My mother's older sister. I'm going to drive over later this afternoon, but I will be back on Thursday."

"You've finished all the conference stuff, then?"

"Pretty much. All the program related work, anyway. The finance people will be going at it for a while, sorting out bills and invoices and things like that."

"Why don't I give you my number, you can call me when you get back."

"Good idea."

York took out his phone and entered Rashford's details into his contact list, then sent a confirmatory text. Rashford's phone pinged, and he glanced at it.

"Message received," he said.

"Good. I'll let you know when I get back. Right, I'll leave you to it. I need to go and get myself organized."

He started to stand but Rashford interrupted him.

"Hang on a minute," he said. "What about you. What did you learn?"

York sat back in his chair.

"Me? Nothing much. Except maybe that I was really tired this morning."

"Yes, you said."

Rashford waited, patiently. After thinking for a few minutes, York spoke.

"One thing I learned was that even though I'm too old to keep up, I've got a year to get fit."

He chuckled.

"What do you mean?" said Rashford.

"Apparently, Shyanne's brother, Piapot, he runs a small travel agency. They organize cheap flights to the Caribbean for students. They have them during university holidays like Christmas and spring break, but also every spring after final exams. And another one in the late summer, I think, a back to school special. Shyanne and Josee are planning on going next year, as a sort of graduation present when they finish their studies. She wants to stay with me for the week!"

"That might be interesting for you," said Rashford.

"Yes mon, no doubt. At least Josee will stay in the hotel that comes with the flight, and this way they'll both get their own space."

"Right," said Rashford, slowly, drawing out the word. "Anything else?"

"Not really, no. Like I said, we didn't spend much time talking."

York got to his feet.

"I've really got to go," he said.

"Say hello to your aunt," said Rashford.

"What? Oh, yes, of course. She'll be so glad to hear that we're making some progress on finding out what happened to Chad."

Rashford stood and shook hands.

"Have a good drive," he said. "Safe travels."

"Thank you," said York. "I'll call you on Thursday."

He turned and left the room. Rashford sat back down at the table and picked up his coffee. He took a sip, then got out his notebook. He was reviewing his notes and jotting down a few other thoughts when his phone rang. It was Mandy.

"Hello," she said. "What are you up to?"

"Just finishing my coffee," he said. "I had lunch with Patrick York. What about you?"

"I've finished my exam and I'm just heading back to my apartment to study," she said. "Two more to go!"

"You only took three courses?"

"No, I took five, but one was continuous evaluation so no final exam, and the other is an online exam. I can pick my own time to do that, as long as I finish it before Friday."

"So, when is your next exam?"

"Wednesday," laughed Mandy, and dropped her voice to a husky whisper. "Why? Do you want to come over and help me with my revision?"

"I think that would be more of a distraction than a help," said Rashford. "Anyway, I've got a really busy afternoon."

"Spoilsport," she said, then paused. "Just a minute. I thought you were leaving today?"

"I was, but I've changed my mind."

Her voice brightened, and she spoke quickly. "That's good. For how long? I thought this would be my last chance to see you, it's great that you're staying. What about dinner?"

"Whoa, slow down," said Rashford, laughing. "I'm going to stay until next weekend, so there's no rush."

"We can celebrate my end of university together," she said, delightedly. "My last exam is on Friday."

"I might be working on Friday," said Rashford. "We'll see. It may have to be a deferred celebration."

"Well, I've waited over ten years for this, so another day won't hurt. Anyway, what about dinner tonight?"

"That might work," said Rashford. "Where, and what time?"

"Seven o'clock at my place," she said. "I'll cook my famous Chicken Cacciatore for you. Bring a good red wine. Italian."

"Yes, Ma'am," said Rashford, laughing.

They said goodbye to each other, and he clicked off his phone. Looking at the time, he saw that it was almost one thirty, so he got up and walked over to the bar. The young man standing at the till looked at him.

"Can I help you?"

"Yes, could you give me directions to the Office of the Registrar, please?"

"Sure," said the young man, and came across to where Rashford stood.

After memorizing the directions that he had been given, Rashford first returned to the residence and collected his bag. A lot of the conference delegates were trying to check out at the same time and the elevators were busy, so he used the fire escape staircase and walked down the five flights. He noted the chipped and faded paint on the walls, and the poor ambience of low-wattage lightbulbs. It reminded him of the passages he had taken to get to the Secret Quadrangle. There was nobody else on the stairs, and he had ample time to reflect on the fact that institutions seldom spent money on the less-public aspects of their buildings.

As he came through the doors into the reception area, he was surprised to see Marc Claydon in the line to checkout. They nodded to each other and Rashford joined the line. It moved quickly, and he was soon collecting his receipt. He saw that Claydon had already left so when he had completed his formalities he walked after him to the door. Claydon was standing on the steps.

"Where's Josee?" said Rashford, teasingly.

Claydon turned to him with a serious look.

"She's not here," he said.

Rashford laughed.

"I can see that, Marc," he said. "But why not? I thought she'd want to see you off."

Claydon shook his head.

"No, we had our time," he said. "I went back to her place last night and had fun. But, there were two sessions I wanted to go to this morning, so I left early."

"You're a love 'em and leave them kind of guy, are you?"

Claydon shrugged.

"She said she doesn't like farewell scenes," he said. "We didn't even say goodbye. She said there's no word for that in her language, they only say 'see you later'. So that's what we said."

"And will you?"

"Will I what?"

"See her later?"

"I don't know," said Claydon, ruefully. "Perhaps, but probably not. She doesn't go to the sort of conferences to which I go, I don't think we're going to bump into each other."

"You could always invite her down for a visit," said Rashford.

Claydon just stared at him.

"I don't think she'd have enough money," he said. "And anyway, she wouldn't really fit in with my friends. Plus, I think I've learned all I can from her."

Rashford shook his head in disbelief.

"So, what, you got what you wanted, now you're gone? You met a pretty young girl and slept with her, now you can add that to your knowledge of Métis customs and move on."

Claydon shrugged again, turning to scan the car park as he spoke.

"She didn't want anything else, and neither did I. Anyhow, how is that different from you and Mandy, or Patrick York and Shyanne?"

Rashford thought for a moment.

"We didn't have ulterior motives," he said. "It sounds like your main goal is to thicken up your doctoral thesis."

Claydon stopped and turned.

"And your point?"

Rashford stopped and stared back.

"My point is that you're just using Josee as a source. You don't care about her, do you? You just wanted information. It's neo-colonialism, asset-stripping. But the resources you're after are the intellectual ones."

"I'll give her a credit in my acknowledgements," said Claydon, stiffly.

"Whoopy-do," said Rashford, and walked out of the residence. Claydon followed and caught up with him at the bottom of the steps. He grabbed hold of Rashford's arm.

"That's not really fair, you know," he said. "It's a conference, for God's sake. Everyone knows that even if you get lucky, you're only going to get a quickie, a one-night stand. It's not a mating circle."

"But you only wanted her knowledge."

"Exactly. Her knowledge, not her body. I wasn't expecting that, for Christ's sake. I wanted to meet a Métis person and I did that. I wanted to learn about the Métis sash, and I did that. The music at the pub and the *Red River Jig* was a bonus. Then when Josee took me home and invited me in, I couldn't believe it. But it was just sex."

He nodded towards a car that had just arrived and parked at the curb.

"That's my Uber," he said. "I'll say goodbye now."

"Not 'see you later'?" said Rashford.

"I doubt it," said Claydon, and got into the car.

Rashford watched him drive off, then walked across the car park.

The hotel he had booked was just down the road from the university, past the steps leading down to the riverside path. He drove past the bollards, wondering where the next pedestrian access point might be. The traffic rumbled steadily along.

After about a kilometre he came to the gates of the hotel, which was set on a bluff overlooking the river. He turned into the small driveway, which held a turning circle and a sign saying, 'Parking for check-in only'. As he walked towards the steps a small group of people emerged from the door and walked to his right, carefully following a path with a sign reading 'To the river'. They disappeared into the woods as he reached the entrance.

His room was a basic hotel room, with a double bed, a flat-screen television, and a banal abstract print on the wall. Opening the curtains, he saw that the car park was adjacent to the building, directly below his window, and then there was a screen of trees and bushes. Beyond that, he was pleasantly surprised to see that he had a good view of the river.

He hung his last clean shirt in the small closet, and then called down to reception. After accepting the ludicrously expensive charges for laundry and hoping that the Chief Superintendent would agree that this was an essential expenditure, he placed his dirty clothes into the small plastic bag provided and placed it by the door.

He had just finished setting up his laptop computer and connecting to WiFi when there was a knock on the door. Opening it, he saw an elderly hotel employee standing there. Rashford passed over the bag, glancing at the man's name tag as he did so.

"How long will it take, Richard?" he said.

"It will be ready tomorrow morning, sir," said the man. "The maid will bring it to your room when she's doing the cleaning."

"Thank you," said Rashford, handing over a five-dollar bill.

"No, thank you, sir," said Richard, the bill disappearing from sight before he turned and walked off down the corridor.

Rashford finished unpacking, then went down and moved his Jeep to the car park. The receptionist had given him a small card, which he left displayed on the front dash as directed. Making sure the vehicle was locked, he left the hotel and walked back up to the Three-Legged Rabbit.

CHAPTER 14

Following the directions that he had been given, Rashford found himself able to walk from the pub to the Office of the Registrar in less than ten minutes. Once he arrived at the correct building, he followed the signage and went down a wide flight of steps into a small reception area. Three hard wooden chairs were lined up against one of the walls, which itself was covered in posters.

A laminated desk extended most of the way across the room, with a levered flap that obviously served as an entry to the office area. A clear Perspex shield about thirty centimetres high divided the desk into a front and back area. The back contained numerous pens, month-by-month plotters, university calendars, and open notebooks, as well as two laptop computers. The area in front of the Perspex was empty, except for a small silver bell, a spray bottle of hand sanitizer, and two coffee cups marked with the insignia of the university. One, which had a label stating 'new', contained a dozen or so ballpoint pens. The second, with a label indicating 'used', was empty.

Rashford looked around. There was nobody at the desk, but five feet into the main office a lady who appeared to be in her early fifties sat at a smaller desk, typing on a keyboard. She did not look up, even after he cleared his throat, so he went to the counter and rang the bell. The lady kept typing.

After a minute had passed, Rashford rang the bell again, this time with more force. The woman looked up sharply.

"Someone will be with you in a moment," she said. "Please sit down."

Rashford stood still for a moment, taken aback by her tone, then turned and went over to the chairs. Before sitting down, he looked at the posters, which mainly depicted smiling young people clustered under trees. 'Our mission is to provide you with a diverse and welcoming experience' read one of the posters, and 'together we can!' proclaimed another. He sat down.

When, after a few minutes, nobody had appeared, Rashford took out his phone and started scrolling through his e-mail. He was interrupted by a loud 'harumph' sound. Looking up he saw the woman had stopped typing and was staring at him crossly. She pointed over to the opposite wall, where there was a large photograph of a cell phone with a red line drawn through the middle. Rashford put his phone away, and the woman resumed typing.

It was seven minutes, almost eight, before anyone appeared at the desk. Rashford had started to take it as a personal challenge, to see how long he could stare at the typist before she cracked and looked back, but she had been the clear winner. Other than when he had used his phone, her eyes had never left the screen the whole time he sat staring at her. When the young woman appeared from a side door, Rashford almost did not see her, he was so focused on the typist.

"Yes?" said the young woman, in a tone that implied she was busy and did not appreciate being disturbed from her work. "Can I help you?"

Rashford stood and approached the desk. He tried to put on his most disarming smile.

"Yes, please. I would like to see the Registrar for a few minutes, if I may."

"Do you have an appointment?"

"No, I'm afraid I don't."

"Then you will have to make one."

"It's only a few questions."

"It doesn't matter. She's a very busy person. We're all very busy here. It's getting close to the end of the semester, and we need to get all the student grade audits completed so they can graduate."

"I understand," said Rashford, "but it really is quite important that I see her."

"Then make an appointment," said the woman, folding her arms.

"Okay," said Rashford. "Please can I make an appointment to see the Registrar?"

"You can only do it online," she said. "We've gone paperless."

She smiled and passed a business card across the Perspex divide.

"Here's the website address. Fill in the form and submit it. We normally respond within three business days but, as I said, we're terribly busy at the moment. And don't forget to put down your student number, otherwise you won't get a reply at all."

Rashford had had enough. He moved a step closer to the counter and leaned forward with his hands on the laminated surface. He stared straight at the young woman but raised his voice so he could be clearly heard by the older lady, who had stopped typing.

"There seems to be some confusion," said Rashford, slowly and distinctly. "I am not a student. I am a police officer. And I wish to speak to the Registrar. Now."

The young woman froze in place, then slowly turned her head and looked at the typist. The latter nodded. The young woman turned back to Rashford.

"I'll see if she is free," she said, her voice squeaking. She cleared her throat. "May I tell her what this is about?"

"Not in detail, no," said Rashford, feeling that he had won at least one round of the exchange. "You may tell her that it is confidential, and extremely urgent."

The young woman turned and left through the side door. The older woman resumed typing. Rashford stood patiently.

After a few minutes, the young woman returned, her face pale.

"I'm sorry," she said, stammering a little. "The Registrar is on a zoom conference with all the Alsama university Registrars right now. She is not sure how long it will take; they are trying to develop a common response to plagiarism. She said you can wait and hope, or else speak with the Deputy Registrar."

Rashford considered this for a moment, then made a decision.

"Sure, I'll speak with the Deputy Registrar," he said. "At least to see if my questions get answered."

The young woman nodded, then turned to the typist.

"Ms. Greenfield, do you have a moment? There is someone to see you."

"Just a second, let me save this," replied the typist, clicking at the keyboard and then standing up. She was wearing a tweed skirt and used the palm of her hands to smooth it down over her thighs as she approached the counter. She looked straight at Rashford.

"I'm Betty Greenfield, the Assistant Registrar," she said, sweetly. "How may I help you?"

Repressing a large sigh, Rashford repeated his point that the matter was both confidential and urgent, and suggested they find a less public place.

"It's exam week," said Greenfield, "nobody is going to come in here, and you've terrified Celia, so she won't be back."

Rashford looked at her.

"I didn't mean to terrify Celia," he said. "But you must admit, she was a bit obtuse."

Greenfield nodded.

"Yes, she's one of my best proteges," she said. "This is soul-destroying work, officer …"

She looked at him with the question obvious on her face.

"Rashford," he said.

"Officer Rashford. Quite. Well, at this time of the year, and I mean no offence, but when people your age come in here, it's usually to scream about the low marks one of their intellectually enriched children has received from some obviously degenerate professor who only gives good marks to the lackies who agree with him. Or who have large bosoms."

Rashford could not help himself. He smiled.

"Drone parents," he said.

"Quite," she said, then folded her arms and looked at him.

"Well?"

Rashford was confused.

"Well, what?" he said.

"Well, Officer Rashford, do you have some identification, so that I know you are not a drone parent in disguise, a modern-day Trojan Horse come to pierce our defences?"

"Not on me, no," he said, noting the raised eyebrow as she took a step back. "However, if you would call this number, you can talk to my Chief Superintendent. She will vouch for me."

He took a pen from the coffee cup and scribbled Pollard's phone number on the back of the card he had been given, then passed that across the divide to Greenfield. She took the card and glanced at it, then turned back to her desk, speaking over her shoulder.

"Will she indeed? Very well. Wait."

Rashford placed the pen in the 'used' cup, then waited. The woman sat down at her desk and picked up the phone before dialling the number. It rang a few times, then was answered. Rashford could hear Sarah's voice, but not what she said.

"May I speak to Chief Superintendent Pollard please," said Greenfield.

The reply was indistinct.

"It's about an Officer Rashford."

There was more murmuring.

"I'm not at liberty to say."

Rashford realized that Sarah was enjoying this, and that Greenfield was playing along. He started tapping his fingers on the counter, as the questions apparently took on a bizarre nature. At least, the replies did.

"No, I don't think so. It doesn't look freshly cut."

"Yes, it looks ironed."

"I wouldn't say 'fat', not really. Starting to get plump. Perhaps."

"Yes, he is, now. Quite red in the face, in fact."

"Yes, we probably should."

"Thank you."

There was a pause.

"Chief Superintendent Pollard? Hello. My name is Betty Greenfield, I am the Assistant Registrar at ... Oh, you were expecting my call? Excellent."

Rashford could hear Pollard's voice. It was sharper and more to the point than Sarah had been.

Greenfield listened.

"That is correct, yes. Every assistance. Certainly. Thank you, Chief Superintendent. Goodbye."

She slowly returned the telephone to the cradle, then stood up and came back over to the counter. Opening the flap, she ushered him through to the back. They walked past her desk to a door in the far corner, which lead into a small office that was empty except for a small round table and four padded chairs. There was a single computer terminal and keyboard on the table. Greenfield closed the door behind them.

"Your bona fides have been established," she said. "Now, what can I do for you?"

Once Rashford had explained the situation, things moved quickly. Greenfield was both intrigued and horrified by the suggestion that three students had disappeared.

"I've never heard even a rumour of this," she said, shaking her head. "Not a thing."

She sat behind the computer and turned it on, then quickly logged on. Rashford smiled when he saw her automatically use her left arm to shield the keyboard as she entered her password with her right hand.

"Okay," she said. "I'm in the data base. This is searchable, so let's see what we've got."

Rashford took out his notebook, and a pen from his inside pocket.

"The first name is Emmanuel," he said, "often known as Manny. He was a first-year general arts student here, four years ago."

"He will be under Emmanuel, not Manny," said Greenfield. "This is the official data base."

Rashford nodded and waited as she typed.

"Okay," she said. "I have three Emmanuels who were in first year four years ago. Let me see."

Her fingers flew across the keyboard and pages of text appeared on the screen, moving by so quickly that Rashford could not read them. Greenfield seemed to scan them in seconds and then move onto the next page. Never taking her eyes off the screen, she spoke as she read.

"Bredalbane, Emmanuel. Nope, he made it to the end of third year, then transferred to a university down east."

The keyboard clacked.

"Montague, Emmanuel. No, he's graduating this year, so he's still around."

Another pause.

"Ah, here we go. Tealeson, Emmanuel. Did not complete his first year. Let me see what details we have."

She kept typing but at the same time nodded to Rashford that he should go and stand at her shoulder. He did so.

A formal photograph of a young Black man came up, together with his name, date of birth, and home address. Greenfield clicked a key, and the screen went to his academic record.

"Just a minute, go back," said Rashford.

The photograph appeared again.

"Can you print that for me, please?" he said. "That will help me confirm that this is the right person."

"Sure," said Greenfield, clicking another key. "The printer is in a different office; we can pick up the photograph when we're finished."

Rashford nodded. The Assistant Registrar made some more keystrokes, and the academic record came back up on the screen.

"That's printed," she said. "Now, let's see ... Hmmm, it looks like he was doing well, good marks, a B+ average in his first semester, midterms in the second look okay as well. The only course he completed in second semester was Introduction to Language, he got an A. The other four are all marked incomplete, I assume he didn't sit the final exams."

"Does it say who was the instructor for that Language class?"

"Yes, one second. Ah, here it is. Professor Benoît."

"Professor Linda Benoît?"

"Oh, yes, we only have the one by that name."

"Thank you."

Rashford made a note, then asked Greenfield to look up the records of Chad Sobers and Simon Lepani, both of which came up instantaneously. Greenfield read the screens and then turned to Rashford.

"This can't be right," she said.

"What can't?"

"These transcripts are almost identical. It's uncanny."

"Tell me, please," said Rashford.

"Well, they both have poor to middling marks, a C average in their first semester and that's consistent to the second semester mid-terms as well. Then four incompletes at the end of the semester, the only completed course was Introduction to Language, and they both got an A."

"And the instructor?"

"The same; Professor Linda Benoît."

Greenfield swivelled in her chair and stared at Rashford.

"What's going on?" she said.

"I'm not sure yet," he said, answering truthfully. "Can you run off their photographs for me, and also look up one more name?"

"Of course," she said, turning back to the computer. A few clicks on the keyboard later, she spoke again.

"Those are printing, who's the fourth?"

"Jeremy Beals. I don't know if that's 'ea' or 'double e'."

"I'll check both ... ah, here we go. It's 'ea'. Oh, he's in first year now. His marks are a little better, a B average in his first semester and B or B+ in the second semester mid-terms. He's enrolled in five courses this semester."

"Including Introduction to Language?"

"Including Introduction to Language," she said.

Rashford nodded.

"Ms. Greenfield, I must ask you to keep this confidential," he said.

"Of course, but I will have to tell the Registrar," she said.

"Very well, but absolutely nobody else," he said, looking her straight in the eyes. "Please impress the importance of the information. If it becomes public, it may jeopardise an ongoing investigation."

"Absolutely," she said.

They walked to a small office crammed with four printers, two large photocopiers, and a fax machine. One wall was covered in shelves, which held reams and reams of paper, spare toner cartridges, and a variety of envelopes. Rashford looked around.

"I thought you were going paperless," he said.

Greenfield laughed.

"We are," she said. "You should have seen the old print room!"

Rashford looked at the small squat machine sitting on its own table.

"Do you still send faxes?" he said.

"Yes, I'm afraid we're still mid-twentieth century in that regard. Well, not us, *per se,* but some of the previous institutions attended by our international students still have limited internet access, so we get a lot of paper copy records that are transmitted by fax. Most files come electronically, of course."

Rashford nodded. Greenfield gestured to the other machines.

"We still need some paper records, so we can print and copy them here. And over in the corner, there, that's a scanner so we can send them on as e-files."

She picked up the photographs and handed them to him.

"They're only black and white, I'm afraid," she said, then blushed and held her hand to her face.

"Oh dear, that didn't sound right. I'm sorry."

Rashford smiled.

"It's alright," he said, "I won't report you. Monochrome prints are just fine, thank you."

Greenfield escorted him back to the main entrance, where Celia was standing, holding a sheaf of papers in her hand. Greenfield ignored her, holding open the flap so Rashford could exit. Once he was on the other side of the counter, they shook hands.

"Thank you for your help," he said.

"Shush," said Greenfield, looking around. "Someone might hear you, and then everyone will want some."

Rashford laughed, then walked up the stairs to the main exit door. As he walked out into the late afternoon sunshine, he heard Greenfield's voice.

"Don't gawp, woman," she said, crossly. "What have you got for me there?"

Rashford left the campus and walked back to his hotel. As he approached the bollards, he heard a bicycle bell and stepped to the side. Shyanne pulled up alongside him.

"Hello," she said. "What are you up to?"

"Oh, I just had a few people to meet," he said, vaguely, waving the papers he was holding in the air. "Now I'm going back to my hotel. What about you?"

"Your hotel?" she said, ignoring his question. "I thought you were leaving today."

"I was," he said, "but I've decided to stay for a few more days."

Her eyes glinted.

"Really? Mandy will be happy!"

"Perhaps, but she does have to study for her exams."

Shyanne laughed.

"So do I, but I still have to work. We women find ways to have our cake and eat it too, you know."

Rashford shook his head.

"Is that where you're going, to work?" he said.

She grimaced.

"Yes. It was supposed to be my day off, but Josee never turned up for her shift, so I have to fill in."

"Is she okay?"

"I guess. She's not answering her phone. She's either moping over Marc leaving or else just focusing on her exams. She's not confident about the one we have on Friday."

Rashford nodded.

"Well, I hope it's a quiet day and you get to do some revision in-between the customers," he said.

They reached the bollards.

"I might see you around," said Shyanne, then with a wave she bumped her bicycle down the steps and onto the riverside path.

CHAPTER 15

The Chicken Cacciatore was as good as Mandy had promised. Rashford had stopped at the liquor store and bought a bottle of Ruffino Chianti, the Riserva Ducale. Mandy looked at the bottle with some trepidation.

"It's a bit old," she said. "Won't it be vinegar?"

"The salesperson told me it was a good vintage," said Rashford, defensively. "And 2017 wasn't that long ago."

"It was the first year I went to university," said Mandy, "but whatever. Let's try it."

Rashford kicked himself for not making that connection. The last thing he wanted was Mandy bringing back memories of those first few weeks on campus.

"I'm sorry," he said. "I didn't think it would be a trigger. I just told the guy that you'd asked for a good Italian red wine, and then I went for what he sold me."

She leaned up and kissed him.

"It's okay," she said. "I'm not upset. It's just the stupid little things that come out of nowhere and remind me."

He put his arms around her and squeezed tightly. She slapped him on the back.

"Come on, let me go. This chicken won't cook itself. You can set the table, and open that wine. Let it breathe a bit. We can have a beer while we're waiting."

They chatted as they did their various tasks. Rashford complimented her on her dress, which accentuated her figure, and she commented that she 'loved a man in linen' as she stoked his arm. He didn't mention that it was his last clean shirt until the laundry was returned in the morning. Once the wine was opened, Mandy handed Rashford a litre carafe and a plastic funnel.

"Pour it in there," she said.

"Why?"

"It aerates the wine, makes it much smoother. When I worked retail, our store owner was a proper wine freak. He taught me and the other girls how to do this. He used to say, 'it will add about twenty bucks to what people think you paid for the wine'."

Rashford did as he was told.

"Be careful at the end," she said. "Look out for the lees."

"The leaves? What leaves?"

"The lees. The sediment stuff that sometimes sits at the bottom of a bottle, especially an old bottle like this. Do it slowly."

Rashford tipped the bottle back, slowing the flow of wine, then stopped altogether.

"This sludgy stuff?" he said.

Mandy looked over.

"Yes, don't pour that, just leave it in the bottle."

Rashford held the bottle up to the light.

"There's half an inch in here," he said.

"Trust me," said Mandy. "You don't want to drink that. Rinse out the bottle, please."

He poured the last of the wine down the sink and then rinsed out the bottle with cold water, swishing it around to make sure all the sediment was removed.

"Good," said Mandy. "Now, pour the wine back into the bottle."

Rashford looked at her, then took the funnel and did what he was told.

"There's a bit more of that sludge here," he said, as he got to the bottom of the carafe. "Shall I toss that as well?"

"Yes, please," said Mandy, busily adding some chopped herbs to the big pan that was bubbling away on the stove.

Rashford took the bottle to the table and then watched as she gave the pan a final stir, turned down the element to it's lowest setting, and then placed the lid on top. A second pot, this one full of water, was starting to boil. Mandy waited until it was at a full boil and then carefully placed some wide strips of dry pasta into the pot. She gave it a quick stir with a wooded spoon, added a pinch of salt, and then set the timer.

"Right," she said, taking her beer and leading him to the couch.

"We have thirteen minutes," she said. "Tell me about your day."

"Thirteen minutes?" said Rashford. "That seems a bit ... precise."

"People wait for pasta," said Mandy, definitively. "Pasta doesn't wait for people. Especially pappardelle. Twelve and a half."

"I went to see the Assistant Registrar," said Rashford, and proceeded to make her laugh with his descriptions of their interactions.

"That was absolutely delicious," said Rashford, once he had cleared away their dinner plates. "Where on earth did you learn to cook like that?"

"That's just normal food where I come from, Stanley Mission."

Rashford stopped and stared at her.

Mandy laughed.

"During my break from university, my gap years as I call them, I worked in retail. Like I said, the owner was a wine freak, what do they call them? An oenophile."

"Oweenofeel?"

"Something like that. I might not be saying it properly. Anyway, someone who really likes wine. He used to open a bottle every Saturday, after we closed. He'd call the girls into the back room and give us each a glass, then talk about it for ten minutes, its structure, the floral notes, all that. Most of us just wanted to glug it back and go home, but he made us drink it slowly. It was kinda fun. At the end, he'd always say, 'another empty bottle and still no genie, we'll have to try again next week.' Then he'd pay us, and we'd go home."

Rashford nodded.

"Sounds like a good team-building exercise," he said.

"Yes, it was," said Mandy. "And Peter preferred Italian wine to French, for some reason. So that's what we usually drank. Naturally, I saved my money and went to Italy on a holiday. It was beautiful. I was there for two weeks, mainly in Florence. One day I saw this sign saying that there were cooking classes, with an English-speaking teacher. I had been to the Uffizi, twice, and the Boboli Gardens, and the cathedral, and the palaces, but they were all in the city. I wanted to see the countryside.

"This was like a make and take thing, where you went to the market and did some shopping with the teacher, then got a minibus up to a farmhouse in the Tuscan hills, where you cooked what you had bought and then ate it for lunch. So, I signed up. And it was brilliant. We even made our own pasta! Afterwards, you're on this e-mail list, and they keep sending you recipes, so when I got home, I just kept practicing. My mom started calling me 'Mandybella' but she liked the food!"

"I bet she did," said Rashford. "What's your secret ingredient?"

"Apart from chicken, you mean?"

Rashford laughed.

"Yes, apart from that!"

"It's nothing special, really. Most recipes say you should use chicken legs, but I use boneless breast meat, it's softer and more tender."

Rashford smirked.

"Yes, I prefer breasts to legs," he said.

She flipped a tea-towel at him.

"You've got a one-track mind," she said. "Do you want to hear this or not?"

"Yes, please. Sorry."

"Mmmpfh. Well, good chicken, and then fresh herbs, oregano, thyme, not dried stuff. Good garlic cloves, not the ones that come from China, I've no idea what they use to grow those. And wild mushrooms, if possible, not those white button ones. I couldn't find any proper wild mushrooms, it's too early for the morels, so I used a couple of portobellos, they have a decent taste. You stir them all together and let them simmer in the bean and tomato sauce. Easy-peasy."

"Just like that?" said Rashford. She nodded.

He poured the rest of the wine into their glasses and carried them over to the couch. Mandy went to her phone and scrolled through, then put it down as music started to come out of a hidden speaker.

"Thank goodness for streaming," she said, moving to the couch and sitting next to him. She took her wine glass and had a sip, then placed it on the side table. He listened to the music.

"Is that you?" he said, realizing that he was hearing a fiddle.

She laughed.

"No," she said. "This is classical violin. Beethoven's Sonata number nine. It's a mix, so there's lots of different composers. I just like the sound."

She leaned across and kissed his cheek.

"It's romantic," she said.

Rashford put his arm around her and kissed her hair.

"Indeed, it is," he said.

They sat quietly, listening to the music and drinking their wine.

"Do you remember how we were talking about triggers, earlier," she said, nestling her head in his shoulder. He stroked her hair.

"Yes, I remember," he said.

"Well, it reminded me of the boy who wanted doggy, and I didn't know what it was."

"Mm-hmm," said Rashford, absently.

She stood up from the couch and took his hand.

"I know what it is, now," she said, smiling, and led him into her bedroom.

The next morning, they slept late. Mandy had a ground floor apartment in a multi-unit building. There were two bedrooms and a living room with a galley kitchen. In the master bedroom she had a high bed, with an ornate carved headboard. The walls were painted ivory and reflected the soft light from the mock candles in the wall sconces. She had a nightstand, a chest of drawers, and a full bookcase as well as two built-in closets and an en-suite bathroom.

The walls and ceiling of the second bedroom were covered in large squares of thick felt. 'It's my practice room', she had told him, 'I don't want to disturb the neighbours.' There were three violins, each on its own stand, and a lectern for holding sheet music. In the corner was an old card table, on which a small portable keyboard reclined.

From her living room, the windows opened up onto a low-walled balcony, beyond which was a lawn edged with mature trees. Rashford made coffee and took it outside. He sat in the shade and lit a cigarette. It was his first one since he had met Shyanne the day before, and he felt the familiar frisson of nicotine running through his arms and legs. 'I should probably stop,' he thought, for perhaps the eight hundredth time, tapping the ash into a saucer he had brought from the kitchen.

Mandy appeared, still wrapped in a towel from the shower, and sat next to him. She leaned across and took the cigarette from his fingers, then took a long drag.

"I didn't know you smoked," said Rashford, surprised, as she handed the cigarette back.

"I don't," she said. "But I used to, until I went back to university. All that talk of Italy last night reminded me of sunny evenings on a patio, people watching, with a caffè corretto and a Muratti. It was heaven!"

Rashford looked at her, her long hair cascading down below her shoulders, the thick towel with its Hudson Bay stripes wrapped around her breasts. He imagined her on a dark green metal chair at the edge of a paved stone patio, her espresso cup and ashtray on a rickety table, wearing a pale-yellow summer cotton dress, idly kicking one tanned leg over the other, attracting the attention of every man around.

"You must have had a hell of a holiday," he said.

"Sì, signore," she said, laughing. "And I never paid for my coffee either!"

Rashford shook his head.

"I'm going to get dressed," she said, then stood and walked into the bedroom. Rashford followed her.

"You forgot your towel," he said.

Later, after Rashford made another pot of coffee and went back out to the balcony, Mandy was fully dressed when she joined him. This time she took a cigarette from the package. He lit it for her, noticing how she closed her eyes as she inhaled.

"God, that's good," she said. "I've quit for four years, you know."

"Well, I don't want to be responsible for you starting again," said Rashford.

"Too late," she said, smiling.

She noticed the look of panic on his face.

"It's okay," she said. "I'm not starting again. But this one is nice, post-coital as it were. So, if you can keep your hands off me, then I won't smoke."

"So, it *is* my fault," said Rashford.

"Fifty-fifty," she said. "Right, what's the plan for the day?"

Rashford looked at her.

"Don't you have to revise?"

"Yes, but I'd like a break, just for a couple of hours. Can we go somewhere for lunch?"

"Of course. I was thinking of having a walk around campus, a proper walk. I've only seen the bits of it where there was the conference."

Mandy chewed her thumbnail.

"Well," she said, "we can do that. If we cut across campus from the Three-Legged Rabbit then we'll see the library, the main quad, some of the fancy buildings."

"That sounds good."

"There are a whole bunch of little restaurants on that side as well, where we can find somewhere to eat."

"Great."

"Then I'll come back here and study while you do whatever you're doing."

Rashford nodded.

"That would be good. The rest of this week might be a bit busy; can I make a date for Saturday?"

"Sì, signore," she said, coquettishly. "Pick me up at seven?"

"It's your celebration," he said. "Where would you like to go?"

"Surprise me," she said.

<hr>

They walked arm-in-arm along the road leading to the Three-Legged Rabbit, then cut across the car park to a path Rashford had not noticed before. This lead them alongside a small pond, filled with ornamental lilies not yet in bloom and fringed with yellow marsh marigolds, which were. An early-arrived red-winged blackbird chattered at them from the bushes, marking out his territory.

A large glass-sided tower rose up on their left, some of the recessed windows open.

"That's the new library," said Mandy. "It's a smart building, apparently. The windows open by themselves to moderate the temperature inside."

Rashford looked at her with raised eyebrows and she nudged him with her elbow.

"The university is very proud of it," she said. "It's in all the brochures. It's got a big circular nook for storytelling, a computer centre, musical instruments you can borrow, gaming consoles, a maker space with 3D printers, a conference room with a kitchen for catered events ..."

"Does it have any books?"

"Philistine," she huffed, but laughed with him as they kept walking.

They came to a large lawned area, bisected by diagonal paths which met in the middle. The lawn was square, with formal flowerbeds along the edges. These were still covered in a layer of leaves, left as winter mulch to protect the soil.

"This is the main quadrangle," said Mandy.

"Is there another one, a lesser quadrangle?" said Rashford.

"Not unless there's a secret one," said Mandy, laughing.

Rashford said nothing.

The library tower paralleled one side of the quadrangle; the other three sides were flanked by three and four storey buildings constructed from some sort of sandstone brick; the facings glowed warm under the sun. As they walked along the path from the library, Rashford saw that the grass was almost ready for its first cut of the spring, the leaves of violets and dandelions starting to show through the lawn. Where the paths crossed there was a gravelled circle, in the centre of which stood a large boulder. This had been painted black, over which bold capital letters announced that the end-of-exam happy hour would continue from three to ten p.m. at the Three-Legged Rabbit every day until Friday.

"Not maths graduates, then," said Rashford, laughing.

"That's the Notice Rock," said Mandy. "Anybody can write a message or an announcement there. The only rule is that it has to be left up for twenty-four hours before being repainted. Right now, that's the only important announcement, it's been there all week."

They circled the boulder and continued across the quad on the same diagonal path. There were a few other people, walking either alone or in pairs, and a few students had spread blankets or ponchos on the grass and were sitting, reading books. Mandy suddenly pulled Rashford onto the lawn and walked quickly across towards the opposite path, cutting laterally across the grass.

"Prof! Prof!" she shouted, almost dragging him towards a woman walking alone on the other diagonal.

"Hello," said the professor, stopping to wait for them.

"This is our Gender and Women's Studies professor," said Mandy, coming to a breathless halt and pushing Rashford forward to say hello.

"Gavin?" said Bettina Blackeagle.

CHAPTER 16

Rashford disentangled his arm from Mandy's and stared at Bettina. She smiled.

"Tân'si," she said.

"Mânan'tow, ki'ya maka?" he replied, automatically.

Then she stepped forward and he gave her a hug, opening his arms to embrace her.

Mandy looked from one to the other.

"You two know each other?" she said, incredulity in her voice.

Bettina ignored the question but broke the embrace and stepped back, looking at Rashford carefully. Her gaze seemed to go from the top of his head to the bottom of his boots, drinking in the detail of his pale-blue linen shirt, his dark blue jeans. He realized that he had taken a breath and pulled in his stomach, so he consciously relaxed. She laughed, and her eyes found his face again.

"You're looking good, you," she said, nodding.

"Tê'nikeh," he said. "As are you."

She was as coolly composed as when he had last seen her almost six months before, and her hair was still long and bound in a tight braid. She was still wearing long silver earrings studded with turquoise but had changed from her habitual blue jeans and black shirt to black trousers and a cream blouse, over which she wore a charcoal grey jacket.

Rashford remembered his manners.

"Bettina, this is my friend, Amanda Robicheau. Mandy."

The two women exchanged a soft handshake. Bettina nodded, slowly, looking carefully at Mandy.

"You were in my class, last year I think."

Mandy nodded.

"Yes, Doctor Blackeagle," she said. "I shall be graduating this year."

Bettina smiled.

"How time flies," she said. She turned back to Rashford.

"And you? What brings you here? I had heard you had retired?"

"Yes, I have," he said. "Well, almost! It's a long story but I came here to talk about the FILTER program."

"Ah, good. It is important that people understand how that works."

"Indeed. And you? I didn't know that you taught here. I thought you were only at Swift Current."

"Another long story," she said, smiling. "I teach the Gender and Women's Studies course each year, to the third-year students."

"I've heard a lot about that course," said Rashford, laughing. "I might have guessed it was you!"

"Really?" said Bettina. "How intriguing!"

Rashford looked at Mandy, then back at Bettina.

"We were just going for lunch," he said. "Would you like to join us?"

She looked at her watch.

"I'm sorry," she said, "but I have an appointment. My students have their final exam this afternoon, I am going to help invigilate. I find people welcome a known face during these stressful days."

"I know that I did, last year," said Mandy, laughing.

She looked at Rashford.

"Gavin, you know that after lunch I have to go back and revise. Why don't you meet Doctor Blackeagle then?"

He looked at her, and then at Bettina. She nodded.

"That might work," she said. "It's a three-hour exam but even the slowest student should be finished before then. I will be free by four, if you'd like to meet for tea?"

"That would be great," he said. "Where should we meet?"

"Let's meet there," she said, nodding towards the boulder. "At the Notice Rock."

Rashford nodded.

"Four o'clock. See you then."

Bettina gave him another hug, then shook hands with Mandy before walking away. Mandy stood and stared at Gavin, her hands on her hips. He grinned at her.

"I know," she said. "It's a long story. It's okay. You can tell me over lunch."

She linked her arm through his and they continued walking down the path.

They found a small café that served Italian style food. Mandy asked for a seat outside, and they sat at a small table with a red and white checked tablecloth. She took control of the menu and ordered for them, speaking rapidly in Italian, so Rashford just sat back and looked around.

They had left the quadrangle and followed a passage between two of the large buildings, which Mandy had informed him housed the Arts Faculty and the School of Business. Once through the passage they were in a large square paved with cobble stones. It was not as large as the quadrangle but still substantial in area, and two narrow rows of two-storey buildings extended like arms from the School of Business. The top floor of these buildings looked like offices, but the bottom floor had been converted into cafés and shops. At the end of the gap between the arms, the area was filled by food trucks, and picnic tables dotted the cobble stones.

It was early afternoon, and the area was busy with students, staff, and faculty. Rashford saw some groups bringing fast-food options from the food trucks to the picnic tables, and others entering into one of the dozen or so cafés along the perimeter or, like them, choosing an outside table. The café about twenty metres from them advertised bratwurst and schnitzel, and from the flagons of beer being delivered to the group sitting outside, it was going to be a celebratory afternoon.

Their waiter returned with a large bottle of San Pellegrino sparkling water, a dish of mixed olives, and a wicker basket of bread. He left but soon came back with two small carafes, one each of red and white wine, which he carefully placed on the table. Rashford looked at Mandy and raised his eyebrows. She smiled.

"White wine for the starters, while it's still cold. We're having tuna crudo and caprese salad. By then the red wine will have opened up a bit, and we'll have that with the duck confit risotto and the gnocchi fries. In case we're still hungry, I ordered us a pizza diavola, nice and spicy, but we can always take that home if we don't eat it."

Rashford just looked at her.

"You speak Italian," he said.

"You hug my Gender and Women's Studies prof, who hates men," Mandy retorted.

She reached over and poured the white wine carefully into one of the three glasses in front of Rashford, then put the same amount in her own glass. She replaced the carafe on the table, then raised her glass in a toast. Rashford reciprocated and the glasses clinked.

"You first, I think," she said, taking a small sip of her wine and smacking her lips in satisfaction.

Rashford took a larger swallow of his wine. He wasn't particularly keen on white wines, but he felt that, given current circumstances, any type of alcohol would be useful.

He put down his glass and started talking, explaining about Kôhkum Christine and his Cree lessons, and the relationship of Bettina to her grandmother. This led him into the story of the tracking and capture of Simon Wolfe, the targeting of Roxanne, the trickery of Alf in claiming compensation, the roles of Fox Woman and Cicily in the story, and then his decision to retire. It was only as he was describing the view of the lake through the windows of the Prince of Wales Hotel that he realized his fish was cold. And raw.

"Ugh, this isn't cooked," he exclaimed, putting down his fork and trying to discreetly lift a napkin to his mouth. Mandy just looked at him.

"I told you, it's tuna crudo. It's supposed to be raw. That's why they marinade it in the olive oil and lemon juice."

"Oh," he said.

"If you don't like it, I'll eat it. The rest of the food is cooked. Except the salad. That's raw as well."

Rashford raised his hands.

"Well, duh, salad is always raw. That's why it's called salad."

Mandy raised her voice a fraction.

"Well, duh, that's why it's called crudo, which means crude, original, uncooked."

She sat back and folded her arms, then leaned forward again and hissed at him.

"What about egg salad?"

Rashford was confused.

"What?"

"Well, in egg salad, you cook the eggs first, right? Before you mix them with the mayonnaise. They're not raw."

She sat back, then leaned forward again.

"And potato salad. They're not raw either."

Rashford put up his arms again, this time in surrender.

"Okay, you win, not all salads are raw," he said. "I'll eat the crude fish."

Mandy started to say something and then saw the grin on his face. She just shook her head, then savoured another slice of the tuna, mopping up the oil and lemon sauce with a piece of bread. She sipped her wine, then looked across the table. Rashford looked back, thinking she was going to talk to him about learning Italian. Instead, she said:

"Who's Roxanne?"

The waiter had cleared away the plates and brought the pizza in a cardboard box before Rashford had convinced Mandy that Roxanne was no longer part of his life. He had been as open and honest with her as he could, believing that she deserved no less after sharing such intimate details of her own story. He had admitted to feeling deserted and betrayed when Roxanne had determined to stay in Charlottetown but had not reported his subsequent dalliance with Sarah. That, he thought, might be a truth too far.

"Anyway, that's all over now," he concluded, finishing his wine. "It's no longer relevant. Where did you learn Italian? Surely not in two weeks in Florence?"

Many laughed, then called the waiter over. He nodded as she spoke, then disappeared. She focused back on Rashford.

"No, of course not. I learned a few words, but that was all. When I came back, and started cooking the recipes for mom, I also started to learn the language. We were in Saskatoon then, so I went down to the Italian Cultural Centre on 24th Street and took conversational lessons."

"There's an Italian restaurant near there, in two old railway carriages," blurted Rashford, then blushed and bit his tongue as he realized that was where he had met Roxanne. Mandy didn't notice.

"Yes, we used to go there for lunch," she said.

"We?" said Rashford.

It was Mandy's turn to blush.

"Oh, some of the other students, and me," she said.

"And ...?" said Rashford. He had conducted too many interview interrogations not to sense when someone was being economical with the truth.

"Sometimes our instructor would come as well," she said, at last.

"Would he," said Rashford, arching his eyebrows.

Mandy ignored the gendered choice of pronoun, thereby confirming it.

"Most of the class were older couples who were planning a trip to Rome for their holidays," she said. "I was the only younger person there. It was natural that we got along."

"I'm sure it was," said Rashford, grinning.

"It was really good that he was from Fiesole, which is up in the hills near Florence, and was actually the place where I had gone with the cooking group. So, we had common places to talk about."

"Huh-hmm," said Rashford, non-committedly.

The waiter returned and placed two small cups on the table, one in front of each of them.

"Caffè corretto, signora," he said with a flourish. "Alla grappa."

"Molte grazie," she said, and he went off with a smile.

"Anyway," said Mandy, "it was a long time ago and only a bit of fun.

I'm not ashamed. I found it a lot easier to learn the language when I had a pillow dictionary."

Rashford just about choked on his espresso, coughing violently. Mandy laughed.

"Serves you right," she said. "You asked. Anyway, who helped you learn Cree?"

Rashford recovered enough to speak.

"An old lady in her nineties," he said. "And some books. No pillow dictionary there!"

"I bet my way was more fun," said Mandy. "Capisce?"

They walked across the cobbled area and past the food trucks to the street beyond. They were now outside the boundaries of the university, so they sat on a low wall near a bus shelter and Rashford lit a cigarette. He offered the packet to Mandy.

"Want one?" he said.

She shook her head.

"No, thanks. If we'd been able to smoke in there, I'd have loved one with my coffee. But not now, it's too late."

Rashford nodded.

"Fair enough," he said. "You don't mind if I do?"

"Not at all. I still like the smell."

Rashford chuckled.

"I've got an hour to kill before I meet Bettina," he said. "Can I walk you home?"

"No, it's okay," she said.

She nodded at the glass shelter in front of them.

"This bus does a loop around the outside of campus; it goes right past my apartment. I'll just catch it. You should go and look at the gallery."

"Gallery? What gallery?"

"If you go back across the quad, the building on the other side of that passage we took is the Faculty of Arts. In their main hall is a beautiful gallery of Indigenous artefacts that have been found in the area. It's well worth seeing."

"Thank you, I will."

They were silent for a moment, Rashford smoking his cigarette, Mandy idly kicking her legs back and forth. Rashford took a deep breath.

"Can I ask you a question?" he said.

Mandy stopped kicking and turned towards him, a quizzical look on her face.

"Of course," she said. "What?"

Rashford tried to pick his words with care.

"I've heard that Pia runs a trip to the Caribbean after the exams are finished," he said, slowly. "It seems that a lot of graduates go on the trip. I was wondering, is that in your plans?"

Mandy looked at him. When she spoke, her tone was withering.

"You're wondering if I'm going to dump you and head to the beach?"

"Not really," protested Rashford. "Well, perhaps. Sort-of."

"Not really perhaps sort of?"

"I'm not being clear," he said.

"Nope," said Mandy, chuckling to herself.

"What I mean is, are you planning on going on that graduation trip and if so, when? And if not, why not?"

"Those are clear questions," she said, leaning across and kissing his cheek. "Thank you."

Rashford stubbed his cigarette out on the bricks of the wall on which they were sitting, then put the butt in his pocket. A bus pulled up to the shelter, but Mandy ignored it. Two people got off, but nobody boarded, and it quickly pulled away.

"Yes, there is a Caribbean trip and no, I'm not going," she said. "Two reasons, I guess."

She put her hand to her temple and twirled her hair around her forefinger.

"First, I like Pia, and he's my cousin, but I'm not sure about the deal he gives people. It's only three hundred dollars to go to Barbados for a week, accommodation included. That doesn't seem right. My mom always said you get what you pay for, and it seems to me that a deal like that is trouble."

Rashford looked at her.

"What do you mean? Drugs?"

She shook her head.

"I don't mean anything, and I don't know anything. It just seems really cheap. And I don't like his business partner."

"Who's that?"

"His name is Dave Leblanc, but most people call him Slider."

Rashford looked surprised.

"The biker?"

It was Mandy's turn to look surprised, then she nodded.

"Oh, right, you'd have seen him at the pub when I played," she said.

Rashford confirmed this, and Mandy continued.

"But that's not the main reason," she said. "I had a big decision to make, a couple of months ago, and that means I can't go to Barbados."

She looked at him, and he saw her eyes were shining with excitement.

"We're going on a tour," she said. "Me and the band. How cool is that!"

Rashford clapped his hands together.

That's brilliant," he said. "When? For how long? Where?".

Another bus drew up to the shelter. Mandy jumped down off the wall and gave him a kiss on the cheek.

"See you on Saturday," she said. "Seven o'clock!"

"Text me after your exams," he shouted as she walked away.

She blew him a kiss.

"And the tour?"

"We leave at the end of June," she called back over her shoulder. "It's a six-week tour."

He stood up.

"Of where?" he yelled.

"The Maritimes!" she cried, waving back at him, and got on the bus.

CHAPTER 17

Rashford found the museum interesting, although he could not differentiate among the seemingly endless array of different types of arrow heads and spear points. The diorama of a buffalo jump was spectacular, extending over the full height of the atrium, with a bison caught seemingly in mid-fall. It was only when he paused on the stairs leading up to the second floor that Rashford noticed the thin filament wires holding the beast in place.

On the second floor was a room devoted to textiles, and Rashford could not help but be reminded of Marc Claydon. He admired the beadwork on a series of buckskin jackets and tried, unsuccessfully, to distinguish the difference between Dene and Cree designs. At the end of the room there was another diorama, this one of voyageurs manhandling a trade canoe over some rapids. Their sashes were tied around their heads as tumplines, and they carried large bales of furs on their back. A side panel described how the voyageurs may have individualized their garments by colouring them with plant-based dyes, predominantly as a means of identifying their clothes from those of someone else.

The exhibit continued into a second room where there was another diorama, this time of a family in a winter cabin. The man was outside, carrying a gun and holding a brace of rabbit pelts. His wife was inside, using her fingers as a loom on which to weave a sash. A lengthy side-panel described the history of the Assomption Sash and explained why it was also called the 'ceinture fléchée' or arrowed sash.

The last panel provided a summary of recent academic thought on the matter of the Métis sash and quoted a prominent scholar who described it as 'an early example of gendered expressionism, in which the display of the sash was no doubt influenced by the interaction between two distinct cultural traditions.' After a reproduced painting that showed two voyageurs meeting a stereotypical Plains warrior outside a tipi, the quote continued: 'the masculine heterogeneity found among European trappers of the time, who were forced to rely on each other in order to survive, both reflected and conflicted with the collective communalism of the First Nations people with whom they traded."

Rashford nodded to himself. This was what he recalled from Claydon's talk, more or less, and it was apparent that the PhD student's research was solid. Finishing the last panel, he left the room and went downstairs by the other staircase. As he descended, he passed a large painting depicting a circle divided into quadrants. The circle itself was blue, and the quadrants were painted black, yellow, red, and white. The work was entitled "The Sacred Directions of the Lakota" and was accompanied by a small panel that described the meaning of each colour, adding that green was also a sacred colour. Rashford paused and re-read the panel, thinking of the pattern of stripes on the Hudson's Bay towel with which Mandy had dried herself that morning. He shook his head and continued down the stairs.

Rashford was a few minutes early at the Notice Rock. He amused himself by trying to decipher the words covered by the latest coat of paint but found it a frustrating task. He was relieved to see Bettina Blackeagle making her way across the quadrangle and walked a few steps to meet her. She shook hands again, then turned and walked back down the path.

"I thought we could go to the Faculty Club for our tea," she said. "They also serve coffee. Did you eat well?

"Yes, thank you," said Rashford, and described the Italian restaurant they had visited.

"That's got a great reputation," she said. "Good choice."

Rashford admitted that he had just followed along, and that Mandy had selected the restaurant, and the meal. Bettina laughed.

"Oh, Gavin," she said, "you were always good at letting someone else take responsibility!"

Rashford wasn't sure whether he was being teased or insulted, so he said nothing. They walked to the passage that led through to the food court area, then Bettina turned and guided him along the front of the large sandstone building that housed the School of Business.

They entered via a wide staircase, the ends of each step flanked with large stone urns, from the top of which bright flowers cascaded.

"Those are pansies, lobelia and dianthus," said Bettina. "The gardeners raise them in the greenhouses and try to get them planted before the end of term, so we can all enjoy them."

"Isn't it still too cold?"

"Well, they're early annuals, so they're usually okay. If we get a bad frost, sometimes they have to plant them two or three times."

They went in through the double doors and then took the elevator up to the fourth floor. They exited into a small vestibule, the only furniture a desk on which a large book lay opened. A pen was chained to the edge of the desk, and Bettina used it to sign the book, noting both their names and the time of their visit.

"It's an honour system," she said, leading him through another door and into a large open room with windows that looked out over the quadrangle. The walls had been left as exposed brick, and the high ceiling was painted white. There were perhaps thirty tables, most of them empty, and Bettina led him across to one by a window. A young woman appeared and placed two menus on the table, together with a pen and a pad of paper. She stepped off to the side.

"I'm going to eat as well," said Bettina. "I trust you don't mind?"

"Not at all," said Rashford, looking at the menu. "I might be tempted by one of the sweets as well!"

Bettina laughed, then picked up the pen and started to write on the top sheet of the pad.

"I'm having the salad bowl," she said, "and a mint tea. What about you?"

"I'll have a coffee, please. Black. And a slice of the raspberry cheesecake."

Bettina wrote down their order, signed with her name and what Rashford assumed was a membership number, then handed the pen and pad back to the waitress.

"Thank you, Alex," she said. The waitress nodded and then left the room. Bettina looked at Rashford, tapping her fingers slowly on the tablecloth. Rashford looked back.

"You're looking well," he said, at last.

She gazed steadily.

"Yes. You said."

"How is Kôhkum Christine?"

"She is as well as the Creator wishes," said Bettina, switching to Cree. "She is still able to live on her own, with my help, and so I am grateful for the chance to repay her many kindnesses."

"That is good to hear," said Rashford, also in Cree. "Please give her my best regards,"

"It would be better if you gave them yourself," said Bettina, her voice tight. "We have not seen or heard from you since before Christmas."

Rashford bowed his head but remained silent.

"We had to learn from Gayle that you had closed the case and been promoted."

Rashford kept his head down.

"Later, it was she who told us that you were planning to retire."

She paused.

"We had to learn from Alf that Roxanne had left you."

Rashford looked up at this news.

"Alf? How did he know?"

Bettina smiled.

"Apparently his nephew's girlfriend's brother ... have I got that right?"

Rashford sighed.

"Pete. Yes, that's right."

"Okay. Pete. Apparently, when he was down east Pete met someone, whose roommate is a friend of someone called Darryl, who is a friend of Roxanne ..."

"Anne," said Rashford, quietly. "She prefers to be called Anne now."

"Indeed," said Bettina, then sat back as the waitress returned with their food and drink. She switched back to English.

"Thank you, Alex," she said.

The waitress nodded.

"Would there be anything else, Doctor Blackeagle?"

"No, thank you."

The young woman left. Bettina poured herself a cup of tea from the small ceramic pot, then opened the lid and fished out the teabag with a spoon.

"I find that it gets bitter if you leave it to steep too long," she said.

She picked at her salad.

Rashford picked up his coffee and took a sip. It was quite hot, so he grimaced and replaced the cup on the table. He cleared his throat.

"I apologise," he said. "It was not my intent to hurt the feelings of anyone, or to ignore Kôhkum Christine. I have just been ..."

He paused.

"Busy?" said Bettina, her fork halfway to her mouth.

Rashford shrugged.

"Perhaps. But everyone is busy. That is not an excuse."

Bettina nodded, then ate a mouthful of the salad. Rashford took a great sigh, then sat upright, placing his right hand flat upon the table.

"It's not just being busy," he said. "I was ... embarrassed."

"Embarrassed? Why? Because Ro ... sorry, because Anne sent you away?"

"A bit."

"I understand that she sent you away because she wanted you to close your case."

Rashford nodded.

"And that she decided to stay in Charlottetown, with her mother."

Rashford nodded again.

"Did she tell you not to go back to her?"

Rashford thought back to the last telephone call he had had with Anne.

"She told me that I was a prairie boy and didn't really want to live by the ocean," he said.

"And how did that make you feel?"

Rashford slumped back.

"I was hurt. But also, I think, perhaps, I was ... relieved."

Bettina nodded.

"That is what she thought," she said.

Rashford sat forward again.

"'What she thought?'," he said. "You've talked to her?"

"Of course. I called her after I had spoken with Alf."

Bettina took some more salad. Rashford just stared at her. Once she had swallowed, she smiled at him.

"It's easy, Gavin. You just pick up a phone and dial a number."

As they finished their drinks, Bettina explained that since that first call, she and Anne now spoke nearly every week. Anne had moved into her own apartment but still saw her mother every day. She had no steady partner but had made lots of new friends and was enjoying her work. As she came to the end of her description, Bettina looked across at Rashford.

"And what shall I tell her about Amanda?" she said.

Rashford shook his head.

"She's a friend," he said. "I've known her for less than a week."

Belinda stared at him in surprise.

"Really? You seemed very ... comfortable ... together."

Rashford nodded.

"We are. But as she said when we met, 'it's just a bit of fun, it's not like we're going to get married'."

Belinda shook her head.

"For a famous detective, you sure miss a lot of clues," she said.

"I'm not famous," protested Rashford.

Belinda just laughed and drank some more tea.

"Anyway, said Rashford, "enough about my love life. What about yours? How is Cicily?"

Belinda looked down at her lap. She spoke softly.

"She is still in Toronto," she said. "But I have told her that I cannot be there, I have to stay with my nôhkum. She understands, but it is difficult. She wants to go to concerts, to exhibitions, to travel. I worry that we are starting to come apart."

Rashford nodded.

"I noticed that you were not wearing her ring," he said. "The one that Gayle made, with that yellow-stone that Cicily found."

Bettina inhaled, then smiled sadly.

"The Chemawinite. Yes. I keep that at home now. That helps keep the sadness away."

"I am sorry."

"Thank you."

Bettina sat up and smiled.

"Enough maudlin'," she said. "My nôhkum is still well. Even though they are not with us, our friends are keeping themselves busy. I am healthy and enjoying my work. You appear to be happy. These are good things to celebrate."

"Yes," said Rashford. "But thank you for making me talk. It is hard to keep things inside. They become bitter, like the tea that has been steeped for too long."

Bettina nodded, then laughed.

"So, tell me," she said, still smiling. "What have you heard about my course?"

An hour later, Rashford left the Faculty Club and took the elevator back to ground level. Bettina was waiting to meet a colleague and Rashford had declined her invitation to join them for supper. He had too many things going on in his mind and felt the need to simply sit and think. He walked in the opposite direction from the quadrangle, following a series of paths and service roads that wandered through the campus. It was nearly fifteen minutes before he saw what he was looking for, and he cut across a flower bed to speak to the two women who were on their hands and knees, weeding.

"The SQ?" said one, looking at him carefully. Her Tilly hat was pulled low over her eyes, and she squinted as she considered his question.

The second, younger, woman sat back on her haunches.

"What do you want to know that for?" she said.

Rashford smiled.

"I'm going for a smoke," he said. "LBC sent me."

She nodded, looking across at her colleague.

"Shall I show him?" she said.

The older woman nodded, then returned to her weeding. The younger one rose quickly and lithely to her feet.

"This way," she said.

Rashford followed her, admiring the cut of her jeans and the way her body moved. They had only gone about twenty metres when she stopped and turned to him.

"Would you prefer it if I took off my jeans?" she said.

Rashford blushed crimson.

"No, sorry ..." he stammered.

She nodded.

"Why don't you walk ahead," she said, pointedly. "Follow the path."

He did as he was told, still blushing furiously, and very cognizant of every step he took, how his muscles were moving, what he must look like from behind. He reached the building at the end of the path and saw a small grey door.

"In there," said the woman, still behind him.

Rashford stopped and turned around. He had recovered his composure, and was no longer bright red. He looked at the woman, who was smiling.

"You were in front of me," he said, slowly. "How did ..."

She shrugged.

"You're a man," she said. "It's what you do."

She turned and walked away. Rashford tried not to watch her go.

He found his way through the grey corridors and emerged from yet another door, one he had not noticed before and about fifty metres from the picnic table. He walked across the grass to the wooden structure, which he saw was still not planted. A new bag of sheep manure stood propped against the side, and the surface was raked clear, but there were no seedlings in sight.

Rashford nodded slowly to himself, then walked to the picnic table and sat down, He had just lit a cigarette when a young man emerged from the closest door. He walked over and nodded to Rashford, then sat down on the other side of the picnic table.

"Afternoon," he said, lighting his own cigarette.

"Good afternoon," said Rashford, trying to place the man's face and then remembering.

"We met before," he said. "You were with Fred."

The man nodded.

"That's right," he said. "My name's Jeff."

"Gavin," said Rashford, shaking hands.

The two men were silent, smoking their cigarettes.

"Fred figured you for a cop," said Jeff, looking straight at Rashford.

Rashford nodded.

"Used to be," he said. "Why would he think that?"

Jeff exhaled a long plume of smoke.

"He thought you was asking too many questions, especially about that garden bed."

He nodded across at the wooden structure.

Rashford smoked, pensively. Then he broke the silence.

"And you? What do you think?"

Jeff shrugged.

"Me? I think Bruce needs to get those geraniums planted right quick. They're still in pots and will be getting all root bound. We already put out all the cool season annuals."

He stubbed out his cigarette in the ash tray bucket, nodded at Rashford, then rose and walked back out of the same door through which he had arrived. Rashford lit another cigarette and sat back, looking at the sun shining on the empty planter, thinking.

CHAPTER 18

The next day passed quickly for Rashford. It was Wednesday, and he had no appointments or telephone calls scheduled, so he hung a 'Do not Disturb' sign on his hotel room door and spread out his note-books on the bed. At ten o'clock he called down to Reception and asked for some extra coffee pods. The uniformed woman who delivered them asked him if he was going to need room service and seemed relieved when he told her that he would make his own bed. She left, then came back a few minutes later and handed him two wrapped bundles, which when he unravelled the plastic turned out to be his clothes, neatly ironed and folded. He put those in the drawers and made fresh coffee.

It was mid-afternoon when he came back from his fourth visit to the bathroom and decided he had probably had enough coffee. He had arranged and rearranged his notes, both physically and in his mind, and had a fairly good idea of what might have happened. Now, he just needed proof, and he decided that a walk might help him figure out how to get that piece of the puzzle.

He looked out of the window and saw that clouds had rolled in, turning a fine morning into a grey and overcast afternoon. Grabbing his jacket from the closet, he checked to make sure he had his phone, wallet, and room key, then left the room. The uniformed maid was standing outside the next room, putting some cleaning supplies back on her trolley, but when she saw that he had left the sign on the door she simply nodded. He went back into his room and came out with his soiled towel.

He took the clean towel from the maid and returned it to his bathroom, then picked up his cigarettes and lighter and put those in his jacket pocket. Closing his door and nodding once more to the maid, he walked past her to the elevator and then changed his mind, going down the stairs instead.

Once outside he felt the chill of the wind and fastened his jacket. He crossed the car park and headed for the marked path, which he then followed down to the river. He saw that small buds were starting to emerge on many of the shrubs, and that one bush was covered in the silver catkins of a pussy willow. Once he was down on the riverside path he turned to his left, in the opposite direction from the previous day. He walked briskly for thirty minutes, passing a few couples who were dawdling along, hand in hand, and being passed by a number of joggers whose trim Lycra-clad bodies indicated that they were serious runners.

When his phone pinged to mark the thirty-minute timer, he stopped and turned. He took a more leisurely pace on the walk back, and it was almost four-thirty when he reached the path that led back to the hotel. He stopped for a moment, then ignored the side path and continued on the riverside route. He walked for another few minutes and found himself at the 'Dances with Gravy' food truck. The aromas emanating from the truck reminded him that he hadn't eaten that day, so he went to the serving hatch and perused the menu. He ordered the venison patty on bannock, and a can of ginger ale, and the harried-looking man inside the truck said it would only take a few minutes.

Rashford took some napkins from a glass jar on the shelf beneath the hatch, together with some sachets of tomato sauce and a reasonably clean ashtray and carried everything to the table nearest the river. There was nobody else on the dock patio, so as he waited for his food, he lit a cigarette and looked for the Canada geese. He heard a splash and a sizzle from inside the truck, followed by a not-very-muffled curse, so he had decided to just sit and relax when Shyanne appeared.

She stopped her bicycle next to the patio and said hello. Rashford asked her how her exams were going, and she was just telling him about the trick questions set by her Gender and Women's Studies prof when there was another curse from inside the truck. Shyanne laughed.

"Poor Antoine," she said. "He's been here on his own all day, again. I'd better go and help."

She wheeled her bike to the area behind the food truck and then ran lightly up the steps, knocking once before opening the door.

"Thank the Gods you're 'ere," Rashford heard an accented voice declare, just before the door closed. "No Josee again today."

***

Rashford had smoked a second cigarette before Shyanne appeared with his food.

"There you go, one Bambi Burger," she said, placing it on the table in front of him. "I got you fries as well."

Rashford looked at the meat patty, visible between the bannock halves and obviously topped with lettuce, tomato, and some sort of sauce.

"Bambi Burger?" he said.

Shyanne laughed.

"That's the unofficial name," she said. "Like the rabbit stew, we call it Triple C. That stands for Customized Cottontail Cutlets."

Rashford shook his head.

"Why don't you put that on the chalk-board menu?" he said.

Shyanne huffed,

"We did," she said. "Then the Bylaw people made us change it. Wimpy settlers can't take a joke!"

Rashford laughed, then bit into his sandwich.

"Well, this is delicious, whatever you call it," he said.

Shyanne nodded.

"Yeah, Antoine is a really good chef. He used to work in a top kitchen, up in the city, but he had to leave, there was so much racism."

"Really?" said Rashford. "In a kitchen?"

"Yes," said Shyanne. "For example, every time he went to flambé something in brandy, this other chef would say something like, 'check the level in the bottle, someone, otherwise Antoine will drink it.' Or he'd ask him to 'pass the hatchet so I can scalp this steak'. Just stupid stuff, but all the time."

"What did Antoine do?"

"He held the guy over the deep fryer and told him that if he said another word, he was going to dunk his head. The guy was terrified and peed his pants. Then he reported him, and of course Antoine was fired."

Rashford nodded.

"I can see that," he said. "Has he been tempted to put 'Roast Racist' on the menu?

"Don't give him ideas, you," said Shyanne, laughing.

"Baked bigot? Marinaded môniyâw?"

Shyanne slapped his arm.

"Stop it," she said, still laughing. Then she turned serious.

"I still haven't found Josee," she said. "I'm getting worried."

"You called her, right?"

"Called and texted, yes."

"Have you been to her place?"

"No, not yet. I was waiting until after today's exam, but she didn't show up for that either."

Rashford nodded, slowly.

"When do you think you will go?" he said.

"This evening, after my shift."

"Would you like me to come with you?"

Shyanne looked at him, then started to cry.

"Would you? Oh, yes please. I'm scared to go on my own."

Rashford put out his hand and stroked her shoulder.

"Don't cry," he said. "We'll do this together. I'm staying at the Island View, that's the hotel just up on the main road."

Shyanne nodded.

"I know it," she said.

"I'll come downstairs just after seven," said Rashford. "I'll meet you in the lobby, okay?"

"Okay," said Shyanne, sniffling and nodding at the same time.

"Now please, let me finish my lunch," said Rashford.

At five past seven Rashford was waiting outside the front doors of the Island View Hotel. He had finished his meal and then dashed back to the hotel through a sudden shower of rain. Now he was leaning against a tree at the edge of the circular drive, smoking a cigarette, and waiting for Shyanne. A car turned off the main road and swept past him, spraying up water from a puddle in the gravelled drive. Rashford cursed at the silver SUV, a European model of some sort, then gaped in amazement when the passenger door opened, and Shyanne got out.

As she started to walk up the steps to the lobby, Rashford stepped out from his tree and called her name. She stopped, then turned around, looking for him. Once she saw him, she ran lightly back down the stairs.

"Sorry, we didn't see you," she said, opening the back door of the SUV and starting to get in.

"You go in the front," she said.

Rashford walked towards the vehicle, which he now recognized as an X-7, one of the BMW models. He held the door open for Shyanne, then closed it behind her. Moving to the passenger window, he peered inside and recognized the driver. He opened the door.

"Hello, Pia," he said, smiling. "Nice wheels."

"Mmmppfh," said Pia, snorting. "Five years old, pre-owned, eighty-seven thousand kicks, and they still wanted forty-five grand. Bandits."

Rashford laughed and fastened his seatbelt. Pia pulled away in a spray of gravel.

"Easy, tiger," said Rashford.

"Remember, we're the lions," said Pia, not stopping at the gate and driving into the traffic without regard for the cacophony of horns that erupted. Rashford leaned forward with his left hand flat on the dashboard, then reached up with his right and grabbed the safety handle that was attached above the door.

They reached Josee's apartment in just over twelve minutes. It was in a leafy suburb on the far side of the university, the corner unit of a row of townhouses. Pia pulled up outside and parked in a space marked 'Tenant's Only', ignoring the 'Visitor Parking' sign three spaces down. They got out and looked at the buildings, which were faced with brick and had looked well maintained.

"She shares it with two other girls," said Shyanne. "The main floor is a common area, then they each have their own bedroom, and there's a basement for storage."

Pia sat on the hood of the BMW and pulled out his phone.

"I'll wait here," he said.

Shyanne looked at him, then tossed her head and started towards the front door. Rashford followed.

"Don't mind him," she said, muttering. "He's mad because I invited you as well. He wants to be the hero."

"For Josee?" said Rashford, surprised.

"Yeah. He really likes her; he's always thinking of reasons to visit."

"But isn't she his cousin?"

Shyanne shrugged, as if this was of little consequence.

They opened the gate and walked through a small, neatly maintained garden. A square of lawn had a welded metal bowl at its centre, the remnant ashes identifying it as a small firepit. Heavily mulched beds edged the outside of the lawn, a few early shoots starting to pop up through their winter protection.

They reached the door and Rashford heard music from inside the house, some sort of pop song. Shyanne knocked, loudly. There was no answer. She knocked again, even harder, and this time the music stopped. A window on the second floor opened and a young woman stuck her head out. She had long black hair, nearly as long as Mandy's, which framed a laughing face.

"Yes? Oh, hello, Shyanne. I don't think Josee's here."

"That's what we've come to see," said Shyanne. "May we come in, please?"

"Sure!" shouted the girl. "Let me just put some clothes on."

She disappeared inside and closed the window. Rashford looked at Shyanne, who shrugged.

"She's a nudist," she said. "Wears no clothes around the house, unless there are visitors who she doesn't know, of course."

"Of course," said Rashford, wondering not for the first time what he was missing about the culture of the young.

They stood outside, then heard footsteps on the stairs. The door opened and a fresh-faced young woman stood looking at them. Her hair was now covered with what to Rashford's eye looked like a hijab, the headscarf worn by Muslim women.

In addition to the hijab, she wore a long blue caftan, the neckline of which was edged in gold thread, a pattern which continued down the edges of a long zipper that ran from the neck to the hem. The caftan clung to her body like a second skin, revealing her to be tall, slim, and curvaceous. Her feet were bare.

"Salaam alaikum," she said, bowing her head slightly.

"Wa alaikum salaam," said Shyanne. "Petra, this is my friend, Gavin. Gavin, this is Petra. She's from Afghanistan."

Petra laughed.

"A long time ago," she said. "My parents left when I was three!"

She looked around, then waved.

"Hello, Pia," she called.

Pia got down from the hood of the car and walked towards them. Rashford noticed that he had a sheepish smile on his face.

"Oh, hi, Petra," he said, "I'm just the driver."

He stood next to Rashford and shuffled his feet as they listened to Shyanne explain the purpose of their visit. Petra shook her head.

"I've not seen her since last Sunday," she said. "She was getting ready to meet you guys at the pub. She wanted me to go but I can't, there's just too much alcohol."

She looked at Rashford.

"I'm Muslim," she said. "We don't drink."

He nodded.

"That's okay," he said. "Lots of people don't. Even Pia, here – he drinks blueberry soda!"

Pia went scarlet, blushing furiously, while Petra looked across at him.

"Really?" she said.

"Anyway," said Shyanne, breaking into the conversation. "Josee. We haven't seen her since she left my place on Sunday night, well, early Monday morning. I thought she was coming back here."

"I haven't seen her or heard her," said Petra, "but you can have a look. We all keep a spare key for each other, so nobody gets locked out."

She turned and walked into the house, followed by Shyanne. Rashford glanced at Pia.

"Sorry," he mouthed.

Pia just glared at him, then walked back to the car. Rashford followed the women and went inside.

Petra went to her room first, leaving the door open. Rashford saw that the space was largely empty, the floor covered in rugs woven in abstract designs. Apart from a small dresser, there was no furniture other than a number of large cushions placed against the wall, and a small single bed, which was covered with a white and gold duvet. The walls were bare.

Petra opened the drawer of the dresser and leaned down to look inside. The afternoon sun shone through the window behind her and Rashford could clearly see the silhouette of her breasts, and legs, through the thin cotton. He only realized he was staring when Shyanne kicked his ankle. Petra closed the drawer and came to the bedroom door, holding out a key.

"Thank you," said Shyanne, and walked across the hall to one of the other doors. She inserted the key, then paused and knocked loudly.

"Josee," she called. "You in there?"

There was no answer. Shyanne looked across to Rashford, who nodded. She turned the key, then the handle, and pushed open the door. Taking a deep breath, she glanced at Petra, and then they both looked at Rashford. He sighed, then walked inside.

Rashford paused just inside the door and looked around. The two women crowded in behind him, one at each of his shoulders.

The room was empty, apart from furniture. It held a double bed with a light blue coverlet, a small chest of drawers, painted white, and a comfortable armchair situated in the nook next to the window. A disarrayed fan of blouses and t-shirts lay on the bed, and a pair of black denim jeans were rolled in a ball on the chair. A black-handled hairbrush lay on the chest of drawers, together with an open display box of different coloured lipsticks and two small vials of perfume. Three pairs of shoes were scattered on the floor. Rashford moved to the side so that Shyanne and Petra could step forward.

"This is normal Josee," said Petra. "She was trying on different things and then just left everything she didn't want. She would clean it up when she came back."

Shyanne nodded.

Rashford cleared his throat. They both looked at him.

"So, I don't want to be indelicate," he said. "But does this mean she wasn't expecting to be bringing someone back with her?"

Shyanne and Petra looked at each other.

"She wasn't like that," said Petra. "She's never brought anyone home, not as long as I've lived here."

Shyanne nodded.

"We were brought up Catholic," she said. "And Josee never lapsed."

Rashford looked at her, noting the faint blush that was beginning to rise on her cheeks, and decided to leave that question for later. He simply nodded.

"Right, then," he said. "Let's go back to your place and see if she's turned up there."

They all walked back down the stairs and paused at the front door.

"Thank you for your help," said Rashford, shaking Petra by the hand.

"You're welcome," she said, then turned to Shyanne.

"Let me know when you find her, 'kay?"

"Of course," said Shyanne, giving the other woman a hug. "Talk soon."

As they left the doorway, Petra waved to Pia, who was back sitting on the hood of the car.

"Goodbye, hope to see you later!" she called.

He waved back, then got in the car and waited for Rashford and Shyanne to arrive.

"Where to now?" he said.

"Shyanne's place, please," said Rashford.

Once they were back in Shyanne's house, she left them in the front room while she went into the kitchen. She reappeared with three cans of soda water, handing one to each of them and gesturing to the chairs. Rashford and Pia each sat in one of the armchairs, while Shyanne threw herself down on the couch.

"Where can she be?" she cried.

"Calm down," said Rashford. "Let's start with what we know. What happened on Sunday night, after Mandy and I left?"

Shyanne sniffled.

"We sat talking, the four of us, for another thirty minutes or so. Then Josee said she was tired and needed to get some sleep, we had a big exam on Monday."

Rashford nodded.

"I said she could stay here, she often did that when we were out late, but Marc said he would walk her home. So, they left."

"And Patrick?"

"Josee asked if he'd like to walk with them, but he asked me if he could stay to finish his drink," said Shyanne, blushing.

Pia looked at her but said nothing. Rashford hurried the conversation back to Josee.

"So, Josee left with Marc. Have you been in contact with him?"

"How? He never gave me his number or anything."

Rashford thought back to his interactions with Marc Claydon and realized that he had no contact details either. He reflected on this for a moment.

"Do you have a computer?" he said.

"Of course," said Shyanne, gesturing to the Secretary's Desk. "I work over there."

She walked over and carefully lowered the lid, revealing a laptop computer on the shelf in front of a series of small cubicles and drawers. She slid the computer forward and opened the lid.

"Here you go," she said.

Rashford walked over and joined her. He hit the enter key and then turned back to Shyanne.

"Can you enter your password, please," he said, looking across the room at Pia while she did so. Pia got to his feet, gesturing with his phone.

"It's open," she said.

"I have to go," said Pia. "I need to meet someone. Are you going to be okay?"

Rashford and Shyanne nodded, distractedly.

"Sure," said Shyanne. "See you soon."

"Thanks for the ride," said Rashford. "Take care."

Pia started to walk across the room but stopped when Rashford suddenly called his name.

"I need to talk to you," said Rashford. "I'll give you a call tomorrow, okay?"

"Sure," said Pia, leaving the room.

Rashford turned back to Shyanne.

"Can you open your browser, please," he said, at the same time getting his wallet out from his jacket pocket. He looked through the contents and picked out his name tag, which as he hoped had a URL address on the back.

Once he had access, he went to the conference website and looked up the speaker list. Marc Claydon was listed, with an affiliation of Toronto University.

"I thought it was the University of Toronto," said Shyanne, looking over his shoulder.

"So did I," said Rashford. "And why is it a Hotmail address, instead of a university one?"

Shyanne shrugged.

"Lots of students do that," she said. "The spam filters on the university account mean you miss half the messages from your friends."

Rashford brought out his phone.

"Well, let's try it," he said, typing in the address and a quick message, then pressing send.

Almost immediately his phone pinged as a reply was received. Rashford read the message out loud.

"It's a Delivery Status notification," he said. "The address could not be found."

"It could be his mailbox is full," said Shyanne, her voice quivering.

"I think it would say that, if that was the case," said Rashford, gently.

He turned back to the keyboard and brought up the main search engine.

"Let's see what happens here," he said, typing in 'Toronto University', then pressing enter.

"Eight point six million results!" exclaimed Shyanne.

"Yes," said Rashford, "but look. Toronto Film School. Toronto Metropolitan University. University of Toronto. No mention of a Toronto University."

He sat back in the chair and put his hands behind his head.

Shyanne went back to the couch, sat down, and started to cry. Rashford got up, walked over, and sat next to her. He put his arm around her shoulders.

"It's going to be okay," he said. "Let's just think this through."

She nodded, still sniffling, and reached for a box of tissues that were on the arm of the couch.

"Pia has gone now," he said. "So, tell me again, what happened on Sunday night?"

Shyanne blew her nose on a tissue, then wiped her eyes.

"After you and Mandy left," she said, "we all had another drink. Well, three of us did. There was no more IPA, so Marc just had water."

"He didn't have another drink?"

"No. Josee and I finished the bottle of Pinot Grigio between us, Patrick had another couple of glasses of red. Marc stuck to water."

"Then what happened?"

"At some point we must have all moved around, because I was sitting on the couch with Patrick, and Josee was sitting on the arm of Marc's chair."

She blushed.

"Patrick started getting amorous, you know, he had his arm around me and was feeling me up."

She glanced at Rashford and bit her lip.

"I know I should have stopped him, but I didn't."

Rashford nodded.

"Josee obviously noticed, she told Marc that she was tired and wanted to go home. That's when she invited Patrick to walk with them. Now she's gone and it's all my fault! Patrick asked me if he could stay and finish his drink, and I knew it wasn't his drink he wanted, and I still said 'yes'."

She started crying again. Rashford stroked her arm.

"It's okay," he said. "You're not to blame for anything. We don't know that anything has happened. They could be in a hotel room somewhere."

Shyanne shook her head.

"Josee wasn't like that. She has never been with a guy; she was waiting until she got married. You heard what Petra said. She never even invited anyone back to her place."

"So, they left, and Patrick stayed with you. What time was this?"

"Maybe half an hour or so after you'd left. Around one o'clock, I guess."

"And you didn't see them again, or hear from Josee?"

"No. Nothing."

Rashford thought for a moment.

"What about Patrick? When did he leave?"

Shyanne pulled away from Rashford's arm and edged to the side of the couch. She blushed and looked down at the floor.

"About four," she said, mumbling something else afterwards.

"Sorry, I missed that," said Rashford.

She looked up.

"I said, we didn't have sex."

Rashford looked at her, surprised.

"What? What did you do, then?"

She scoffed.

"Well, we were on the couch, getting frisky. He had my shirt off and I could see he was excited, so I helped him, you know?"

Rashford shook his head. She sighed, loudly.

"I blew him, okay? Then we went to bed, but he was done. He's an old man, you know. 'Once a night' is his limit, that's what he said."

"Really?"

"Yes. So then, we talked. He told me about his house, it's on the coast near Bridgetown, in Barbados. He's got miles of sandy beaches, and from his deck you can look out over the surf towards the sunset. I'm going to go and visit him, next year."

"Will you meet his family?"

"He's not got any, except for his mom, who lives in a different part of the Island. I checked that first. I don't do husbands."

"You just lie in bed with men for three hours, talking?"

She blushed furiously.

"I have some toys, you know? I showed him how to use them. Why do I have to tell you this?"

Rashford held up his hands.

"Sorry, you don't. I didn't mean to pry. Let's get back to Josee. You say she is a Catholic?"

"Yes. It's the way we were brought up. I stopped going, all those stories about the residential schools made me sick. Josee said that was all in the past and anyway, it was people who did those things, not Jesus. We used to argue so we stopped taking about it."

"Do you think she would have 'helped' Marc, if he had gotten excited or had any needs?"

"No way. Like I said, she was waiting for marriage. She would kiss and cuddle, but nothing else."

Rashford stood up.

"I'm just going outside for a smoke," he said. "I need to think."

When he came back inside, Shyanne was standing in the doorway of the kitchen.

"I've made tea," she said. "How do you take yours?"

"Just some milk, please," he said.

She turned away and then came into the main room a few moments later, carrying two mugs. She put one down on the table and took the other to the window. They sipped their tea quietly.

Shyanne broke the silence.

"Do you think he's hurt her?" she said, quietly.

Rashford shook his head.

"I honestly don't know," he said. "This whole thing is weird."

He drank some more tea.

"I saw him, you know. When I was checking out. He was taking an Uber to the airport. At least, that's where he said he was going."

"Did he say anything about Josee?"

Rashford decided not to mention what Marc had said about his sexual interactions with Josee. Instead, he focused on the other part of the conversation.

"He told me that they didn't say goodbye, because there's no word for that in her language, so they only said, 'see you later'."

"Pfft," Shyanne snorted. "That's a Cree language thing, not Michif."

"Michif?"

"The Métis language. They say 'bon swear', or sometimes 'meena kawapimitin'."

"That sounds like French for 'goodnight' and Cree for 'see you later'," said Rashford.

Shyanne paused.

"I guess," she said. "I hadn't really thought of that."

Rashford finished his tea and put his cup back on the table. He saw the small stain that had been left by a previous cup and inhaled sharply. Then he clicked his fingers.

"Shyanne, when do you take out your recycling?" he said.

"The third Thursday of each month," she said. "It goes to the curb for pick-up."

"Even the cans and bottles?"

"Yes. Unless Derek is broke, which often happens. Then he'll sometimes take them to the bottle depot to collect the money. Why?"

"Where do you keep them?" he said, walking through into the kitchen.

"There's a blue bag under the sink," she called.

He came back with the bag, which was slightly more than half full, together with two additional empty bags.

"Do you have any newspaper," he said, "or an old cloth?"

Shyanne looked around.

"I've got the flyers," she said. "They're from last week."

"That's fine," he said. "Can you put them on the table, please."

She did so and he spread the sheets out to cover the surface, then upended some of the cans and bottles onto the newspaper. Patiently he sorted through, picking them up and putting them into one of the clean blue bags. Every so often, he would use the edge of the bag to pick up a can and place it in the second new bag. When the table was empty, he lifted up the original bag and tipped out the rest of the bottles and cans. Only one of these made it to the second new blue bag.

When he had finished, he took the bag with most of the bottles and cans back into the kitchen and returned it to its place under the sink. He came back out to where Shyanne was looking at the second bag, which held four cans.

"These are all the same beer," she said.

"Yes," said Rashford. "The IPA. We know that's what Marc drank; he may have left a fingerprint."

"But Josee gave it to him," she said.

"Yes, and we'll get her fingerprints from her room."

He decided not to mention that he thought they would also take DNA from her hairbrush, just in case.

"We might also need to take your prints, for comparison. Then we can exclude you. Who else used to drink this beer?"

"Just Derek. He buys them, nobody else touches them normally. We all find they taste funny."

"That would be the hops," said Rashford. "Tell Derek that someone might need to come and take his fingerprints as well, please".

Shyanne nodded. Rashford asked her to let him know as soon as she heard anything from Josee, and then he left, carefully carrying his blue bag.

CHAPTER 19

____

Rashford slept late on Thursday. The previous evening, he had returned to his hotel room just after ten, and carefully placed the four tins, still in the blue bag, into the bottom drawer of the dresser. Then he'd gone back downstairs, to the bar, and ordered a double scotch, with a small glass of water on the side. It was a Balvenie single malt, only the ten-year-old but quite drinkable, nonetheless. Before taking his first sip he had poured in a couple of drops of water and watched the essential oils swirl around.

There were few others in the bar. A group of five young people were watching a late season hockey game, one of the playoffs he presumed, and a couple sat talking quietly at a corner table. Two other single men were sitting at the bar, each nursing a drink, and between them a young woman in a red jacket was finishing her glass of white wine. As soon as she replaced her glass on the counter, the man on the far side called over and asked if he could buy her another drink. She nodded, and he moved over to sit next to her, waving to the bartender as he did so.

The man closer to Rashford had scowled into his drink, drained it in a single swallow, then got unsteadily to his feet and left the bar. Rashford stopped the bartender as she moved towards the new couple.

"Excuse me, is there a place I can smoke?"

She barely broke stride.

"Not in here, but you can take your drink out onto the terrace," she said. "Just bring the glass back in, would ya?"

She went on down the bar, pausing only to pick up a bottle of white wine on the way. Rashford took his scotch and walked outside by way of a small door set into the wall between the large windows. There were four tables outside, each with an ashtray, but the terrace was empty. He picked a table out of the direct light from the bar, and sat quietly, smoking and sipping his scotch, and mentally prioritizing what he had to do the next day.

When he had finished, he walked back inside, taking his empty glass with him and leaving it on the bar. The bartender waved an acknowledgement, and he nodded back in return. As he passed the couple, he saw that the man had his hand on the woman's knee, and that she was not as young as she had first appeared. Rashford had idly wondered whether she was another stranded guest, or whether she was working, then decided it was none of his business and had gone to bed.

Now, stretching in the light of day, he put on the coffee percolator and then went for a shower. Afterwards, as he dressed, he realized that he was once again running low on clean clothes. He did not think that Pollard would cover a second set of laundry, so he decided he had to wrap things up fairly quickly. Drinking his coffee, he scribbled down the list of tasks he had decided upon while sipping scotch.

He first person he called was Senior Constable Gayle Morgan. She picked up the phone almost immediately and he could tell from the background noise that she was in her cruiser.

"What have you done now?" she said.

"Hello to you too," said Rashford.

She snorted.

"A social call? At this time of the morning? I don't think so."

"It's after nine," protested Rashford.

"Yeah, well that's like sparrow fart for you retired fogies, isn't it?"

Rashford laughed.

"I'm not retired yet."

"Yes, I heard," said Morgan. "Pollard said I might get a call from you. What's up?"

Rashford gave her a brief summary of what he knew, and an even briefer one of what he suspected, then asked if she could drive up and join him the next afternoon.

"What time?" said Morgan.

"About five, if possible," he said. "But it might be a long night."

"I'm doing now't else," she said, laconically. "My social life is buggered since Brian went off with that hussy from the diner."

"You can tell me all about it tomorrow," said Rashford, trying not to laugh.

"Aye, and you can tell me about this girl who's fiddling you," she retorted.

Rashford was silent for a moment, once more reflecting on the fact that everyone seemed to know all about his life.

"Deal," he said at last.

"Okay, five o'clock where?" said Morgan.

"Do you know the Island View Hotel?"

"I can find it," said Morgan, and clicked off the call.

His second call was to Piapot Starblanket, who did not seem as cheerful as Morgan had been.

"It's not even daytime yet," he protested.

Rashford laughed.

"It's nearly ten," he said. "I'm calling to see if I can take you to lunch."

Pia muttered for a moment, then spoke clearly.

"A late lunch," he said. "One o'clock."

"Okay," said Rashford. "Anywhere particular?"

"You're paying, right?"

"Yes."

"Somewhere expensive, then."

Rashford thought for a moment.

"Do you like German food?"

"What? Schnitzel and stuff like that? Sure."

"Okay then. There's a German place in that food plaza area at the university, behind the Faculty of Arts building."

"Yeah, I know it."

"See you there at one."

"Later," said Pia, and disconnected the call.

Rashford's third call was to Chief Superintendent Pollard. To his dismay, Sarah answered.

"Well, hello, stranger," she said. "Are you trying to avoid me?"

Rashford stumbled over his words.

"No, not at all," he said.

"So, calling at eight o'clock, before I get to work, wasn't a cunning strategy, then?"

"No," said Rashford. "That was just when I was awake and needed to talk to the Chief."

Sarah scoffed.

"Right," she said. "Of course."

Rashford felt himself blushing, although he couldn't understand why.

"Hmmm, how are you?" he said.

"I'm fine, thank you for asking," said Sarah. "How are you?"

"I'm good," he said. "You know, keeping busy. What are you up to?"

"Well, I've had no more two-notch weekends, if that's what you mean."

Rashford was stunned into silence. From the heat he felt on his face, he knew he was turning scarlet. He was pleased he was in the privacy of his hotel room.

"No, I didn't mean, no ... I was just ..." he said at last, sputtering.

Sarah laughed, loudly.

"I'll put you through now," she said.

When Chief Superintendent Pollard picked up the phone, Rashford knew he was still blushing and discombobulated. He tried to pull himself together, but she sensed his discomfort.

"Are you and Sarah still mad at each other?" she said.

"No, Ma'am."

"Good. Office romances between consenting adults are fine as long as the sex doesn't get in the way of the work. Capisce?"

"Yes, Ma'am," said Rashford, noting the use of the Italian phrase and wondering what message was being sent. "We're not, Ma'am."

"Not what?"

"Not having an office romance, Ma'am."

"Figure of speech, Staff Sergeant, figure of speech. A dirty weekend is as good as, if you can't get past it."

"Yes, Ma'am. I mean, no, Ma'am."

Pollard laughed.

"Anyway, I understand you're frying other fish now. Decided you like bannock better than perogies, have you?"

'How does she *know* this stuff?' thought Rashford, keeping silent.

"What's your report?" said Pollard, returning to the business in hand. "I assume that's why you're calling?"

Rashford agreed that it was and proceeded to give the Chief Superintendent a somewhat more detailed summary than he had provided to Gayle. She murmured quiet responses to his retelling of what he knew, then paid more focused attention when he described what he suspected. He concluded by confirming that he had asked Gayle Morgan to drive up and join him the next afternoon.

Pollard was silent for a few minutes. Rashford could hear the pencil tapping on her teeth and knew better than to interrupt. Eventually she spoke.

"Okay, item one. I'll make some calls and get back to you before you meet this guy for lunch. That's at one this afternoon, right?"

"Correct," said Rashford.

"Item two. I'll have a car drop round your hotel in about thirty minutes. Give him the cans and I'll look after that."

"Yes, Ma'am."

"Item three. Senior Constable Morgan has already reported your request. I have approved it, but only for the weekend. You'd better get this sorted out, Rashford. As I said to you earlier, I expect you here with a full report next Monday morning."

"Yes, Ma'am."

"And when you get here, be nice to Sarah."

"Yes. Ma'am."

Chief Superintendent Pollard became the third person to hang up on him that morning.

At one o'clock Rashford was already sitting at one of the tables outside the Gaststätte Lederhosen. He had rendezvoused with the police driver and handed over the beer cans for fingerprint analysis, then made another two telephone calls. At noon his phone had rung, and he had answered to Sarah, who was still being cool to him. She informed him that the Chief Superintendent had been called to a meeting, but wanted a message passed on. He listened carefully, then thanked Sarah and wished her well. He thought they parted on slightly more cordial terms.

After reviewing his notes again, he made his way slowly across the campus to the eating area. He looked inside the Italian trattoria, just in case Mandy was there, but was not surprised that she was not to be seen. Two restaurants down the checkered tablecloths at the German restaurant were a pale-orange colour with darker tan squares.

Pia arrived about fifteen minutes late, sliding into the seat opposite without a word of apology. His bulk filled the small chair, making it seem like he was overflowing the edges. His hair had been pulled to the sides and tied in two braids. He was wearing the same buckskin jacket that he had worn at the bar, dark and stained, the small round lapel button still the only decoration.

Pia nodded at Rashford, then waved for a waiter. Rashford was surprised that the man simply waved back, then disappeared into the inside rooms of the restaurant. He emerged a few minutes later with a tall blue drink, which he placed in front of Pia.

"Danke," said Pia.

"Bitte," replied the waiter, then looked at Rashford.

"Would sir like to order?" he said.

"Yes," said Rashford, annoyed that he had been sitting there for fifteen minutes without anyone apparently noticing his existence.

"I'll have one of those as well."

The waiter nodded, then turned and walked off. Pia chuckled softly.

"That's what it's like to be invisible, môniyâw," he said. "Welcome to our world."

Rashford looked around.

"But why here?"

Pia shrugged.

"The waiter, Nicholas, he's nehiyâw," he said. "A third cousin. He can smell a cop at a thousand metres."

Rashford looked at him, shaking his head. The waiter returned and put another tall glass of blue liquid in front of Rashford.

"Tê'nikeh," he said.

"Bitte," said the waiter, automatically, then looked confused as he processed the reply. Pia laughed.

"Got you good, bro," he said.

The waiter shook his head, then held out his arm for a fist bump. Rashford complied, and the man walked back to the inner sanctum of the restaurant.

Pia sipped his drink.

"Why am I here?" he asked.

***

Rashford had been thinking about how best to proceed and started by talking about Mandy and the proposed tour of the Maritimes which was scheduled for the band. This brought him to the fact that she would be missing the graduation flight to Barbados, and he was able to finish with a question asking Pia how that enterprise was organized.

Pia sat impassively as Rashford spoke. The tattoo on the side of his neck pulsed. When Rashford finished speaking, Pia leaned forward.

"Let's order some food," he said, and waved to the waiter, who came immediately and held out two menus. Pia ignored the outstretched hand.

"What's good today?" he said.

The man thought for a moment.

"The Wiener Schnitzel," he said. "With potato salad and green beans,"

"We'll have two," said Pia.

The man nodded.

"And two more blueberry soda, please."

The man nodded again, then walked away. Pia looked at Rashford.

"Okay?" he said.

"Yes, that's fine."

Pia studied him for a moment, then spoke.

"That was a long way to get to the question. Thank you. I respect you giving me the context of what you want to know."

He paused as the waiter returned with two full glasses and took away the empty ones. Once he had left, Pia resumed.

"If I understand you properly, you want to know how my business works. Is that right?"

"Yes."

"Why?"

"It will help me understand some other things better."

Pia raised his eyebrows.

"Very enigmatic," he said.

Rashford looked at him steadily. He made no response. Pia nodded.

"Very well. I will tell you the basics, but not the financial details. Okay?"

Rashford nodded.

Pia took a long drink of his blueberry and soda water. Rashford waited.

"Three times a year," said Pia, "we charter a plane."

"We?"

"My company."

"Go on."

"Three times a year, we charter a plane. Each charter is for twenty-four hours and covers the plane, the crew, fuel, landing fees, everything."

"It's a fixed cost?"

"Yes, negotiated each time."

"And where does it fly to, this plane?"

"It starts and finishes from Saskatoon, and flies to Bridgetown, in Barbados."

"There and back in one day?"

"No, our twenty-four hours is split into two halves, each a week apart."

"So, it goes down, waits a week, and comes back?"

"More or less, yes. Our passengers do, anyway."

Rashford decided to return to that point later in the conversation and changed the topic.

"Who or what is on the plane?" he said.

Pia scoffed.

"Students, of course! That's my bread and butter. I sell them seats to go down to Barbados for a week's holiday. Sun, sand, booze, the lack of parental oversight; they love it!"

"Where do they stay, when they're there?"

"We, the company, we have a deal with a resort that's on the beach a bit south of Oistins. That's a small place halfway between the airport and Bridgetown. Most of the famous beaches are along the west coast, the Caribbean side north from Bridgetown, and you can't really go in the water on the east coast, the Atlantic side, because of the surf. We're on the southern tip, near Kendal Point, so the real estate is a lot cheaper."

"So, you can get a good deal?"

"Exactly. Plus, you get both the sunset and the sunrise. And the resort makes extra money because people who want to go to Bridgetown, or to Oistins for the fish fry, or anywhere really, have to rent cars or take local transport. Win-win."

"And if someone didn't want to leave the resort?"

"That's okay. There's a restaurant and a bar, and a couple of rum shops on the street outside if you want street food. The beach isn't as fancy as the ones further north, but it's got white sand, and it's safe for swimming."

Rashford nodded.

"It sounds tremendous. And you do this three times a year?"

"Yes. In the spring, at the end of the final exams. In late summer, just before classes start for the year. And in December, after the Christmas exams."

"How many people can you take?"

"The plane we charter is usually a 737, we sell a hundred and fifty-six seats and keep a dozen back for special guests."

"And how much is a ticket?"

"For the round trip, including accommodation at the resort, three hundred bucks."

Rashford scratched his head.

"Three hundred bucks, with a hundred and fifty-six people, that's less than fifty grand. How do you cover your costs?"

"It's enough. Like I said, the company negotiates good prices for services, so we do okay."

Rashford returned to the question which had been bothering him earlier.

"What does the plane do, for the week you don't need it?"

Pia shrugged.

"No idea," he said. "That's not my side of the business. My partner looks after that."

"Your partner?"

"Yeah. Dave Leblanc. Me and him went to school together. He looks after the plane; I just sell the seats. As long as the plane is at Saskatoon when the people are ready to leave, and at Bridgetown when they want to come back, then it's all good."

Rashford thought for a moment.

"I know you don't want to talk financial details," he said, "but are you set up as a double company, so you sell the seats, but in the first place you buy them from Dave?"

Pia nodded.

"Yeah. In and out accounting. It's all perfectly legal."

Rashford raised his arms to waist height, palms up.

"Oh, I'm not arguing that at all. But if you don't mind me asking, how much do you buy the seats for?"

Pia looked at him. He smiled.

"I do mind," he said. "But I don't think you'll give up. So, I'll tell you. Fifty bucks."

"Each?"

"Yes,"

"Plus, accommodation?"

"No, that's included. Dave deals with the resort. I told you; I just sell tickets."

"So, you sell a hundred and fifty tickets, three times a year, at a profit of two hundred and fifty bucks each?

"More or less."

"That gives you an income of over a hundred thousand dollars a year!"

"That's what my accountant tells me, yes."

Rashford stared at him.

"No wonder you can afford a BMW X-7," he said.

"Used, remember," Pia laughed.

***

The waiter appeared with their meals at that point, so they stopped talking and concentrated on the food. The Schnitzel was superb. The breadcrumb coating was crunchy, the egg layer not overpoweringly cheesy, and the veal itself tender and moist. The *Speckbohnen* was done in the traditional style, the freshly boiled beans glistening with butter and dotted with crisp fried onions and neatly trimmed squares of Speck. Only the potato salad had been adjusted to meet the tastes of the local community; Rashford had expected the mayonnaise, but was taken aback by the small, chopped pieces of dill pickle that made him scrunch up his eyes with each bite. He smiled to himself as he realized that Mandy was correct, as usual; the potatoes were cooked.

Pia ate methodically, stopping every so often to wash down his food with a drink of his blueberry and soda. He ate more slowly than Rashford, who finished first and then waited patiently until Pia placed his knife and fork together in the centre of the empty plate.

Rashford took a sip of his own drink.

"Good call for lunch," he said. "That was magnificent."

Pia nodded.

"Yes, this is one of the best places on the square. That and Trattoria d'Arno, the Italian place just up there."

He pointed with his chin to the restaurants behind Rashford, who nodded.

"Yes, Mandy took me there," he said.

Pia laughed.

"Loves her Italian, Mandy," he said. "That and her fiddle."

Rashford agreed.

"That's why she can't go on the graduation flight this spring," said Pia. "She's my cousin so I offered her one of the twelve special seats, up front in business class. Same price. But the band is going on tour."

"Mandy told me that your business partner, Dave Leblanc, he's that Slider character, right? One of the bikers."

Pia nodded.

"Yeah. Like I said, we went to school together."

"And then into business together?"

"Not straight away, no. I think Shyanne told you, I started university but then dropped out, too many parties. I was messing about, doing this and that, drinking a lot, when Mandy told me she was going back to university. She'd dropped out as well, earlier."

Rashford nodded.

"Yes, I know."

Pia glanced at him, looking like he was going to say something else then deciding against it. He coughed.

"Right. So, anyway, we decided we'd try it together. Going back to school. To motivate us, I quit drinking, and she quit smoking. Things went fine for a while; our marks were doing okay. Then I started hanging out with this group, a mix of Indigenous and international students."

"The IDIOTS," said Rashford, nodding.

"You know about them?" said Pia, surprised. He shrugged, then continued.

"Well anyway, I hung out with those guys a lot. I still wasn't drinking, but I wasn't studying either. My marks started to drop, and my first semester results were terrible. The second semester started out the same way, and I was starting to rethink my decision. One Friday in early

February, I was in the pub as usual, and Dave came over. He asked if he could see me, outside the pub, to 'discuss a business venture'. I said yes."

"This was what, four years ago?"

"About that, yes. We met the next week, at a coffee shop in town. He told me that Edward and some associates were setting up an import-export business, and because of that they would have an empty plane, and was I interested in selling seats to the students. Kind of as backfill for the flights. They figured I had better access to campus than they did, the bikers aren't very academic."

He laughed. Rashford drummed his fingers on the table.

"So, you sell the seats, but that's it. Everything else is organized by Leblanc?"

"I'm not stupid, you know," said Pia. "I figure that this is Edward's gig, he's just using Slider as a conduit to me because we know each other from school. But what do I care? I'm doing nothing wrong. I buy tickets from Slider's part of the company, sell them for a profit, and pocket the difference as income. I declare it and everything, even pay taxes. The rest is none of my business."

Rashford looked at him.

"You'd still be incriminated, if anything went sideways. Nobody would believe that you didn't know what was happening."

Pia shrugged.

"I'm sorry," said Rashford, "but I've got to ask this question. What's in it for them?"

"What do you mean?"

"Well, you're filling the plane for two of the four flights. What are they putting on the other two? What would they bring back from Barbados that makes it worthwhile? And what do they take back with them?"

Pia shrugged again, at the same time shaking his head.

"Don't act dumb, Pia. You know what I mean."

"Hey, I'm just a simple Indian, so maybe I'm being taken advantage of by those merciless white bikers. I thought I was helping my people, giving them the opportunity to move along in the world, to celebrate their successes. I didn't know I was being screwed. It wouldn't be the first time that's happened to my people."

Rashford laughed.

"Come on, Pia. The bikers are selling you a plane fare and accommodation combo for fifty bucks. I can see the attraction for you, but I repeat, what's in it for them?"

"Don't know and don't care," said Pia.

He lay his hands flat on the table and levered himself upright.

"We done here?"

Rashford nodded.

"Thanks for lunch," said Pia, and walked off, picking his way through the tables.

Rashford ordered a coffee to go, paid the bill and then followed Pia across the cobbles and past the food trucks. He sat on the wall by the bus shelter and lit a cigarette.

Chapter 20

Rashford had smoked two cigarettes and was just thinking about a third when his phone rang. He saw from the call display that it was Patrick York, so he answered it.

"How was your aunt?"

"What? Oh, she was fine. Thanks. What are you up to?"

"Nothing right now," said Rashford. "Just contemplating what to do with the rest of the day. If you're free, I wouldn't mind a chat. I've got a few questions that need answering."

"Maybe in an hour," said York. "I just got back and need to check a couple of things first."

"Sure," said Rashford. "It's almost three now. How about four o'clock somewhere?"

"How about six at the Three-Legged Rabbit? I'll be ready for a beer and something to eat by then."

"See you then," said Rashford, and hung up.

Carefully dismounting from the wall, he walked back along the road to his hotel. Once he was in his room, he took out his notebook and entered the gist of his conversation with Pia. Once that task was finished, he spent forty minutes reviewing his notes. Then, for the next two hours, he lay on his bed, his arms behind his head, and thought.

Patrick York was back in his gangster clothes, dressed in black and with his head freshly shaved. He was already sitting at the table, beers in front of him, when Rashford joined him just after six.

"Sorry I'm late," said Rashford, shaking hands. "I just went back to the SQ for a moment."

York stared at him.

"Really? Why?"

"I wanted to see if Bruce the gardener had planted those geraniums yet."

York looked puzzled.

"Okaaay," he said. "And has he?"

"Nope," said Rashford, raising his glass and taking a drink of beer.

York rolled his eyes.

"Okay, I'll bite," he said. "And that's important because ..."

Rashford shrugged.

"I'm not sure yet. How was Calgary?"

"Oh, it was fine, you know? Big city, long lost nephew visiting, my auntie laid on everything to make it a memorable day. We went to the Glenbow in the morning, then to the River Café for lunch. Wandered around Eau Claire, window shopped on Stephan Avenue, had dinner at the top of the Tower, in that revolving restaurant. Normal touristy stuff."

Uh-huh," said Rashford.

"You?"

Rashford put down his beer.

"Do you want to eat first, or talk?"

York paused, his glass halfway to his mouth.

"That sounds ... serious," he said, slowly.

"Oh, it is," said Rashford, nodding. "It will really spoil your appetite."

York nodded.

"I think it already has," he said, taking a mouthful of beer and then getting to his feet.

"I'll just go and get refills," he said. "It sounds like it might be a long night."

He put his half-finished glass on the table and walked towards the bar. Rashford watched carefully. He didn't think York would run, and if he did then he wasn't sure what he would do about it, but he need not have been bothered. York spoke to the young person behind the bar and returned with two pints of beer.

"They serve food until nine," he said, passing one glass to Rashford. "Will that give you enough time for all your questions?"

Rashford laughed.

"It depends on the answers I get," he said.

York rolled his head on his shoulders, then sat back straight in the chair, smiling.

"Go ahead, mon," he said.

Rashford took his time, looking steadily at York for over a minute before he spoke. Then he cleared his throat.

"You don't normally work undercover, do you," he said.

York stared back.

"Is that a statement or a question?"

Rashford smiled.

"Let's say it's a statement. People who work undercover ... sorry, police officers who work under cover, they're trained to keep personal information to a minimum. Not to tell lies. It gets too easy to make a mistake, to forget the details. That's what catches you out."

York said nothing.

"So, when you tell me that you are looking for your half-nephew, your wife's sister's son, and then you tell Shyanne that you're not married and have no family, then I get confused. When you tell me how upset you are with Linda Benoît making a play at you, because you're a happily married man, and then encourage Shyanne to give you a blow job, then I get confused."

"It sounds like maybe you should be confused with Shyanne," muttered York.

Rashford ignored him.

"When you're an academic who would prefer to organize a conference instead of talking about your research, I'm confused. When you're too busy with the conference to meet but then appear at an end-of-the-road pub in the middle of the evening, I'm confused. When you dash off to meet your auntie but according to the Calgary police never leave your room at the Westmount River Inn, I'm confused."

"I'm still not hearing any questions," said York.

"Oh, they'll come," said Rashford. "Once we set the context a bit. I've been making some phone calls while you were away, and I'd like to tell you a story."

York sighed, then sat back and folded his arms.

"I'm listening," he said.

"Once upon a time," said Rashford, angling his hands in front of him and touching his lips to the ends of his fingers, "the good people at the Royal Barbados Police Force headquarters building on Roebuck Street in Bridgetown had a conundrum. They were getting this plane load of students coming down three times a year, but their intelligence people told them that the costings didn't work. Or should I say, their undercover beach patrols told them that drunken students were bragging they got their flights and accommodations for three hundred bucks. Which didn't make sense.

"The bosses figured there had to be some scam going. Were the students being used as drug mules? Was there some sort of money laundering taking place? They put on extra dogs at the airport, they tried to infiltrate the parties, but they never got anywhere. Then some bright spark thought, what if it's not the students coming down that's the problem. What if it's the plane going back?"

He paused and looked across at Patrick York.

"How am I doing so far?"

York shrugged.

"It's a good story," he said.

Rashford smiled, then continued.

"Roebuck Street tracked the plane and decided that someone needed to come up here and have a look around. They knew from the Inter-Island Bulletin that Chad Sobers had gone missing, so that was a convenient cover story. They needed someone who was a bit brighter than your average cop, someone with a degree at least, someone who could fit in as a prof. Where did they find you, 'Fraud and Financials'?"

York shook his head.

"Pharmaceuticals," he said.

"Really?" said Rashford. "That's interesting. Why ...?"

"Pharmaceuticals make up over seven per cent of exports from the Island," said York. "Our chemists make medicines for prophylactic and therapeutical purposes and export them all over the world. We figured they must be smuggling them back up here, but we couldn't figure out why. So yes, I was sent to look into things."

Rashford nodded.

"I'm glad we agree on that," he said. "And I assume that your trip to Calgary was to debrief with someone?"

"Yes," said York. "Two someone's, actually. One who'd flown up from Bridgetown especially for the meeting, and one who'd driven across from here in their own car. I'd like to keep them confidential, if you don't mind. Operational security, you know."

"Fair enough," said Rashford. "What have you found out?"

"Further investigations at home have discovered a little enterprise that has been established off the books, as it were. Just along the beach from this resort where the students stay, in the cliffs near Kendal Point, we found a lab. Two fellows from one of the big pharmaceutical companies have set up shop there, adding hallucinogenic medicines to their prophylactic and therapeutic ones."

"Hallucinogenic?"

"Yeah. They'd figured out a way to take lysergic acid diethylamide and stabilize it in small enough doses that people had controlled trips."

"And then they were bringing it up here on the empty planes?"

York shook his head.

"They weren't as stupid as that, no. After dropping everyone off, the return flights were packed with legitimate exports like rum, fish, nuts, even authorized pharmaceuticals. Then the second flight, coming back to pick up the holidaymakers, was full of machinery like washing machines, fridges, farm equipment. Things we need but don't make."

"And the LSD?"

"We're not sure. We think they were putting it in panels on the plane, in the hold. Then using the same space on the way back for cash, which was being laundered on the island. We've got nearly fifty offshore banks, you know, they have to be kept fed."

"So, the passengers were basically ballast?"

"They provided some income to what would have otherwise been an empty plane, and I guess they provided some camouflage as well. But they weren't the main money-makers."

"Then why are you here?"

"I'm officially seconded to the Caribbean Financial Action Task Force. Cee fat eff is linking with your Financial Crime Unit on this one."

"Cee fat eff?"

"It's the way we say the acronym, CFATF."

"Oh, right," said Rashford, laughing.

There was a pause while the two men regarded each other. York broke the silence.

"Shall we order that food now?" he said.

They both ordered 'curried chicken and chips', a dish which apparently the Three-Legged Rabbit chef had imported from England. Rashford looked at his plate in surprise.

"Those are not chips, they're fries."

York sighed.

"In England, they're called chips."

"Well, what do they call chips, then?"

"Crisps."

"Weird."

Their server came over and asked if they would like any ketchup.

"On curry?" said York, horrified.

"Yes please," said Rashford.

Once they had each shaken their heads at the idiosyncratic culinary intransigence of the other, York continued their conversation.

"I was tasked with finding out as much as I could about how things work at this end. At first, I thought this was a gang thing, that Pia was the head of an Indigenous cartel that was running everything. Now, I'm not so sure."

"Really? Why not?"

York looked at him quizzically.

"Do you know something I don't?"

"No," said Rashford. "Actually, I agree with you. I'm just wondering what evidence you've got?"

"Well, from talking with Shyanne and others ..."

Rashford had never seen a black-skinned person blush. He tried not to smile. York coughed to hide his embarrassment.

"From talking with them, I figured out that all Pia does is sell cheap tickets. It's where he gets them from that I'm wondering about."

"I can help you there," said Rashford, and proceeded to explain the arrangements that Pia had made with Slider and the rest of the biker group.

"So, you think that Edward fellow is behind all this?" said York, once Rashford was finished.

"Perhaps," said Rashford. "I have no evidence, though."

York nodded.

"I agree," he said. "But I didn't know that before. Pia is the face of the operation, and so I've been trying to get close to him for a while. It was only when you hooked up with Shyanne that I saw the opportunity."

"You followed us to the pub?"

"Yeah. I got an Uber. He thought I was joking when I said, 'Follow that bus!'. Then I saw that it was a biker bar, so I waited outside for a bit. I thought maybe you'd made a mistake and would come out after one drink. When you didn't, I went in. And, well, you know the rest."

Rashford finished his beer and stood up.

"Refill?"

"No, I'm good, thanks."

Rashford went to the bar and replenished his glass, then returned to the table.

"What happened last Sunday, Monday morning, after Mandy and I left?"

York looked at him.

"Truth?"

Rashford nodded.

"Yes, please."

York cleared his throat.

"I don't usually drink," he said.

Rashford raised his eyebrows.

"Truth, not excuses."

York looked down, nodding.

"Fair enough. Okay, I'd had a couple of drinks at the bar, and then that wine at Shyanne's. We were sitting close together on the couch, and she sort of cuddled up to me. I put my arm around her."

"So, it was her fault?"

York scoffed.

"Hardly. Anyway, I had my arm around her and my hand sort of ended up touching her breast. It felt good, and she didn't complain, so I kept going."

"She said you were feeling her up."

"I guess I was. Not very professional, I know, and I regret it. But that's what happened."

"Then what?"

"Well, you and Mandy left, and there were just the four of us. I could see that Josee wasn't very impressed with me, she kept glaring at us while she was talking to Marc. But Shyanne and me ignored her. Eventually she stood up and said she was tired, and Marc said he'd walk her back to her place. She asked me if I wanted to go with them, but I didn't, and Shyanne said I could stay to finish my drink, so they left."

Rashford nodded.

York squirmed on his seat.

"Then Shyanne said that I looked uncomfortable, and she could help me with that."

"I'm not interested in the gory details," said Rashford. "My problem is, nobody has seen or heard from Josee since she left that house."

York stared at him.

"What? I didn't know that. Have you checked with Marc?"

Rashford barked a dismissive laugh.

"I've tried," he said. "He seems to have disappeared as well."

"What, both of them?"

"Well, not exactly."

Rashford explained the conversation he had had with Marc at the residence check-out, and the discoveries he'd made since then.

"So, what are you saying? That he was a con man?"

Rashford shook his head.

"No, I think he was hunting. And I think Josee became his prey."

"That's an awful lot of planning," said York.

Rashford agreed, then told the other man about his trip to the museum at the Faculty of Arts building.

"I think he must be a student somewhere," he said, "or perhaps even a prof. He knew enough about the way academic events work, and he knew how to do research. He was able to create a reasonable persona. I certainly believed him."

"Me too," said York. "Shit, mon, what are you going to do?"

"I'm not sure yet," admitted Rashford. "I've had a couple of other things on my plate. Including your missing step-nephew or whatever he is."

York bent his head.

"Yeah, sorry about that as well. He does exist, and his name is Chad Sobers, but he's no relation. He's just a missing person report and we're trying to figure out what happened to him."

Rashford nodded.

"Oh, I know he's real," he said. "I found him in the university records, remember. And so were the other two."

York scratched his chin.

"You don't think they're related to Marc and Josee, do you?"

Rashford shook his head.

"No, not at all. And I don't see a link to Pia and the travel agency either."

Both men were silent, drinking their beer. Once he had finished, Rashford put down his cup.

"Well, I'd better get back to it," he said. "It's going to be a busy couple of days."

"You're leaving this weekend, right?"

"Yes," said Rashford. "I have to go back to Regina; I've got a meeting first thing Monday."

"Do you fancy dinner on Saturday night?"

Rashford shook his head.

"Sorry, no. I have a previous engagement."

York laughed.

"Ah, with the Adorable Amanda, I guess!"

Rashford nodded.

"Yes. We're going to celebrate her finishing her exams and getting ready to graduate."

York inclined his head.

"That's good," he said. "We should celebrate things more. How about earlier? We could meet for coffee, or an early drink?"

Rashford looked at him.

"You just want to know what happens tomorrow," he said, laughing.

York spread his hands.

"What, me mon?"

Rashford stood up.

"Okay," he said. "Here at three o'clock, Saturday afternoon."

Chapter 21

Rashford slept late on Friday. He had nothing planned until the afternoon, so he decided to walk back along the river and think though what he knew, hoping to link some of the facts with his hunches and suppositions. The morning was cold, made raw by the perimeter winds from a Colorado Low which was bringing an April snowstorm to Regina. He walked briskly, seeing no other pedestrians, then returned to the hotel, made coffee, and called room service to order some lunch.

He was in the middle of a club sandwich when he received a text from Mandy telling him that she had just finished her last exam, and that she was looking forward to their date. He texted back to congratulate her but didn't want to spoil her mood and so decided not to mention the situation with Josee.

In the afternoon he re-read his notes, made some telephone calls, and generally planned what he was going to say to Gayle Morgan. Then he lay on his bed and watched a 24-hour news channel, waking up just after four. He quickly dressed and then went down to the lobby to wait.

Gayle Morgan arrived at five o'clock as planned and they parked her car in the hotel car park. It was a Pay and Display operation, but Gayle refused to buy a ticket for a marked police cruiser.

"Let's see who's got the nerve to tow me," she muttered.

The two of them drove to Linda Benoît's house, where they spent the early part of the evening sitting in Rashford's Jeep. They were in a leafy suburb where well-maintained houses stood behind well tended gardens. They had both agreed the Jeep would be less conspicuous than a police car, and they had watched as different women arrived, knocked on the door, and were admitted.

"That's four altogether," said Morgan. "Interesting. Do you know any of them?"

Rashford shook his head.

"No. The third one looked a bit familiar; I think I saw her at one of the conference things, but not the others."

Morgan turned to him.

"Ah, yes. How was the conference? I hear you found yourself a pretty young thing to play with. Is that true?"

Rashford blushed.

"I made a friend, yes."

He tried to change the subject.

"Talking of friends, how's Brian?"

"Don't change the subject," said Morgan. "This isn't about me."

Rashford ignored her.

"I thought you two were getting along," he said.

"So did I," said Morgan, exhaling a sad sigh. "Then I had to pull three double shifts in a row, we were having all sorts of problems with an environmental group targeting the oil derricks. For three days, all I basically did was went to work, and slept. I was knackered."

Rashford nodded.

"Been there," he said, remembering the constant grind of police work.

"Anyway, I got off late on the last night, so I thought I'd surprise him. I drove over and there was a strange car in the driveway, Manitoba plates. Yada yada yada. You can guess what happened."

Rashford heard the hurt in her voice.

"I'm sorry, I didn't mean to pry," he said.

Morgan sniffed.

"Whatever. He said he'd met her at the bar, she'd just been hired at the diner and had gone over to see if the pub had any rooms for rent. He told her she could stay in his spare room."

"Well, lots of people do that, share a house with someone," said Rashford. "It doesn't always mean there's something else going on."

Morgan nodded.

"True. But it seems she had no money, and the diner wouldn't pay her for two weeks, so she decided to pay her damage deposit and first month's rent in kind, as it were. When I went in, she was naked on the couch, and he was naked on top of her. I was still in uniform, and I think that at first, she thought I was some sort of dress-up party girl he had invited to join them. I soon corrected that impression."

"I bet you did," said Rashford, then had a thought.

"You didn't shoot her, did you?"

"Tempting, but no. I just stood watching while she beat her hands on his back, trying to make him stop. He thought she was egging him on, got quite the surprise when she eventually kneed him in the balls. That stopped him. He asked her what the hell she thought she was doing, then saw where she was looking, and turned round. I looked at him, then walked out."

"Did he follow you?"

Morgan huffed.

"Don't be so bloody daft! He was starkers, and I had a gun, he just wailed and wilted."

They sat together in silence, watching the house. The front room window had flimsy curtains made from a gauzy material and they could see people moving around inside. After a short time, they all sat down.

"They must be having dinner," said Rashford.

Morgan nodded.

"You're probably right. Anyway, about this fiddle player ..."

Although Morgan was the officer in charge of the case, it was Rashford's car, and he drove the first shift. He followed slowly behind the couple as they left Linda Benoît's house and ambled down the suburban street. It took them nearly twenty minutes, and at one stage Rashford pulled over so that Morgan could get out. He then drove off, past the couple, and waited in a side street while Morgan crossed the street and began walking in the same direction.

"They might suss the car," she had said, "but if I follow them on foot for a bit then that will break the pattern. If they get to wherever she's taking him then I'll call you, otherwise park up and we can switch for a bit."

Rashford saw the pair walk past the end of the cul-de-sac where he had chosen to park and walked to intercept Morgan as she crossed the end of the street.

"Here you go," he said, handing her the keys to his Jeep. He then sauntered off down the sidewalk, trying to look nonchalant and yet purposeful at the same time. He hoped that if either of them turned around, they would simply think him another robotic commuter, homeward bound from the bar after a long day. He also hoped that he was far enough away that Jeremy would not recognize him, should he decide to look back.

Jeremy had looked back, but only as he stood outside the town-house, waiting while the woman searched through her bag for the keys. Rashford was on the other side of the street, keeping his head down and trying to reduce his height by slumping his shoulders. He pulled his phone out of his pocket and held it to his ear, hoping that would further conceal his features. Jeremy ignored him, turning back as the woman opened the door and gestured him inside.

Rashford phoned Morgan and his car appeared in front of him, pulling alongside the cars parked by the curb and flashing its lights. He walked over and got into the passenger seat.

"Now what?" she said.

"Now we wait," said Rashford, "while that lady get's her money's worth."

"If he's anything like the guys I know, it won't be long," muttered Morgan, pulling out and then parking two gates up from the house to which Jeremy had escorted the woman.

The rain came suddenly, icy slivers blown on the prairie wind, and they watched the young man turn up his collar as he left the house. He moved as close to the garden walls and fences as the path would allow, trying in vain for some shelter. The early leaves on the trees were just starting to unfurl and did little to shield him from the deluge. The road was empty at this time of the evening, the only other movement coming from fast-food wrappers skittering across the asphalt. There were a few other cars parked along the street, wheels tight to the curb. A few distantly spaced streetlights provided a sickly yellow illumination.

"There he is," said Gayle Morgan, watching as the young man navigated small piles of dog faeces and the regurgitated remains of what looked, from their vantage point, like a Chinese meal. "About time, you know. I mean, four hours! What a show-off! It's after midnight, one of them should be a bloody pumpkin by now."

As Morgan straightened in her seat and reached over to start the engine, Rashford laid a hand on her arm.

"Wait for a minute," he said.

"Wait for what?" said Morgan.

"Just a hunch," he said, turning slightly so that he could look over his shoulder.

A set of headlights came on, and a vehicle pulled out of the line of parked cars behind them. As it drove slowly towards them, Rashford turned back and embraced Morgan tightly, kissing her passionately on the lips. For a moment she responded, closing her eyes, then opened them and pushed him away.

"You could at least look at me!" she said, "instead of out of the window."

"Mmmm, yes, sorry," said Rashford, watching the taillights of the white truck moving down the road ahead of them.

"Just wait another moment," he said.

He caught Morgan's glance.

"Please."

They watched as the pick-up approached Jeremy; his shadow suddenly clear in front of his as the headlights shone on his back. The truck slowed, matching his pace, and drew up alongside the pedestrian.

Jeremy looked across at the truck, seeming to hesitate, and then dashed across to the curb. He paused at the open window and spoke to the driver. The door opened and he climbed into the cab. The driver accelerated away, sheets of rain dancing through the headlights as the windshield wipers beat out the metronome of the night.

"Now we follow," said Rashford, settling back into his seat with a nod of satisfaction.

Morgan started the engine and pulled away from the curb.

Morgan kept a hundred metres behind the truck, slowing down as it approached traffic lights or intersections and then accelerating to keep it in sight. They drove into another residential area, this one characterized by single-family homes set on their own lots. Most had an attached garage, with a small, manicured lawn adjacent to the paved driveway.

The truck indicated, then turned into a single-story home where the lawn had been replaced with small shrubs and flower beds. The garage door rolled up and the truck drove inside. The brake lights flashed, then the door rolled down and closed. Morgan drove past the house and pulled into the next available parking space.

"Now what, Sherlock?" she said.

"Give him ten minutes," said Rashford.

They sat quietly, watching the house. A light came on in the living room, and then another, further back in the house. A car drove past them and pulled into a driveway, four houses away. The door opened and the interior light switched on, illuminating a young woman as she made to step out of the vehicle. The driver put his arm out and she leaned back in for a lengthy embrace, then pushed him away and disembarked. The driver said something, indistinctly, and they could hear her laughing as she ran up the drive, her jacket pulled over her head to protect her from the rain. The reversing lights came on and the car backed out into the road, then drove past them.

"He could have made sure she got inside safely," muttered Morgan. "She's not even at the door yet."

They watched as she fumbled in her purse for a key, then opened the door. A light came on in the hallway, then the door closed. After a few minutes an upstairs light appeared, then the hall light went out. They saw her enter the bedroom, taking off her shirt as she did so. She unclasped her bra and then stood for a moment, weighing her breasts in her hands.

"What's she doing?" said Rashford, bemused.

"Just checking she's still got it, I reckon," said Morgan. "There'll be a mirror there."

The woman suddenly seemed to realize that she was on full view to the street, and came to the window, drawing the blinds and turning into a silhouette.

"Show's over," said Morgan, nudging Rashford with her elbow. "Are our ten minutes up yet?"

"I reckon," said Rashford. "Let's go and see our friend."

Rashford stood to one side while Morgan rapped on the door. There was no response, so she knocked again, louder. This time a light came on in the hallway, and they heard footsteps. These stopped as the person approached the door.

"Yes, what is it?" said a voice.

"Police," said Morgan. "Open up, please. We'd like a word."

There was a moment of silence.

"Police? Can't it wait until tomorrow? It's not very convenient right now."

"We'd appreciate a few minutes of your time now, please," said Morgan. "It's quite important, sir."

She rolled her eyes at Rashford, who nodded supportively. There was a longer silence, then they heard the noise of a deadbolt clicking open. The door opened a fraction, still attached to a security chain.

An older man in a white undervest peered out.

"Can I see some identification, please," he said.

"Of course, sir, can't be too careful these days. Here you go."

She held her laminated police identification up to the crack in the door. The man nodded.

"Just a second," he said, closing the door and unlatching the chain.

He opened the door properly and looked at her through the screen door.

"Yes?"

"Inside would be better, sir," said Morgan. "Instead of us standing outside where all the neighbours can hear."

"Us?"

Rashford stepped into the light.

"Yes, this is Mr. Rashford, my colleague," said Morgan.

Rashford nodded.

"It will only take a few minutes, sir," he said.

The man huffed, hesitating, then opened the door.

"Very well," he said. "It's one in the morning! What do you want?"

They stepped inside the small entry hallway, their very presence crowding the man so that he stepped backwards, into a small living room. His white singlet was stained yellow in a few places, with tufts of white chest hair poking from the neck. He had on a pair of black trousers, held up by a pair of old-fashioned braces, and comfortable carpet slippers.

The room was tidy, with nothing out of place. There was a single chair, placed so as to face a large television mounted on the wall, and a row of glass fronted curio cabinets along another wall. A tall pink amaryllis plant stood to one side of the television, a pot of purple lavender to the other. A small dining table with two chairs completed the furniture. Rashford stood just inside the door while Morgan walked over and looked inside the cabinets.

"You collect china dogs, sir?" she said.

The man looked from one to the other, confused.

"Yes, I do. But they're pugs, not dogs. Is that what you wanted to talk about?"

Rashford grunted.

"No, sir. We're here to check on the well-being of Jeremy Beals."

The man looked at him.

"Who?"

"And what's your name, please, sir?" said Morgan.

He turned to her.

"Smithson. Bruce Smithson."

He looked back at Rashford and spread his arms.

"There must be some mistake," he said. "I've never heard of anyone called Jeremy whatever."

Rashford stepped forward, crowding the man's space even further.

"That's strange," he said. "We just saw you pick him up and drive him into your garage."

"Not ten minutes ago," said Morgan.

The man looked frantically from one to the other.

"Wait. You mean the hitch hiker? I don't know his name."

Morgan looked at Rashford.

"Hitch hiker?" she said.

"Well, I ... It's not a crime, is it?"

"It is if you were soliciting," said Rashford, grimly.

"No, I wasn't. I was just driving. If you saw me, then you will have seen that. It was raining. I offered him a lift, that's all."

Rashford looked around.

"Where is he, then?"

The man seemed surer of himself now. He stood a bit straighter.

"In the truck, we got to talking, and ... well, we realized we like the same things. So, I invited him to ... umm ... to stay over."

"He's in the bedroom, then?" said Morgan, going through the doorway into a small hall which led towards the back of the house. There was a kitchen visible through one open door, with two doors opposite. They were both closed. She knocked on the panel of the first door.

"Mister Beals?"

There was no answer. She turned back to Smithson and raised her eyebrows.

He wrung his hands, and Rashford noticed that a sheen of sweat had appeared on his upper lip.

"He's not there."

Morgan waited.

"He's ... umm ... in the playroom."

"The playroom?" said Morgan. "Interesting. And where is that?"

Smithson deflated again. He looked miserably at the second door and nodded.

"Down there," he whispered. "It's in the basement."

Morgan went to open the door and Smithson moved towards her. Rashford stepped up quickly and laid his hand gently on the man's arm.

"We'll stay here, shall we, sir?" he said, but it wasn't really a question.

Morgan opened the door. Light spilled out into the hallway, and she carefully went down the stairs, descending out of sight.

Smithson turned to Rashford, tears starting to well up in his eyes.

"We were just going to have a bit of fun," he said.

Morgan walked into the police station canteen and slumped into a chair. Rashford pushed a paper cup of coffee across the table.

"Thanks," she said, taking a sip and then pulling a face. "God, this is awful!"

"It's all they've got," said Rashford. "Probably been here since the night shift went on duty five hours ago."

"Yuck."

She put down the cup and looked across at him.

"I think we're going to have to let him go," she said.

Rashford stared at her.

"What? Why? We have him bang to rights."

"That's not the way the lawyer sees it."

"What do you mean? Jeremy was tied naked to a cot, spreadeagled, gagged and blindfolded. That's got to be common assault at least."

"Smithson says he asked for it, he volunteered to that. It was all part of a sex game."

"Garbage! Jeremy says he forced him down there."

"The lawyer says it's a case of 'he said, he said', find some evidence or let my client go. Hard to beat that."

Rashford lunged to his feet and started to pace around the small room, bumping into tables and chairs in his anger.

"Fuck fuck fuck," he said.

Morgan remained seated.

"The only evidence we have is the polaroid photograph that was on the floor next to the cot. In that picture, Jeremy is sitting on the cot with one arm tied to the bedpost. And he's smiling."

Rashford stopped and threw out his arms.

"Yes, I saw that. And so did Jeremy. He says it's not a smile, he was terrified, it just looks like a smile."

"Again, he said, versus he said. Not evidence."

"What about the tiled floor and walls, and the hose pipe hanging next to the tap?"

"The lawyer suggests that's because Smithson is a gardener and starts his new seeds down there, so he needs to be able to wash all the dirt away when he's finished potting on."

Rashford stomped once more around the canteen.

"And the secateurs and utility knives hanging on the wall?"

"Same thing. Common gardening tools, apparently."

"But we saw him wait for him and pick him up!"

"No, we didn't. We saw the truck pull up in the rain, we saw them talk to each other, we saw Jeremy get in the truck. Willingly. There was no coercion."

"Fuck shit fuck."

Morgan stood and went to him, reaching up to put her arms on his shoulders.

"We need more, Gavin," she said. "Right now, we don't have anything to hold him."

Rashford gently took her hands off his shoulders, walked to the side of the canteen, and banged his forehead against the wall.

"Fuck shit fuck shit fuck."

"Pollard will charge you for it, if they have to redo the gyprock," said Morgan, laughing.

She walked to the door.

"I'm going to go down and release him with a caution," she said. "He'll be more careful in future; he knows we're onto him now."

"What about Jeremy?"

"The duty doctor has checked him, he's physically okay, just a bit shaken up. One of the uniforms will run him back to his residence."

"Can I talk to him?"

"Later. We'll let this settle down first."

Rashford nodded.

"We need to have a chat with Professor Benoît, as well," he said.

"Not now, no. Perhaps tomorrow, or rather later today, when we've all had some sleep. Wait here. When I've finished with Smithson you can drop me off at my car on your way to the hotel."

The next morning Rashford slept in until his watch alarm woke him at nine-thirty. Morgan had dropped him back at the hotel just before four, but it had taken some time for his anger to dissipate enough that he could sleep. Throwing his sheets to the floor, he went straight into the shower and turned it as cold as possible. Awake, if not refreshed, he dressed and went to the hotel restaurant for breakfast. He was not amused to find that they had stopped serving at ten and would not be open for lunch until noon. He found an urn that still had some luke-warm coffee and poured a cup. Grumbling to himself, he went outside into the parking lot, where he drank it while smoking a cigarette.

His 'breakfast' complete, he walked back up the road until he came to the university. He went to the residence, but the front door was locked and there were no students around to let him in. Unlike him, for them Saturday morning was a lazy affair.

Feeling frustrated at every turn, he made his way to the Three-Legged Rabbit. This was open, and he was able to order a fresh coffee and a bacon sandwich. There were only a few other customers, so he sat at what he now considered 'his' table and ate a solitary meal. 'Just like a Hobbit', he thought, 'having my second breakfast'. The idea cheered him, and he smiled as he called Gayle Morgan to tell her where he was.

He was on his fourth cup of coffee when she pulled up outside the pub and blipped her siren. A few of the other diners looked up, and one made a rapid exit towards the gentlemen's toilets at the rear of the building, but most ignored Rashford as he paid his bill and made his way to the door.

CHAPTER 22

"Good morning," said Morgan, "did you get any sleep?"

"A bit. You?"

"Not really."

They drove in silence for a while.

"Do you know where we're going?" said Rashford.

Morgan glanced at him.

"The professor's house. Where we went yesterday, where they had dinner."

He looked back at her.

She huffed.

"Honestly, Gavin, you're not the only one with special powers! When I've been somewhere, I pay attention, and I can usually find it again."

He kept silent as she navigated a series of intersections, including one where an elderly lady pushing a small shopping cart was still on the road when the light turned green.

"Three points if she doesn't bounce," muttered Rashford.

Morgan smiled.

"Extra points if I get the wally wagon as well," she said.

The exchange broke the ice between them, and they spent the next five minutes talking about Bruce Smithson.

"Mebbe he is just a punter who got lucky," said Morgan. "We've got nothing on him except for Jeremy saying he was coerced. And that was only after the fact. We never saw that. He might well have been only offering him a ride in the rain, and then they decided to play some games."

"You don't really believe that?"

She shrugged.

"I've seen now't to prove otherwise," she said.

They pulled into the street where Linda Benoît lived and drove slowly down until they reached her house. Morgan parked the cruiser in the driveway, behind a lime green Fiat 500 Cabrio. She looked at it with disdain.

"Why would you drive something that colour?"

Rashford shrugged.

"Easy to find it in a parking lot at the mall," he said.

Morgan nodded.

"Still, hard to make an illicit visit somewhere. Everyone would know where you were."

Rashford shook his head.

"You really surprise me sometimes."

"Me? Why?"

"The way your mind works, for one."

Morgan laughed.

"You gotta cover all the angles, Gavin," she said.

They looked at the house.

"Do we have a plan?" said Rashford.

"Let me lead," said Morgan. "You just hover and look menacing."

Rashford nodded.

"Okay," he said. "But before you get to talking about Jeremy, can I ask them a couple of questions first? I'll soften them up for you."

Morgan pondered this for a moment.

"Only a couple," she said. "I want to get this nailed down today."

"Scout's honour," said Rashford, holding two fingers up to his ear in a mock salute.

Linda Benoît led them into their tidy living room and offered coffee. They were dressed in what Rashford supposed were their 'relaxing clothes', brown corduroy trousers paired with a red and white checked shirt. It reminded him of the tablecloths at the Trattoria d'Arno, and he checked his watch. Morgan raised her eyebrows.

"Need to be somewhere?" she whispered.

"Not until later," he said.

He looked around the room. There were two matching leather recliners in a shade of light tan which he could not name, a two-person couch with grey cushions, and a straight-backed wing chair covered in a burgundy fabric. A television was mounted on one wall, with a long bookcase extending beneath it. There was a large painting of a nude woman on one wall, and an abstract on another. Rashford walked over to the bookshelves and scanned the titles, noting that most were mystery novels by authors whose names he recognized.

Benoît returned with a tray carrying a French press, three cups and saucers in a matching Blue Willow pattern, a small jug of milk, three teaspoons, and a bowl of sugar cubes. They placed the tray carefully on the small table.

"Please, sit down," they said, arranging the cups and saucers and pouring the coffee. "I'll let you add your own mixings."

They poured some milk into their own cup and took one of the recliners. Morgan went to the wing-back chair, so Rashford lowered himself onto the couch. They each held their coffee cup carefully.

"So, how can I help you?" said Benoît, pleasantly.

Rashford looked at them.

"I have a couple of questions of a personal nature," he said. "I'd like to ask those first, please."

Benoît raised their eyebrows.

"How intriguing," they said.

Rashford put his cup and saucer on the table.

"I was at the conference last week," he said.

Benoît nodded.

"I knew I'd seen you somewhere. We met after the MacDowell lecture. And you were at Ben McHale's talk."

Rashford nodded.

"That's right. During the conference, I met a young woman, a mature student. She seemed very pleasant. Then I heard some rather negative things about her, so I thought I'd ask for your opinion. Before I, umm, pursue things further, as it were."

Benoît looked from Rashford to Morgan, and back.

"We have a lot of students," they said. "I couldn't possibly know them all."

Rashford scoffed.

"No, no, of course not. But I think you know this one."

"Curiouser and curiouser," said Benoît. "Do continue."

"Amanda Robicheau," said Rashford, watching closely to see the response. Benoît paled and shook their head slightly.

"Yes, I know that one," they said, quietly.

Rashford waited.

"She first started at university here about fourteen or fifteen years ago. We were all much younger then, of course. Things did not go well for her. She was very promiscuous and left before Christmas. Ten years later she came back and tried again. She appeared a lot calmer."

Benoît paused and drank some coffee.

"In the first semester of her third year, she took my Contemporary Poetry class and did very well. I had great hopes for her. Then, after Christmas, she got back to her old ways and started having relationships. Towards the end of the second semester, she came storming into one of my first-year classes, screaming that I had taken her lover. It was terribly embarrassing, both for me and for her."

Rashford nodded.

"That would have been your Introduction to Language class, I assume?"

Benoît raised their eyebrows.

"You are remarkably well-informed, officer, Yes, that is correct."

"Thank you. Perhaps you could tell us what happened when Ms. Robicheau came into your class?"

"I asked her to leave, of course. She refused, and started shouting at the students, telling them that I taught poems of love and beauty but practised sex and debauchery."

Benoît looked up, sadly.

"I'm afraid I lost my temper," they said. "I slapped her face and told her that at least I hadn't spread my legs for everyone I met, and that my nickname wasn't Randy Mandy."

Rashford stared at them.

"How did she react?"

Benoît shrugged.

"She went very still, very pale. Then she said, 'I'll get you for this, you fucking bitch,' and left the classroom."

"Have you spoken with her since?" said Rashford.

"No. I've seen her around campus, of course, but we haven't spoken."

Gayle Morgan coughed and interrupted.

"I think that's enough of that topic," she said. "Do you agree, Staff Sergeant?"

Rashford nodded.

"Excellent," said Morgan. "Thank you."

She turned to Benoît.

"My turn," she said. "Perhaps you can start by telling us about Jeremy Beals."

***

"Jeremy?"

Benoît laughed.

"A lovely young man. He is ... was my teaching assistant."

"Was?"

"Yes. The semester has finished now, and so have his duties."

"I understand that his duties were somewhat ... varied?"

"The normal range, I think. The big difference was the conference we had last week. He helped me with that."

Benoît looked at Rashford.

"You were there, I know. You saw him."

"Correct. Actually, I also presented at the conference."

"Yes! That's right. I'm sorry, please remind me. What was your subject?"

Morgan coughed.

"Excuse me. Perhaps we can remain on topic ..."

Benoît glanced at her.

"We are on topic, Senior Constable. Your colleague here witnessed Jeremy in action, engaged in what you rather dismissively refer to as 'varied responsibilities'."

Morgan smiled. Rashford thought it was a very good imitation of the barracuda smile perfected by Chief Superintendent Pollard. 'Here we go', he thought.

"Actually," said Morgan, "I was referring to his duties at your weekly dinner parties. Would you like to tell me about those?"

Benoît flushed.

"Oh, that was just a bit of fun. I needed some help serving my guests."

"Serving or servicing?"

"Excuse me?"

Morgan smiled again.

"Come now, professor. We all know that you were pimping him out. Why shouldn't I charge you with living off the avails of prostitution?"

Benoît went white.

"What? Living off ... I didn't pimp him!"

Morgan waited.

"He just served the food. Nothing else."

"And afterwards?"

"What?"

"Afterwards, he walked them home."

Benoît nodded.

"Yes. But that was all. If there was anything else, I didn't know about it."

Rashford glanced towards Morgan and received a small nod. He leaned forward.

"That's not quite true, is it, Professor? He had to work for his 'A'."

Benoît looked rapidly from one to the other.

"I've heard all about the contract," said Rashford, gently. "The women paid you for his services, didn't they?"

Morgan spoke, her voice hard.

"Just like they had for the others, right? For Manny, Chad, Simon …"

Benoît sat back in the chair. When they spoke, their voice was quiet.

"My friends made a donation. To a charity."

Morgan resumed the questioning.

"Which you then forwarded to the charity?"

Benoît nodded.

"Yes," they said, in a relieved voice. "There's nothing wrong with that, is there?"

Morgan smiled.

"In that case, perhaps the charge should be fraud. You got a tax receipt for money that wasn't yours."

Benoît looked shocked.

"No! No."

There was a long pause. Morgan and Rashford sat patiently.

"I kept it," Benoît whispered.

Morgan shrugged.

"Still fraud, then," she said, "plus theft. If you told them you were going to make a donation, but instead kept the cash."

Benoît started to cry.

"We know about your sexuality," said Rashford, gently. "This is all related to that, isn't it?"

Benoît nodded, sniffling.

"Why don't you tell us how this all worked," said Rashford.

Benoît took a tissue from a pocket and noisily blew their nose, then wiped their eyes. They looked across at Morgan, who nodded encouragingly.

"Go on," she said.

"As you've already guessed, I'm a person in transition," said Benoît. "It's a difficult time."

Morgan sat with folded arms, expressionless. Rashford nodded.

"Yes," he said. "It must be. Is that why you kept the money?"

Benoît looked at him.

"Yes. I'm saving up for my surgery. It's going to be really expensive, thousands of dollars. Jeremy was going to be the last one. I've saved enough now, and I've got an appointment booked. It's in three weeks, once I've finished marking."

Morgan and Rashford glanced at each other. Rashford spoke quietly to Benoît.

"Sorry," he said. "I'm afraid you'll have to tell them you've made other plans."

"What? Why?"

Rashford shrugged.

"Unless you tell us the truth, the whole truth, then this investigation could take months."

Benoît was silent. Rashford and Morgan waited.

After three minutes had passed, Morgan started to get up from her chair. Benoît looked at her.

"No, wait," they said. "I'll tell you everything."

Morgan sat back down.

Benoît cleared their throat.

"As I said, I need the money for my surgery. I've legally changed my gender, all my paperwork is correct now, but I need to medically transition as well. This is not on our health coverage, not here in Alsama. It used to be covered, back when I lived in Ontario, but it's not here."

"Can you even get the operation here?" said Rashford.

"I don't know," said Benoît. "I never checked. This is a small place; everyone would soon know if I started asking those kinds of questions. No, I'm going down to the States for the operation."

Rashford nodded.

"Go on," he said.

"A few years ago, I had this idea. I started having dinner parties, and I got a student to help me."

"The one you called a 'teaching assistant'?"

"Yes. That way they could get some benefit, I could give them a good grade."

Rashford nodded.

"Did they understand everything that would be involved?"

"Oh, yes. 'No surprises', that's my motto. I invited three or four possible candidates to a pre-Christmas luncheon and explained what I was doing. Then I let them think about it over the holidays. They were asked to give me their answer at the beginning of the next semester, and that's when I would choose."

Morgan broke in, shaking her head.

"So, you picked your gigolo and then you sold tickets to these, these dinner parties?"

"He wasn't a gigolo! And no, not exactly. I asked for donations."

Morgan shook her head.

"That's the bit I can't figure out," she said. "How did this determine who he got to 'walk home', as you euphemistically put it?"

Benoît made a big sigh.

"There are twelve weeks in a semester, right? Thirteen really, but the middle one is the reading week break, when the students can go away and relieve their tensions. They're supposed to be studying for their mid-term exams but few of them do, they just party. I invite twelve friends to my first dinner party, in January. They get to meet what I call our 'special waiter.' He's the person who is my teaching assistant for the semester. At the end of the meal, I give them each an envelope with their name on it. They leave it in a bowl by the door as they are leaving."

"With a donation inside?"

"Some of them, yes. Some don't bother, they're not interested in my choice of special waiter. The ones who do leave a donation are invited back the next week. The others are not."

"What if everyone leaves a donation?"

"Then the one who left the smallest amount is not invited back."

Morgan nodded.

"So, week two will have eleven guests?"

"Yes. Sometimes fewer."

"And then what?"

Benoît shrugged.

"We eat and talk, just a normal dinner party. They get a chance to interact with the special waiter, get to know him a little bit. At the end of the meal, they get another envelope and decide whether or not to leave a donation. This continues until the seventh dinner, or until the group is down to six members. Two get eliminated that week."

"Leaving four guests for week eight?" said Morgan.

"Yes."

They were silent, looking down at the floor.

"And then?" nudged Rashford, gently.

"Then the rules change. Each of the guests still leaves a donation, but the lowest bidder gets to be walked home."

Rashford and Morgan looked at each other.

Morgan cleared her throat.

"And, umm, does the lowest bidder get to come for dinner the following week?"

"For dinner, yes, but only to share stories."

Benoît blushed.

"If they want to, of course. But they're not allowed to bid again, unless we have a very small group."

"So, normally, in week nine there are three bidders, and week ten only two?"

"Correct."

"So, that must mean that in week eleven, the last person, the one who had lost because they bid highest in week ten, automatically wins?"

"Correct."

There was a silence.

"It's quite strategic," said Benoît. "That's what makes it fun."

Morgan looked at them,

"Strategic? How?"

"Well, if you're the lowest bidder for week eight, you get to 'set the bar', as it were. Plow new ground. Make things memorable. But if you're one of the later winners, especially if it's week eleven, then you get to benefit from all the little tricks he might have learned from the others."

Morgan exhaled softly and sat back in her chair. Rashford leaned forward.

"What happens on week twelve?" he said.

Benoît smiled at him and raised their hands.

"That's the bonus week," she said. "The special waiter chooses who he wants to walk home."

Morgan was still shaking her head as they returned to the patrol car. She opened the back door and unceremoniously helped Benoît climb inside. The door closed with a click as it locked.

Morgan turned to Rashford, who was standing by the front of the car.

"Absolutely un-fucking-believable," she said.

Rashford laughed.

"Theft under five thousand dollars. Do you think that will stick?"

"I've no fucking idea what else to charge them with. Pimping? Fraud? Common mischief?"

Rashford looked at her.

"Mischief?"

"Yeah. Conning those women that there was strategy involved! They were just trying to maximise their profit. Sorry. Maximise the donations."

"Did they say how much has been raised?"

"No. I'll get all that on Monday. At least with this charge they can't leave town and have got the weekend to think about things. I'm taking them in, do you want a lift?"

Rashford looked at his phone.

"It's only one," he said. "I'm meeting a fellow at three, so I'll walk back to campus. I could do with the exercise.

Morgan nodded.

"See you around," she said, getting into her car. "Thanks for the assist on this one."

She drove off and Rashford walked slowly through the suburban estate, admiring the ingenuity that had been invested in some of the small gardens. He was crossing the large quadrangle when he saw Patrick York, who was following one of the other diagonal paths. He waited for him at the Notice Rock and shook hands.

"Still fancy a coffee?" said Rashford.

"I need a smoke first," said York.

***

The secret quadrangle was empty. They sat at the table and Rashford explained that the search into the missing men was still continuing, but that another scam had been unearthed and an arrest made.

"Senior Constable Morgan is happy," he said, "she's got a good arrest. At the same time, it's not clear whether this other guy is involved at all, or whether it was just a coincidence that he picked up Jeremy the other night."

"It's all smoke and no mirrors," muttered York. "Me, I don't like coincidences."

"Me neither," said Rashford. "Anyway, what have you been up to?"

York lit a second cigarette, then expanded further on his investigation.

"We're not going to tip our hand," he said. "When the next plane arrives, we'll let things proceed as normal, and then once everyone has disembarked, we'll do the normal random testing. We might focus on the people in those business class seats, though. If anyone is a courier, it's them. Then, when the plane is ready to leave, we'll have an unannounced safety check. But if we find anything, we'll just photograph it and leave it. Then when the plane comes back a week later to pick everyone up, we'll have a proper look inside."

Rashford nodded.

"That sounds like a plan," he said. "Will you tell the Mounties if you think there's something of interest on the first return flight?"

"Of course. That was what we spent most of Wednesday talking about. Some people from your firm came and we argued over whether they should do a big raid or not. We agreed that they'll track and trace but not move in until after the second flight. That way we can wrap this up properly."

"Do you think it's the bikers?"

York shrugged.

"I think it has to be. At the bar, they seemed to be looking out for Pia and his friends, the Indian and Métis folk. The bikers I know don't usually give a shit about anyone else. I'm guessing they were protecting their investment."

Rashford nodded.

"They used the school connection to get Slider close to Pia, then set him up with a pretty sweet deal."

"Yeah. He must have figured something was going on, but he decided not to ask questions. They were hiding in plain sight."

Rashford nodded. He looked around the quadrangle, noting that the planter box was still empty. A second bag of compost was leaning up against the wooden frame, blocking his view of the folded-up stepladder and the spade. Suddenly, he clicked his fingers.

"Hiding in plain sight?" he said, excitedly. "Of course."

He jumped to his feet and pulled his phone from his pocket, hitting the keys with passion. York looked up at him.

"What's up, mon?"

Rashford waved at him to be quiet, then spoke into his phone.

"Gayle. It's Gavin. Where are you?"

He listened to the response, tapping the fingers of his left hand rapidly against his leg.

"Okay. ... Okay. Listen, can you get to the university ASAP, please? And bring a couple of constables with you."

He listened again.

"I'll tell you when you get here. See you at the Three-Legged Rabbit. Twenty minutes? Great."

York looked at him with a question in his eyes.

Rashford shrugged.

"Just a hunch," he said.

CHAPTER 23

R ashford and York were standing outside the Three-Legged Rabbit when Morgan arrived, followed by a second police car. Two constables emerged from this vehicle and joined her in the car park.

"This better be good," she said. "I was still processing Benoît."

York stared at her, then at Rashford.

"Lin-Lin?" he whispered.

"Later," said Rashford, then spoke to Morgan.

"It's just a hunch but if it proves correct then yes, this will be worth it," he said. "Anyway, I think they're linked."

He turned and led the way to the door marked 'Garden tools for repair: Maintenance Personnel only' and pushed it open. Inside he paused and picked two spades from the collection of tools hanging on the wall, handing one to each of the constables.

"Follow me," he said, walking down the bleak corridor and then leading them out into the secret quadrangle. Morgan stopped and looked around, taking in the details. She nodded towards the picnic table and bucket ashtray.

"This your secret lair, Gavin, is it?" she said.

He shook his head.

"Not mine, a lot of people know about it. But only one person works on that planter over there."

He pointed towards the wooden structure, which still had two 60L bags of potting soil leaning against the side.

"Who's that?" said Morgan. "Is Professor Benoît a secret gardener?"

"Sort of," said Rashford. "She built and pays for this container, but she doesn't do the work."

Morgan gazed at him, her head to one side.

"Go on, I'll bite. Who does the gardening, Gavin?"

"Bruce Smithson," he said.

She rocked back on her heels, then looked at him carefully.

"And you think this is important because …"

He shrugged.

"Let's go and have a look," he said.

The group walked across the grass and arrived at the container. Rashford picked up the stepladder and opened it to its full shape, then stood it next to planter. He gestured to the two constables.

"Up you go," he said. "One at each end. Dig slowly and carefully."

The constables looked at each other, and then at Morgan. She nodded and held out her hands to receive the two spades.

"You first," said the taller constable, an athletic looking Black woman, and stood back while her shorter, fatter, and older ginger-haired colleague climbed the stepladder. Once he was balanced at the top, she joined him, and Morgan passed up the spades. They started to dig, then stopped.

"Where shall we put the dirt, Ma'am?" asked the woman. Morgan looked at Rashford.

"Wait," he said, and walked back across the grass to the door through which they had entered. A few minutes later he came back with a folded tarpaulin, which he proceeded to spread on the grass.

"Throw it on here," he said. "Carefully! If I'm right, there might be all sorts of trace evidence."

The constables took it in turns to shovel a spade full of earth and carefully decant it onto the tarpaulin. Morgan, Rashford, and York watched intently. Other than the sound of digging, the Secret Quadrangle was silent.

The taller police officer suddenly straightened, holding her spade down to soil level.

"Ma'am?" she said.

Morgan looked at her, then went to the stepladder and climbed up. The officer held out her spade. There, sticking out from the mound of soil, was a bone.

"Shit," said Morgan, then looked down at Rashford.

"Mebbe your hunch was right," she said.

"Now what happens?" said York.

He and Rashford were sitting at the corner table in the bar of the Three-Legged Rabbit, both having decided that a beer was more suitable than a coffee. Morgan had taken the female police officer with her to arrest Bruce Smithson and left the shorter one to guard the planter until the Forensics team arrived. Rashford, she had implied, would simply get in the way.

Rashford shrugged.

"Forensics will excavate the planter properly, then we'll ask Mister Smithson to explain himself. If my hunch is correct, there will be at least three sets of human remains in there."

"Including Chad?"

Rashford nodded.

"Sadly, I think so."

"What's Lin-Lin got to do with this?"

Rashford explained about the dinner parties, and how it seemed that Smithson had followed the couple to the lady's house, then picked up the student on his way home.

"What, this guy knocked them off after their last dinner party, then buried them? Why?"

"Sorry, Patrick, you know the drill. I'm not going to speculate. This is all something that will come out in the investigation. And if they think Chad Sobers is involved, they'll be asking your guys to provide some DNA."

"Right."

They sat quietly, sipping their beer. York looked up from his glass.

"Can you tell me, what made you think of this? Not speculation on what they might find, but what led you to your hunch?"

"I couldn't understand why the geraniums hadn't been planted. If Smithson was the only person allowed to put things in the planter, why wasn't that done? Every other year, they were planted the Sunday after the end of semester. The only thing different was that Professor Benoît's final dinner party had been postponed for a week. But what was the link between those two things? It didn't even click when we picked him up yesterday, in the act of taking Jeremy to his basement. Then you said something about 'hiding in plain sight', and everything just came into focus."

"Glad to help, mon," said York, laughing.

Rashford drained his beer.

"Thank you," he said. "Now, I have a date to get ready for, so if you'll excuse me, I'm out of here. I'm heading back to Regina tomorrow so, if I don't see you again, good luck. Keep in touch, eh? You've got my number."

York got to his feet.

"Thanks," he said, shaking hands. "I'm staying around until the plane leaves. Plus, I've got to go and see Shyanne, see if I can help with finding Josee. I'll keep you posted."

Rashford nodded, then turned and left the bar.

At seven o'clock he knocked lightly on the door to Mandy's apartment. She opened it almost immediately and threw her arms around his neck.

"Hello, you," she said, giving him a long and passionate kiss.

Rashford held the clinch, then put his hands on her shoulders and pushed her away. He looked at her with a smile.

"Hello yourself," he said. "How were your exams?"

She lifted his arms, then deftly slipped around so that she was leaning with her back against his chest. She lowered his arms to her waist, then tilted her head back and sighed.

"The exams were fine, I think," she said. "I'll find out next week. As long as I passed all my courses, so I can graduate, I'll be happy. It's this awful news about Josee that's upsetting me."

Rashford tightened his grip.

"You heard, then?"

Mandy shivered.

"Yes. Yesterday afternoon. I always turn my phone off for exam week, everybody knows that. It's the only way I can focus. I don't do e-mail either. So, when I finished my last exam, I turned on my phone and found I had all these messages from Shyanne, asking me to call her. I called her and she told me. I went over yesterday and stayed last night."

Rashford nodded.

"It's an awful situation," he said. "We have no idea where she might have gone."

"Do you think she's with Marc?"

"We have no idea about that either, I'm afraid."

Mandy shivered and choked back a sob. Rashford held her tightly.

"Do you still want to go out tonight?" he said, gently.

Mandy stiffened slightly.

"Of course," she said, her voice breaking. "I came back and got ready especially. You don't want to cancel on me, do you?"

Rashford squeezed her again.

"No, it's all organized and booked," he said. "But only if you want it."

She reached up and put her hand on the back of his head, then pulled him down so he was nuzzling her neck.

"Oh, I want it," she said, breathily.

He raised his hands from her waist to her breasts, slowly squeezing them through her dress and flicking his thumbs.

"I really want it," she whispered, rolling her shoulders against his chest.

He kissed her neck then lifted his lips and nibbled on her ear. She moaned.

Dropping his hands, he slapped her on both buttocks.

"Later," he said, laughing. "We have a dinner reservation."

Rashford had booked a table at Ristorante d'Arno, the fanciest Italian restaurant he could find, a repurposed merchant's house he'd noticed during his walk along the riverbank, a kilometre or so past the food truck. He had spoken to the maître d'hôtel and to the sommelier and had left what he felt was some serious money to confirm his arrangements. The maître d' had organized a table with a view over the terrace and promised that they would have wait staff who spoke Italian; he would not allow them to smoke with their meal, but he arranged for a string trio to stop by their table during dessert.

The food had been left to the chef's choice, Rashford only asking for dishes made famous in Florence, and the results were superb. The sommelier had recommended Franciacorta Spumante to accompany their caprese salad, then a Chianti Colli Fiorentini for the meat course and a Lugana Riserva del Lupo for the fish, followed by a Vendito Grappa Riserva Brunello with their tiramisu and coffee.

Mandy was mesmerized by the food, the drink, and the ambience, especially when the violinist played a haunting version of Paganini's *Caprice d'Adieu* before the trio wandered off to serenade other diners with more contemporary fare. Rashford decided not to even look at the total bill; he simply hit the twenty per cent tip option and entered his PIN number, relieved when the electronic beep signalled a successful transaction.

It was almost ten o'clock before they left the restaurant. The evening was cool and Rashford was glad he had encouraged Mandy to bring a sweater; even in his jacket he could feel a chill. They had travelled from the apartment by Uber, but Mandy suggested they walk back along the river. She folded herself under Rashford's arm and sighed in contentment.

"What a wonderful evening," she said. "Thank you so much."

Rashford leaned over and kissed the top of her head.

"You're welcome so much," he said.

They made their way down the riverbank path, nodding at the few other couples they met, some of whom were walking and some sitting on one of the wooden benches that they passed along the way. After ten minutes they came across an empty bench, set back slightly from the path, with a cleared view over a narrow strip of lawn to the river itself.

Light from a nearby streetlamp spilled over the edge of the clearing but, as they sat down, they were in semi-shadow from the overhanging trees.

"I think I'd like a cigarette now," said Mandy, smiling.

Rashford nodded and brought out his packet, pushing a cigarette forward with his thumb. Mandy took it and placed it between her lips, then waited for him to light it. He did so, and she took a deep drag. He started to push out a cigarette for himself, but she put her hand on his arm, stopping him, then took the cigarette from her mouth and placed it between his lips.

"Let's share," she said, breathing out a gust of smoke in the form of a perfect smoke ring. "Can you do that?"

Rashford tried, but the smoke simply billowed from him with no form or structure.

"It's all in the lips and the tongue," she said, after blowing another perfect ring and then sending a second, smaller, one through the centre of the first. She grinned at him, then lowered her head so she was looking up at him through her eyelashes. She dropped her voice to a throaty whisper.

"I can do all sorts of tricks with my lips and tongue," she said, reaching over to undo his belt. "Especially in a nice shadowy place like this."

Rashford gasped, but did not stop her, lifting himself slightly so she could gain the access she desired. One part of him kept watch for anyone who might walk up on them, but most of him simply gave himself to her. He ran the fingers of his left hand through her hair and held the cigarette in his right. He had just shuddered out the last billow of smoke when she raised her head and smiled at him.

"Thank you for a wonderful dinner, and my second dessert," she purred.

Rashford could hardly talk, his mind felt numb of all emotion except the intense pleasure he felt. His toes were curled, the little one on his right foot somehow locked over the one next to it. He simply nodded, then dropped the cigarette on the floor and reached blindly with his heel to stub it out.

"I hope you'll pick that up," said a male voice, and a couple emerged from the darker side of the path. They came into the light thrown by the lamp and he saw that the man was short, dressed in a tuxedo, the bow tie unravelled at his throat, while his much taller companion wore a tweed jacket over a mid-length skirt and high black boots. Rashford tried to cover himself with his arm as the woman laughed and leaned forward, lifting the front of her skirt in order to brush pine needles from her knees.

"It's a beautiful night for it, isn't?" she said, winking at Mandy, who burst into giggles and buried her face in Rashford's chest.

The man looked helplessly at Rashford as the woman laughed, then led him by the hand onto the path. Mandy was still chuckling and shaking as the couple disappeared into the night, and Rashford belatedly corrected his clothing.

"You have a Class Four driver's licence, right?" said Mandy, once they were both settled back on the bench, and each had a cigarette in hand. "Because you were a policeman?"

Rashford shook his head.

"I have a Class Four, yes," he said. "But not because I was a police-man. I used to do some volunteer coaching, kids' soccer, and I needed it to drive the team to games in other communities."

Mandy nodded.

"Good," she said, taking a drag on her cigarette.

Rashford waited.

"You ask because …?" he said, eventually.

She turned and looked at him.

"Remember I told you about the tour?" she said. "The one the band is doing."

Rashford nodded.

"Well, you mentioned it, but I don't know the details," he said.

She looked at him, smoke drizzling from the corner of her mouth.

"It's a five-week tour of Atlantic Canada. Mainly the Maritimes, really, but we're starting with a Canada Day show in Saint John's, Newfoundland. Then we come back and play in Nova Scotia, Prince

Edward Island, and New Brunswick. We're playing twenty-four gigs altogether."

"Twenty-four? Wow! That's a lot of playing."

"Yes. Tours are hard work, you know. Crammed in a van with all the gear, staying in cheap hotels, fast food and arguments. They're not holidays, that's for sure."

Rashford looked at her, intrigued.

"How many have you done?"

"This will be our third, but the first one in eastern Canada. The first one outside Alsama, actually. A couple of years ago we did a short one, only a week, playing bars from here up to the north, places like Prince Albert and La Ronge, Meadow Lake and Île-à-la-Crosse. Then last year we went a bit longer, nearly two weeks down through southern Alberta and Saskatchewan before coming home. That tour we did both bars and clubs. But nothing this big."

"Bars and clubs again?"

"Yes. And some festivals. Those are what will make it worth the hassle, we have a chance of getting properly noticed if we play well."

Rashford nodded.

"It's a great opportunity, for sure," he said. "I'm still not sure what me having a Class Four licence has to do with anything, though."

Mandy laughed, then leaned forward and stubbed out her cigarette with her heel.

"No more of those for me," she said, reaching over and kissing his cheek.

Rashford looked at her.

"You're stalling," he said.

She nodded.

"I know I am," she said. "I'm just not sure how to say this. I don't want you to feel any obligation, either way."

Rashford waited, intrigued. Eventually he gave up.

"Come on, spit it out," he said.

She punched his arm.

"You didn't say that earlier!"

"Amanda Robicheau!" he said, pretending to be shocked.

She laughed.

"You sound just like my dad," she said, then looked at him, mischievously. "Are you going to spank me later?"

Rashford just stared at her.

"If I ask nicely?" she said, winking.

He took a deep sigh.

"The tour," he said, slowly and patiently.

She pouted, then sat back.

"Okay; but let me finish before you say anything. Promise?"

"Promise," said Rashford.

Mandy looked across the path, her gaze focused on the river.

"Gordon, our roadie, has gotten sick," she said. "Well, not really sick, more injured. He was humping some of the gear out to the van after our last show and tripped over a body in the car park."

Rashford looked at her but did not interrupt.

"He twisted his ankle and pulled a muscle in his shoulder, but the worst thing was he did something to his back. Now he's been told he can't lift anything for at least three months. So, we're looking for a roadie, but it needs to be someone who can lift stuff like speakers and amps, who can get on well with everybody and who can drive the van. I was wondering if you might be interested?"

She paused. Rashford waited a moment, then decided it was okay for him to speak.

"Me?"

He had not been expecting this.

"Yes. I asked the band if it was okay to ask you and they said it was. But you don't have to say yes, I'll still like you anyway."

Rashford laughed.

"That's good to know," he said. "Seriously, I'm flattered. But I don't think you need someone with a Class Four."

"We do, because he'll be driving all of us, and the gear."

"There's just the five of you in the band, right?"

"Yes."

"Then you should be okay. It's like driving a big car. You only need a Class Four if you've got fifteen people."

"Yes, that's what I mean. It's a fifteen-seater van."

"But there are only going to be five people in it, six including the driver. That's the number that counts."

Mandy was silent.

"Oh," she said. "We didn't know that."

Rashford snuggled her in closer to him. She tapped her fingers on his chest, then sat up suddenly, pulling away and looking at him with shining eyes.

"The rest don't know that, even now," she said. "Let's not tell them."

Rashford laughed and pulled her back in close.

"What's this about a body?" he said.

She shrugged.

"One of those stupid farmers, the ones who were giving Patrick a hard time. He must have annoyed someone."

Rashford remembered that after they had entered the Uber, he had looked back and seen the farmers clustering on the steps. Pia and his friends were standing in the parking lot, and the bikers had formed a guard across the gate. He cleared his throat.

"Was this body ... umm ... a live body or a dead body?"

Mandy shrugged again.

"I don't know. Gordon didn't say. He was too busy complaining about himself."

Rashford decided that unless a dead body turned up, he wasn't going to worry about this information either. The idea of spending six weeks with a band, though, was intriguing.

"I tell you what," he said. "Let me think about it and tell you in the morning. It's getting late, we should be heading back to the apartment."

Mandy got to her feet and pulled him upright next to her. She took his hand, then yawned.

"Time for bed," she said, and led him off down the path.

The next morning Rashford's phone rang at eight o'clock. He reached over and picked it up, aware of Mandy's naked body pressing into his back. He checked the call display then looked back over his shoulder.

"I've got to take this," he said.

Mandy kept her eyes closed, pretending to be asleep, but he could feel her fingers dancing across his back. He clicked to accept the call.

"Gayle," he said, resting his chin on his hand.

"Is this a good time?" she said.

"Umm ... give me a second."

He slipped out of the bed, leaving Mandy grasping at air. She kept her eyes closed but he saw a moue of amusement on her lips. Naked, he padded into the bathroom and picked up a towel, then wrapped this around himself as he walked into the front room. He sat down on one of the armchairs.

"Go ahead," he said.

"Sorry for the early call," she said, "but it's been a busy night."

"I bet. What's happened?"

"Well, first, Smithson wasn't at his house when we arrived. Neither was his truck, and when Sheri looked in his bedroom, it looked like he'd packed in a hurry."

"Sheri?"

"Constable Hayleyson."

"Okay."

"I put out an All Points Bulletin on him, apprehend on sight, but nobody reported seeing him."

"Remind me, when was this?"

Morgan was silent, then let out an exasperated sigh.

"Really? It was yesterday, Gavin. Today's Sunday. What has that girl done to you?"

Rashford shook his head.

"Sorry, I was still asleep," he said. "We had a late night, last night."

"Uh-huh."

"We were celebrating the end of her exams. Anyway, I'm awake now. Carry on. You went to Smithson's, and he wasn't there."

"Correct," she said, patiently. "It seemed like he'd done a runner, so I put out the APB and then went back to that planter. Forensics was there so I stayed around and watched. They have been working all night and have found what appear to be the skeletal remains of five people."

"Five? Who are the other two?"

"No idea. Perhaps he'll tell us."

Rashford thought for a moment, considering her words.

"You've caught him," he said.

He could hear the triumph in her voice.

"Yes. The silly pillock was in such a rush that he got stopped for speeding about two hours from town. The constable recognized the name and called in to get a description. It was patched through to me, and I told him to check to see if he had that tattoo on the inside of his left wrist."

Rashford thought back.

"What tattoo?"

"The one of the pug dog, or whatever he called them," she said. "I saw it when he was gesticulating about something, waving his arms about."

"I missed that," said Rashford. "Well done."

"Thank you," said Morgan, pleased. "Anyway, the speed cop checked and sure enough, there it was. So, he nicked him."

"Where is he now?"

"The speed cop was based out of Regina, so that's where he took him. They left him in the cells overnight. I'm going down this morning. Do you want to come?"

Rashford scratched his head.

"I've got to report to Pollard at nine tomorrow," he said, "so I was going to go down this afternoon anyway. I guess I can leave a bit early. What time are you going?"

"I've got to go and do the paperwork before I chat with him," she said. "You've got your own car. Why don't we meet at the station at one thirty. Does that give you enough time to say goodbye to your girlfriend?"

Just then Mandy walked slowly through the living room, making sure that Rashford realized she had not bothered to get dressed. She blew him a kiss as she sashayed past.

"Hmmm ..." said Rashford. "Well, I have to be checked out of the hotel by twelve ..."

Mandy came out of the kitchen and walked back across the living room. Still naked, she was holding a pastry brush in one hand, and a pressurized tube of cream whip in the other. She disappeared into the bedroom.

"One thirty, that's fine," said Rashford, starting to stand up and losing his towel in the process. "Albert Street?"

"Yes."

Rashford ended the call and left his towel on the chair. He followed Mandy into the bedroom and paused at the door. She was sitting on the bed, leaning up against the pillows. She held out the pastry brush to him. He shook his head as he crossed the room, then took the brush from her hand and placed it on the bedside table, next to the cream whip.

"That was work," he growled.

She looked down and spoke softly, her eyes sparkling.

"Sorry. I was only teasing. I didn't mean to upset you."

"You didn't upset me, but you were naughty."

Mandy smiled at him, then slid down the pillows and turned over so that she was lying face down on the bed.

"Time for that spanking, I think," she said.

CHAPTER 24

With one thing and another, Rashford did not manage to check out of his hotel until just after noon. He kept about ten kilometres above the speed limit all the way down and arrived in Regina just after one o'clock, then made his way through the quiet Sunday streets until he reached the police station. He parked on Albert Street, not sure of his status as an almost retired officer and went inside to check in at the reception desk. They phoned for Gayle Morgan, and she came downstairs to meet him. The constable at reception gave him a visitor's pass to pin on his jacket, and Morgan escorted him to a small office.

She sat behind the desk and pointed at a rickety wooden chair with her chin.

"Sit," she said.

Rashford sat.

She considered him carefully, then spoke.

"You look like shit," she said. "Don't you have any clean shirts?"

Rashford snorted.

"I've been living out of a suitcase for nearly two weeks," he said. "How much laundry do you think Pollard will pay for?"

"What about the Marvellous Mandy?" said Morgan. "Doesn't she know there are other ways to serve, not just on her back."

"Gayle," said Rashford, in a low voice.

She coloured.

"Sorry. That wasn't fair. I take it back. But really, that looks like you slept in it."

"I promise you I didn't," said Rashford, grinning.

Morgan looked at him and started to grin as well.

"Touché," she said, then looked at him cautiously.

"Are you okay? Really? I don't want you getting hurt again. It's not good for any of us."

Rashford met her gaze.

"It's just a bit of fun, that's all she wants," he said.

Morgan shook her head.

"And you, Gavin? What do you want?

He shrugged.

"Right now, to get this bastard to confess," he said.

They went to a small interview room which contained a table and four chairs. A video camera blinked from a wall mount, and a control panel stood on the edge of the table nearest to the wall. Smithson was already there, seated next to a young man with pimples who introduced himself as the duty lawyer. A police constable standing against the wall stepped forward and pulled one of the chairs out for Morgan, who sat down.

"Thank you, Sheri," she said.

The constable nodded and left the room. Rashford pulled out his own chair. They all looked at each other, then Morgan leaned forward and clicked a switch on the control unit. She gave the date, time, and her name, and noted that the interview was with Bruce Smithson. Then she sat back and folded her arms.

"Thank you for joining us, Mister Smithson. You are not obligated to say anything, or to repeat anything you may have said earlier, however anything you do say will be recorded and may be used as evidence against you in a court of law. Do you understand?"

Smithson nodded.

"For the tape, please, I need verbal confirmation."

"Yes, I understand."

"Thank you. Where would you like to start?" said Morgan.

Smithson looked at her, then at his lawyer.

"My client has nothing to say, Senior Constable," said the lawyer. "Except that he would like an explanation for why he was dragged in here in the middle of the night."

Morgan nodded.

"Fair enough," she said. "He's been dragged in here because he ran away during a police investigation, and was caught speeding two hours later. In the middle of the night. Now, as I was saying. Where would you like to start? Emmanuel Tealeson? Simon Lepani? Chad Sobers? Jeremy Beals? One of the others?"

Smithson looked down at the desk but remained silent.

"For the tape, Mister Smithson has no comment," said Morgan. She glanced at Rashford, who took his cue.

"The Forensics people are taking your house and truck apart as we speak, Mister Smithson," he said. "They're going to find traces. It doesn't matter how many times you've sprayed down the tiles in your playroom, it doesn't matter how many times you put WD40 on your secateurs, it doesn't matter how many times you vacuumed out the cab of your truck. Somewhere there will be a droplet of blood, just the smallest speck, and that will give us DNA. Somewhere there will be the souvenirs you kept, the locks of hair or the pieces of clothing, because you had to keep a record, didn't you? We will interview Jeremy again, and when he knows you're in prison then he won't be too scared to talk, will he? So why don't you just answer the question. Where would you like to start?"

Smithson took a deep breath. The lawyer looked alarmed and put his hand on Smithson's arm.

"You don't have to say anything," he said. "In fact, I'd advise you not to."

Smithson nodded.

"Thank you," he said. "Advice noted."

He looked at Morgan, then sat back in his chair and folded his arms in mimicry.

She raised her eyebrows.

He smiled.

"Have you ever fucked a Black man, Senior Constable?" he said. "Or perhaps you prefer women?"

Rashford had an instant mental image of Sheri Hayleyson and Morgan together. He shook his head to clear it. Smithson saw the movement and spoke to him.

"Don't shake your head," he said. "It's true what they say, they're different."

Rashford just looked at him.

Morgan remained silent.

"I helped her set it up, you know."

"Who?" said Rashford.

"Professor Benoît. When she came and asked for help in building a flower garden, I helped her. I made the planter, I looked after it, nobody else."

Morgan nodded.

"It was her planter. I just helped."

Morgan unfolded her arms.

"Helped with what?" she said.

"With putting in the soil, picking the seedlings, planting the geraniums, keeping it watered."

He stopped speaking, wiping his lips on the back of his hand.

There was silence. Then Smithson began to speak again.

"They're taking over, you know. And they don't appreciate all the help they're given here."

"Who?"

"Darkies. They're happy to take the easy grade that the Professor gives them, and they're happy to dress up so that they get to fuck the women at the dinner parties, but they don't appreciate it."

Rashford broke in.

"I'm not sure I understand. How should they show their appreciation?"

Smithson scoffed.

"After all we do for them, they should let us have a piece as well."

Morgan looked puzzled.

"Us? You mean, you and Professor Benoît?"

Smithson nodded.

"Yes."

Rashford and Morgan looked at each other. Rashford leaned forward again.

"You mean, they should let you have sex with them?"

Smithson nodded.

"Yeah. We set everything up and then they get all coy and closed-minded. They'll fuck a woman in the ass, but they won't let me touch them. It's just discrimination. Professor Benoît says it's a post-colonial reaction against the proper order of society."

Morgan stared at him.

"A post-colonial ..."

"Yeah. Basically, they're happy to be on top, but they won't return to their proper place. So, we have to teach them."

"We? I didn't see anyone else at your house, Mister Smithson. I think you're just trying to shift the blame, here. Nobody else is involved, are they? You pick them up on their way home from the last dinner party, take them to your house, assault them, murder them, and bury them in the planter. All by yourself."

Smithson shook his head.

"No," he said. "I pick them up, yes, but how do you think I know where they'll be? The Professor phones me and gives me the address. Check my phone, you'll see when she called me."

Morgan nodded.

"We will. Thank you. Then what happens?"

"I take them home and give them a drink, just friendly like. Mostly they're teetotal so I just give them a soft drink, made with my own recipe."

"How does that help?"

"Usually, they start to feel nauseous and disoriented straight away. That's the *Amaryllis belladonna*. The lavender makes them feel sleepy."

Morgan clicked her fingers.

"The plants on your shelf. You use those to poison them."

"No, not poison them. Just calm them down, so they don't hurt themselves."

"Right. I can understand you're worried about that. Okay, so you've got them disorientated and sleepy. Then what?

"I take them down to the playroom."

"And tie them to the bed, naked?"

Smithson nodded.

"Why the photograph?" he said.

"That's for the Professor. I take it and then scan it to her, so she knows I'm in the playroom."

"Why not just take a photo with your phone?"

Smithson was silent. He looked down.

"I know," said Morgan, smiling. "That's your souvenir, isn't it? Somewhere we will find an album or a scrapbook, with those photographs. One for each victim."

She looked across the table.

"You're in the playroom, the fellow is tied up. Then what?"

"I play with them until the Professor comes. Then they play as well. We want them to have a good time, then we can let them go. It's only when they don't participate that there's a problem."

"How do you mean, don't participate?"

"If they won't show that they're excited, or they won't, you know …"

"I don't know. Won't what?"

"Open their mouths," he mumbled.

Morgan sat straight in her chair, sucking in her cheeks. Her stare seemed frozen. Rashford cleared his throat.

"How do you solve that problem?" he said.

Smithson shrugged.

"With the clippers," he said. "Or a hammer. That helps them participate."

"You torture them?"

"Well, not exactly. We're just trying to get them involved. Give them some encouragement."

"How long does this go on for?"

"It depends. The Professor has less patience than me."

Morgan resumed the interview.

"So, you kill them, and then dispose of the bodies in the planter?"

Smithson shook his head.

"Usually they die first, we don't actually have to kill them," he said.

"Okaaay," said Morgan. "Then what?"

"We wrap them in a tarp and put them in the back of the truck, then go to the Secret Quadrangle and bury them in the planter. I drive us back and we wash out the playroom, then the Professor goes home. The next day I plant the geraniums."

The young lawyer had edged away from his client. He was sitting with a shocked look on his face. Rashford nodded at Morgan. She took a deep breath.

"Bruce Smithson, I am charging you with the murders of Emmanuel Tealeson, Simon Lepani, and Chad Sobers, as well as the abduction and administration of a toxic substance to Jeremy Beals. You are not obligated to say anything, or to repeat anything you said earlier, however anything you do say will be recorded and may be used as evidence against you in a court of law. Do you understand?"

"Yes," said Smithson.

"Interview terminated at two forty-seven," said Morgan, rising to her feet. Rashford beat her to the door and opened it for her. She stepped outside and spoke to Constable Hayleyson.

"Take him back to the cells, please."

The constable nodded and entered the interview room. She stepped out a moment later, guiding Smithson by the elbow. The lawyer, looking pale, came out after them, nodding at Morgan before hurrying away. Morgan leaned against the wall and looked at Rashford.

"Is it too early for a drink?" she said.

CHAPTER 25

On Monday morning Rashford put on his uniform for what he felt might be the last time and walked out to his car. There had been a light dusting of snow overnight, so he swept off his windshield before driving cautiously to the headquarters building. A few minutes before nine o'clock he was standing in the outer office of Chief Inspector Pollard. Her administrative assistant sat at her desk, which he noticed had a new outer ledge along the rim. She leaned back in her chair and smiled at him.

"Hello, Gavin," she said.

"Sarah," he nodded. "How are you?"

"I'm fine, thank you. Did you have a good weekend?"

Rashford scoffed.

"I helped Senior Constable Morgan with a couple of things," he said. "You?"

She smiled, running the tip of her tongue across her lips.

"Oh, the only person I helped was myself," she said. "See, I needed a new ledge."

Rashford shook his head.

"Another canola farmer?" he said.

She laughed.

"No. These were shoe salesmen. Twins. They do everything together, apparently. I met them when I went to buy some new pumps, they told me they had something I could slip into. Right there in the back office! That was a first for me, I can tell you."

"TMI," said Rashford, as always not sure how much she was telling him was truth and how much was concocted to hide her shyness or her low sense of self-esteem. Or to wind him up.

"How is your mom?" he said.

Sarah laughed.

"Always the considerate one, aren't you? She's fine, thank you. You should join us for our perogy dinner one Saturday."

"I'd like that," he said. "Just let me know."

The phone on her desk buzzed and she picked it up, then nodded towards the door.

"You can go in," she said. "You're expected."

Rashford nodded, then walked into the inner sanctum.

<hr>

Chief Superintendent Pollard stood to her full five feet four inches and glared at him from across her desk. Rashford stood at attention and stared forward at a place a foot above her head.

After thirty seconds of accusatory silence, she spoke, enunciating each word with precision.

"I sent you to give a talk. Is that correct?"

"Yes, Ma'am."

Rashford tried not to move a muscle, not even in his lips as he spoke.

"Did I send you to investigate missing students?"

"No, Ma'am."

"A multiple homicide?"

"No, Ma'am."

"Living off the avails of prostitution, fraud, and theft?"

"No, Ma'am."

"International drug smuggling and money laundering?"

"No, Ma'am."

"A possible addition to the growing list of Missing and Murdered Indigenous Women?"

"No, Ma'am."

She regarded him, shaking her head and nodding at the same time. Then she picked up the phone.

"Coffee, please, Sarah. Extra strong. I've a feeling that I'm going to need it."

She looked back at Rashford and sighed.

"Sit down, Gavin," she said.

He did so, maintaining an erect posture. Sarah entered with a tray and placed the coffee cups and French press carefully on the table. Pollard turned to her.

"Go and get your notebook, Sarah," she said, "then pull up a chair. I'm going to need a record of this conversation. And bring a cup for yourself."

"Yes, Ma'am," said Sarah, looking at Rashford in disbelief. Her heels clicked as she went back into her office, then again as she returned. She put her own cup next to the others, then waited as the Chief Superintendent carefully poured the coffee.

"Help yourselves to the fixings," said Pollard, adding sugar to her own cup and then leaning back in her chair. She fixed her gaze on Rashford.

"Right," she said. "It's time for you to tell me a story."

It was almost eleven before Rashford was able to leave the office. He had been as concise as possible in his report, but Pollard had teased at the edges with a series of penetrating questions, each requiring a substantive answer. Sarah had taken rapid notes, using some sort of shorthand if the scrawled loops and dots were anything to go by, and every so often had looked across at him in amazement as some new detail was revealed.

When he had finished, Pollard swivelled in her chair and looked out of the window. Sarah shifted her position, crossing one leg over the other in a way that caused her skirt to ride up, exposing a long view of her leg. She smiled when Rashford looked at her.

"Stop that, Sarah," said Pollard, still looking out of the window.

Rashford grinned when Sarah turned crimson and hurriedly placed both her feet flat on the floor. Pollard turned back around and faced them.

"We were able to lift a fingerprint from one of those cans of beer," she said. "The rest were ruled out because they belonged to Derek, Shyanne, Josee, or Alvita."

"Alvita? She spoke to you?" said Rashford.

Pollard laughed.

"Not to me personally, no. But yes, she spoke to us once we had explained the situation. Interesting lady, that one."

"What situation was that, Ma'am?" said Sarah, her pen poised over her note book.

"That if she didn't talk to us about the beer cans, we'd talk to the Immigration people about her student visa, and the drug squad about some of her habits, that sort of thing. No need to write that down, Sarah."

"Yes, Ma'am. I mean, no, Ma'am."

"I sent her a text message to her private telephone number assuring her that her fingerprints would only be used in this case, and only to rule out any contact she might have had with the cans. It turns out that Derek wasn't the only one who liked a hoppy IPA. She said she used to sneak sips when he wasn't looking."

Rashford laughed, then turned serious again.

"So, there's a good chance that the extra fingerprint might belong to the person I knew as Marc Claydon," he said. "I assume there haven't been any matches in the system?"

"Not in ours, no," said Pollard. "But we've just sent it off to the Mounties, so they can check the Canadian records. That might take a week or so before we hear anything back, sadly it won't be a high priority."

"It's a potential case for the MMIW squad," Rashford protested.

Pollard shrugged.

"Potentially. Right now, it's a missing adult woman in her twenties, who's actually only been missing for a week. She was last seen leaving on her own volition, under her own steam, no suspicious circumstances at all."

"She missed her final exams!"

"Lots of students do that. Nerves. Pressure. Fear. It doesn't mean they've been abducted or murdered."

Rashford shook his head.

"They're checking, okay?" said Pollard. "Maybe not as quickly as we would like, but it's on their to-do list."

"Yes, Ma'am," he said.

Pollard nodded.

"Good. Moving on. Gayle Morgan had an interesting talk with Linda Benoît yesterday evening, after the two of you had finished your little chat with Smithson."

Rashford nodded, remembering his disappointment when he had realized that Gayle had been joking about a drink, but was really sending him off while she continued on the case.

"She summarized his story," said Pollard, "but made it sound like Smithson was putting all the blame on Benoît. Then the good professor sang, oh how they sang."

She took a sip of her coffee and smiled her barracuda smile. Rashford and Sarah waited expectantly.

"Their version was that they had always been teased by the women, who assumed that they were sleeping with the student all the rest of the time, except those last five Fridays. They never corrected the assumption but thinking about it made them both ashamed and excited at the same time. So, when Smithson came to them with a plan, they thought it was a great idea."

Rashford scoffed.

"I can't see Smithson coming up with this on his own," he said. "How did they meet, anyway, those two?"

Pollard smiled.

"Good question," she said. "Morgan asked that as well. It turns out that they met back in Toronto, at some club in the gay village. This was years ago. Benoît was still trying to figure out who they were and Smithson, well, I guess he knew. When they both ended up out here, at the university, they recognized each other."

Rashford shook his head.

"Just coincidence," he said, "and now at least five people are dead. Do we know who the other two are yet?"

"No," said Pollard. "It doesn't look like they're students, though. That Assistant Registrar, Greenfield, can't find any other cases where people seemed to suddenly disappear for no reason."

"So now we have to search through missing persons?"

"Yes. They're each blaming the other for the actual murders and burials. They don't seem to have a problem admitting to illegal confinement, torture, and sexual assault, but I suppose even psychopaths draw the line somewhere. No matter, we've got more than enough to charge both of them, and the interviews will continue until we have all the details."

She drank more coffee, then looked up at Rashford.

"Changing the subject, Chief Superintendent York sends his regards."

Rashford stared at her.

"Chief Su ..."

She laughed.

"He said that might surprise you. Yes, anyway, he asked me to thank you for all your work on his case. Apparently, you clarified quite a bit of detail for him, and were able to get him to places that he would otherwise have never gone."

Rashford thought of Shyanne and smiled to himself.

"He told me, hang on ..."

She searched around on her desk and found a piece of paper that looked like it had been torn from a diary or Day-Timer.

"Here we are ... 'we have followed the chrome trail, the natives are free'. He said you would understand."

Rashford nodded.

"Yes, Ma'am. It means ..."

Pollard raised her hand to stop him.

"I don't want to know," she said, then looked at Sarah.

"We don't want to know," she corrected. "All I know is that when he walked in here, he was followed by the heads of the Drug Squad, Gang Squad, Fraud Squad, Financial Crime Unit, and Border Services. And they'd told Sarah to go to the washroom for fifteen minutes. That's way over my paygrade. So just accept the thanks and move on."

"Yes, Ma'am."

She flipped over the paper.

"The other message was, 'don't worry, we'll look after S, she'll have a great time'. Again, I don't need to know."

Rashford smiled.

"Yes, Ma'am."

Pollard cleared her throat and nodded at Sarah, who got to her feet and went into the outer office. Rashford wondered what was coming next. Sarah returned and put a large manilla envelope on Pollard's desk, then returned to her seat. Pollard picked up the envelope and turned it around in her hands. Then she looked at her administrative assistant.

Sarah blushed pink, then took a deep breath and spoke to Rashford.

"Gavin, I'm sorry if I upset you. I didn't mean to, sometimes I just say the wrong thing."

Rashford stared at her, mystified.

"It was after our weekend at the Stone Hall Castle," she said. "You had just been promoted to Staff Sergeant, remember, and you had a meeting here to get your first assignment. Then you got all upset with me and stormed off. Then two days later, you told the Chief that you were going to resign and take early retirement. I don't want to be responsible for that. You're too good at what you do."

She reached out and put her hand on his arm.

"Please, Gavin. I'm sorry."

Rashford looked across at Pollard, who was sitting quietly. She cleared her throat and leaned forward, holding the manilla envelope.

"In this envelope are your official retirement papers," she said. "HR said I couldn't delay things any longer. The only way they can be negated is if you rescind them, before I serve them to you."

He stared at her.

"*You* were delaying things?"

"God, yes, these have been ready for ages. HR aren't that incompetent, you know."

Rashford shook his head.

"Why?"

"Because like Sarah says, you're a good cop. A very good one. And you're just going to get better. I don't want to lose you."

He looked at the envelope.

"I can't see what's in it?"

"Sorry, no. You have to receive it unopened. It's even got a seal, look."

When she flipped over the envelope, he saw the small knob of wax across the seal, impressed with some sort of mark.

Rashford coughed.

"What if you forgot to give it to me today, what with all the excitement that's going on?"

"If I forgot?"

"Yes."

"Well, I guess you'd stay in this netherworld you've been inhabiting since early January, not a proper policeman but not retired yet either. Somewhere in-between."

"And still getting paid?"

She stared at him.

"Are you?"

"Yes, Ma'am."

Pollard looked sharply at Sarah.

"How did that happen?"

Sarah blushed.

"You've been signing off on his timesheets, Ma'am."

"Have I?"

Sarah paused, then looked down at her feet.

"Electronically, Ma'am."

"What? Don't mumble, woman, you're worse than he is."

Sarah looked up.

"I said, you signed off on his timesheets, electronically, Ma'am."

"Did I indeed?"

She looked at Rashford.

"Well then, I needn't feel guilty about all this work you've been doing, need I?"

"No, Ma'am," said Rashford, trying not to smile.

Pollard stood and went over to her window, looking out. She spoke to the horizon.

"What do you think, Staff Sergeant?"

He looked at Sarah, then at the back of Pollard's head. Then he stood up, and Sarah rose with him. Pollard turned to face him; her eyebrow raised.

"Thank you for your confidence in me," he said, slowly. "I truly appreciate that."

She nodded.

"But?"

"But I really was going to retire, I've been making plans."

"What kind of plans? I heard that at one point you were thinking of becoming a private detective."

'How does she know all this', he thought.

"Not that, Ma'am. At least, not at the moment. No, I was planning on taking a summer holiday, down around eastern Canada."

"That's where Roxanne is, correct?"

"Yes, Ma'am," said Rashford, deciding that wasn't a lie.

"I see. How long would it be, this holiday?"

"I was hoping for about six or seven weeks, Ma'am. From the end of June until mid-August."

"Six weeks? That's more than our normal annual leave allowance," said Pollard.

"Yes Ma'am. If HR would approve, perhaps I can take what I'm owed as holidays and the rest as an unpaid administrative leave?"

Pollard stepped forward and picked up the envelope, tapping it lightly on the edge of her desk.

She paused for a moment, thinking, then spoke.

"I can live with that," she said. "From now until the end of June, you'll be posted here, to my personal unit. On deck every morning at eight thirty, finish when I say so. Got it?"

"Yes, Ma'am."

"Then take your holiday, and when you come back, we'll talk about your next assignment."

"Thank you, Ma'am."

Pollard gave the envelope to Sarah.

"Keep this in a safe place," she said. "You never know when we might need it."

Yes, Ma'am."

Pollard waved them towards the door, then sat down at her desk and picked up her pen. Rashford stood back to let Sarah leave the room first. He was just about to follow her through the door when Pollard spoke.

"And for the record, I would have paid for two sets of laundry. You only had to ask."

"Yes, Ma'am," he said, wondering again how she knew these things.

***

In the outer office he stood by Sarah's desk, running his fingers over the smooth surface of the ledge. She looked up at him. He cleared his throat.

"I'm sorry, as well," he said.

She looked surprised.

"Why?"

"This is your business, your life. I don't care whether your stories are true or false, whether you're Walter Mitty or Casanova, it's got nothing to do with me."

She nodded.

"Thank you, Gavin. I appreciate that."

"We had fun," he said. "That's all that matters. Nobody would give me a hard time for sleeping with you. Why should the other way be any different?"

She bit her lip, nodding slowly.

He paused, then looked directly into her eyes.

"Which reminds me, I need the name of someone in IT, someone who's good, and discreet. Someone who can track a posting on the internet back to the phone it came from, and who won't have any qualms telling me whose phone it is. Or where the owner is now."

"Why?" she said.

He told her, and she smiled the barracuda smile.

'Does everyone who works here learn how to do that?' he thought.

Sarah picked up a pencil and tapped it against her bottom front tooth. Then she nodded to herself.

"I know just the person," she said. "No morals, very discreet, and terribly adept."

Rashford looked at her.

"Is he a notch as well?" he said.

"No comment," she said, grinning as she picked up her phone.

***

Rashford drove back to his townhouse, stopping along the way at a grocery and the liquor store. He carried everything inside and put them in their correct places. Then he vacuumed the carpet, picked up some books and various pieces of clothing, and rinsed out both the sink and the bath. Only then did he take out his phone.

Mandy answered on the first ring, sounding breathless.

"Did you find Josee?"

"Not yet, no. Are you okay?"

"What? Yes. I'm fine. I'm with the band, we're rehearsing, I was just playing the *Red River Jig*."

Rashford remembered the night in the bar and smiled.

"Oh, right. Listen, I have a question."

"Hang on, let me just grab some water."

He heard Mandy pouring out a glass, then the chugging as she drank it. Her voice came back.

"Okay, go on. What's your question?"

"When's your next rehearsal?"

"What, after this one?

"Yes."

"Today's Monday, so, Thursday, I guess. Yes, Thursday."

"Do you want to come down here for a couple of days?"

"What, to Regina?"

"Yes."

Mandy was silent.

"Why?"

"There's a few things I'd like to talk to you about."

"I thought you were working."

"During the day, yes. Not all the time."

There was a pause.

"Jody, our bass player, is going to visit his nôhkum in Indian Head this afternoon. He's got his own car, so he can give me a ride."

"That would be great. Call me when you're in the city and I'll come and pick you up."

"Can I bring my fiddle?"

"Of course, I'd like that. My place is new and has good insulation, you can practice all you want."

Mandy laughed.

"And what else would we be doing, when you're not working and I'm not practising?"

Rashford hesitated.

"I'm sure we can think of something," he said.

She huffed.

"Is it still just enthusiastic sex, Gavin, or are you starting to spoil it all by making it a relationship?"

He was silent, sensing a test of some sort. He was pretty sure that whatever he said, it would be the wrong answer. He decided to prevaricate.

"I'm not sure," he said at last.

He could hear the chuckle in her voice as she responded.

"Well, then," she said. "I guess I'd better come down and find out."

CHAPTER 26

Rashford and Mandy sat on the couch, snuggling together as they waited for Final Jeopardy to start. They were dressed in sweatpants and tee-shirts, both of which belonged to Rashford. He knew that they were both naked underneath, for he had watched her get dressed, and he reached around her back with his arm and slowly massaged her breast. She shrugged his hand away.

"Stop trying to put me off. I'm still going to win, you know."

He had met her in the car park outside the Regina Casino, as that seemed to be the only place that Jody knew how to find. She had climbed down from the cab of the pick-up, handing her fiddle case to Rashford, and had then undone the tailgate before reaching in for her bag. A bag, he noticed, that seemed rather extravagant for a two-night stay. Slamming the tailgate shut, she had banged on the soft-top cover and shouted thank you to Jody, who had driven off in a cloud of exhaust.

On the way back to his townhouse they had passed a Thai restaurant and gone in to order some food. There were not many customers on a cold Tuesday evening, and their meal was prepared quickly. They had put the tinfoil dishes in the oven and turned it on low, then dropped clothes across the living room floor as he pulled her into the bedroom.

Afterwards, he had passed her his spare gym clothes, and then left her to use the bathroom while he spooned their noodle dish, crispy rolls, and sticky rice out onto two plates.

Sitting on the couch, Mandy had scrolled through the television channels while they were eating their food, stopping for a few moments at various stations before moving on. They had arrived at Jeopardy just as the last questions in the first round were being asked.

"Do you like this?" said Mandy.

Rashford nodded, his mouth full of food.

"Bet I can beat you," she said.

He swallowed, then looked at her with a smile.

"Deal," he said. "Loser makes breakfast."

They half-watched the commercials as they finished their meal and put the plates on the floor beside the couch.

"I'll have eggs Benedict, please," said Mandy, "hollandaise sauce on the side."

Rashford scoffed and put his arm around her just as the theme music started.

"That's ridiculous," said Mandy. "Who is supposed to know what Canada gave Queen Elizabeth the Second as a Diamond Jubilee gift?"

"I did," said Rashford.

"Yes, well you cheated."

"I cheated? How?"

"It was a horse, and it came from the RCMP, and you used to be a Mountie, so you had insider information."

She folded her arms and plumped back into the couch pillows, pouting.

Rashford laughed.

"Don't pout," he said, sliding his hands under her tee-shirt and tickling her. "I'm trying to think what I want for breakfast."

She laughed and pushed his hands away.

"Stop it, no fair," she said, giggling, then stabbing her hand down between his legs.

"I'll squeeze," she said.

Rashford removed his hands and sat back against the cushions.

"Don't pout," she said.

They sat quietly; Mandy curled up under his arms. He ran his fingers through her hair.

"Why did you choose me," he said.

"Mmmm?"

"Why me?"

She leaned her head back and looked up at him.

"What do you mean?"

"Well, you're smart, you speak two languages ..."

"Four," she said.

"Four?"

"Yes, English, Michif, French, and Italian."

"Wow. Okay, you're smart, you're quadrilingual, you're an incredible fiddle player, you're a marvellous cook, and you're probably the most beautiful woman I've ever met."

"Probably?"

"Well, there was this girl in high school ... ouch! No pinching!"

She laughed, then lifted up his tee-shirt.

"Don't be a wuss, there's not a mark on you," she said.

Rashford pulled the hem of his tee-shirt down.

"As I was saying, you're amazing, and I'm just a plebian cop, so why did you come to my room that first night of the conference."

Mandy was silent for a minute, stroking his hand.

"You were the only one who listened," she said. "When I was explaining what the Social Committee does, everybody just started talking. Nobody paid any attention to me. Except you."

Rashford remembered the look she had given him when she had seen him clapping. The smile, he now realized, had been one of gratitude.

"Most people can't get past the tits and the hair," she said. "They think I'm some blonde bimbo, only good for blow-jobs or a quick hand job."

"Well ..." said Rashford, and she elbowed him in the side.

"I'm being serious," she said. "Do you know how hard it was

growing up with a big chest? I was fourteen and looked eighteen, at least that's what they used to tell me. I know some guys like girls who look young, but where I grew up, if you looked old enough then you were old enough."

She huffed.

"There was a clapped-out old bar at the edge of town, it's gone now. Me and some other girls would wait out the back. Guys would pretend to go to the Gents, but instead they'd come out the back door, pick one of us, then drop their pants. Afterwards they'd give the girl five bucks and go back inside to their friends or their wives. My dad could never figure out where I was getting the money to buy new clothes. My mom, I think she knew, but she never said anything."

"I'm sorry," said Rashford.

She shrugged.

"Why? You weren't one of them, were you?"

"No!"

"So then, don't worry. It was what it was, life in a small northern town. And I couldn't get pregnant, not like some of the other girls."

"Were you playing the fiddle, while you were at school?"

"That's when I started, yes. One of my uncles, I think he must have heard about what was happening at the back of the bar, he came and told my dad that I needed something to keep myself busy. He had been down to Prince Albert and studied under John Arcand, who was one of the best Métis fiddle players ever, and he offered to teach me. He gave me one of his old fiddles, for my sixteenth birthday, and I've been playing ever since."

Rashford was silent for a few minutes.

"Thank you for sharing," he said. "And for choosing me."

"Like I said, I like fit older men!"

Rashford thumped her over the head with a cushion, and she thumped him back, which led to a wrestling match on the couch, and then on the floor, and then their sweatpants came down and they made love on the carpet.

The next morning Mandy had finished her shower and was standing in the bathroom, looking over her shoulder to examine her reflection in the mirror.

"Gavin, I've got rug burns on my butt," she complained.

He came in, already fully dressed, and reached into the medicine cabinet.

"I've got some salve here," he said. "Shall I rub it in for you?"

She took the tube from his hands.

"No way," she said. "I know how that will end up, and I've got things to do today."

"That's true," agreed Rashford. "What's for breakfast?"

She flipped her towel at him, and he walked back into the living room, laughing.

He was sitting at the table, reading an old copy of the Regina *Leader Post*, when she appeared and walked into the kitchen. She was wearing her apron, the one with rabbits gambolling on the front, and not much else. The bib barely contained her breasts, and it was only as she went into the kitchen that he realized she was wearing panties. He peered at the design, which as far as he could see was a picture of a bucolic rural scene. There were some trees in full leaf, underplanted with flowers, and what looked like a tractor harvesting wheat.

"Are you looking at my bum?"

"No."

He cleared his throat.

"Well, yes, actually. I'm trying to figure out the picture on your panties."

She turned around and faced him, lifting the hem of the apron. The front showed the same picture.

"They go with the apron," she said, then turned a full circle. He shook his head.

"Sorry, I don't get it."

"Under the trees," she huffed. "There's a rabbit hole."

She went back to the kitchen and Rashford returned to his paper, deciding that in future he would try to avoid stupid questions. Mandy clattered about, muttering under her breath, opening and closing cupboards, looking in the fridge. He heard something cooking but kept quiet. She came out with a fresh pot of coffee, which she left on the table, then again with two plates, on which he found a pile of fluffy scrambled eggs on toast.

Rashford took a bite, then looked at her.

"This is delicious," he said, meaning every word. "Thank you."

"You're welcome. Even if you cheated."

Rashford just smiled and kept eating. He finished his plate, and then poured them both coffees.

"So, what are things you're going to do today?"

She looked at him.

"First, I'm going to find a grocery store, and buy some real food. There's nothing here! The eggs are okay but for them to be good I needed some chives, parsley, some rock salt, some decent olive oil, and some Asiago cheese I could grate into the mix. Italian, not American. I will pick us up some herbs and spices, and some things you can always use, even when I'm not here. Cannelloni beans, some decent pasta, vegetables, fruit. Don't worry, I'll stock your kitchen."

"I've not been here for nearly two weeks," he protested. "I didn't have time to shop!"

She grinned at him.

"It's okay, no need to be defensive. I understand."

"I'm not being defensive," he said, then grinned back. "No, you're right. I am, just a little. Sorry. And it would be great if you had time to go shopping, I probably won't be back until late afternoon."

"What would you have done for supper, if I wasn't here?"

He shrugged.

"Probably stopped at that Thai place again."

She huffed.

"All the more reason for me to get us some real food, then. The additives are fine in small doses, but you don't want to live on them."

Rashford put his hands up and laughed.

"Guilty as charged," he said. "What else are you going to do, apart from shopping?"

"I've got some clothes shopping to do, as well. I need a couple of new shirts for when we play shows, and I saw on Facebook that a store I like is having a sale. Then I've got to practice. We've got another big gig this weekend."

"Will you be okay for lunch?"

"Yes, I'll grab something when I'm out."

He smirked.

"Watch for additives!"

She snorted, then got up from the table and cleared the dishes. Rashford followed her, carrying the cups out to the kitchen. She turned and faced him, leaning back against the sink. He bent forward and carefully kissed each rabbit.

"Keep the warren safe for me," he said. Mandy kissed the top of his head.

"You go and keep the world safe for us," she said.

He straightened up and kissed her on the lips, leaning into her so her back arched over the sink.

"Are you going to dress like this for dinner as well?" he growled.

She pushed him away.

"Off you go. See you tonight."

He kissed her again, then went through to the living room, collecting his bag and coat as he left. At the door he stopped.

"I nearly forgot," he said. "There's a key for the apartment here, on the side. So, you can get back in."

"Rats," she said, coming out of the kitchen.

"What?"

"I was going to wait until you had left and then hang out of the window and wave my apron at you, shouting that you were holding me captive."

He shook his head and laughed.

"They're here," he said, pointing at the keyring, and then left the room.

Outside, he was still grinning as he walked to his Jeep. He said good morning to his neighbour, who was loading her three teenage sons into the car for the school run.

'That would have been the talk of the neighbourhood', he thought.

When he got to the office, Sarah was already there. She handed him a cup of coffee and told him to sit on one of the guest chairs. He did so and waited as she pulled some papers together from a series of files. When she had finished, she handed them to him.

"The Chief says you're to read these," she said, "then come back here at ten for a meeting to discuss."

He nodded, taking the file, then looked around.

"Do I read them here?"

"No, in your office."

He looked at her.

"What office?"

"Has nobody told you? Honestly, sometimes I think I'm the only person who actually does anything around here."

She rummaged on her desk and then passed him a key.

"Room 303, down the hall."

"Thank you."

He took the key, the file, and his coffee and walked down the hall, checking off the numbers. At 303 he unlocked the door and found himself in a small office, with a desk, chair, filing cabinet, and computer terminal. There was a window which looked out over the car park, and a fluorescent light that spluttered and spat when he turned it on. He found a desk lamp which worked, and turned off the overhead light, then sat at the desk and opened the file.

At five to ten he left the office, locking the door, and walked back to see Sarah. She nodded that he should go straight through, so he did. Chief Superintendent Pollard was sitting at her desk.

"Ah, Staff Sergeant," she said. "Right on time. Did you read the file?"

"Yes, Ma'am."

"And?"

"It seems like we have a lot of missing persons, Ma'am."

"Indeed, we do. Thirty-seven at last count, from the last year alone, and just from this province. Ninety-two if we go back five years. Who knows how many if we were to include all of Alsama. Where do you think they've gone, Staff Sergeant?"

"I've no idea, Ma'am."

"Exactly. Nobody does. For the next ten weeks I want you to try and find out. Your computer has full access to our system database, and to the RCMP system in Toronto. Your job is to try and cut the list down to those who are really missing. I want you to try and find those who have run away, those who have changed their name, those who decided to make a new life. Let's see if we can get this down to manageable proportions, and then we can put resources into finding them as well."

"Yes, Ma'am."

"If you need to go out and do follow-up work, visits and interviews and the like, just tell Sarah where you're going and when you expect to be back. I don't want to lose you as well."

"Yes, Ma'am."

Pollard paused, then looked at him.

"In case you're wondering, Josee is on that list. Nobody admits to having seen or heard anything of her. But please, give them all your equal attention."

"Yes, Ma'am. Excuse me, but did we hear back about the fingerprint?"

"Not yet. In your capacity as special investigator on this file, you can follow up as you see fit."

"Yes, Ma'am. Thank you, Ma'am."

"Right. Off you go, then."

She turned her attention back to the papers on her desk. Rashford saluted and left the office.

At lunch he went down to the canteen. He was picking his way though a casserole of indeterminate meat and vegetables when he felt a hand on his shoulder and Gayle Morgan slid into the chair next to him, placing a paper cup of coffee on the table.

"'ey up, Gavin," she said. "Back in't fold, are ya?"

She looked at his plate.

"Strewth, what are you eating?"

"I've no idea," he confessed, pushing the plate to one side. "The menu says it's boeuf bourguignon, but I've got my doubts."

She laughed.

"Stick to the salads," she said. "They're better for you, and they can't really screw them up."

"Have you eaten?"

"Yes, I stopped on my way in. I just came down for a coffee. I'm meeting Pollard at one-thirty."

"Any news?"

"Oh yes," she said, then looked around. "Not here, though."

Rashford nodded.

"Why don't you come to my office after your meeting?"

She stared at him.

"Your ... You have an office?"

He nodded.

"Room 303," he said.

She shook her head.

"Wonders never cease. See you then."

She stood up, collected her coffee, and left the canteen. Rashford took his plate to the trolley, dumping the stew into the compost bin and making sure his plate and cutlery were in the correct plastic trays. Then he went outside and had a cigarette in the designated smoking area before returning to his office and continuing his search through the databases.

At two-fifteen there was a knock at his door and Morgan walked in. She looked around and sniffed.

"Not very homey," she said. "You should get a spider plant or something."

"I just got here this morning," he said, laughing. "Hang on, I'll go and find you a chair."

He walked down the hall and asked Sarah if he could borrow one of the guest chairs.

"'Borrow' means 'and bring it back'," she said, nodding at the one with a cracked seat. "Take that one."

He carried it back and found Gayle Morgan standing at his desk, idly leafing though the file.

"This'll keep you busy," she said, nodding.

He put the chair in front of the desk; she sat down gingerly, testing the structure.

"I don't want that crack biting me bum," she said.

Rashford thought immediately of Mandy, standing at the sink in her apron and rabbit hole panties, and grinned. Morgan huffed.

"It wouldn't be funny," she said.

"No, of course not," he agreed, trying to remove his smile as he looked at her. "So, what's your news?"

"We've got Benoît and Smithson bang to rights," she said. "For all five bodies."

Rashford whistled.

"Well done," he said. "Who are the other two?"

"Apparently, they're a couple of hitchhikers who were passing through. Smithson picked them up and got chatting, he said they indicated to him that they liked things a bit kinky. They were on a journey of exploration, he said, and wanting to explore their sexuality. So, he invited them back to his playroom, and called the professor. She came over, and it turned out that what the hitchhikers' thought was kinky and ground-breaking was a bit vanilla for the tastes of the hosts. They showed them 'some proper S&M', in Smithson's words, which sadly they didn't survive. This is where the idea of the planter box came from. They stored them in a freezer until it was ready."

"Holy mackerel, that's good police work. Well done!"

"Thank you. We're having a bit of a celebration this evening, down at the Grey Goose. Do you want to join us?"

"Umm ..."

"You can bring this Ravishing Robicheau woman I've been hearing about. I understand she's down for a visit?"

Rashford looked at her.

"How can you possibly know that?"

"Bettina told me. That guy who drove her down and dropped her at the casino, his grandmother is Bettina's auntie."

Rashford shook his head.

"Incredible," he said. "Okay, what time?"

"Anytime after seven," she said. "We've booked the back room. Pollard might show up as well."

He nodded.

"Yes, she'll want to show support, That's a great result for you."

Morgan nodded and got to her feet.

"Thanks. See you later."

Rashford stood up as well.

"Hang on," he said. "These hitchhikers. When was this?"

Morgan shrugged.

"Four, five years ago."

"Do you have their names, or a photograph, anything like that?"

She nodded.

"Both, actually. Smithson kept his polaroid, of course, though it's a bit yellowed now. But for some reason he kept their driver's licences as well. Why?"

Rashford tapped the file on his desk.

"They might be in here," he said. "It would be good to cross two off the list on day one of the job."

Morgan laughed.

"I'll check when I'm back in the car, the details are in my report. I'll text you the names."

"Thanks."

"See you tonight?"

"Wouldn't miss it."

CHAPTER 27

Rashford got home just after five, having decided to stop early for the day. Gayle Morgan had texted him the two names, both of which were on his list, and he carefully noted the details of their abduction and murder in his file. He had also tracked down a sixteen-year-old girl who had disappeared the previous year. She, it turned out, had joined a small commune in the wooded hills east of North Battleford. It was run by a religious sect who maintained a strict code of obedience to the man who had founded the church. Rashford discovered this by reading the transcript of an interview with the Founder's wife, who had found herself supplanted in the marriage bed by the sixteen-year-old.

"She looks older," the woman had sobbed to the detective, "but it's still illegal, isn't it?"

The police had conducted a check, but the girl swore she was living on her own and showed them her room, a monastic cell which contained a bed, a crucifix, and a dresser that contained all her clothes. The Founder said his wife had been having psychological issues recently and, in his opinion, should be medicated, not interviewed. The woman had refused to return to the commune, disappearing into the streets of Regina, and the police file indicated that no further action was required.

Rashford found the number for the commune and called it; he was able to confirm that the girl was who he thought she was, that she still lived there, and that she was expecting her first child in two months. She refused to give him permission to contact her parents, who she referred to as 'hypocritical bigots and non-believers out to destroy the world'. He emailed a summary of his findings to the detective who had conducted the first investigation, receiving a terse reply which did not give him confidence that anything further would happen. He sighed and crossed the girl's name off his list.

"Three successes on your first day!" said Mandy. "That's wonderful. Shall we have a glass of wine to celebrate?"

She was dressed in jeans and a sweatshirt and had smears of flour on her cheek and around her nose. Pleasing smells emanated from the kitchen.

"Perhaps later," said Rashford. "What's for dinner?"

"Boeuf bourguignon," said Mandy, then looked at his face.

"What?"

Rashford explained his lunch-time disaster and she laughed, saying that she hoped hers would be better. Then he told her about the invitation to the celebration. Mandy sat down on a kitchen stool.

"Who'll be there?" she said.

"Just Gayle and her team, the people who've made these arrests. And the Chief Superintendent might drop in as well."

"Do we have to go?"

He shrugged.

"I should probably drop in, at least for one drink," he said. "These kinds of things, they're important for morale. That's why the Chief will go."

"Do you need me there?"

Rashford paused, looking at her.

"I don't *need* you there, no. But I'd be happy if you came. It will give you a chance to meet some of the people with whom I work."

"Who will all be getting plastered."

"Maybe later, yes. But we don't have to stay for that bit."

She looked at him.

"Just one drink?"

"Yes."

"Promise?"

"Yes."

She gnawed at a fingernail.

"Okay then. Let's eat, and have that glass of wine, and then I'll get changed."

"You're fine like that," Rashford protested.

"Ha! I'm not going to meet the famous Gayle Morgan dressed like this," she said.

Rashford shook his head and opened a bottle of wine, carefully decanting it into a flagon and back into the bottle. Mandy nodded approvingly, then brought out a lidded casserole dish which she placed on a pair of place mats in the middle of the table. Wearing an oven mitt to hold the dish, she carefully ran a sharp knife under the lid. Rashford looked on, perplexed.

"What are you doing?"

She looked up at him.

"Opening the lid," she said.

"Is it stuck?"

"Yes. You put a flour paste around the lip to seal it, so the casserole doesn't dry out in the oven."

"Oh."

Once she had cut around the perimeter, the lid popped off easily and a rich aroma swirled out. Rashford breathed it in and smiled.

"This is nothing like what I had for lunch," he said, reaching for a serving spoon.

"Wait," said Mandy, returning to the kitchen. She came back with a loaf on a wooden carving board, a serrated knife lying alongside.

"I made bread," she said. "It's good for dunking."

They got to the Grey Goose just after seven. It was a gastropub just down the block from the Albert Street police station and was used to hosting events to both celebrate success and commiserate failure. Not many local residents were regulars at the pub, preferring to do their drinking away from police officers, and the licensee was an ex-officer himself. Rashford led Mandy into the back room, which legally held forty people and was currently packed with at least fifty.

Mandy had settled on a dark grey maxi skirt which brushed the tops of her polished cowboy boots. These had three-inch heels, which made her stand out even more in the crowd. She wore a cream-coloured silk blouse under a dark blue linen jacket and had braided her hair in one long strand. Rashford thought she looked fabulous, and had told her so, but on the drive over she had constantly worried what people would think of her.

Rashford was wearing what he called his 'dress' jeans, dark blue Wranglers with a fancy leather belt, an open-necked white dress shirt, and a black leather jacket. She made him enter the room first, so he stood just inside the door and surveyed the crowd while he waited for her to join him.

"Don't be nervous," he whispered. "They're only people."

She nodded, and he took her arm, leading her towards the bar.

"Over here, Gavin," someone called, and he turned to see who it was. At a table in the centre of the room, somehow separated from the throng elsewhere, sat a small group. He recognized Chief Superintendent Pollard, Sarah, Gayle Morgan, and, looking very comfortable sitting next to her, Constable Hayleyson. There were two empty seats. Rashford gulped, then led Mandy to the table.

He introduced her to the group, who each stood in turn to shake hands. In the process he discovered that Sarah's last name was Pacholuk, a name of Ukrainian heritage which made him reconsider the perogy theory. She was still in uniform, as was Pollard, but Gayle had changed into a burgundy-coloured pant suit. Sheri Hayleyson was wearing a skirt, albeit one shorter than Mandy's, and a tight burnt-orange tee-shirt that glowed against her dark skin.

"Red wine?" said Pollard, holding out a bottle. They both nodded, and she poured them each a glass.

"Are you driving?" she said.

Rashford admitted that he was.

"Give the keys to Sarah," said Pollard. "You can get a taxi home."

"We can only stay for one drink," he said. "We have to get home. Mandy has to practice."

Gayle Morgan raised an eyebrow.

"Practice what, one wonders," she said, quietly. Sarah giggled.

Pollard shook her head and put her hand on Mandy's arm.

"You'll have to forgive them, dear," she said. "Rude and crude the lot of them."

Mandy laughed.

"It's okay," she said, then turned to Gayle.

"I play the fiddle," she said. "In a band. We have a big show coming up this weekend."

Hayleyson leaned forward.

"Where are you playing?" she said.

"The Majestic, out towards Swift Current. Saturday night at seven."

Hayleyson nodded.

"I live out there," she said. "I'm usually based at Speedy Creek. Are there any tickets left?"

Mandy shrugged.

"I'm not sure," she said. "But I'm sure I could get you one, if you'd like to come."

"Two, if possible," said Hayleyson, glancing towards Morgan, who nodded.

Sarah interrupted. "They grow canola out that way, don't they?"

Morgan nodded, looking at Rashford, who had choked on his wine. He wiped his lips.

"Sorry, it went down the wrong way," he said.

"It happens," said Sarah, smiling. "I find it best to breathe through the nose when I'm swallowing."

Rashford choked again, Morgan giggled, and Sarah innocently looked at Mandy.

"I'd love to come as well, if there's room," she said.

Mandy nodded, then looked across at Pollard.

"Sorry, I have a prior engagement," she said.

"Three tickets, then. I'll see what I can do."

"Good," said Morgan, then looked at Rashford.

"Come on Gavin. Sarah got the short straw; she's driving the Chief tonight, so she gets to hold the keys."

Rashford noticed that Sarah was drinking a fruit-coloured concoction with a small beach umbrella decorating the top. She saw his look.

"It's a mocktini," she said. "All glitz and no glamour."

Mandy laughed.

Sarah glanced at her.

"So, what do you do, Mandy, when you're not playing fiddle?"

Mandy shrugged.

"Not a lot, right now. I'm waiting to get my results, then I'll figure out what's next."

"Results? From what?"

"University. I've just finished a degree in psychology, with a major in witchcraft and a minor in sexual deviancy."

Everyone at the table stared at her.

She smiled.

"Don't worry, it was all theoretical, not applied."

Rashford drained his wine, passed his car keys to Sarah, and held out his glass for a refill.

It was just before nine when the taxi dropped them back at the townhouse. They had only had three drinks, but Rashford had taken Pollard's advice not to drive. Mandy was still laughing.

"Did you see their faces?" she said, hanging onto his arm. "Priceless. Thank you for inviting me."

She leaned into him and gave him a deep kiss.

"Get a room," said a voice, and Rashford saw one of the teenagers walking up the next-door path. He waved, then opened the door and dragged Mandy inside.

She dropped onto the couch with a great sigh and lifted one of her legs.

"Can you help me with my boots, please," she said. "My feet are killing me."

He stood in front of her and pulled at the heel, working it back and forth until it came off her foot. She placed her foot back on the floor and raised the other boot. This one slipped off more easily.

"And wine," she said, giggling. "I think we should have more wine."

Yes, m'Lady," he said, wandering into the kitchen and returning with two glasses of wine from their earlier bottle.

They toasted each other, then Rashford sat down on the couch. Mandy swivelled her legs so that her feet were on his lap, and he started to rub them gently with his spare hand. He looked at her, shaking his head.

"Witchcraft and sexual deviancy?"

She scoffed.

"I figured those two out straight away," she said. "Gayle and Sarah. I figured I'd get my shots in first."

She'd done that, he thought. Hayleyson had looked on in amusement as the innuendo, double entendres, and general sexualized comments had come thick and fast between the three women, getting more and more ribald as they consumed more wine. It was only after one particularly suggestive exchange that Chief Superintendent Pollard called a halt.

They had been in the pub about forty-five minutes when Gayle suggested they get something to eat, "summat to mop up t'booze" as she phrased it. Sheri Hayleyson had offered the opinion that the food at the Grey Goose was good, especially the chicken, and Sarah had smiled provocatively.

"Oh, yes, you like your chicken, don't you, Gavin? But I forget. Are you a breast or a leg man?"

Mandy reddened as Gayle scoffed.

"Geez, Sarah, look at her, what do you think he likes? Look in the mirror as well, while you're at it."

Chief Superintendent Pollard nodded and spoke for the first time since they had arrived.

"That's enough, ladies," she said.

Sarah blushed pinkly. Rashford noticed that her uniform did not really diminish her chest, which he now remembered was quite generous, if not to Mandy's proportions.

Pollard turned to Mandy.

"What program did you really take, at university?" she said.

Mandy smiled, her blush slowly subsiding.

"I did a double major in politics and philosophy," she said, "with a minor in musicology."

Rashford half-turned in his seat and stared at her. Pollard nodded.

"I thought that must be you. Your full name is Amanda, correct?"

Mandy nodded.

"I looked you up," said Pollard. "You're in the running for the President's Prize this year, I hope you get it."

Mandy blushed again, this time with pride.

"It was an honour to be nominated," she said.

"And you're becoming quite a famous fiddle player, aren't you? One blog I read even said that you were thinking of leaving the band to pursue a solo career."

Mandy shook her head.

"That's just idle gossip on a fans' forum," she said. "I don't respond to that stuff, it's better just to leave it alone and let them have their conspiracy theories. Unless it get's too crazy, then I might say something."

As he rubbed Mandy's feet, he voiced his doubts regarding their relationship.

"How long will me listening to you be enough?" he said.

She sipped her wine, her eyes closed as she relaxed, and spoke drowsily.

"What do you mean?"

"Well, you're going to get really famous soon, aren't you? Either that or go off to graduate school somewhere. Why would you be interested in an old policeman like me?"

"Is this us having the 'is it a relationship or just sex' conversation?"

"I don't know. Maybe. Perhaps."

She opened her eyes and looked at him.

"Gavin, can we talk about this another time? Right now, I'm just having fun. I haven't got my marks back so I don't know if I passed my courses, I can't even think about graduate school. And the band has this big tour I told you about, I'm not leaving them at anytime soon. I can survive on the enthusiastic sex theory for now, can't you?"

He squeezed her foot and then her ankle. Keeping his fingers lightly rubbing on her skin, he pushed his hand under her skirt and up her calf, stroking the back of her knee, and then reached beyond that to her inner thigh.

"I guess I'll have to," he said.

The next two days passed quickly and Rashford was able to cross another four names off his list. He also got permission to leave work an hour early on Thursday and drive Mandy back for her rehearsal. They chatted as they drove, and he told her about his conversation with Pollard.

"So, you can come on the tour?" she said, grabbing his arm excitedly and almost making him swerve onto the shoulder of the road.

"Careful," he laughed, "or we won't be going anywhere."

He got the vehicle back in lane and then continued.

"If they still want me then yes, I've got permission to be away for the tour."

Mandy clapped her hands together.

"That will be so good," she said. "I don't think anyone else has found a possible roadie."

When he then told her that Shyanne had confirmed that she could meet with him that evening, to talk about Josee, Mandy invited him to stay at her apartment overnight.

"I'll talk to the band tonight," she said, "and tell them that you're interested. Tomorrow we'll have an early breakfast, and you can still be in the office by eight-thirty."

They made good time, and he dropped her off at her apartment just before six.

"I'll be back around ten," she said, kissing his cheek as she got out of the Jeep. "Sorry but I don't have a spare key here, so you'll have to wait for me."

He nodded.

"You should have one somewhere," he said. "In case of an emergency."

"I do. Shyanne's got it, I just don't have an extra one."

Rashford waited a beat, then spoke.

"I could ask to borrow hers," he said.

Mandy shook her head emphatically.

"Nope. Definitely not. The place is a mess. I didn't clean up before I left. Please, just wait until I get back, okay?"

He nodded.

"Sure," he said. "Have a good evening."

She waved and walked into the apartment building. Rashford drove slowly through the early evening traffic until he reached the Island View Hotel. He entered the numbers for his vehicle registration and credit card numbers, and the machine spat out a ticket that was valid for six hours, one of four options available to him. Leaving the car park, he followed the path to the riverbank and then followed the path to the 'Dances with Gravy' food truck.

There were only a few customers and so he took a seat at one of the tables on the edge of the floating dock. As he had hoped, Shyanne was still working. She waved at him, finished serving plates of food to two customers, and then walked over to his table.

"Hi, you," she said, leaning in for a hug. "I thought you were coming here after seven?"

"I was," he said, "but we got in early, and Mandy had to get ready for her rehearsal."

Shyanne nodded.

"And she kicked you out? That figures. Mandy can be a bit focused when it comes to her music."

"Yes, I'd noticed," said Rashford, laughing.

"Did you eat? Antoine prepped too much food, we were expecting a bigger crowd tonight, so I can give you a good deal on the buffalo chili and bannock."

"Sounds great," he said. "And a beer if you've got it. Something light."

She shook her head.

"Sorry, we're not licensed for booze. Lots of soft drinks, though."

"Ginger ale?"

"Coming up."

She left him and went back to the food truck, returning a few moments later with his drink and an ashtray.

"The chili is ready," she said, "he's just making you some fresh bannock. It'll be a few minutes, so I thought you might want a smoke."

He nodded his thanks, bringing out his cigarettes and angling his chair so he could watch the river.

At seven o'clock Shyanne called goodnight to Antoine and then collected her bicycle from behind the food truck. Rashford walked over to meet her and together they strolled down the embankment. She was not her usual chatty self, so he waited patiently until she spoke.

"Have you heard anything?"

"Not yet, no," he said.

She wiped her eyes with the back of her hand.

"Where can she be? She's my best friend, she should have told me."

"Maybe she was going to but just didn't have the chance," he said.

"That means she could have been hurt, or worse. I don't want to believe that. It's just not fair."

She burst out crying properly now. Rashford awkwardly put his arm around her, pulling her to his chest. She let go of the bike and it dropped on the path as she threw her arms around him and leaned tightly into his chest, sobbing uncontrollably. He patted her back and stroked her hair, ineffectually he thought, and her weeping and shaking slowly subsided. At last, she stood back and turned away, blowing her nose lustily. He picked up her bike.

"Come on," he said, "let's get you home."

This time he wheeled the bicycle while she walked next to him, clutching his hand. They may have looked like lovers, he thought, but this contact was desperation, not romance. They didn't speak until they reached her house.

"Do you want to come in?" she said, still sniffling.

Rashford nodded.

"Yes, please. I do have some news."

She paused on the step and looked at him.

"No, nothing bad," he said. "Nothing good either, really. A bit of both, I guess. Just informational."

"Okay," she said, opening the door and going inside.

He looked at the bicycle, which he was still holding.

"What's the combination?" he said.

She shouted it out and he went round the side of the house, chained the bike to the metal grill, then ran lightly up the steps and joined her in the living room. The black bear stared at him balefully, so he leaned down and scratched its ears.

"Hello, boy," he said. "We're back."

Shyanne laughed quietly, still blinking back tears, and asked him to wait while she got changed. This she achieved in less than ten minutes, coming back down in jeans and a sweatshirt, her cheeks pink from washing and her hair brushed straight. She walked over and hugged him tightly, then stepped back and looked at him, her hands on his elbows.

"Thank you," she said. "I needed that. Now, what else are you going to tell me?"

He nodded and led her to one of the armchairs, then crossed the room and sat in the second one. They looked at each other.

Rashford cleared his throat.

"First, I have to tell you that I'm now unretired," he said.

She looked at him.

"Unretired? Is that even a word?"

He shrugged.

"It is now. Anyway, I've been asked to look into all the missing persons cases here in our province and then, if I have time, all across Alsama. The bad news is that Josee is now officially on that list. The good news is that I might be in a position to do something about it."

Shyanne nodded.

"So Josee is now considered a missing person?"

"Yes," said Rashford. "It's been more than ten days now, and we have a credible independent eyewitness report that when she left your place, she wasn't in distress or upset about anything."

"You mean, like, suicidal?"

"Well, that's always a concern," said Rashford, gently.

"But I told you, she's a Catholic. She doesn't believe in that."

"Yes, I know. And we've ruled that out."

She huffed.

"And who's the credible eyewitness? Not me, I guess?"

"Correct. You were her friend, and you worked with her. You could have had a falling out. I know, I know …"

He broke off, trying to calm her down as she pushed up angrily out of the chair.

"Shyanne, listen. We get to see all sorts of things in my work. And sometimes, it's the easy options that we ignore, and that can be bad for the investigation. We had to check whether you and she were getting on okay. We had to check her and Antoine. We had to check her friends at university, and her family back home. This is what we do."

She subsided in the chair, still grumbling.

"It's because we've done all those things, and because Patrick York has made a sworn statement that when she left, she appeared calm, relaxed, and unthreatened, it's because of all those facts that we can now officially declare her a missing person. We know what and where she isn't, now we have to find where she is."

She looked at him.

"And you're doing that? Personally, I mean."

He nodded.

"I am."

***

She made some herbal tea, some kind of personal blend of mint, ginger, and sweetgrass, then sat and answered his questions as he tried to piece together the disparate elements of Josee's life. It was only as she mentioned Pia going to visit her that he stopped the conversation.

"Josee tried to tell him that they were cousins," she said, "but he wouldn't listen."

"I think you've got that wrong," he said. "Pia isn't interested in Josee."

"What do you mean? He went over there two or three times a week."

Rashford sat silently and waited. He saw her face scrunch up in a parody of deep deliberation, then realization dawn on her face.

"Petra? No way. She's Muslim!"

"So what? She's lived here since she was three, her worldview is probably more western than traditional. You said she was a nudist, for heaven's sake."

"I know. But Pia, and Petra?"

She shook her head, but Rashford detected that she was asking herself questions. He waited patiently.

"I will ask him," she said, glaring at Rashford. "He's my brother, I should know these things."

He shrugged.

"Maybe ask Mandy first. Sometimes outsiders see things more clearly than family, especially if he wasn't or isn't ready to tell you."

She nodded.

"I will," she said, firmly. "Tomorrow."

They sat in silence, sipping their tea. Eventually, Rashford spoke.

"Do you have your exam results back yet?"

"No, we don't get ours until next week. They try to get all the fourth-year students finished first, so they know who is going to graduate. They were going to get theirs' today."

"Today?"

"Yeah, the e-mail was supposed to come out at six. That's why I was surprised you were at the food truck."

Rashford shook his head, sadly.

"She didn't tell me," he said. "Why wouldn't she trust me?"

Shyanne looked at him.

"Like I said, she can get very focused. She probably wanted to just be by herself when she got the news, good or bad. That way she's not vulnerable, there's nobody else there to see her reaction."

"I sort of get that, but I should be part of these things."

"Why?"

"What?"

"Why should you be part of these things. Are you married now?"

"No ... umm ..."

"Are you in a common-law relationship?"

"No ... umm ..."

"Are you in any sort of relationship other than a sexual one?"

"Yes! She wants me to be her roadie."

Shyanne stared at him in disbelief, then burst out laughing.

"Well, there you are, then. Of course, she should have shared one of the most meaningful moments of her life with you, you might be her roadie!"

Rashford nodded his head, feeling sheepish.

"You're right," he said, looking down at the floor. At the edge of his vision, he saw that the black bear had raised its head and was laughing at him.

"What's that?" said Shyanne. "Don't mumble."

He looked up.

"You're right," he said, clearly.

She smiled.

"A girl can never hear that enough from a man," she said, leaning back in her chair and stretching her arms high above her head.

He sighed.

"You're right," he said, pronouncing every syllable.

Then he glanced across at the bear and saw that it was back in its usual place, staring at the door. He shook his head to clear it, but the image of the bared teeth grinning at him would not go away. Shyanne laughed.

"Mandy is bear clan," she said, as if that explained everything.

Chapter 28

He left Shyanne's and got back to Mandy's apartment just after ten, as requested. He saw the lights were on, so he knocked at the door. When she opened it he saw that she was wearing a pair of track pants, emblazoned with the university logo, and an over-large sweatshirt. Her hair hung loose across her shoulders and over her chest, and she held a hairbrush in her right hand.

"Great timing," she said. "I just got out of the shower. It was a hard rehearsal tonight."

She reached up to kiss him, then led him inside. He saw there was a large map spread out on the table. She took his arm and they stood next to the table, looking down.

"Atlantic Canada," she said, then looked at him.

"They said you can come, if you still want to, but I have to show you the route first."

He nodded.

"Fair enough."

"And then, if you're still interested, they want to meet you. Tomorrow morning. Can you be late for work?"

He nodded.

"I'll figure it out," he said.

She leaned over and placed her finger on Newfoundland, continuing to brush her hair as she spoke.

"We'll fly into Saint John's on the twenty-eighth of June," she said, "and then play the big Canada Day concert on Signal Hill. Then we fly back across to Halifax."

She moved her finger around the map as she spoke.

"We're going to loop down the south shore and back up the Annapolis Valley, then across to Cape Breton. We have a couple of small festivals there, plus the normal gigs. We'll come back round to Antigonish and Pictou, here, then get the ferry to PEI. There's a great show called the Rollo Bay Fiddle Festival and we're playing there for three days."

"Three days? Wow," said Rashford. "That sounds intense."

She nodded.

"It is. Then we come across the bridge to New Brunswick, do some gigs there, then get the ferry from Saint John across the Bay of Fundy to Digby, here. We have a couple more gigs in the Annapolis Valley, at Digby and Kentville, then we go to Halifax and close the tour with two shows at the big arena there. Then we have a day off before we fly home. That will be in early August."

Rashford shook his head.

"Will you be playing every night?"

She laughed.

"No, we have a number of days off. We're usually too tired to do much sightseeing, though. Most days we get up, drive to the next gig, set up, do a sound check, have a rest, then play. I tell you it's pretty boring."

She looked into his eyes.

"I only want you to do this if you want to do it," she said. "And I should tell you, there will be six of us in the van, plus you."

"Who's the new person?"

"We're going to bring a sound guy with us. We usually use the local talent but for a tour like this, we want the sound to be right every night. So that's an extra mouth to feed."

Rashford shrugged.

"No problem for me," he said. "As long as you and the band trust him."

She nodded.

"He's never been on tour," she said, "but we've used him here and he seems okay. He's doing the sound on Saturday, at The Majestic."

"Can I come to that?"

"If you'd like, sure. That will also give you a chance to look at the gear, make sure you're okay with it all."

She looked at him.

"I think Petra's coming as well," she said. "Plus, your police officer friends. Are you okay with that?"

He nodded.

"Gayle and Hayleyson will only have eyes for each other, and Sarah will be hunting for another notch," he said. "What about Pia? Is he coming?"

Mandy said nothing until she had finished brushing her hair.

"Why do you say that?" she said at last.

He considered his words carefully.

"I ... umm ... I think he'd like the opportunity to spend some time in Petra's company," he said.

Mandy grinned.

"You're right, he would," she said, putting down her brush and clapping her hands. "And luckily, Shyanne can't come, so he doesn't have to worry about his little sister getting in the way."

Rashford looked at her.

"You knew?"

She shrugged.

"It became obvious that he was starting to 'drop-in' on Josee whenever he knew she was working her shifts at 'Dances with Gravy'. I asked Petra if she needed me to say anything, to him or to Shyanne, but she said she quite liked him. Apparently, he believes in the principles and benefits of nudism as well."

Rashford stared.

"Pia?"

She giggled.

"The mind finds that hard to compute, right?" she said.

Rashford thought for a moment of the lithe young Petra and the large, older Pia, each without clothes, then decided Mandy was right. He changed the subject.

"Why can't Shyanne come?"

"She's going to a movie, apparently," said Mandy. "With Patrick."

When he had finished coughing and choking, Mandy led him to the couch and made him sit down. She went into the kitchen and came back with two tall, fluted glasses and a bottle with a gold-coloured label. She handed it to him.

"Do the honours, could you?" she said. "Please."

He looked at the bottle.

"Veuve Cliquot?" he said, tearing the foil from the top. "What's the occasion?"

She just smiled. He removed the foil and then carefully unwound the metal frame that kept the cork in place. He put it to one side, then slowly worked the cork backwards and forwards with one hand while holding the bottle in the other. The cork popped out, knocking his arm backwards, but he held it firmly. Then he reached forward and tipped the foaming bottle over the first glass. He moved the bottle from one flute to the other, waiting each time for the foam to subside, until they had two well charged glasses. Then he put the bottle and the cork down on the table.

Mandy held out one of the glasses. He took it and looked at her. She smiled.

"I assume this is for more than the tour?" he said.

She nodded.

"I got my marks tonight," she said, softly. Then she looked at him, her eyes shining.

"I passed everything. I'm going to graduate!"

He clinked his glass against hers.

"Well, that's one thing I never doubted," he said. "Congratulations!"

She huffed.

"I doubt everything," she said. "Then I'm never disappointed."

Rashford laughed.

"That's one way of looking at it," he said. "What about that award, the one Pollard mentioned?"

"The President's Prize?"

"That's it."

She shrugged.

"I don't know. They don't announce that until the convocation ceremony."

He took a sip of champagne and looked at her over the top of his glass.

"Can I go to that?"

She laughed and kissed him, then looked seriously at him.

"Unfortunately," she said, "each graduate is only allowed up to six tickets for the convocation ceremony. I've got all mine, for my parents, my uncle, and my cousins."

Rashford felt intensely disappointed but nodded with a smile.

"Fair enough," he said. "Perhaps I can take everyone out to dinner afterwards?"

"That would be nice," she said. "But I hadn't finished."

He looked at her.

"Oh?"

"Unless she turns up in the next week, you can have Josee's ticket," she said. "They don't care who actually uses the tickets."

Rashford nodded.

"You know," he said, "put like that, I rather hope I don't get to go."

Mandy put down her glass and reached over for his, placing it next to hers on the table. She stepped into his embrace, and he held her tightly, her head pushing against the front of his shoulder. Her voice was muffled.

"Me too," she said.

They stood quietly, pressed close together. Rashford spoke over her head.

"When is it, this convocation?"

"Next Saturday. A week or so from now."

"What will you do until then?"

"Well, we have this gig on Saturday, and then I need to find somewhere to live. My lease here runs out at the end of the month, so I need to find somewhere for two months before the tour."

"Can't you extend here?"

"No. The landlord has already told me they're going to renovate this building, and then put the rents up."

Rashford thought for a moment, then took the plunge.

"You could always come and live with me," he said.

She hugged him even tighter and spoke into his chest.

"I didn't hear that," he said.

She raised her head, smiling.

"Thanks, but no thanks," she said. "It's too much hassle to come back and forth for rehearsals. And I don't want to sit at your place watching daytime television while you're at work."

She reached up and ran the palm of her hand along his cheek.

"Don't pout," she said. "I'll ask Shyanne if I can stay with her for four months, until the end of August. It's likely that Derek or Frieda will be going home for the summer, one of them usually does, so I can have their room until they get back. By then I'll know how the tour went, and what's happening with the band."

Rashford nodded.

"You're right," he said.

She smiled and stretched her arms high over her head.

"You're right," he said, a second time. "Will you be able to come down for weekends?"

"If we're not playing a gig, why not? Or you could come up here."

He looked at her.

"Why would I want to do that?"

She stretched her arms high again, this time lifting the hem of her sweatshirt with her hands.

"I'm sure I can tempt you," she said.

Chapter 29

Rashford called Sarah at eight-thirty the next morning and told her that he would not be in the office until the afternoon.

"Sorry, I got tied up," he said.

"I'm sure she'll let you go before lunch," said Sarah, giggling. "Say hello from me."

Rashford huffed and clicked off the phone, then shouted to Mandy that he was ready. She called back that she was nearly done, then a few minutes later emerged from her rehearsal bedroom, wiping her hands on an old towel.

"Sorry, I just had to rosin my bows," she said, "and clean the dust off the bridges."

He looked at her.

"If I agree to become the roadie, do I have to understand what you just said?"

She laughed.

"Oh, you'll pick it up along the way," she said. "Come on."

They left her apartment and jumped into his Jeep, then he followed her directions until they reached a strip-row of shops and restaurants. He found a parking spot and they walked across to a small independent coffee shop.

"Who was 'Timothy'?" he said.

Mandy shrugged.

"No idea. He makes good coffee, though."

Inside they found a long bar, behind which stood two baristas. The daily specials were written on a chalk board attached to the back wall, and small display units were filled with different pastries.

"Medium latte please, extra hot," said Rashford.

"Make that two," said Mandy, "and two *pain au chocolat* please."

She grinned at Rashford.

"No crumbs, remember," she said.

He felt himself blushing as he paid the cashier, a tall young man with a hipster beard, red hair tightly woven into cornrows, and pale pink fingernails.

"Sit where you like," they said, "I'll bring it over."

"We're with the band," said Rashford, recognizing the lead singer and pointing to the corner table where a group of five were sitting. As they walked across the room he leaned over and whispered in Mandy's ear.

"I've always wanted to say that!"

She was still laughing as she made the introductions.

The lead singer had short, cropped hair, a dirty blonde in colour, and smiled at Rashford in welcome.

"How lovely to meet you at last," she said, surprising Rashford with her Australian accent. "I'm Monica. We've heard a lot about you."

He wasn't sure what to say, so went for the obvious.

"You've cut your hair," he said.

She laughed.

"No, the red hair is a wig," she said.

Mandy shook her head as Rashford started to redden.

"This is Jody," she said, hurriedly, "he plays bass."

A tall, skinny, dark-haired man in a black tee-shirt stood up and shook hands.

"Cheers," he said.

"Bass players talk like they play," said Mandy. "Quietly and in the background, but the heartbeat of the conversation."

Jody nodded and returned to his cappuccino.

"I'm Mick," said a short, laughing and somewhat rotund man with a multicoloured Mohawk haircut. "Lead guitar's my gig, so don't bender my Fender."

He laughed, then coughed violently.

"Sorry, need a smoke," he said.

"Mick and Josee didn't see eye to eye on a lot of things," murmured Mandy. "But she always said he was the best lead guitarist she's ever seen."

Mick shrugged.

"She always told it like it was, that girl," he said. "Mandy says you're gonna find her?"

"I'm going to try," said Rashford.

Mick nodded then subsided back into his seat. A bald Black man who appeared older than the others stood up. He had on a black tee-shirt emblazoned with a stylized orange drum-kit and the word Ginger, depicted in a 70s style psychedelic font.

"You must be the drummer," said Rashford.

"What was your first clue?" said the man, in a carefully modulated voice. "Was it the haircut?"

Rashford laughed.

"Even I know of Ginger Baker," he said. "Great band, Cream."

The man nodded.

"Plus, that's the only instrument left," said Rashford.

"Kit. Drums are a kit, not an instrument."

"Sorry."

"Not a problem," said the man, holding out his hand. "Gary. Short for Garfield."

Rashford shook hands.

"Like the cricket player?" he said.

"The man looked at him.

"Yes. My dad was a big fan. I hadn't taken you for a cricketer, though."

"Oh, I'm not," said Rashford, quickly. "A friend of mine was telling me about him, that's all. He's from Bermuda. My friend."

Gary nodded.

"Lot of good players from there," he said, then sat down.

Rashford turned to the last person at the table, a man in his early twenties who was focused on a game he was playing on his phone. He was wearing a linen dress shirt without a collar, pale green in colour with red stripes. There were two short horizontal black lines tattooed under his left eye, and a blue star with fuzzy edges on the side of his neck, under his right ear. Mandy coughed, loudly, and he looked up. He removed two earbuds and nodded.

"Sorry. Miles away. Hello."

Rashford held out his hand and the man half rose from the table. They shook hands.

"Hello," he said.

They looked at each other.

"Who are you?" said the man.

Rashford flashed a look at Mandy, then turned back.

"I'm Gavin," he said. "I might be the roadie for the tour."

The man nodded.

"Yeah, I heard about that. Shame about Gordon. He was a good bloke."

Rashford stood for a moment. The man started to replace one of the buds in his ear.

"And you are?"

The man stopped, then laughed in a high-pitched falsetto voice.

"Oh, didn't I say? Silly me. I'm Nigel. Nigel Woods. I'm the sound guy."

"Nice to meet you," said Rashford, but Nigel had already replaced the buds in his ears.

Mandy shrugged, then turned to the table.

"Guys, this is Gavin. I've told him what's involved and shown him on the map where we're going. If you're okay with it, then he'll come to our concert at The Majestic tomorrow and help us move the gear around. That will give him a sense of what it's really like."

The band members looked at each other.

"Works for me," said Gary, rapping out a tune on the table with his hands. Jody and Monica both nodded, and Mick turned to Rashford.

"Looks like you're good for tomorrow, then," he said.

Rashford nodded.

"Thanks," he said.

"Final decision by Monday morning, yeah?" said Mick. "We need to know if you're in or not."

Rashford nodded, then followed Mandy across to a small adjacent table, where the barista had placed their coffees and pastries.

From the coffee shop they went to a thrift store so that Mandy could look for a new top.

"New to me, anyway," she'd laughed. "I didn't find anything I liked in Regina. Sometimes there are great bargains here."

Rashford followed her around as she picked at items on the racks, selecting three to take into the changing rooms. Two she threw over the door, saying that they were the wrong shape for her, but she was wearing the third when she stepped back into the store. Rashford whistled.

"Wow," he said.

The top was a sort of tee-shirt, deep burgundy in colour, with short arms and the tops of the shoulders cut out and left bare. The front started as a round neck but then transformed into a deep vee, with four buttons on each side from which thick cords laced across her cleavage, which had been accentuated by the side bars of the shirt pushing her breasts together. The top fell to just over the belt of her jeans.

"Is it okay?" she said.

"It's perfect," said Rashford. "How much?"

"Five bucks," she said, laughing, then went back into the changing room.

"I'll be outside," he called, and left the store. He walked a dozen paces and joined another man who was standing on the corner, smoking. Rashford nodded at him and pulled out his own cigarettes, lit one, and then called Sarah to tell her that he wouldn't be in until Monday.

"Still tied up, are you?" she said, laughing.

Rashford tried to erase the image of the cords across the decolletage of Mandy's new top and kept his voice light.

"Just following up a few leads," he said. "Can you look up someone for me, please? Name is Nigel Woods. Caucasian male, about five feet eight inches tall, maybe a hundred and eighty pounds. Star tattoo on his neck, under his right ear."

"What's he done?"

"No idea," said Rashford. "But my gut tells me he's done something."

"Right," said Sarah. "I'll check."

"Thanks."

He paused, then cleared his throat.

"Are you really going out to The Majestic tomorrow?" he said.

She was silent for a moment, then replied in a soft voice.

"I was going to, yes. Are you okay with that?"

"Yes, of course. But I wanted you to know, I might be working."

"Working? On a case?"

Rashford laughed.

"No, nothing like that. As a roadie. Mandy wants me to help them shift their gear around."

"Really?" said Sarah. "How cool. Will you come out to the front and walk around with me a bit, during the break?"

Rashford nodded, then realized she couldn't see him.

"Sure, yes," he said, mystified. "Why?"

Sarah laughed happily.

"Then I can tell people, 'he's with the band'," she said. "They'll think I'm a groupie!"

Rashford smiled to himself.

"If it makes you happy," he said, and finished the conversation just as Mandy came out of the store and stood looking around. He walked over to her and they went back to the Jeep.

"Where next?" he said.

They had ended up back at her apartment and he had spent the afternoon acting as a clothing advisor. Mandy kept coming out of her bedroom in various combinations of clothes and Rashford had to score each outfit out of ten. He also had to develop a shorthand to identify the various clothes in each pairing, and soon discovered that 'black pants' was not sufficient information. After seeing twenty-one combinations over a three-hour period, Rashford called for a break.

"My eyes hurt," he said.

"Poor boy," said Mandy, coming out of bedroom wearing only jeans and a bra. "Let's have a glass of wine, that will help you."

"It's only four o'clock," said Rashford.

"Your point?" said Mandy. "Were you planning on taking me out somewhere?"

Rashford was silent but shook his head.

"Well then," she said.

She went into the kitchen and came back with two glasses of red wine, then sat next to him at the table and nudged the various sheets of paper with her finger.

"What scored highest?" she said.

Rashford clinked his glass against hers, took a sip of wine, and then started to sort through the paper. He pulled out five pages and handed them to her.

"These five were all in the "wow!" category," he said.

He pulled out another three.

"These were excellent."

He sorted through the pile that were left, placing them in three piles.

"These were very good, good, and more-than-acceptable," he said.

"Which ones did you triage out?"

"None of them. The worst you got was 'more-than-acceptable'."

Mandy shook her head.

"You'd never make it as a catwalk journalist," she said. "You need at least three in the 'I wouldn't bury my worst enemy if they were wearing that' category."

Rashford threw up his hands.

"How can I help it if your worst taste is 'more than acceptable'?" he said.

She kissed him on the cheek.

"Right answer."

She took the eight papers with the 'wow!' and 'excellent' combinations, and her wine, and returned to the bedroom.

"Now we'll focus on just these," she said. "Oh, hang on."

She came back into the room carrying a large standing lamppost with two hooded lamps at the top. She plugged it in and aimed it into the middle of the floor, then turned off the room lights as she returned to her room.

After the first walk through, Rashford had dropped two of the outfits and Mandy was left with six. After the second walk through, she was down to five.

"I'm hungry," Rashford complained. "It's nearly six o'clock."

She glared at him, her hands on her hips.

"We stay until we're finished, buster," she said. "This is important."

"But they're all amazing."

"Two were only 'excellent' the first time," she said, "and three were 'wow!' I want to get beyond those categories. The final three will make every woman at the show want to have them for themselves. And every man will want to rip them off me to give to them."

"Pretty high bar," muttered Rashford, then looked at her.

"Can I make a suggestion?" he said.

"Of course."

"Why don't you try the pants from this one and the top from this one, together," he said. "And the same with these."

He pointed at the various pages and Mandy nodded.

"I'll give it a try," she said, doubtfully, then went back into the bedroom.

When she came back out, Rashford could feel his jaw drop.

"Stunning," he said. "Just stunning."

She smiled, then went back and returned wearing the second set.

Rashford could hardly speak, she looked so beautiful. He just nodded vigorously and mumbled incoherently.

The third time she came out wearing the combination that had been first in the initial 'wow' category and had been front-runner of the final five. He nodded.

"I would gladly rip any of those three off you," he said.

Mandy grinned at him.

"Well, let's start with this one," she said. "It's in third place so it won't matter if it gets torn."

The Majestic was an old country pub that had fallen on hard times when stricter drink-driving laws came into effect. Many of those who ignored the new rules were arrested and had their vehicles impounded and their driving licences suspended. Others fell victims to Neo-Darwinism, wrapping themselves and their vehicles around power poles, misjudging distances between trains and unmanned railway crossings, or forgetting laws of motion as they attempted to take 'recommended speed: 80 kms' bends at a hundred and twenty-five.

The Majestic had limped on for a few years, supported by the local ranching community and the three hundred residents of the village, then stood derelict for a while before a couple from Vancouver had decided to make a lifestyle change. Selling their small one-bedroom condo for enough money to buy and refurbish The Majestic, with sufficient funds left over to buy matching Subaru Cross-Treks, Herbert and Arthur had embraced rural life and, after a period of readjustment, been embraced in return.

They had gutted the old pub and refurbished the upstairs, keeping half as a spacious apartment for themselves and making the other half into four self-contained rooms which they rented out to passing tourists. The three original saloons had been expanded into a large single space, with a bar along one side and a good-sized stage at the end. Dressing rooms for the musicians were clean and well-stocked and had the luxury of an additional outside entrance. The toilets had been updated and upgraded, and the kitchen produced simple but filling pub food three nights a week.

The Majestic had returned to being just that, its name spelled out in multicoloured lights that could be seen across many kilometres of prairie. Recognizing that tourists were now stopping just to take photographs, the new owners repainted the outside trim and installed replica original barn boards as walls. They also constructed a mini barn, which Arthur laughingly called a 'barnette', and took local artwork for sale on commission. Rashford was delighted to see that the name above the door to the gallery read 'Not Herb'n Art'.

"Very droll," he said to Mandy as they arrived to help set up for the show.

Mick had hired a young local man to set up the equipment and so Rashford tried to make himself useful during the sound check, moving microphones, amps, speakers and stools around as directed. He found it hard, physical work, and discovered a side of Mandy he had not seen before. She was a perfectionist in anything related to her music and insisted that her demands be met exactly as specified. There was, he discovered, no margin for error or initiative, as shown when she marched up to him when he was outside enjoying a break and a smoke.

"Gavin, I told you, the third stage monitor has to be exactly two feet in from the edge of the stage," she said.

"It is."

"It is not. Come and look."

She was not shouting, her voice was very precise and controlled, and he was all the more worried because of that. He stubbed out his cigarette and went back inside with her, then took the tape measure from her hand and knelt down.

"See, it's exactly 60 centimeters."

She glared at him.

"Yes. But that is only 23.6 inches. That is not two feet."

He looked up at her.

"When I come onstage, Gavin, I stand exactly there."

She pointed to a white cross made out of masking tape, just to the left of Gary's drum kit.

"Then I walk across to there, and then I come here to play the *Red River Jig.*"

At each point she indicated a cross taped to the floor. Looking around, he saw others as well, constructed from red and orange tape.

"The red ones are for Monica," she said, "and the orange ones for Mick. They help us make sure we don't get in each others way. And I know what the sound should sound like through the monitors when I am standing in the right place. But the monitors must be in the right place as well, exactly in the right place. Okay?"

He nodded.

"Sorry. I hadn't realized the precision involved."

"It's a performance, Gavin. Every step is choreographed, every note is practised until it's perfect. It's like Ron Stewart said in that old song, our *'ad lib* lines are well rehearsed'. That's why we're good. Because we work at it, and because we take care of the details. Capisce?"

"I'll move it," he said.

"Thank you."

She gave him a quick kiss on the cheek and then walked off backstage. Gary did a staccato sequence on the snare drum and grinned over at Rashford.

"Wait until we've been on tour for three weeks and she's tired," he said.

CHAPTER 30

Rashford met Gayle Morgan and Sheri Hayleyson at the entrance thirty minutes before the doors opened. He escorted them inside and showed them to their seats, which were at a table about a third of the way back from the stage.

"Not front row seats, then?" said Morgan, looking around.

Rashford shook his head.

"No, this is the best table. If you're too close then you're looking up all the time, it's bad for your neck. Here you're looking straight at the band and apparently this is the 'sweet spot' for the sound. We made the passages around a bit wider than the others as well, so you can pull your chairs back and have more leg room."

Hayleyson nodded.

"Thank you, Staff Sergeant. I appreciate that."

"Gavin, please. We're off-duty here.

"Thank you, Gavin. Long legs get in the way sometimes."

"Not very often," said Morgan, grinning lasciviously.

She was wearing what she referred to as her cowgirl clothes, modelled on either late Patsy Cline or early k. d. lang, Rashford was never sure. In addition to a plaid pinafore dress that flared out over ribbed black leggings, she wore a white men's dress shirt and soft-leather, sandy-coloured, short-rise cowboy boots with an intricate design. Hayleyson accentuated her figure with tight fitting blue jeans and a pale pink roll-neck shirt that was at least a size too small across the chest, and in her zip-sided black leather boots she towered over Morgan.

"Would you like a beer?" he said.

"Why not?" said Morgan. "We've already had a bottle of wine, before we came out, so why not beer. This looks like a beer kind of place."

Rashford laughed, then went to the bar to set up a tab for the table. Looking round, he saw that there were twenty-five tables, each with six seats, and from the sign on the wall he noticed that, according to the Fire Marshall, the room had a capacity of a hundred and fifty people.

"Someone knows how to do maths," he said to the bartender, who laughed.

"Yeah. After Herbert got the first fine, he just about had a fit."

"Fine for what?"

"They put on a karaoke drag night and must have had two hundred people crammed in here, whooping and hollering. What made it worse was that the Fire Marshall was here, then came round the next day with pictures he'd taken on his phone! Herbert told him that he'd thought it was a guideline, not a regulation, but he still had to pay a thousand dollar fine."

"So now the numbers are controlled?"

"Completely. Ticket only, nothing at the door. It's the only way."

Rashford nodded.

"How are sales for tonight?"

"Sold out. They went in less than two days. Luckily the band had asked for a table to be kept back."

"Cheers," said Rashford, taking the beers in hand. "Just FYI, two of the people who'll be at the table this evening are teetotalers. One likes soda water with blueberry juice, if you've got it."

"Not cranberry?"

"Apparently not."

"Okay, I'll dig out a bottle, we must have one somewhere. What about the other person?"

"I don't know what they'll have," said Rashford. "Sorry."

"No worries. Have a good evening, and we'll settle up at the end of the night, yeah?"

"Yeah. I'll come and see you before we start hauling the gear away."

The bartender nodded and moved away, and Rashford walked the drinks over to Gayle and Sheri, who were deep in conversation. They accepted the beers with thanks.

"I'll be back in a minute," said Rashford, and walked back to the main door. He nodded at the ticket collectors and then stepped outside, where he found a lengthy queue had formed, waiting for the doors to open at seven thirty. He walked to the corner of the building and lit a cigarette, then looked around. The sun went down at around eight o'clock and was already close to the horizon, silhouetting an old barn and a grain silo against the multicoloured layers of sky.

"Isn't it gorgeous," said a voice beside him.

He turned and found Sarah standing there, a long thin cigarette in her hand.

"I didn't know you smoked," he said, surprised.

She shrugged and exhaled a plume of smoke.

"Only on a Saturday night," she said. "It's one of my special treats."

He refrained from asking her what the others were, and instead complimented her on her clothes.

"You look nice," he said, taking in the black bustier dress, a series of pleated layers descending to just below her knees. Her hair was brushed out over her bare shoulders, the straps from the dress disappearing beneath her tresses. She was wearing a black velvet choker collar around her neck, with an imitation pearl suspended from a narrow chain and nestled between her breasts. The scalloped top of the dress reminded him of the notched edges of her desk, and her red pumps had yellow ankle straps and a four-inch heel. He wondered if they were the ones she had slipped into with the twins.

"Why thank you, kind sir," she said, pirouetting in a way that flared the bottom of her skirt.

"Don't peek," she said, grinning. "I'm going commando tonight."

They finished their cigarettes and stubbed them out in a metal biscuit tin that had been nailed to the wall, then she took his arm.

"Shall we?" she said, and they stepped out from behind the building.

Rashford led them past the queue and up the steps to the door. There were a few disgruntled mutterings as they passed, but Sarah simply smiled and waved.

"We're with the band," she said, and even autographed a small book which was thrust at her from the line. Rashford nodded at the ticket collectors as he passed.

"There will be two more," he said. "I'm not sure where they are yet."

"Just bring them down the line," said the older volunteer, who was wearing a striped black and white smoking jacket, and green velvet trousers. His colleague, who was wearing a tuxedo, nodded.

"We'll hold the mob back for you, old chap," he said.

Rashford nodded and walked Sarah into the building. Her heels clipped on the parquet floor as she made her way through the tables towards the other officers. Morgan appraised her as she approached.

"Red and yeller, catch a feller," she said, smirking.

Hayleyson punched her on the arm.

"Be nice," she said, then turned to Sarah.

"You look great," she said.

"Thank you," said Sarah. "You're looking pretty good yourself."

Morgan looked from one to the other.

"Hello," she said. "I'm still here, remember. And I outrank you both."

Rashford laughed, then asked Sarah what she would like to drink. He brought her tall gin and tonic to the table and then left to go and find his other guests. Sheri followed him, saying she needed to use the powder room. He had just pointed out the location when she tapped him on the shoulder, so he stopped. She leaned in to speak softly in his ear.

"I think I'm the only one at the table you haven't slept with," she said, smiling. "I know you're busy right now but when you're free, can you put me on the list?"

He looked at her, stunned, then hurriedly closed his mouth. She laughed, then let her hand trail along his face and across his shoulder, before turning and walking away.

He was still tingling when he arrived at the two gentlemen who were to collect the tickets. They were standing at the top of the steps, looking out over the crowd.

"Surely a minute or two early wouldn't hurt," said the tuxedo.

"We said seven thirty and we shall open at seven thirty," said the smoking jacket. "There's probably another damned regulation about early admittance."

"Mmpfh."

They looked at Rashford.

"Off to find the tardy ones, eh?" said the tuxedo.

Rashford admitted that he was, then introduced himself. The men smiled.

"I'm Herbert," said the smoking jacket. "This is Arthur. We own the place."

"You've done an incredible job with it," said Rashford.

Herbert nodded.

"Thank you. It's been a labour of love, hasn't it, Art?"

"It certainly has," said Arthur. "It's put years on our lives, living and working here instead of in the city. We're having a blast."

"Will you come and see the show?"

"Wouldn't miss it, old chap," said Arthur, nodding vigorously. "What's the point of owning a concert hall if you don't watch the concerts?"

"Even the strange ones," said Herbert, smiling. "We make a point of going to every event. We had no idea what an S and M themed party was going to be, did we, Art?"

Arthur shook his head.

"None at all. That evening was an eye-opener, I can tell you."

Herbert tsked.

"I could never use the whisk to whip cream ever again," he said. "We had to buy a machine."

Rashford laughed and left them counting down the seconds to seven thirty, an achievement marked by the sudden surge forward of people in the queue. He went to the edge of the car park and looked around, then saw a white BMW X-7 parked over by the trees. He looked around but couldn't see anyone, so he ambled across to the car and peered in the side window. Pia and Petra were sitting upright in the front seats, looking forward, holding hands across the console.

For a moment, Rashford thought they had been shot. He knocked on the window and was relieved when the pair turned to him as one. Pia pressed a button and the window wound down.

"We're coming," he said. "Just getting our chakras centered before we go in there."

He pressed the button and they both turned to face the front as the window purred closed. Rashford went over to the edge of the trees and lit a cigarette. He had smoked it, and was contemplating a second, when the doors opened, and Pia and Petra left the vehicle. They shook hands, then walked together to the doors of The Majestic.

Herbert looked at Pia, who was wearing his hair in a long braid and had traded his tattered old vest for a brocade smoking jacket worn over a Cowessess Powwow tee-shirt, and fringed buckskin trousers.

"Come to any show you like," he said. "Wear that and you get in free."

"The same goes for you, dear," said Arthur, looking admiringly at the body-hugging long black dress worn by Petra, a sparkling red and gold scarf around her hair the only colour. "You look exquisite."

They both nodded gravely, then followed Rashford into the room. The tables were already beginning to fill up, so he walked them to the group and then went to the bar for their drinks.

"Two sodas with blueberry, please," he said, and the barkeeper nodded. "And I'll have a beer."

<hr>

The concert was a huge success. The band played two forty-five-minute sets, and then a ten-minute encore, so it was ten thirty before the crowd started to disperse. Rashford went to the bar to pay the bill, adding a twenty-per-cent tip and leaning against the counter as he watched people make their way to the exit.

"One for the road?" said the bartender.

"Thanks, but I've got to move the gear now," he said. "I should try to stay sober; I don't want to drop anything."

"We're open until midnight if you'd like something after."

"Cheers."

He hadn't seen Sarah since the intermission. She had come up to him and given him a big hug, pressing herself closely into his body. He tried to push her away, but she resisted.

"Just hold it for a moment," she whispered. "There's a guy over there who's been trying to get his hands up my dress all evening. I don't like him. I told him I was yours and you'd kill him if he didn't leave me alone. So, make it look good."

Wary of revealing whether or not the commando comment was true, he kept his hands on her waist as he kissed her on the forehead, then put on an angry face before looking around the room. He caught the eye of a short, stocky youth in his early twenties, sitting at one of the back tables. The youth, who looked vaguely familiar, held his gaze for a moment and then looked down. Rashford pushed Sarah away and took a step towards the man, who hurriedly got to his feet and headed for the washrooms.

"He's gone," said Rashford, and she stepped back to kiss him on the lips.

"For old times sake," she said. "Oh, and by the way, I pulled a file on that Woods guy. He's got form, but nothing major. Some low-level breaking and entering, suspicion of stalking, driving while impaired. He did a three month stretch for assault, but he's never done real time. I've left the file in your office."

"Thank you," said Rashford, trying to kiss her on the cheek but laughing when she moved her head, and he landed on her lips. She kissed him back, then patted his behind, turned, and disappeared into the crowd. A few minutes later he saw her talking with an older man in a white suit, who laughed at something she said and then took her arm as he led her to the bar. Now he looked around and realized he hadn't seen either Sarah or the white suit since the start of the second set.

Gayle Morgan and Sheri Hayleyson walked over to say goodnight.

Their faces were flushed and shining, both from the alcohol and from their frenetic dancing.

"She's damn bloody good, Rashford," slurred Morgan. "She's gonna be a big star. Where you gonna be then?"

"I'm just enjoying the ride," said Rashford.

"I bet you are," purred Hayleyson, winking at him. "Don't forget that list, now."

"What list?" said Morgan, confused.

"Nothing," they both replied, simultaneously, then burst out laughing. Morgan looked even more confused, so Hayleyson put her arm around her shoulders and gently led her away, Rashford watching the blue jeans until they disappeared.

"Mandy will know," said a voice next to him. "She's bear clan, they know everything."

He turned to Pia, nodding to Petra at his side.

"Know what?" he said, innocently.

"Dogging the denim," said Pia.

Rashford smiled.

"I haven't done anything," he said, holding out his hands, palms up.

"Like that American president said, it can still be adultery even if it's only in your mind."

"Adul ... That would mean we were married!"

Pia laughed as Petra slapped his arm.

"Even when there is mince in the shop you can look at the steak at home," she said.

Rashford paused; Pia looked at her.

"What?"

"It is one of those English sayings that people here say."

Rashford shook his head.

"I think what you mean is, 'why go out for hamburger when I have steak at home'?"

"Exactly," said Petra. "That's what I said."

Pia laughed.

"It was a great concert," he said. "Please thank Mandy for sharing her talents with us."

"I will," said Rashford, then waved as they walked away.

Checking that all his group were safely out of the room, and that the last of the other patrons were following, Rashford made his way backstage. He found the band sitting in the main dressing room, still sweating and shivering. There were trays of food, beer, and wine on the tables, but everyone seemed to be holding a bottle of water. He went over to Mandy and sat on the arm of her chair.

"What a great show," he said, leaning over and kissing her on the head. "You were fabulous."

He looked around.

"All of you. I've not heard one negative thing from anybody out there. It was just brilliant."

Mandy put her hand on his arm.

"Thanks, Gavin," she said. "Just leave us alone for a minute, could you? We need to get our breath back. You can start moving the gear if you'd like, it needs to go back into the van."

Feeling dismissed, and childishly upset, Rashford stood and left the dressing room. On the stage he found the temporary roadie who Mick and Monica had hired to move equipment. As their eyes locked, he realized that it was the young man who had tried to hit on Sarah. Rashford held out his hand.

"I wouldn't have killed you," he said, laughing. "She just wanted you to go away, she had another guy in mind and you were ruining her pitch."

The youth nodded.

"I thought you were with the fiddle player, Robicheau," he said.

"I was, I am," said Rashford. "That other lady was just someone I work with."

"You must have an interesting job," said the youth, picking up one of the stage monitors and carrying it out to the van.

Rashford picked up two of the microphones, carefully rolling the cables, and dismantled the stands. Together he and the youth had the stage cleared and the van packed inside forty minutes. Once they were finished, the youth went behind the van and lit a cigarette.

"Mind if I join you?" said Rashford.

The youth shrugged, which Rashford took as assent. He lit his own cigarette and looked across at his companion.

"What's your name?"

"Seabass."

"Seabass? That's an, umm, interesting name."

The youth laughed.

"It's really Sebastian but one of my uncles used to call me Seabass, when I was a baby, and it kind of stuck. It's better than Sebby, anyway."

Rashford nodded.

"My name's Gavin. What do you do, Seabass, when you're not being a temporary roadie?"

"Whatever's around. I help Arthur and Herbert here, doing general cleaning up stuff. I cut the grass and fix anything that breaks, and sometimes work in the gift shop. During harvest I might get a job with a farm, and in winter I put a snowplough on my truck and clean peoples' driveways."

"That sounds like you work hard," said Rashford. "Do you have a girlfriend or anything?"

"Not yet," Sebastian laughed. "I'm still playing the field, when I can find one."

Rashford laughed, then stubbed out his cigarette.

"So, you're driving the van tonight?"

"Yeah. That fiddle player, she's with you, right? I'll take the others home when they're ready, then leave the van at Mick's place."

"How do you get home?"

"I call my dad and he comes to get me. He works an evening shift so he's home now."

"Nice dad," said Rashford, then went to find Mandy.

<hr>

They woke up late the next morning. Rashford disentangled himself and went into the kitchen to make coffee. He ground the beans and added water, then turned everything on and went to the bathroom. When he had finished his ablutions, and cleaned his teeth, the pot had just finished brewing. Mandy came in, her robe wrapped around her, her hair tousled, and gave him a sleepy kiss. He handed her a mug and they went into the front room.

He sat on the couch, and she snuggled up next to him, her feet pulled up beneath her and her head on his shoulder.

"This is nice," she murmured. "Thank you for coming last night."

"It was an awesome show," he said, "and you looked fabulous."

"Thank you," she said, sighing contentedly. "I thought it went well." Rashford kissed her head.

"Did you hear, we had another body last night," she said.

"What?"

"After the show, Mick went out for a smoke and tripped over some geezer. He was sure surprised!"

"Was the 'geezer' okay?"

"I guess. It looked like he'd been beaten up by someone. It looked like he had a broken arm and stuff. We called 911 and an ambulance took him away."

"Are your concerts always this exciting?"

She laughed.

"No, they're usually pretty tame. They go smoothly and everyone's happy."

She paused, stroking his arm.

"The only thing I didn't like," she said, "was that new sound guy, Nigel. He kept giving too much bass on the mix, the back beat overwhelmed some of the vocals. And during the two-step, when I did my opening notes there was a bit of feedback. I spoke to him at the break and the second set was better, but we'll need to get that sorted before the tour."

Rashford murmured in agreement.

"How was being a roadie?" she said. "Did you have any problems?"

"No," he said, and then made her laugh by telling her the story of Sarah and Seabass.

"Seabass, what a great name!"

Rashford sat quietly, not laughing with her. Mandy looked up at him.

"What?"

He cleared his throat.

"Mandy, I'm not sure about this," he said.

"About what?"

"About the tour. You're such a perfectionist, I think we'd spend the whole time with you being mad at me."

"Why? If I tell you something should be twenty-four inches in from the stage, can't you just do that? Why would I be mad?"

"Exactly," he said.

She was quiet, her eyes downcast.

"I was looking forward to us having a holiday together," she said, softly.

He hugged her with his free arm.

"I think we can," he said. "I've booked time off already. But I'll hire my own car and my own hotel rooms, and just follow the band around, like a groupie. Then on your days off, or on nights when you need a cuddle, you can come and visit me. The rest of the time you can focus on your music."

She drank her coffee, thinking this over.

"What do we do about a roadie?" she said.

"I think you should hire Seabass."

She was silent for a moment.

"It would be awfully expensive for you," she said. "We can't pay you if you're not working, and we're going to be away for six weeks."

"I know," said Rashford. "And I might not be able to be there for the whole tour. But I've got some money saved up, and I always wanted to spend time in the Maritimes. I've only been once, for a brief visit. I'd like to go for longer. Even if I don't manage the full six weeks, it'll be fun."

"Would I travel in the van, or with you?"

"Whichever you liked."

Mandy giggled.

"So, I'd have my very own groupie-on-demand," she said.

He nodded.

"That's right."

"My every whim?"

"Within reason. If you want to yell about stage monitors, you'll have to find Sebastian."

"I didn't yell. I asked nicely."

"Uh-huh."

She dug her elbow into his ribs.

"I did!"

He took her cup and put it on the floor next to his.

"Perhaps I can show you some of the whims on offer," he said, leaning over to kiss her. She untied her robe as she reached her arms around his neck.

"Please do, she said."

CHAPTER 31

Rashford arrived at work in good time on Monday and took his coffee down to his small office. He was looking forward to an uninterrupted week. Mandy was preparing to meet her parents and was concerned at how they would respond to Josee's disappearance. She had asked him to drive up after work on Friday so they could all have dinner together but had warned him that he would have to rent a hotel room for the weekend.

"They wouldn't be able to handle us sleeping together," she said. "I've told them we're just good friends."

He was scanning the internal news feed on his computer when there was a tap on the door and Sarah entered. She was in uniform, and her hair was tied back into its regular bun. She also had a black eye, partially concealed by make-up.

"I just wanted to thank you for letting me go to the concert on Saturday," she said. "I had a great time."

Rashford looked at her.

"I'm glad you enjoyed yourself," he said. "What happened to your eye?"

She laughed.

"Too many gin and tonics," she said. "I walked into a door."

"Clumsy," he said, nodding.

She shrugged.

"It happens. Did you find that file I left you?"

Rashford picked it up and waved it at her.

"Yes, thanks. I didn't read it yet. I was just checking what else is going on. That sounds like a terrible car crash out on the highway."

"Yes. Three dead at last count, two in critical. Apparently, a car full of students celebrating the end of their university year."

Rashford made a mental note to call Shyanne and make sure she wasn't involved. Sarah waved and left, then poked her head back in the door.

"Oh, the Chief wonders if she could have a quick word? In about twenty minutes?"

"Sure, I'll drop down."

She nodded and left.

He took out his phone and called Shyanne's number. It rang four times, and he was preparing to leave a voicemail message when the line clicked open.

"Shyanne's phone," said a voice he recognized. He cleared his throat.

"Umm, Patrick? It's Gavin. Is Shyanne there."

There was a pause before he spoke.

"Yes, she's just in the washroom. She asked me to answer ..."

There was an awkward silence.

"How was the movie?" said Rashford.

"What? Oh, it was fine, thank you. Ah, here she is."

There was a slap as a hand was held over the microphone, and Rashford could hear a whispered conversation. Then the line cleared.

"Hello, Gavin. This is early," said Shyanne. "Have you heard something about Josee?"

"Sorry, no. I was just checking on you. There was a big crash on the highway, and I wanted to make sure you weren't involved."

"Me? Why would I be involved?"

"They were university students."

There was a pause.

"No, we've not been out driving," she said.

"That's good."

"Yes."

Rashford shook his head.

"Well, listen, I'll let you get back to it," he said.

"Okay. I should go, we were just ..."

She coughed.

"Excuse me, sorry ... I was just in the shower, I'm dripping everywhere."

Rashford chuckled to himself.

"I'll let you know if I hear anything about Josee."

"Thanks. Bye."

Rashford clicked off his phone and smiled at the ceiling, then got up and walked down to the Chief Superintendent's office. Sarah was at her desk in the outer office, and he laughed as he saw a fresh notch on the sill. As she looked up at him, he leaned in and peered more closely at her eye, noting also a scratch across her forehead and a graze on her chin.

"That was no door, Sarah," he said. "What happened?"

She shrugged.

"A misunderstanding."

He scoffed.

"A misunderstanding with a white suit?"

She nodded, then glanced at Pollard's door.

"We had a quickie out the back," she said, her voice low. "A traditional knee trembler. Then it turned out he wanted me to be a bit more subservient than I was comfortable with. I think he thought that me being commando meant I was all access, but I'm not. He tried to persuade me otherwise."

Rashford looked at her, remembering that she had been the Women's Mixed Martial Arts champion for the Regina Division, three years in a row.

"What did you do?" he said.

"I dissuaded him," she said. "Nothing serious, I just broke his arm and a couple of ribs. And rearranged his personal equipment, those pumps have a nice firm toe."

"Where did you leave him?"

"Out by the back door. I figured someone would find him. Then I called an Uber and went home."

She held a hand to her eye.

"I didn't want Gayle to see this, she and Sheri would have gone out and stomped him, given him a right kicking. I'd got my notch; my night was done. How was the second set?"

Rashford was telling her about the three ovations that Mandy had received for her solo on the *Red River Jig* when the inner door opened, and Pollard looked out.

"I thought I heard you," she said. "Come in, Staff Sergeant."

He followed her back into her office and stood at attention in front of her desk. She walked behind it and picked up a piece of paper, then looked at him.

"We've had two hits," she said.

"Ma'am?"

"Claydon. The Mounties found two matches. But don't get too excited. They're both old ones, from ten and fifteen years ago."

Rashford nodded.

"He would have been younger then. Just starting out. Made some mistakes."

"Perhaps," said Pollard. "I'll leave you to follow it up."

"Where was it, Ma'am?"

"One was in Sault Ste. Marie, Ontario. That's the one from fifteen years ago, it's considered a cold case. The other one was in Halifax, Nova Scotia. That was ten years ago. It's considered 'active' but they're not really doing anything with it. Here are the contact details for the officers who are still holding the cases."

She handed over the paper.

"Thank you, Ma'am."

She looked at him.

"Aren't you heading out that way?" she said. "On this groupie tour of yours?"

"My holiday, Ma'am."

"Right. Your holiday. Well, if you get a moment, when the Adorable Amanda is otherwise engaged, I'm sure someone would be happy to have a chat with you, seeing as you're in the area."

"Yes, Ma'am."

"How did she do, by the way? On her exams?"

"She passed all her courses, Ma'am. She graduates at the end of this week."

"Are you going to the convocation?"

"Yes, Ma'am. She's letting me use Josee's ticket."

"Time to meet the family, is it?"

"Yes, Ma'am."

She laughed.

"Well, good luck with that. Dismissed."

He saluted and left the room, returning to his office holding the piece of paper like it was a sacrament. Josee might be missing, but he was one step nearer to finding out where she might be. He closed the door behind him and sat at his desk. He visualized her laughing at him as she directed him to hold his cigarette over the water, and the smile on her face as she had proudly touched the earrings which displayed her Métis identity to those who knew how to look.

Rashford took a deep breath and picked up the phone.

His calls to both Sault Ste. Marie and Halifax were disappointing. It was lunchtime in Ontario, and he had to leave a message, asking the detective to return his call. It was early afternoon in Nova Scotia, and he got through to the contact person straight away. That officer, however, was not very helpful.

"It's only a partial print," she said. "We've put it in the system but we're not hopeful of any matches."

"What was the offence?"

"There was a thing at one of our universities. A young woman claimed that in her first year, during orientation, she was taken away from her room and held captive by a guy. She escaped after a couple of days, and reported it, but by the time anyone got to the apartment, he was gone. She said that he didn't touch her, just kept her chained up, like a pet. She said that, at first, she had thought it was just a hazing thing, but after the second night she was starting to get seriously concerned. Anyway, we found the partial on the toilet handle, so it's in the system. I don't know what we'd do if we found him, though. A ten-year old student prank with no visible victim? That would be hard to prosecute, even if the woman wanted to press charges."

"Did you have a name for the fellow, the guy with the apartment?"

"The lease was paid cash, by someone called Marvin Chesapeake, but we could never identify who that was. That's why we took it a bit seriously. It did look like there was some planning and premeditation involved."

They chatted a bit longer, and she agreed that he could call her when he was in the area later in the summer.

"Here's my number," she said. "But remember, I'll be on holiday for the last two weeks of July, and it will take something really serious for me to give that up."

He had laughed and promised not to interrupt her vacation unless it was absolutely necessary.

An hour later he was trying to find some reference to the next name on his list when the phone rang. It was the detective in charge of the Sault Ste. Marie case.

"We've got nothing," he said. "A girl claimed she was dragged into a van by a young guy. She was twenty-five and she didn't think he was as old as she was. She said that she fought him off and ran away."

The man sniffed. Rashford waited patiently.

"I think it's a load of hooey," said the detective. "She was a native girl from the reserve, and the street where she said he grabbed her was well-known as a hooker hangout. I think they just disagreed on price."

"Where was the print from?"

"From her backpack, she said that's what he grabbed to pull her into the van. She had a black eye, and she said she'd scratched his face."

Rashford thought for a moment.

"Was there anything under her nails, something we could use for DNA?"

The detective scoffed.

"First thing she did was wash her hands and face; we've got nothing except this fingerprint. No name, no description, nothing."

"Did she see him? To say that he was young?"

"Dunno. She didn't report anything. He pulled her off the street, punched her, she scratched him and got away. Just a day in the life."

Rashford thanked him and hung up the phone.

After lunch, he chatted with Mandy and was pleased to learn that the band had hired Seabass as their roadie for the tour.

He was leaving the building when Constable Sheri Hayleyson fell in beside him.

"That was a wonderful evening on Saturday," she said. "Thank you so much for inviting us."

"You're welcome," he said, smiling.

They walked to the car park together. Rashford left her by a sleek canary yellow Miata and walked off towards his Jeep.

"Do you have time for coffee?" she called.

He stopped and waited for her to walk over.

Rashford's phone rang about forty minutes later. He saw from the call display that it was Pia, so he took it out into his living room and answered. There was no small talk.

"Twenty-seven Oakfield Drive, Saskatoon."

"What about it?"

"That's where he took Josee."

Rashford was silent for a moment, then cleared his throat.

"And you know this, how, exactly?"

Piapot laughed.

"Old fashioned detective work, bro. We asked people."

"We?"

"Yeah, well you didn't seem to be getting anywhere. So, I talked to some friends, and they talked to every Uber driver in town. And one of them remembered picking up the Indian Agent."

Rashford thought for a moment.

"There's a lot of Uber drivers in town. And that sort of information is supposed to be confidential."

"Uh-huh."

"But ..."

"But it's easy to get around town if you've got wheels, and a large guy on a motorbike can be very persuasive. We checked all the ones we knew, and they suggested other names we might have missed. Brian was able to describe who we were looking for, so that helped."

"Tell me what happened."

"The Uber guy took him to an address just out of town. I got that address, and we went to visit."

"You and your friends?"

"Other friends. You know some of them. Leon, Johnboy, friends like that."

"Go on."

"There was nobody here. We waited a while, then left, but kept checking back. Six days later this dude turned up. He'd been on holiday and had let his house out on Airbnb. We chatted. He gave us the name and address of the renter."

"Again, confidential information."

Piapot scoffed.

"In your world, maybe you need a warrant. In my world, Leon is usually enough."

Rashford sighed.

"Go on."

"You're looking for Michael Carmichael, who lives at that address."

"Have you been there?"

"Not yet. I just got the details confirmed twenty minutes ago. A friend in Saskatoon did a drive by and there is a car in the driveway and lights on in the apartment. Then I called you."

"Twenty-seven Oakfield Drive?"

"Correct."

"I'm on my way."

"My friend is watching the place, with some of his friends. I'll meet you up there, you'd better be introduced, or they might get nervous. It's gonna take you at least a couple of hours to get there. There's a Tim's on the corner, about two blocks away, we'll be in the parking lot."

"Copy that."

Rashford clicked off the phone and called out through the bathroom door.

"I've got to go out. Work. Can you see yourself out? I'll see you tomorrow."

"Work? Can I come?"

"Gayle will be there; I'm going to call her now."

"So what? We live separate lives. And you and I haven't done anything. We just had coffee."

"I know, but not for want of trying."

"That's not the point. Coffee isn't a crime or a sin."

"But ..."

"My uniform is here somewhere. Ah, here it is."

Sheri Hayleyson came out of the bathroom, buckling her belt. She held her dress shirt in her hand.

"Now where the hell's my bra?"

Rashford called Gayle Morgan as he drove, giving her the directions to the restaurant. She was already waiting in the car park when they arrived, her patrol car parked in the Blue Badge Only parking area. Morgan raised an eyebrow when Sheri Hayleyson got out of Rashford's Jeep but did not say anything. Sheri hurried over and gave her a hug.

"We were just finishing a coffee when you called," she said. "I asked if he would bring me up here."

"Where's your car?"

"At the office. We'd just gone for coffee."

"Yes, you said."

Morgan looked from Hayleyson to Rashford, then shook her head.

"Whatever," she said, then nodded over to the far side of the parking lot. "I'm assuming those are your friends."

Rashford looked over and saw a number of large motorbikes, three pick-up trucks, and a white SUV.

"I'll go and chat," he said.

"I think we should all go, Staff Sergeant," said Hayleyson, emphasizing the rank. Morgan shot her a glance and nodded.

Rashford considered this for a moment.

"Very well," he said. "Come on."

As they walked across the parking lot, four men stepped forward to meet them. Rashford nodded in greeting, holding out his hand as they approached. He shook hands with each in turn and introduced his colleagues.

"Pia, Leon, Malcom, Slider, I'd like you to meet Senior Constable Morgan and Constable Hayleyson."

Pia nodded in recognition.

"We met already," he said. "You were both at The Majestic."

Morgan nodded.

"We were," she said. "Good to see you again."

Malcom coughed.

"Enough with the 'old friends' routine," he said. "How are we going to play this?"

Rashford smiled.

"Is someone at the house?"

"Brian and Johnboy," said Malcom. "They can both recognize him."

"Will they spook him?"

Piapot scoffed.

"He won't even know they're there," he said. "I bet even you could walk around that place twice and not spot them, and you're looking for them."

Rashford nodded.

"I'll take your word for it," he said. "Maybe they can keep watch while we go inside."

"Sure," said Piapot and Malcom, simultaneously. Malcom cleared his throat.

"Do you, umm, need any assistance with entry?" he said.

Rashford shook his head.

"I called back to the office on our way here," he said. "I have a warrant to search the premises."

"I've always wanted to a legal B&E," said Slider, grinning. "Can I open the door?"

Rashford smiled back.

"Sure," he said, "but only after we've identified ourselves, okay? No surprise incursions. If we find anything, I need this to stand up in court."

Piapot shrugged.

"Whatever," he said, glancing across at Malcom, who nodded, then looked around at the rest of the bikers.

"You guys stay here," he said. "But be ready to move as soon as I call. Okay?"

Several of them nodded, so he turned back to Rashford.

"Let's rock 'n roll," he said.

Piapot was correct. Rashford looked but did not see either Brian or Johnboy, although he was confident that they were there. The seven of them quietly approached the building, a vinyl-clad bungalow on a raised concrete foundation.

"Look at the windows," said Slider, pointing to the ones set in the concrete. "There's a good-sized basement."

Leon grunted. "They're all blacked up," he said. "And even the main floor has blinds."

They walked down the drive, stepping to each side of an old Ford Escort that was parked by the house. It had two tires missing and the rear chassis was supported by bricks. As they approached the steps leading up to the front door, Brian materialized from the sides of the building. He nodded at Rashford.

"Not a sign of him," said Brian. "And no noise inside. The windows are all covered. It looks like there are some lights on, though."

Rashford raised an eyebrow.

"There are some gaps at the edges of the curtains," said Brian. "Don't worry, we didn't bang anything."

"Is there a back door?"" said Rashford.

Brian nodded. "Yeah. Johnboy's watching it."

"What about the sides?"

"It's weird. There are no side windows. There's not much space between the houses here, I guess they're all those whatchamacallits, 'infills'. There're these windows here, at the front, and the same at the back. But that's it. The sides are all dark."

Rashford looked more carefully, noting that there was a single large window to the right of the door and two to the left, the latter a bit smaller and placed higher on the wall.

"It's probably a split level," said Hayleyson. "My brother has one. Once we get inside there'll be steps up to the left, and that side will have the bedrooms and the bathroom. There's enough room for there to be a proper basement underneath. The door to that will be next to and under the stairs. To the right will be a living area and kitchen, and there will just be a crawl space underneath on that side."

Rashford nodded, then looked around at the group.

"Right, we know what to expect from a room layout point of view," he said. "Please be careful. I'm hoping we'll find information about Josee, so don't touch anything unless you can't avoid it. Slider, you come with me."

The biker puffed out his chest and grinned at Malcom and Brian, then followed Rashford up the steps and stood at his shoulder. Rashford knocked on the door.

"Police," he said. "We have a warrant to enter these premises. Please open the door."

There was no answer. He waited a moment, then repeated the invitation. When there was still no reply, he nodded at Slider. The biker gestured him to stand back, then moved in close to the door. Six seconds later, it clicked open, and he stood aside to let Rashford enter.

Gayle Morgan shook her head.

"Show-off," she muttered to Slider as she passed, following Rashford into the bungalow. The biker just grinned.

Hayleyson followed Morgan but stopped at the door, examining the lock.

"Simple knob lock," she sniffed. "I could have done it in five."

Slider laughed and turned to Malcom, raising his hands as Hayleyson went inside.

"There's always a challenger," he said, shaking his head.

As Hayleyson had predicted, they entered a small hallway with a flight of steps leading up to the left, and two more dropping to the right. A bare low-wattage bulb, glowing softly, hung from the ceiling on a frayed wire. Rashford nodded up the stairs.

"You guys check up there, I'll look in here."

He went into the sparsely furnished living room, pleased to note that the lights were already on. The carpet was a dull green colour, with a circular rug in a concentric design the only spot of colour. There was a wooden kitchen chair placed in the centre of the rug, facing a reclining armchair made from a tan coloured Naugahyde material. On the left side of the recliner there was a wastepaper basket that overflowed with empty Tim Horton's coffee cups. On the right, a small side table held an overfull ashtray.

Pia had entered behind him and stood by the recliner. He looked around.

"Not much living done here," he said.

Rashford nodded.

"Let's check the kitchen."

They walked to the door in the far corner of the room and passed into a small but functional kitchen. After switching on the light, they saw that the appliances were all old, a green avocado colour, and the floor was covered in a pale cream linoleum. On the pink plastic dish rack by the sink stood two plates, two mugs, and a dinner knife. To the side, next to the toaster, stood a loaf of multigrain bread wrapped in a plastic bag, the ends folded over to keep the remainder fresh. A small cardboard box of Red Rose tea was further over, next to the plugged-in electric kettle.

Rashford touched the kettle but found it was cold. He opened the fridge and found three packages of cheese slices, a half-eaten pizza with four slices remaining, and an almost empty one litre container of 2 per cent milk.

"This is pure seventies chic," said Pia. "Man, not even Indians live like this!"

"I think he's just camping here," said Rashford. "He doesn't live here."

"Upstairs is clear," said Gayle Morgan, coming into the kitchen. "No furniture, just a sleeping bag on the floor."

"Bathroom is clear as well," said Hayleyson, squeezing in behind Morgan. "Toothbrush and toothpaste, toilet paper, a bar of soap and a regular sized towel."

"Where's Malcom?" said Rashford.

"He's waiting at the door," said Pia. "Don't want us to be surprised in here."

Rashford nodded.

"Okay, now the hard bit. I'm going to go down into the basement. Gayle, you hold the front door, please. Sheri, you stay in here. Pia, I think you should stay up here with Sheri, Malcom can come with me."

Pia looked as though he was going to disagree, violently if necessary. Rashford held up his hand.

"You're a relative," he said. "I don't want you down there just yet."

"And us?" said Morgan, her voice controlled but angry. "Why are we staying up here? You want to spare our sensibilities? Don't want us having the vapours down there or summat?"

"No, not at all," said Rashford. "You've never met Josee. Malcom and I know her but are not related. It's better if we go down."

"If not me, then Leon," said Pia, still shaking his head.

Rashford nodded.

"Okay, me, Malcom, and Leon will go down. Gayle and Sheri have the upstairs rooms. Pia has the hall, Slider holds the front door, JohnBoy and Brian are outside on the perimeter. Everyone good with that?"

They all nodded. Rashford led the way back to the small entry hall and paused by the door which was recessed into the wall next to the stairs that led to the bedroom. He held the handle tightly and took a deep breath, then slowly turned the knob. The latch disengaged with a click, and he eased the door open.

Malcom tapped him on the shoulder, and he looked back. The biker pointed to himself, then moved past Rashford onto the top step. Rashford felt another tap, and Leon silently edged through and stood next to Malcom. The basement was dark, but they could see a switch on the wall next to the door jamb. Leon pointed at it, then mimed he and

Malcom going down the stairs before Rashford switched on the lights. Rashford nodded.

Leon placed his left hand on Malcom's shoulder, and they stepped slowly down the stairs. There were eight of them, Rashford counted, and at each one they took a step and then paused, listening. Rashford realized that some light must be coming in from the covered windows, for he could discern the bulk of the two men as they descended. They reached the bottom and stopped. Then Leon waved, and Rashford switched on the lights.

<h1 style="text-align:center">Chapter 32</h1>

By the time Rashford got to the bottom of the steps, Leon was across the room and bending over a small figure lying huddled on a mattress. Malcom was walking around the room, throwing open doors and cupboards, something long and shiny glinting in his hand. Rashford decided not to ask but went to join Leon, who looked up at him with rage in his eyes.

"She's alive," he said, "but she has not been treated well."

"Don't touch anything," said Rashford. "Please," he added, seeing the look on Leon's face. "Let me take some photographs first, okay?"

Leon nodded then stepped back half a pace. Rashford took out his phone and called 911, asking for urgent medical assistance and an ambulance. Then he bent over the body, which was covered in a thick grey blanket. Frightened eyes looked up at him from a tear and dirt-streaked face.

"It's okay, Josee," he said, waving his phone. "I've just got to get some photographs, before we can move anything. For evidence, in case we need it. Okay?"

She blinked, which he took as an affirmative. He pulled out his phone and quickly snapped some photographs, then switched to video and panned out from Josee to encompass the whole room. Leon and

Malcom moved around, keeping out of the shot, and were both standing next to him when he clicked off the phone and returned it to his pocket. He looked at Malcom.

"Can you go and get Senior Constable Morgan, please," he said. "And Pia."

Rashford dropped to one knee next to Josee's head as Malcom nodded and walked quickly across the room, calling out from the bottom of the stairs. He stood to one side as Morgan descended, followed by Pia. Malcom slapped him on the shoulder as he went past.

"I'll take the front," Malcom called back to Rashford, who nodded, then beckoned Morgan over. Pia followed but Rashford asked Leon to hold him back. Morgan knelt down beside him.

Carefully they pulled back the blanket. Josee was still dressed in the clothes she had worn at the bar, dark blue Levi's and a paler blue Wrangler denim snap-button shirt. Both her jeans and top were stained, splattered with what looked a mixture of food, liquids, and blood. Her feet were bare, and a heavy padlock secured a chain around her ankle. She was shivering.

"It's okay, Josee, we've got you now," said Morgan, gently. She put her hand under Josee's neck and cradled her head in her arms. Morgan made soothing noises as Rashford tugged the chain and realized it was fastened to the grate over the sump pump. Sheri Hayleyson appeared and crouched next to him, almost pushing him over, and brought a small leather pouch out of her pocket. She leaned over and fiddled with the padlock, which popped open almost immediately. She put the lock in a plastic evidence bag she brought from another pocket, then gently unwound the chain from Josee's ankle.

Leon came over and took the chain from her, carefully rolling it up and placing it in a corner of the room. Pia sank to his knees next to his cousin and stroked her hair.

"We will get him," he said, quietly. "I will avenge you."

Rashford pulled the blanket down a bit further, taking a deep intake of breath when he saw the unmistakeable scars of cigarette burns on her arm. Morgan reached out and pulled the blanket back to Josee's shoulder.

"Let's leave that to the ambulance folk," she said.

Josee mumbled something and Morgan bent nearer to her head, so that she could hear. She nodded, then looked up at Rashford.

"She says he just went for coffee," she said. "He goes every day at about this time."

Rashford rocked back on his heels, thinking, then got to his feet and ran to the door, calling as he went.

"Malcom, call the guys at Tim's, lock it down."

The next morning Sarah called out to Rashford as he walked past her desk.

"Ten o'clock, back here," she said. "The Boss wants a word."

Rashford paused in the doorway.

"A word?"

"I'm paraphrasing. What she actually said was, 'I want to know what the fuck he's been up to this time.' But you get the gist, right?"

"Ten o'clock?"

"Uh-huh."

Rashford continued down the hall to his office and opened the door. He looked around, then backed out and kept walking along the corridor until he reached the fire escape door. He opened it and descended the stairs, emerging into the grassed area between the building, two car parks, and a maintenance shed.

'My own secret quadrangle', he thought, and leaned against the brick wall as he lit a cigarette. He was on his third when Gayle Morgan came around the corner.

"I thought I could smell smoke," she said. "Can I have one?"

Rashford looked at her.

"You don't smoke," he said.

"After yesterday, I need all the vices I can get."

He grunted and handed her the packet. She withdrew a cigarette, and he lit it for her. She coughed as she inhaled.

"First one for years," she said.

"It's like riding a bike, you'll soon remember what to do."

She laughed, then turned serious.

"How're you doing, Gavin? Are you okay?"

He shrugged.

"I just hope we find the bastard before Pia does," he said. "Did Pollard call you in as well?"

"Yeah. Ten o'clock. I'm a bit early."

They smoked silently for a moment, then Morgan turned and looked at him.

"What really happened yesterday, Gavin?" she said.

He stared back.

"What do you mean? You were there."

She scoffed.

"You know what I mean. Before then. You and Sheri."

He stubbed out his cigarette and took a deep breath.

"Truth?"

She nodded.

"Yes, please."

He blew out his breath in a whoosh.

"Well, like she told you, we bumped into each other after work and went for coffee. We went to that new café, the one with lots of booths. She bought us each a latte and a muffin. Mine was wildberry, apparently."

Morgan gazed at him, impassive. He shrugged.

"We were sitting opposite each other, just chatting, and there was this mom sitting behind her, in the next booth. She had two kids with her, a little one about three and one who was older. She was talking to the older one and the little one poked his head up over the back of the booth. I pulled a face at him, and he pulled one back."

"And Sheri?"

"She didn't notice. She was talking about how much she'd enjoyed The Majestic."

"Uh-huh."

"Anyway, suddenly this kid lifted up his cup and held it over Sheri's head. Before I could say anything, he just tipped his orange juice all over her. She shrieked and jumped to her feet, the kid burst into tears, and then his mom started shouting."

"What did you do?"

Rashford looked at the ground and mumbled something.

"What was that?" said Morgan.

"I said," said Rashford, looking up, tears forming in his eyes again as he remembered. "I said, 'it's a good job you've got short hair', and then I burst out laughing."

He roared again at the memory, and Morgan giggled as she shook her head.

"Anyway," said Rashford, "the mom apologized, and Sheri said it was okay, and I took her back to my place to clean up. She had a wash but her shirt was soaked, and she was just rinsing it out when Pia called. I gave her one of my sweatshirts for the drive and we wrapped her shirt in a towel, it was dry before we got here, and she changed as I drove. Made some trucker's day, he blew his air horn when she took off the sweatshirt."

Morgan laughed and nodded.

"That's why she looked a bit bedraggled?" she said.

"Yup. Why, what did you think had happened?"

Morgan looked at her watch.

"Nearly ten," she said. "We should go."

———

Constable Sheri Hayleyson was already waiting in the outer office when they arrived. She was running her fingers along the notches on the siderail of the desk and smiling at something Sarah had said. Sarah looked up and laughed.

"Well, looks like the gang's all here," she said. "You can go in."

Rashford opened the door to the inner office and then stood to one side to let Morgan and Hayleyson pass through ahead of him. He followed them in, closing the door behind him, and stood at attention alongside his two colleagues. Chief Superintendent Pollard was sitting behind her desk. She put down her tablet and nodded towards the three chairs that were placed against the side wall, under her window.

"Grab a pew," she said. "This might take a while."

Once they were all seated, the chairs arranged in an arc around her desk, she leaned back in her chair.

"Who wants to start?" she said.

They all looked at each other, then focused on Rashford. He explained how he had received the phone call from Piapot Starblanket and immediately called Gayle Morgan. He described his fast drive, up Highway 11, including how he had been stopped for speeding just outside Lumsden.

"We showed our warrant cards and explained the situation," said Hayleyson. "The officer gave us a blues and bells escort all the way to the edge of town."

Pollard made a note, and Rashford knew that one of her follow-up questions would be how the Constable had come to be in his private vehicle in the first place. He hurriedly continued his story, only taking a breath once he was describing the parking lot at the Tim Horton's.

Morgan took over, explaining how they had gone to the house and conducted a legal entry, and then found Josee in the basement. She described how she had travelled in the back of the ambulance and accompanied Josee to the University Hospital, where she had been examined by the on-duty emergency physicians.

"She was dehydrated and malnourished," said Morgan, "and had some superficial physical injuries. That's all curable. It's the mental stress and trauma they're worried about."

"Did you get to interview her?" said Pollard.

"Yes, Ma'am. Sheri, sorry, Constable Hayleyson and I, we interviewed her late last night."

"I took Senior Constable Morgan's squad car and followed the ambulance to the hospital," explained Hayleyson.

Pollard nodded.

"What did she tell you?"

"It's still all a bit mixed up, Ma'am. I think it will be a few days before we can get a coherent story. It seems that he kept her chained up in the basement. He'd let her use the washroom, but she couldn't close the door fully, and he kept hold of the chain around her leg. He brought the food and drink down to her, usually a sandwich and a cup of cold tea. Sometimes he made soup and fed her with a spoon. At first, she resisted and spat things out, but then she got hungry and ate it. Every day he'd take her upstairs and make her sit on the chair we found in the living room."

"The wooden one?" said Pollard.

"Yes, Ma'am. He would sit in the recliner with a cup of coffee and his cigarettes and make her tell him a story."

Rashford looked at Morgan. He hadn't heard this before.

"What kind of story?" said Pollard.

"Anything she liked, as long as it was about the Métis people and their history. Stories she had heard from her grandparents, things she did when growing up, that sort of thing. If he got bored, or didn't believe her, then he stubbed his cigarette out on her. Usually it was on her arm, sometimes on her chest."

Pollard swallowed.

"I see," she said. She looked at Rashford.

"And what were you doing, Staff Sergeant, while the Senior Constable and the Constable were escorting the victim to hospital?"

Rashford cleared his throat.

"I, umm, I went to test a theory, Ma'am."

"Did you indeed. And what, may I ask, was this theory?"

Rashford explained how Josee had told Gayle Morgan that her captor went for coffee every day at about that time.

"I remembered the Tim Horton's cups in the wastepaper basket," he said, "so I asked Malcom to ask his friends to keep people inside until I got there."

Pollard nodded, then rummaged on her desk for a piece of paper.

"Yes, I have the transcript of the 911 call here. Well, one of them, anyway. It says: 'Help! Send police. There's a gang of crazy bikers here who won't let anybody leave the restaurant'. Does that about sum up the situation?"

Rashford looked down as he spoke.

"What's that? I've told you before, don't mumble."

"Yes, Ma'am."

"'Yes Ma'am', what?"

"Yes, Ma'am, it does pretty much sum up the situation."

Pollard leaned back in her chair.

"Okay, so when you turned up, everyone in the restaurant was being held, against their will, by Malcom and his friends?"

Rashford nodded.

"Yes, Ma'am. And some of Pia's friends as well."

Pollard scoffed.

"Good to see inter-gang collaboration in action, Staff Sergeant. Well done."

Rashford decided not to say anything. He kept his gaze fixed above the Chief Superintendent's head.

"Then what did you do, Staff Sergeant?" she asked, sweetly.

"I went inside and told people it was a police operation, Ma'am. Then I asked them all to line up against the wall."

"Indeed," said Pollard, picking up another piece of paper.

"This is a transcript of the 911 call a customer made from the bathroom. 'There's five big dudes here holding us hostage,' said the caller. 'Two bikers, two Indians, and some boss guy who's pretending he's a cop.' Then there's a squawk and the call is dropped."

Rashford nodded.

"Malcom heard him talking and brought him out to join the others," he said.

Pollard stared at him. Morgan choked back a laugh, trying hard to maintain a straight face. Rashford hurriedly continued.

"We separated the women to one side and then checked all the men, looking at their ID and matching them to their photograph. Then we told them that they could go, and I went to see the manager."

Pollard nodded, then lifted another piece of paper from her desk.

"Ah, yes, the manager. This is the transcript of his interview. I'll summarize. 'There was all this chaos outside, people yelling, bikers blocking doors, these big Cree guys wandering around asking people for ID, it was like something from TV. I locked myself in the office.'"

Pollard looked around.

"I should point out that this manager looks to be about twelve. He continues. 'Then someone hammered on my door. I told them to go away, it was securely locked, and anyway I was on the phone to the police. The door opened and this big biker walked in, pulled a knife out of his boot, cut the telephone cord from the wall, and told me not to move. I just sat there waiting to be tortured or killed.'"

Rashford spoke up.

"Slider never threatened him, Ma'am. And he was only there because Constable Hayleyson was busy."

Pollard scoffed.

"Right. Otherwise, you'd have asked her to pick the lock?"

"Yes, Ma'am."

Morgan shook with suppressed laughter, every muscle in her face locked. Pollard ignored her.

"So, the manager sits at his desk, terrified, until you turn up. Then what?"

"I asked to see the CCTV tapes, Ma'am."

"I see. And did you, then or at any other time, show your police identification or warrant card?"

Rashford closed his eyes.

"I honestly don't recall, Ma'am," he said. "It was all a bit hectic."

Pollard made another note on her tablet.

"Carry on."

"The manager said they were on the computer, and I could look as much as I liked, Ma'am."

"Did he offer to help you at all?"

"No. Ma'am."

"Do you know why?"

"I didn't at the time, Ma'am."

"When did you find out?"

Rashford blushed.

"When I requested him to turn on the computer for me, Ma'am."

Pollard nodded, slowly.

"Okay. So, it was only when you persuaded, sorry, requested, this young man to turn on the computer, that you noticed he had soiled himself?"

"Yes, Ma'am."

"Did you blame yourself for his condition?"

"No, Ma'am. I blamed Slider,"

Morgan choked uncontrollably, gasping to keep a straight face. Hayleyson twitched beside her. Pollard glared at them both, then turned back to Rashford.

"Did you show any concern for his condition. Offer him the opportunity to get changed, perhaps? Something like that?"

"No, Ma'am. I needed to see those tapes quickly."

"Right. And what did you discover, Staff Sergeant, when you saw the tapes?"

"He was there, Ma'am. Claydon, or whatever his name is. He can be quite clearly identified on the tape. He's waiting at the counter."

"But he wasn't there later, when you got there?"

"No, Ma'am. There are a number of CCTV cameras at the restaurant, Ma'am, interior and exterior. The films switch from one to another in sequence. You see him there, and then the next one is an outside shot. It shows Malcom and the guys showing up on their bikes, then Pia walks across from his car to meet them. By the time the inside camera switches back on, Claydon's gone."

Pollard stared at Rashford in disbelief.

"You were that close?"

He shrugged.

"Yes, Ma'am."

She looked away and shook her head, tsking to herself, then turned back to face Rashford.

"Do you think he went back to the house?"

"No, Ma'am. Pia had arranged for some of his local, ah, friends, to watch the house. They never saw him or anyone else approach. They explained that to JohnBoy and Brian."

"So, what happened?"

"I think he saw Pia, or someone else he recognized from the bar, and decided to get the hell out. I'm guessing he had a car parked somewhere, street parking, maybe a block or two away. He left through the back door of the restaurant, cut across behind the building, then went down some of the side streets to his car."

"Has he got his ID with him?"

Morgan spoke up.

"We think so, Ma'am. We didn't find anything in the house, and

Josee said that every time he went out, he took this brown murse with him."

"You can see it on the CCTV," said Rashford. "I guess he kept his wallet and stuff in there."

Pollard swivelled in her chair and looked out of the window,

"We've got a heck of a lot of physical evidence now," she said. "DNA. Fingerprints. Multiple aliases that he's used. An eyewitness. But none of that's any good until we have someone to check it against. We need a physical body. All we can do is put the information in the system and wait for him to make a mistake."

She turned back.

"Well done, all of you. I was not expecting a good ending for Josee. I know she's not through everything yet, not by a long shot, but at least she's alive. Congratulations. Dismissed."

They stood up and saluted, then turned and left the room.

***

As they passed through the outer office, Rashford paused.

"We're taking the rest of the day off," he said. "To celebrate. Want to play hooky and come with us?"

Sarah smiled at him.

"Tempting," she said, "but no thank you. I've got to finish all this paperwork."

"That's a shame," said Hayleyson, batting her eyes. "I'd like to get notched."

Sarah giggled, while Morgan huffed and walked out of the office. Rashford smiled and followed her. Hayleyson caught up with them outside the elevator.

"We're really having a day off?" she said.

Rashford nodded, standing to one side as the elevator door opened and then following them as they stepped inside.

"I'm going up to Wheatville," he said. "I'm going to chat with Shyanne and see what can be done to support Josee. I've also got to figure out what's happening on Saturday, with this convocation. You two are free to do as you wish."

Hayleyson grabbed Morgan's arm.

"Oh, I've got some ideas about that," she said, laughing. "Value Village, here we come!"

She pronounced it with a long 'a', villarge, and Morgan smiled.

Rashford shook his head and walked off to his Jeep, waving to them as they stood talking next to Gayle's patrol car. He drove out from the depot and navigated through the city before joining the highway and heading north.

CHAPTER 33

It was mid-afternoon when he arrived in the city. He went first to Mandy's apartment, but there was no answer when he knocked on her door. He called her phone, but it went straight to voice mail, so he left a message telling her he was in town and wondering whether he should book a hotel room for the night. He knew that Tuesday was her normal rehearsal evening, and he simply wasn't sure what time she would be finished.

He then drove to the Island View Hotel and parked in the Pay and Display car park. He followed the path down through the trees and turned along the riverbank, walking until he came to the 'Dances with Gravy' food truck. He walked up to the hatch, where a smiling young man whom he had never met before looked at him.

"May I help you?" he said, pleasantly.

"I'm looking for Shyanne," said Rashford. "Is she working today?"

"Sorry, no. She has had a family emergency."

Rashford nodded.

"Okay, thanks. I'll drop by her house."

The young man looked at him.

"*You* know where she lives?" he said.

Rashford grinned.

"Sure do," he said. "Thanks for your time."

He returned to his car and drove to Shyanne's but found that this was empty as well. He called her number and once again the call went straight to voicemail. He left another message, then stood by his car and had a cigarette as he pondered his next move. He finished his cigarette and picked up his phone.

Pia answered on the first ring.

"Officer Rashford," he said. "Have you found him yet?"

Rashford snorted.

"No. Have you?"

Pia chuckled.

"Not yet. And don't worry, you'll be the last person I inform when I do."

"Right," said Rashford. "Listen, where are you? I'm in town and I can't get hold of either Mandy or Shyanne. Do you know what's happening?"

Pia paused, then spoke, more softly this time.

"They're here, with me," he said. "We are preparing to welcome Josee home."

There was a silence.

"Is this a religious thing?" said Rashford. "Or can anybody come?"

There was a pause.

"It is not religious, no," said Pia. "More spiritual. And no, not anybody can come. Wait."

The line went silent, then after a few moments Pia's voice returned.

"Do you remember where Josee lives?" he said.

"The place she shares with Petra? Yes, I can find that again."

"You may join us," said Pia, then clicked off the phone.

When Rashford pulled up behind Pia's white SUV, the first thing he noticed was a plume of smoke coming from the tiny front garden. Leon was sitting on the wall, watching the street, while behind him Pia sat on a small stool, carefully tending the flames in the firepit. Leon bumped fists with Rashford as he passed.

Rashford stood in the garden and watched until Pia paused, wiped his hands on his trouser leg, and came easily to his feet. He stepped past the firepit and shook hands.

"It is a sacred fire," he said. "We keep it alive for four days. Tomorrow she will be home."

Rashford nodded.

"Where are the girls?" he said.

"They are inside, preparing her room," said Pia. "That is women's magic. You must stay out here. Please, sit."

JohnBoy came around the corner of the house, carrying another stool. He nodded to Rashford, then placed the stool on the grass, opposite to the first one. Rashford walked across and sat down, waiting until Pia joined him before speaking.

"Women's magic?" he said.

Pia shrugged.

"Well, I don't understand it. It's magic to me. They will be out soon."

Rashford looked around the small garden.

"May I smoke?"

Pia nodded.

"Yes. But first, give one to the fire, as a gift."

Rashford took a cigarette from his packet and carefully placed it into the flames. Pia nodded, so Rashford took a second and lit it. The two men sat silently for nearly twenty minutes, the only noise the scratch of Pia's stick as he stirred the burning wood or added a new branch to the fire. Then the door opened, and Petra came out, Shyanne and Mandy following close behind. An older woman brought up the rear, carefully closing the door behind her. Pia stood, so Rashford followed suit. The women walked in single file towards them.

Petra gave Pia a quiet hug, then stepped over and shook hands with Rashford.

"Thank you for coming," she said, softly. "And thank you for finding her safe."

Rashford nodded, choking a little and unable to speak.

Petra stood aside and Shyanne threw herself into Rashford's arms, shaking and weeping as she buried her face in his chest. Through great gulps of air, she said something, but Rashford could not understand a word. He rubbed her back until she had calmed down, then held her at arms length.

"I'm sorry, Shyanne. What did you say?"

She snorted and sniffled, then repeated herself.

"I said, I thought he didn't smoke. Why did he do that?"

Rashford brought her back to his chest and leaned into her hair, speaking quietly.

"I don't think he does smoke. We found an ashtray which was full of cigarettes that were less than half-finished. He was just picking up on one of her fears and foibles. He knew she hated cigarette smoke, so he used that knowledge as a weapon. She was chained to the chair, and he had power; he could blow smoke in her face, and he could burn her."

"It's not fair," she wailed, clinging hard to his shirt.

"I know, I know," said Rashford, rubbing her back and looking helplessly at Petra.

Petra stepped forward and gently took Shyanne by the arm, leading her away and towards the fire. Pia stepped forward and gathered them both in his arms, holding them tightly like a protective bear.

Mandy stepped up to Rashford and gave him a quick kiss on the cheek.

"Thank you for coming," she said. "We're just trying to make her room nice for when she comes home. Luckily, we knew someone who has knowledge of the old ways."

She moved to the side and Rashford found himself face-to-face with Bettina Blackeagle.

"Tân'si," she said, holding out her hand and softly shaking his.

"Mânan'tow, ki'ya maka?"

"I'm fine, how are you?" she said, "It must have been awful finding Josee like that. Are you okay?"

Rashford shrugged, looking across at Pia.

"I've had better days," he said. "At least she was alive."

"We can thank the creator for her survival."

"Have you been here long?"

Bettina shrugged.

"Amanda called me last night and told me the news. She asked me if

I could help, so we arranged to meet today. I showed her how to smudge properly, and what to say in order to cleanse the rooms. She is a quick learner, this one."

Mandy smiled shyly.

"We have a good teacher," she said.

JohnBoy said that he would be honoured to tend the fire while the group took a break, so they took two cars to the university and parked at the hotel. Petra, Leon and Shyanne travelled with Pia, Mandy and Bettina with Rashford. They walked down to the river in silence. Outside the food truck they pulled two tables together and then Pia and Rashford went to the counter to order drinks and food. A few minutes later a young man carried a tray loaded with coffee, tea, and pre-made sandwiches over to the table.

"Thank you, Jean-Paul," said Shyanne, nodding at the waiter. She looked across at Rashford.

"This is Antoine's son," she said. "He's been helping out while Josee has ..."

Her voice broke, and she sniffled before continuing.

"While Josee has been away," she said.

Rashford nodded and glanced at the young man, recognizing him.

"We met earlier today," he said. "I came here looking for you. Pleased to meet you, Jean-Paul."

Jean-Paul nodded, then went back to the food truck and returned with a second tray.

There was silence as everyone took their drinks and selected a sandwich. Eventually, Bettina Blackeagle spoke.

"The house is ready for Josee," she said. "Petra, I think you are ready as well, to care for her?"

Petra nodded.

"With the help of my friends, Insha'Allah, yes, we will care for her."

Shyanne cleared her throat, then spoke gently.

"The doctor told us that physically she will be fine. The burns will heal, although here might be a few scars. It's her mental health that is important. She needs to rest and relax, in a calm place. I think this is something I have been able to organize."

Rashford looked at her.

"Really? How?"

Mandy interrupted the conversation.

"Not yet," she said. "Let's talk about things in the proper sequence. Today we have prepared the house."

"And kept the fire going for the second day," said Pia, nodding. "I will keep it alight until Thursday night. Someone will always be at your house, Petra, for the next two days."

Petra inclined her head.

"There will always be refreshment and a welcome at my house," she said.

"Thank you," said Mandy. "Shyanne, this evening I have rehearsal, but you will stay with Petra until I've finished. Then I will pick you up and tonight you will stay at my apartment."

She looked at Rashford as she spoke. He shrugged and nodded.

"What about Petra?" said Shyanne. "She shouldn't be alone."

"She needs the peace before everything starts to get busy tomorrow," said Mandy. "And anyway, Pia will be outside all night, tending the fire. She can visit with him if she gets lonely."

Rashford noticed that Leon grinned at this comment, and Petra blushed. Shyanne did not seem to notice the implication.

"Tomorrow," continued Mandy, looking at Shyanne, "you can move in to stay with Josee and Petra for a few days. Pia and Leon will always be around, and you will be safe. Then, on Saturday, you will come to my convocation."

She turned to Rashford.

"I'm sorry, Gavin. Josee is back now and will need her ticket."

Rashford nodded.

"I kind of figured that," he said. "My offer of taking the family out to dinner afterwards still stands."

Mandy looked at him.

"You would drive all the way up here, just to take us out to dinner?"

"And to celebrate your graduation," he said, smiling. "Even if I miss the actual moment of you receiving your degree."

Bettina coughed gently.

"I may be able to help, there," she said.

Everybody looked at her. She coloured slightly.

"Faculty members get two tickets," she said. "I never use my extra one. Gavin, you could come as my guest. If you would like to."

Rashford stared at her, then glanced at Mandy, who nodded. He reached out and held Bettina's wrist.

"Tenike," he said. "Thank you so much for this gift."

"You are most welcome," she said. "I will enjoy your company, and also the gossip. This will be a great surprise for my colleagues."

Rashford laughed.

"Always glad to contribute to gossip" he said. "I've got your number; I'll give you a call when I get to town. Mandy, you said you had six guests, plus yourself. With Doctor Blackeagle and me, I shall book a table for nine people for dinner."

Mandy shook her head.

"There will be nine at the ceremony," she said, "but I would like there to be eleven for dinner. Pia and Petra, will you join us?"

They looked at each other, then nodded.

"Eleven it is," said Rashford, smiling.

Shyanne coughed to get everyone's attention.

"I didn't finish telling you about my plan," she said. "I think I should speak now."

Mandy nodded.

"Sorry, cuz," she said. "I got ahead of myself."

Shyanne shook her head.

"No problem," she said, clearing her throat. "Like I was saying, the doctor says that Josee will be okay, she just needs some rest and relaxation. And with the help of my brother, I've got that organized."

She smiled across at Pia, who nodded gravely in return.

"Next week, after the convocation, the graduates who want to celebrate will be flying down to Barbados. Josee and I are going to travel down on that plane."

Mandy and Rashford looked at each other, eyebrows raised. Shyanne ignored them.

"I know we haven't graduated yet, Josee didn't even finish third year, but Pia has said he will make an exception. He's sold us three tickets."

"Three?" said Rashford.

Shyanne nodded.

"Yes. I don't want to stay at the resort with everybody else; that will be a twenty-four seven party. Josee won't get any rest. We're going to stay at Patrick's place, it's on the coast near Bridgetown. He says that there are miles of sandy beaches and not too many tourists in his area, and from his deck you can look out over the surf towards the sunset. He's nearly finished his year here so he's going to come down with us and look after us for the week."

"That sounds wonderful," said Bettina Blackeagle, looking across at Rashford as she spoke. "You are indeed fortunate that this man can make time for you and Josee."

Rashford looked back at Bettina, understanding that he was receiving a message but not being quite sure what it was. Then it clicked.

"Please invite him for Saturday," he said. "I'll make it twelve for dinner."

***

Rashford booked into the Island View Hotel for the night, and at seven thirty that evening he met Bettina outside the long-term stay apartments and suites building where she lived during the semester when she taught in Wheatville. He left his car in a visitor parking spot, and they walked down the gentle hill to the town centre. It was all new to Rashford, and he let himself be guided to a small restaurant on the edge of a strip mall. It was sandwiched between a liquor store and a cannabis retail outlet.

"How did you find this place?" he said, looking around at the fractured parking lot and the desolate fast-food wrappers eddying in the wind.

"Books and covers, Gavin, books and covers," said Bettina, and led him inside. Here it was obvious that she was a known and honoured guest, for although the restaurant was quite busy they were immediately whisked to an empty table located next to a massive aquarium. Small brightly coloured fish fluttered around a variety of differently sized rocks and corals. A small and dark-complexioned man came to their table and served them each a tall glass of ice water. He nodded at Rashford, then brought his hands together, with his palms touching and fingers pointing upwards, holding his thumbs close to his chest and bowing over them at Bettina.

"Namaste, professor," he said.

She repeated the gesture back to him, bowing her head and lifting her fingertips to touch her forehead.

"Namaste, Anil. How are your daughters this evening?"

"They are well, professor. Thank you for asking. Would you like to see a menu?"

Rashford was about to say 'yes' when Bettina shook her head.

"No, thank you. We would like to eat, not too much but enough. Not too spicy but enough. Whatever you think is suitable. And two Arna beers, please."

"Light or strong, professor?"

"Light, please. Thank you."

Anil bowed again and walked away, calling out instructions as he went through the restaurant. The other diners looked across at Bettina and Rashford, no doubt wondering why they were receiving such special treatment. Moments later a young woman appeared, bowed, and placed two glasses on their table. She left, returning almost immediately with two bottles that had blue and white labels. She flipped off the caps and poured into each glass until it was a third full, then bowed and left the table. Rashford picked up the bottle.

"Is that a yak?" he said, looking at the horned bovine whose yellow head was imposed on the edge of the label.

Bettina shrugged.

"I never asked," she said, then raised her glass.

Rashford put down the bottle and picked up his own glass.

"Cheers," he said, and they clinked their glasses together, then each took a long sip of the beer.

"It's very refreshing," said Rashford, licking foam from his lips. "Thank you for bringing me here."

"It's the best-kept secret in Wheatville," said Bettina. "Anil used to own and operate a restaurant in Ottawa, in the Glebe. It was well-known to the local people, and very popular with politicians. I was there on a conference and a colleague took me one evening. It was the best food I had tasted for a long, long time. A few years ago, I was back for some meetings with government, and I was disappointed to find that the restaurant was closed. Then my colleague told me that Anil's wife had passed away suddenly, so he decided to go somewhere new. He took his daughters and moved here. He opened this restaurant just before Alsama was created."

"And the food is good?"

"Trust me on this, Gavin. The food is better than good. There is a two- or three-week waiting list for a dinner reservation."

Rashford looked at her.

"You made one, that long ago?"

She laughed.

"No. Anil always has time for special friends."

Rashford looked at her, thinking through what she had said.

"These daughters," he said. "How old are they?"

Bettina nodded.

"Well done," she said. "You're right, I have provided some guidance to them as they made their way into and through the university. You met one, it was the eldest daughter who brought our beer. She is in third year. Actually, she was in my Gender and Women's Studies class with Shyanne and Josee. The other two are twins, they are in their first year. They will probably serve the food."

Rashford shook his head.

"You never fail to surprise me," he said. "Again, thank you for bringing me here. It's obviously a special place for you."

She nodded.

"It is. But it is I who should thank you, for suggesting we have dinner together this evening."

Rashford shrugged.

"It seemed like a good idea," he said. "Mandy is at rehearsal, and Shyanne and Petra are getting ready for Josee to come back tomorrow. I thought I was just going to get in the way, and hope you don't mind being dragged away?"

Bettina chuckled.

"Not at all. I had done all that I could do, and I think those two were hoping for some quiet time with Pia and this Patrick person. Who is he, anyway?"

Rashford explained the relationship between Shyanne and Patrick, which led to more conversation about how things had evolved to the dinner he was hosting on Saturday. He was interrupted by the arrival of two giggling young women, who repeatedly said 'namaste' and bowed to Bettina as they served dishes of steamed rice, sauteed vegetables, and crispy skinned spiced chicken.

As they ate, their discussion shifted to Maple Creek, and Bettina filled Rashford in on all the local gossip. Alf was still running the car repair business, and Brian was helping. Clara, the 'hussy from the diner', had moved into her own apartment and was no longer providing Brian with rent in kind.

"Now he has to pay, like everybody else," said Bettina.

"Meow," said Rashford, laughing. "Have you told Gayle that he's available again?"

"I wouldn't dare," said Bettina, joining in the laughter.

At some point the older girl returned and exchanged their empty beer bottles for new ones. Bettina thanks her and continued her stories. She said that Kôhkum Christine was still her usual bossy self but getting older, and more frail, every day.

"She is ninety-six now," said Bettina. "She moved into a home last year, I could not look after her and work as well. The last time I visited her, she told me that 'the Good Queen' was ninety-six when she passed, and maybe that was a sign."

"The Good Queen?" asked Rashford.

Bettina laughed.

"That was her name for Queen Elizabeth the Second," she said. "My nôhkum liked her a lot. She's not too sure about King Charles, though. She thinks he needed a bit more time to prepare."

Rashford stared at her.

"What, seventy years wasn't a long enough apprenticeship?"

Bettina shrugged.

"I don't think my nôhkum thinks anybody will ever be able to take the place of the Good Queen."

"Well, he's giving it his best shot," Rashford scoffed.

As the plates were cleared, Anil himself arrived with two tall, fluted glass bowls. Inside each was a creamy looking dessert, topped with dried nuts. One of his daughters placed a long-handled spoon next to each glass.

"Please, this is my special shikarni," he said. "On the house."

"It's yoghurt with fruit," explained Bettina, looking at Rashford's face. "Thank you, Anil. This is very kind of you."

Rashford took a small amount on his spoon and tried it, gingerly. He smiled, then dunked out a spoonful and ate it with relish.

"This is tremendous," he said, digging his spoon back into the glass.

Anil beamed, raised his hands in the namaste gesture, and left them to their food. Rashford finished his half his dessert before speaking again.

"What about Cicily," he said, quietly. "How is she?"

Bettina put down her spoon and looked at him steadily.

"I think I told you, she is in Toronto," she said, slowly. Rashford nodded.

"That is a long way. I cannot leave my nôhkum, my work, my dog, just to run to Toronto for a weekend. And Cicily has a life there, one she does not want to leave to travel here for a day or two. It is difficult, for both of us."

"Are you still ... together?"

Bettina shrugged.

"I'm no longer sure," she said. "I have heard from others that Cicily has a good friend whom she sees often, and who has stayed the night on occasion. But she has said nothing to me, and I choose not to rock the canoe. We talk once a week and, right now, that is enough."

She coughed.

"Enough about me. What about you. This Amanda, isn't she a bit young for you?"

"That's what everybody tells me, yes."

"I have heard, around campus, that she is a very good fiddle player."

"She is, yes. She's excellent. I think she'll go places."

Bettina nodded, then cleared her throat.

"I have also heard that she can be very generous with ... with her favours."

Rashford nodded.

"I know about that part of her life," he said. "It's okay. We're just having fun. I think it will be over before the end of summer. After this tour she is going to really take off; either that or quit music and go to graduate school. But I don't expect to be part of that time of her life."

"Are you going on the tour?" she said. "I heard they asked you to be a roadie."

Rashford looked at her.

"You sure hear a lot, don't you?" he said.

She smiled.

"It comes with my work, and my big family. When I'm having coffee, the students talk as though I am invisible, I hear all sorts of things. And then of course, Jody, the bass player, his grandmother is my auntie."

Rashford shook his head.

"I turned down the roadie gig," he said. "They hired a young lad who I think will do a great job. I'm going to fly down and follow the band for a few weeks during the tour. It will be my summer holiday. I've already told Mandy that I can't be there all the time. I don't think she'll notice, to be honest. She gets so focused in her music, its scary sometimes."

Bettina laughed.

"All the good ones, they follow a different star," she said, then raised her hand to get the bill. Rashford argued and in the end, they decided to split the total, leaving a sizeable tip, and made their way out to the street. As they walked back up towards the building where she was staying, she linked her arm through his, giggling softly as they each made silly comments about the meal and the other diners. When they got to her door, she looked at him. Then she shook her head.

"It's been a lovely evening, Gavin. Thank you. I'm not going to invite you in, I don't think that would be a good idea."

Rashford smiled.

"Not even to show me what I might learn from a more mature person?" he said.

Bettina smiled back, then leaned over and kissed him full on the mouth. She put her hands behind his head to hold him close, and he felt her tongue, and the pressure of her lips. She stepped in and formed her body against his, pushing against him suggestively, and his arms dropped down her back and held her by the waist. Then she suddenly broke away, leaving him gasping, and stood watching him with a glint in her eye.

"Not even for that," she said, then opened the door and went inside.

The next morning Rashford parked outside Petra's house and sat with Pia by the fire. They spoke quietly together, watched as always by Leon from his place on the wall. At eleven o'clock the ambulance arrived.

The paramedics put Josee into a wheelchair and brought her frail figure down the path to the door. Pia, Leon and Rashford all stood up as they passed. The door opened and Petra came out, speaking quietly to the ambulance attendants for a few moments. She gestured behind her, and Shyanne and Mandy came out to help her manoeuvre the chair over the entry sill. Once she was inside the paramedics returned to their ambulance and drove away. The door closed.

After a few minutes, the door opened; Mandy stepped out and came down to the fire. She looked at Rashford.

"She is home now," she said. "We will look after her."

Rashford nodded.

"I will see you on Saturday," he said. "After the ceremony. I have booked dinner at Ristorante d'Arno for six o'clock, so that will give us lots of time for photographs first!"

"Gavin, that's crazy," said Mandy. "That's going to cost a fortune."

He shrugged.

"You only graduate once," he said. "It will be worth it."

"And you're coming to watch, with Doctor Blackeagle?"

"I am."

"Awesome. What are you going to do now?"

"I'm going to go and visit someone in Saskatoon, then I'm heading back to Regina. I've still got a job, you know. I can cross Josee off my missing persons list, but there are an awful lot of people still out there."

She nodded.

"Thank you," she said, leaning over and giving him a kiss on the cheek. "See you on Saturday."

Rashford watched her go back into the house and close the door. He turned back and looked at Pia.

"One more smoke before I go?" he said.

Pia shrugged. "If you wish."

Rashford looked at Leon.

"Would you like one?"

"Sure. Tê'nikeh," he said, taking the packet and withdrawing a cigarette. Rashford brought out a third and placed it carefully in the fire, then lit Leon's and his own. Pia nodded, then gestured to the stool. Leon walked back and sat on the wall, scanning the street as he smoked. Rashford sat next to Pia.

"Three tickets to Barbados?" he said.

Pia shrugged.

"I gave them business class for the same price, more or less. York paid me a grand for the three of them, return. He was happy."

"I bet he was," said Rashford, laughing.

***

Rashford drove directly to Saskatoon and soon found the Tim Horton's restaurant on the corner near to where Josee had been held. He went to the counter and asked if he could speak to the manager. One of the cashiers went to the back, behind the coffee percolators and the ovens, and soon emerged accompanied by the same young man with whom he had spoken previously. The manager blanched when he saw Rashford, but after a moment's hesitation kept walking up to the counter.

"Can I help you?" he said, looking warily across the glass topped display case.

"I want to apologise," said Rashford. "I was out-of-line the other day."

The manager shook his head.

"Thank you," he said. "But it's okay. I've heard what happened over there, at the house. Have you got him yet?"

Rashford shook his head.

"Not yet," he said. "But we will."

The manager laughed.

"That's right," he said. "How could I forget? You guys always get your man, right?"

Rashford nodded.

"Yes, we do," he said, and walked out of the door.

About the Author

J. T. Goddard is a retired educator. Born and raised in Yorkshire, his career took him to every province and territory in Canada, and to many countries around the world. He now happily calls Prince Edward Island home. *Missing* is his third novel. Find out more at: www.jtgoddard.com.